MW00886686

LORD OF WINTER

A MEDIEVAL ROMANCE
PART OF THE LORDS OF DE ROYANS SERIES

BY KATHRYN LE VEQUE

© Copyright 2016 by Kathryn Le Veque Novels, Inc.
Print Edition

Text by Kathryn Le Veque
Cover by Kim Killion

Reproduction of any kind except where it pertains to short quotes in relation to advertising or promotion is strictly prohibited.

All Rights Reserved.

The characters and events portrayed in this book are fictitious. Any similarity to real persons, living or dead, is purely coincidental and not intended by the author.

KATHRYN LE VEQUE NOVELS

Medieval Romance:

The de Russe Legacy:
The White Lord of Wellesbourne
The Dark One: Dark Knight
Beast
Lord of War: Black Angel
The Falls of Erith
The Iron Knight

The de Lohr Dynasty:
While Angels Slept (Lords of East Anglia)
Rise of the Defender
Steelheart
Spectre of the Sword
Archangel
Unending Love
Shadowmoor
Silversword

Great Lords of le Bec:
Great Protector
To the Lady Born (House of de Royans)
Lord of Winter (Lords of de Royans)

Lords of Eire:
The Darkland (Master Knights of Connaught)
Black Sword
Echoes of Ancient Dreams (time travel)

De Wolfe Pack Series:
The Wolfe
Serpent
Scorpion (Saxon Lords of Hage – Also related to The Questing)
Walls of Babylon
The Lion of the North

Dark Destroyer

Ancient Kings of Anglecynn:
The Whispering Night
Netherworld

Battle Lords of de Velt:
The Dark Lord
Devil's Dominion

Reign of the House of de Winter:
Lespada
Swords and Shields (also related to The Questing, While Angels Slept)

De Reyne Domination:
Guardian of Darkness
The Fallen One (part of Dragonblade Series)

Unrelated characters or family groups:
The Gorgon (Also related to Lords of Thunder)
The Warrior Poet (St. John and de Gare)
Tender is the Knight (House of d'Vant)
Lord of Light
The Questing (related to The Dark Lord, Scorpion)
The Legend (House of Summerlin)

The Dragonblade Series: (Great Marcher Lords of de Lara)
Dragonblade
Island of Glass (House of St. Hever)
The Savage Curtain (Lords of Pembury)
The Fallen One (De Reyne Domination)
Fragments of Grace (House of St. Hever)
Lord of the Shadows
Queen of Lost Stars (House of St. Hever)

Lords of Thunder: The de Shera Brotherhood Trilogy
The Thunder Lord
The Thunder Warrior
The Thunder Knight

Highland Warriors of Munro
The Red Lion

Time Travel Romance: (Saxon Lords of Hage)
The Crusader
Kingdom Come

Contemporary Romance:

Kathlyn Trent/Marcus Burton Series:
Valley of the Shadow
The Eden Factor
Canyon of the Sphinx

The American Heroes Series:
The Lucius Robe
Fires of Autumn
Evenshade
Sea of Dreams
Purgatory

Other Contemporary Romance:
Lady of Heaven
Darkling, I Listen

Multi-author Collections/Anthologies:
With Dreams Only of You (USA Today bestseller)
Sirens of the Northern Seas (Viking romance)
Ever My Love (sequel to With Dreams Only Of You) July 2016

Note: All Kathryn's novels are designed to be read as stand-alones, although many have cross-over characters or cross-over family groups. Novels that are grouped together have related characters or family groups.

Series are clearly marked. All series contain the same characters or family groups except the American Heroes Series, which is an anthology with unrelated characters.

There is NO particular chronological order for any of the novels because they can all be read as stand-alones, even the series.

For more information, find it in **A Reader's Guide to the Medieval World of Le Veque**.

AUTHOR'S NOTE

We've got a "genesis" of sorts in this book!

LORD OF WINTER turned out to be the beginning of a few things – for example, you'll see Christopher and David de Lohr, and Marcus Burton, pre-Rise of the Defender, when they were young knights with a lord to serve. And one of the scenes in this book has one of their legendary adventures in it. I was laughing the entire way through it as I wrote it! Typical de Lohr/Burton shenanigans.

We've also got the start of the Unholy Trinity, a series that is slated for 2018, in three knights who are a little darker, a little more "edgy". They have secondary roles here but you get a good feel for the dark side of them. Also in this book is Gart Forbes, hero of *Archangel*, as a squire and his best friend, Erik de Russe. Erik is the brother of Emberley de Russe, heroine of Gart's novel, although by the time the novel took place Erik had already passed way in the Holy Land. Still, it's fun to have a glimpse of the man and perhaps a little sad, even, knowing that he soon meets his end.

More things to note: the weight system discussed at one point in the book is accurate. In 1066, when William the Conqueror arrived, he brought with him the Roman weight system, which is also called the Apothecaries' system of weights and measures. The pound and the ounce are all part of this system. The "stone" system for body weight that the British use now wasn't enacted until 1835, and even that has changed a few times since then.

On to one of the battle scenes in this book – whenever I write battle scenes, I really research the area and the topography to make sure I know what I'm writing about when I put it to paper. Here's an odd tidbit – when I was researching the site for the major battle at the end of the novel, I selected a site because, to me, it seemed the most logical location due to the terrain. I must not have been the only person to think that because, weirdly enough, when I looked at the area most closely, that particular location was known as Battle Hill. Strange coincidence!

Lastly, Bowes Castle is a real castle, exactly where I describe it in the novel. So is Cotherstone Castle, and Auckland Castle, Brough Castle, etc. This novel is unique in that no castles mentioned in it, other than Netherghyll Castle, are fictional. All of them are quite real, as is Hugh de Puiset, Bishop of Durham. Bowes Castle, however, has a bit of a fascinating history but one that, during the time when this novel takes places, is lost to history. We know that it did belong to Henry II and that, at this point in time, it was relatively new. If you want to learn more about it, you can read about it here:

en.wikipedia.org/wiki/Bowes_Castle

Anyway, enough of my ramblings. I truly hope you enjoy this novel and the chance to see some of your favorite heroes again. As always, happy reading!

Love,
Kathryn

TABLE OF CONTENTS

PROLOGUE

Église Saint-André
Five miles from Taillebourg, France
Year of Our Lord 1179 A.D.

"PLEASE DO NOT leave, my love," a woman with pale hair and big brown eyes begged. "You cannot leave us. Please do not go; not yet."

She was clutching the hands of her husband, big hands with big gloves upon them. A knight dressed in heavy protection and loaded with weapons faced the woman as two little girls clung to his legs, whining. Truth be told, he was trying to comfort all three of them.

"I must go now," he assured her calmly. "Have I ever lied to you, Lizette? Do you truly believe I would put you and the girls in danger? You will be safe here."

Lady Lizette de Royans shook her head even though she didn't seem entirely convinced of her husband's reassurance. It was in the pre-dawn hours of a cold morning during the month of March, a hint of winter chill still in the air. But in a stout manor home built on the banks of a quiet creek, it was warm and smoky and pleasant.

Still, there was fear in the air as the big knight gathered the last of his gear, helped by a pair of knights that had come for him in the darkness. The knight was expected to lead a coming battle, not five miles from where they were. The woman, however, was unwilling to let him go so easily. She clung to him.

"I do not want you to go," she said quietly, struggling not to weep. "I saw an owl fly across the moon last night. It is a terrible omen."

The knight gave her a half-smile, kissing her on the forehead. "It was no omen," he said patiently. "It was a night bird looking for a meal. You will be safe here with Lord Annepont. He is a friend and ally. We have been staying here for over a week, my angel. You knew this day would come. You have been brave to this point and it is my wish that you continue to be brave. The girls do not need to see their mother so terrified."

The woman glanced at the two small girls, still clinging to their father's legs. Her expression softened somewhat as she bent down to collect the smaller of the pair, a little girl with her father's curly blonde hair and big green eyes. The child held out her arms to her father, whining, but he was so loaded down with sharp and deadly objects that he didn't dare take her in his arms. He bent over to kiss her unhappy face as she grabbed his long hair, trying to hang on to him.

"I must go," he said, kissing the baby again before kissing his wife. "I do not know when I will return but Taillebourg is not far from here. I am sure you will hear of the battle there but, rest assured, you will be safe here. No one knows you are here."

Lizette was resigned to the fact that no matter how she pleaded, he was still determined to head into the enormous conflict that had been planned for quite some time. "A big army is gathering, no?"

"The biggest."

"Will this be the last one for a time, Juston?"

His warm expression faded. "More than likely not," he said quietly. "Taillebourg is held by Henry and Richard must have it. My angel, you knew this was my life when you married me. I must admit that I grow disheartened with having the same conversation with you every time I go to battle. This is my life and my vocation. We have been married for four years and you knew that the day we wed. Besides… it is not every wife who is permitted to follow her husband from battle to battle. Most women stay home to raise the children, but you have begged to come so I have brought you with me. You should consider yourself very fortunate that I did not leave you at your father's house in Merignac."

Lizette tried not to look too guilty. "It is simply that I did not wish to be without you," she said, touching his cheek. "We have had a good life, Juston. I do not regret following your army, staying in the homes of your friends. If you are injured, I am close enough to tend you, and your daughters are able to see you much more frequently. Nay, I do not regret this at all."

He nodded, his impatience growing. "Nor do I," he said, kissing her swiftly one last time. "Now, I must depart. I will send you word when I can but I can tell you that a massive army is being assembled at Taillebourg and a siege could last months. The fortress is quite impenetrable."

She lifted an ironic eyebrow. "Aren't those the only ones that Richard wants?"

He grinned. "Those are the only ones worthy of my skill."

With that, he began to move towards the entry to the manse with his wife and children scurrying behind him. Lizette could see, through the open door, a host of soldiers and knights waiting for her husband. She could also see the ice on the ground outside.

"Will you be warm enough?" she asked, noting that he wasn't wearing much by way of heavy clothing. "It is very cold outside."

He glanced at the ice as well. "I have the beautiful robe you had made for me," he said. "I will wear that if it grows too cold. But you know that cold does not affect me – I draw strength from it."

He was trying to be jovial at this moment of departure but Lizette couldn't rise to it. "My great Lord of Winter," she murmured with some amusement on a title he seemed so proud of. "The cold is your ally. But that is not why Richard calls you that."

"It is not."

"You destroy everything in battle like the ravages of a great winter storm."

She recited it as if those words had been drilled into her. He simply winked at her. "Indeed, I do." One last time, he bent over to kiss her. "Do not worry. I shall return to you safe and whole."

With that, he was gone, leaving his worried wife and two sleepy, sniffling daughters who did not want to see their father go away again. They stood in the open doorway, watching as he mounted his charcoal-colored war horse and spurred the animal towards the west, heading to Taillebourg Castle and the bombardment that was soon to begin.

Lizette turned away from the door when he was out of sight, leading the unhappy girls away as the panel was closed by one of the house servants.

But this was no ordinary servant. Having heard nearly the entire conversation between the lady and her husband, as well as the conversations over the past week between the knight and his master, Lord Annepont, the servant knew that something very bad was coming. Although he served Lord Annepont, he had ties to Taillebourg and to Lord Geoffrey of Rancon, the lord of Taillebourg.

A siege was coming to Taillebourg.

It was the worst of all possible news but it was something the servant had caught wind of for the past week through snips of conversation he'd heard between the big knight and Lord Annepont. In fact, the servant's sister served Mme. Rancon and he was coming to think that Lord Rancon needed to know that the Count of Poitiers' greatest knight had a family seeking refuge at Lord Annepont's home. Perhaps he would be well-rewarded for such information so his purpose in sending the news to his sister was greed alone. It had nothing to do with whose loyalties he served.

He simply wanted the money.

But he had to act swiftly. The sun had not yet arisen when the servant sent his young son on an errand to Taillebourg, knowing the lad would not beat the knights there but as long as the siege had not yet started, there was a chance the boy could get a message to the occupants so they would know the identity of the guests of Lord Annepont. He told his son to wait for a reply and for a reward. As his son ran off into the icy dawn, the servant settled back into the kitchens to help the cook for the day, making no mention of what he'd done. He was quite sure that by tomorrow, he'd have a good deal of coinage in his hands.

Unfortunately, his greed would not know fruition. Upon receiving word that one of Richard the Lionheart's greatest warriors had a family staying with Lord Annepont, it was the beginning of the end for everyone within the Annepont house and hold. Lord Annepont was now viewed as the enemy by those at Taillebourg and the young man who brought the information ended up in the oubliette.

There was no reward forthcoming, only vengeance. Two days after receiving the news of the disloyal Lord Annepont, a group of knights led by a warrior with the surname of Lusignan slipped from the castle prior to the forthcoming battle and burned Annepont's manse to the ground with the occupants in it. Dorian Lusignan, a cousin to Guy Lusignan of Jerusalem, made sure no one survived.

Juston de Royans did not discover the fate of his family until a month later when he sent one of his knights to Lord Annepont's manse with a message for his wife. The knight returned in tears and Juston was informed that his family was no more, burned alive right along with Lord Annepont. Witnesses said knights from Taillebourg had done it, with whispers of a man named Dorian Lusignan at the head of it. Juston had spent a solid year trying to track down this Dorian Lusignan to no avail. No one could find a trace of him.

That was when the Lord of Winter's heart froze over for good.

CHAPTER ONE

In Dextera Dei

"God's Right Hand" House of de Royans Motto

Siege of Bowes Castle
County Durham
December, Year of Our Lord 1187 A.D.

*A*RMAGEDDON HAD ARRIVED.

Across a winter-frozen landscape that had once been lush with vegetation, the army of the High Sheriff of Yorkshire had laid waste to everything in its path. Entire villages had been burned. Those who fled had been upended at best, and those who resisted had been slaughtered like sheep. The army of England's great Lord of Winter, an informal title bestowed upon the High Sheriff by the Count of Poitiers, Richard *hic leo noster* ("this our lion"), had torn through everything like a deadly winter storm.

A storm of England's greatest warriors.

No one dared challenge the High Sheriff for to do so would be to incur the man's wrath, a fearsome and mighty thing. Even now, as the army of Juston de Royans ripped up and digested a goodly portion of Northumberland and County Durham, the Bishop of Durham (a powerful man in his own right), remained far to the north, unwilling and unable to defend his subjects from the fire of de Royans' army.

Judgement Day had come for those unfortunate enough to be in the High Sheriff's path, particularly disturbing for the occupants of Bowes Castle.

Set along a major road through the mighty and misty Pennine mountains, Bowes guarded the road like a dutiful sentry. Like so many castles in the long and turbulent history between the king of England and his rebellious sons, this castle belonged to Henry. But Richard wanted it, and what Richard wanted, Juston was oath-bound to secure for him. It had always been that way, for many years. Therefore, Juston had gathered his massive army from Netherghyll Castle and marched northward into Durham to lay siege to Bowes and purge Henry's army from it.

It was just as simple as that.

Or so he thought. But Henry's garrison commander had proved strong, something that had infuriated Juston. A student of Roman military tactics, de Royans fought dirtier than most – and also smarter. He brought with him things that most armies couldn't even conceive of, battle engines and tactics and formations that often worked in a matter of days, if not hours. But Bowes and her army had proven quite resistant to what Juston considered to be his genius.

A siege that had started three weeks ago still lingered, a grievous insult to de Royans. He'd hurled burning clay pots of oil over Bowes' outer walls, quite literally exploding bombs when they hit any kind of surface. Oil sprayed and so did the flames. For weeks, they'd seen smoke spilling from inside Bowes' outer bailey but never badly enough to chase the occupants out. De Royans also had his men slaughter innumerable pigs in order to collect their fat to feed his incendiary devices; three weeks later, forty fat pigs had been slaughtered and his men were feasting on pork morning, noon, and evening while the fat from those animals burned through Bowes.

But not fast enough.

De Royans even had archers whose sole purpose was to shoot flaming arrows over the walls and the bombardment was constant. It hadn't let up since nearly the moment de Royans and his army had arrived on the rise overlooking Bowes Castle. Flaming arrows, flaming projectiles, and then when the rains came, siege engines hurling massive boulders at the walls, pummeling them and breaking them down.

It was still raining, which meant Battle by Flame had to be put on hold. But it was of no consequence. The western outer wall had proven the weakest and Juston's army had put such major holes in it that nineteen days after their arrival, nearly half of the wall collapsed. Juston would have been happy but for the fact the garrison commander had most of his men take up bows. The same arrows that Juston had hurled into Bowes' bailey were now the ones coming back out at anyone who tried to breach the western wall. It was quite clever, actually.

But Juston wasn't interested in cleverness. He just wanted that damn castle secured.

Therefore, twenty-one days after his arrival to Bowes Castle, Juston was suffering from one of his many intense headaches after what had been an explosion of temper earlier in the day. While he sulked in his tent, moodily, with salt-soaked rags against his forehead to try and draw out the pain, his men continued with the bombardment of Bowes.

But all of that was soon to change.

A group of dirty, grimy, bloodied knights headed towards de Royans' tent. They'd just come from the front lines of the siege. The weather had shifted from freezing rain to snow and back again. Now, they were being pummeled by rain that was so cold it felt like bee stings to the bare skin. Although the knights were covered with protection, from leather gloves on their hands to the latest design of helms upon their heads, their faces were exposed, leaving all of them red-cheeked from the weather. Exhaustion was playing a heavy role in their manner, as well, trudging through the ankle-deep mud as they headed to de Royans' tent.

"He is not going to be pleased with this offer."

The ominous statement came from one of the group, a young knight with a square jaw and tufts of blonde hair peeking out from beneath his helm. He was bringing up the rear of the group, trailing six other knights as they headed to de Royans' tent. At his quietly uttered words, the man in the lead turned to glance at him.

"He may surprise you, little brother," Sir Christopher de Lohr replied steadily. "This offer will assure our victory."

Sir David de Lohr wasn't entirely sure. His brother was closer to de Royans than any of them, as he had been de Royans' squire many years ago. He'd essentially grown up with him and, therefore, knew his moods and thoughts better than most.

David glanced around to the other men in the group; Marcus Burton, his brother's best friend, as well as Maxton of Loxbeare, Kress de Rhydian, Achilles de Dere, and Gillem d'Evereux. All of them were knights of the highest order, born and bred for battle, with his brother at the head of them. These were all men to be feared, for a variety of reasons.

"Mayhap." David shook his head, gleaning both reluctance and assurance from the expressions of the others. "Do you think he will agree to it?"

"There is but one way to find out."

They had reached de Royans' tent. The canvas was weathered and beaten, the oil used to treat the fabric rubbing off in places and showing mold. But it was the tent of a man who had spent a good deal of time sheltered by it, well-used, with the de Royans crest upon the door flap. Christopher and the others paused near the closed door, not wanting to disturb de Royans in the midst of one of his headaches, but finding it necessary all the same. Christopher cleared his throat softly.

"My lord?" he said, raising his voice to call to the man inside. "We have come bearing a proposal from the garrison commander of Bowes. Would you hear it now?"

The tent flap suddenly snapped back and a young man, eighteen years of age, appeared. Tall and well-built, with a crown of cropped dark blonde hair, Gart Forbes was de Royans' squire, a young man who had been trained by the best and had fought as a knight for the past two years. He had not yet been awarded his spurs, however, considering his young age, but everyone knew that would come very soon. There was no man finer on the battlefield than Gart Forbes. More than that, he was mightily protective of de Royans.

"Chris," he greeted de Lohr informally because of their familiarity and respect for one another. When he spoke, it was quietly. "De Royans is trying to rest. Can this wait?"

"Gart!"

It was de Royans, from inside the tent. As Gart tossed back the flap again, de Royans spoke.

"Admit them."

Reluctantly, Gart motioned the group into the rather large tent. It was surprisingly warm inside considering the cold weather, with two braziers filled with peat giving off a good deal of heat. As the men crowded into the tent, all but d'Evereux who didn't like crowded places, Gart went to light an oil lamp so there was some light. Just as the flame took hold of the wick, de Royans removed the cloth over his eyes and wearily sat up.

"What proposal?" he asked, his voice hoarse from exhaustion. "Explain."

Christopher removed his helm because even the slight heat of the tent mixed with the heavy clothing he was wearing was making his head sweat. A full head of damp blonde hair glistened in the weak light and he raked his fingers through it, slicking it back on his skull.

"The garrison commander of Bowes, Brey de la Roarke, flew a flag of truce about an hour ago," he said. "He asked if I would hear a proposal for an end to this conflict and I agreed, on your behalf. He proposes that we match our finest warrior against his finest warrior and settle this dispute once and for all, two men and one hand-to-hand fight. He swears he will surrender the fortress if his man loses but also says that we must leave them in peace if our man loses."

De Royans stared at Christopher with bloodshot eyes. "A single fight between two men will determine the outcome of a three-week siege?"

It was a rather incredulous question. "Aye, my lord," Christopher said. He grunted, perhaps with frustration. "Truthfully, my lord, I believe he must be in a dire situation to propose such a thing because only a desperate man would make such an offer. We must have damaged Bowes far more than we realized with our bombardment."

By this time, the entire group was looking at their commander for his response. It was true that a proposal such as this was not an unusual one because they'd encountered such things before. But usually, these proposals were always directed at de Royans personally. While he was a man of great physical beauty, he was also a man of great strength, talent, and cunning. He was as agile as a cat and as fast as lightning, and personal challenges had been issued to the man for as long as anyone could remember.

Men would challenge Juston de Royans only to realize, very quickly, that they were in a battle they could not win. As of late, few men wanted to fight de Royans in hand-to-hand combat because it was naturally assumed that he would emerge the victor. In all his thirty-nine years, he'd not lost in combat yet. It was a reputation that de Royans had built upon for many years, something that had grown and taken on dimension until no one knew where the legend ended and the truth began.

Still, some men wanted to test that legend but Juston wasn't particularly eager to prove himself these days. There was no joy in such things any longer and challenges like this only bored him. He'd proved himself enough over the years and was, therefore, disinclined to take on men he considered unworthy, which was, in his estimation, every man with a blade.

No one was a match for the Lord of Winter.

Therefore, after a lingering glance at Christopher, Juston simply closed his eyes and lay back down on the traveling cot.

"Let me guess," he said, throwing the cold rag over his eyes again. "He wants me to meet his challenger."

Christopher shrugged. "He did not say that in so many words, but he knows you lead this army. Your reputation precedes you."

Juston snorted. "Unfortunately, not enough. Had he been impressed by it, he would have merely turned the castle over to me without all of this fuss."

Christopher remained stoic. "I am sure he has heard of your valor during the revolt several years ago," he said. "Every man in England and France has, you know. Your reputation is cemented, my lord."

"By now, I would expect so."

"There was *Castillion-sur-Agen,* for example. You helped Richard pound that fortress into submission."

"That was a bloody nasty bit of chaos."

"And there was Falaise. You led a raid over the walls…."

"No one could have done that but me."

"And there was that smaller castle in the Vexin that you captured with only fifty men."

"Fifty men against several hundred. We captured the gatehouse and slaughtered the men who tried to reclaim it. A damn fine victory, I must say."

Christopher was used to feeding de Royans' ego. The man was great and he knew it. He made sure everyone else knew it, too.

"Do I really need to go on, my lord?" Christopher asked. "It would take the lifetimes of many chroniclers to document the heroic deeds you have accomplished for Richard, and for the crown before him. Clearly, de la Roarke means to challenge you but there are six men in this tent who would gladly accept the challenge in your stead if you do not wish to accept it personally."

Juston ripped the cloth from his eyes. "You would take my glory from me, you savages," he said, half-serious, half-not. He sat up, a hand going to his head as the ache throbbed. "If it will end this damnable siege, then tell de la Roarke that I will meet whatever warrior he selects. But you tell him that he must be prepared to vacate Bowes immediately, for when I defeat his man, I shall not wait to claim it. I will charge in with my weaponry and eviscerate the castle as one eviscerates a slaughtered cow. Is that clear?"

"It is, my lord."

"Who is this fool about to lose his life to me?"

Christopher shook his head. "I do not know, my lord," he said. "But I would not be surprised if it was de la Roarke himself. Do you know of him?"

Juston stood up from his cot, weaving unsteadily. "I have heard of him," he said. "You must remember that Bowes is not too terribly far from my holdings, Chris. I have heard tales from others on his behavior, which is why I did not hesitate to come to Bowes when Richard asked it of me. I have heard of the Bloody Knight of Bowes, a man who treats the road he has been tasked to hold for Henry as if it is his own private revenue source. I've heard how he robs men and kills them. There is an entire section of the churchyard dedicated to his victims. Aye, I've heard of him, so I hope that, in fact, he is the one sent to meet me. I will happily dispense justice for the souls he has sinned against."

Christopher stood back as Gart rushed forward to Juston with his mail and protection. But the truth was that all he really did was help the man with his forearm protection, heavy leather pieces that were tied in place, and little else. When in battle, de Royans would wear some protection but not as much as what the other men wore. He liked to be able to move quickly and found the encumbrance of armor too restricting. When fighting hand-to-hand, de Royans had been known to strip down to nearly nothing, allowing him to move far more quickly than his opponents.

And he'd survived every one of them.

Therefore, no one commented when he didn't put on the full regalia of mail and protection. It was simply his way. As they stood and watched, Christopher sent his brother back to de la Roarke to inform the man that his terms, and his challenge, had been accepted.

"Maxton," Juston said as he strategically placed daggers on his body, tucked into his leather vest or into his boots. "While I am dealing with de la Roarke, you will focus on the weakened western wall. You and Kress and Achilles will form a party that will enter from that weakened side even as I face de la Roarke's challenge. My fear is that his men may not abide by the terms of his bargain when I kill him and we will have wasted the effort entirely. I want to ensure no efforts are wasted. You will get inside and you will lift the portcullis and secure the gatehouse. Is that understood?"

Maxton of Loxbeare nodded; a big man with dark hair and dark eyes, he had served Juston for a few years but by all rights, according to Juston, there was something unsettling about him. There was an edgy gleam in those nearly-black eyes, a darkness in the soul of a man who could easily kill without remorse. Juston liked that about him because Maxton was never a man to question an order, no matter how unsavory it was.

"Aye, my lord," Maxton said. "We will make sure the castle is ours no matter what the outcome."

Juston glanced up at Maxton and his two companions. Kress de Rhydian was an enormous blonde knight who was, at times, even more frightening than Maxton was and Achilles de Dere was simply the muscle of the group. The man had the strength and size of Samson. Even though these three were part of Juston's Praetorian command group, they still tended to keep to themselves sometimes. They were a moody and unsociable collective. *The Unholy Trinity,* Christopher had once joked about them, but the truth was that it was a fitting moniker for the group. If anything questionable needed to be done, those three would do it.

Satisfied that Maxton, de Rhydian, and de Dere would infiltrate the castle while everyone was distracted by the challenge, Juston motioned the three knights to get about their task and turned to Christopher and Marcus Burton, standing as a pair near him. These two were his generals, his closest and most trusted advisors. These were the men he relied the most on, in both friendship and wisdom. He finished shoving a small dagger into a secret place in his leather forearm bands and turned to them.

"I want the men ready to charge the gatehouse the moment I dispatch de la Roarke," he told them. "There is to be no hesitation, Chris – with Maxton and Kress and Achilles inside the compound, look for them to lift the portcullis so my army can enter. Do not wait for me, in any case – your job is to charge that gatehouse and secure the castle. I'm three weeks into this madness and I am eager to be done with it."

Christopher and Marcus nodded. "Aye, my lord," Marcus replied. "I will organize the men. They shall be ready."

"Where is Gillem?"

"Outside," Marcus replied. "You know he does not like crowded spaces."

"Take him with you to secure the gatehouse."

"Aye, my lord."

Juston bent over and collected one of the many swords that were neatly in a rack near his cot. His exceptional broadsword was available but he went for a short sword in a gilt leather sheath, a smaller and lighter version of his big broadsword. It was still very deadly, and very sharp, but it quickly became clear that was the only piece of major weaponry he was going to use.

"Now," he muttered, sword in hand, "let us commence with this foolery and be done with it. Chris, did you see de la Roarke?"

Christopher frowned when he realized that Juston was only going to use his short sword. "I did," he said, "My lord, I think the bigger sword might be of more use to you."

Juston ignored him. "How tall is the man?"

"Enormous. Are you sure you do not want your broadsword?"

Juston pushed his way from the tent with Christopher and Marcus in tow. Gart was trailing after him, as well, helping him secure the leather belt around his hips.

"Nay," he said flatly. "I will be done with de la Roarke in short order. I will take the man down and you will storm the castle and secure it. Those are your orders."

Christopher and Marcus looked at each other, concern in their expressions, but they said nothing. As the freezing rain pounded, Christopher plopped his helm back on his head and headed off with Marcus and Gillem, all of them heading to the bulk of the army that was still laying methodical siege to the walls of Bowes. Now, the army would be called off so de la Roarke's challenge could be met. It would be a good time for the de Royans army to regroup and take a few minutes to breathe while their commander dispatched de la Roarke's chosen warrior.

At least, that was the hope.

As Juston moved off through the freezing rain, heading towards the castle entry and, presumably, the waiting challenge, Christopher lifted a hand to Gart, who was still walking behind Juston and heading in the opposite direction. But Gart saw Christopher's signal and he quickly made his way to the man, freezing rain dripping from his face.

"Aye, Chris?" he asked.

Christopher's focus lingered on Juston in the distance. "He is only taking that short sword."

"I know."

Christopher met Gart's gaze. "Go get the broadsword," he said. "If he loses the short sword somehow, or if it isn't adequate, he will need the big sword."

A gleam came to Gart's eye. "You sound worried."

"Not worried. *Cautious*."

"He will not like that caution."

"I know."

"He will take it as a lack of faith in his abilities."

"So keep it out of sight unless he needs it."

Gart didn't reply. There was, in truth, nothing more to say. Something in Christopher's tone suggested more prudence than de Royans was showing. Without another word, he raced back to de Royans' tent to retrieve the broadsword as he'd been instructed.

JUSTON WASN'T OBLIVIOUS to the fact that his men thought he was daft for going into single combat with only a short sword and a few sharp daggers. He tried not to let their doubts bother him. But the truth was that he was sensitive to those doubts and now, if for no other reason, he was determined to win de la Roarke's challenge simply to show his knights that their doubts were unfounded. He'd served with his generals long enough that their doubts rather infuriated him.

If they thought he was growing soft in his old age, he was about to prove otherwise.

The freezing rain continued to pound him as he approached the battered structure of Bowes Castle. There was an inner and an outer bailey, both seemingly quite vast, and the western wall that had been so damaged was part of the wall that enclosed the outer bailey. Inside, there was still a moat that protected the enormous keep that King Henry had built not too long ago. He'd fortified the place, perhaps anticipating that this son in the midst of rebellion against him would want the strategic fortress.

Juston's family had come over with the Duke of Normandy and it was his ancestor who had been appointed the first High Sheriff of Yorkshire. So, in a sense, Juston was going against generations of his family's loyalties by turning against Henry. But he had his own reasons for what he was doing, and who his loyalties were to, so he had no conscience about defeating Henry's garrison commander and commandeering Bowes for Richard.

In fact, it was time to end this.

So he marched towards the outer wall of Bowes, seeing that the half-burned drawbridge from the gatehouse was down and men were upon it. He could see David de Lohr speaking with some men he didn't recognize, presuming they were de la Roarke's men. But it didn't matter. Juston wasn't willing to wait for the challenge; he bellowed at David, who in turn said something to the men on the crumbling drawbridge. Those men then disappeared back inside of Bowes.

At that point, Juston came to a halt several dozen feet from the entry to Bowes, coiled and ready to do battle. Gart eventually joined him, as did David. The three of them stood there, watching the activity in the gatehouse, knowing that the de Royans army was priming itself to breach both the walls and the entry.

"Where is my opponent, David?" Juston asked.

David was watching the activity at the gatehouse, men shuffling about. "He is coming," he said. "It will be de la Roarke. Evidently, he has been boasting on how he will defeat you."

Juston's expression didn't change. "He is in for a disappointment."

David glanced at Juston, noting that he wasn't carrying a broadsword, only the short sword. He had much the same reaction as his brother and the other knights had.

"De la Roarke is a very big man, my lord," he said. "He will undoubtedly come bearing an arsenal of weapons."

"Hopefully."

"But... you only have a short sword, my lord."

"I know."

David hesitated to say anything more, finally catching Gart's attention. The squire was shaking his head faintly, flicking his eyes in the direction of his hands. It was then that David saw that Gard had Juston's broadsword. David wasn't quite sure what was happening but he kept his mouth shut. Either de Royans was having a serious lapse in judgement in regards to facing another man in armed combat or he was crazy like a fox. David would be willing to bet it was the latter.

There was a commotion on the burned-out bridge and the three of them looked over to see several soldiers emerging, followed by a knight in heavy protection. More than that, the knight was as tall as a tree. The knight crossed the drawbridge to the cheering of his men and he raised his hands as if to encourage their adoration. The weary, beaten men of Bowes cheered on their commanding officer as the man made his way completely across the drawbridge and into the mud on the other side.

De la Roarke was loaded down with enough weapons and protection to take on an army all by himself. He was, quite literally, prepared for battle. But the moment he saw de Royans, who was literally wearing no armor at all, with only a short sword in his hand, he began to bellow with rage.

And that was the moment de Royans had planned for.

A faint smile crossed his lips. It had been very calculated on his part. Juston had been willing to wager that showing up to armed combat lightly dressed would have insulted his opponent grievously and he was very pleased to see that was exactly what happened. He was hoping to convey, purely by his manner of dress, that he thought nothing of de la Roarke's abilities as a knight, delivering a serious insult without uttering a word.

His men hadn't understood what he was doing and he wouldn't take the time to explain it. Knowing the pride of a warrior as he did, Juston was fairly certain his plan would work. It had; de la Roarke began ripping off his protection, raging angrily as he did so.

De la Roarke's men tried to stop him. Several were pleading with him, but de la Roarke was so furious that he shoved men away, even cuffing one of them on the side of the head. His helm came off, as did his heavy woolen tunic and leather gloves. Everything was coming off because he wasn't going to face de Royans dressed to the hilt if de Royans was going to face him without any protection at all.

He would prove who was the better warrior.

But Juston wasn't going to wait until the man was stripped down and ready to face him. He may have been arrogant but he wasn't foolish. He had been biding his time, waiting for the proper moment to charge, to catch de la Roarke off-guard. He had to time it correctly or he would find himself in a serious battle, something he really didn't want to exert himself over, so he waited until de la Roarke bent over to pull off his mail coat. The man's head and arms were wrapped up in the wet mail and he would be unable to fight back. He made a perfect target that way.

Juston knew it was time to strike.

He abruptly charged forward when de la Roarke was bent in half. Even at his advanced age of thirty-nine years, Juston could move like the wind and he did, charging through the mud, startling nearly everyone who witnessed his speed. By the time de la Roarke's men realized what was happening, it was too late. Juston rushed up to de la Roarke and plunged his short sword into the man's back, straight through his spine, so that the blade emerged from his belly.

As de la Roarke fell to the mud, mortally wounded, the situation dissolved into chaos.

CHAPTER TWO

ALL SHE KNEW was that men were rushing into the keep, which contained the great hall where the wounded were being tended. Some of the men were from the garrison at Bowes, but some men she didn't recognize. It took her little time to realize the castle had been breached.

Startled, the woman stood up from the man she had been bent over. She was tending a man who had burns to most of his body and who probably wouldn't survive more than just a few days. There were many burn victims from the incendiary devices hurled over the walls by the opposing army. When the bombardment had begun, they'd had some remnants of snow from an earlier storm that they were able to use for the burn victims, but that snow had melted and now all they had were cold rags and butter to ease the pain, and even the butter was almost gone.

The enemy is inside!

It would have been incredibly easy to panic as the woman watched enemy soldiers pour into the keep. In fact, her sister, the wife of the garrison commander, began to screech from the other side of the hall.

"Emmy!" she cried. "Hurry! Upstairs!"

Emera la Marche wasn't flighty like her sister. She was more reserved, far more in control of herself. She was also weary and hungry from a three-week siege and, as she saw the enemy soldiers enter the keep, her first thought was one of relief. Truly, one of relief. No longer would they be bottled up in a fortress that was slowly starving out, with men dying before their eyes and no way to receive help for them.

At least now, there was some resolution to the conflict, even if it meant she was on the losing side.

"*Emera!*" her sister screamed again. "Upstairs! Now!"

Emera turned to her sister, who was racing towards her, tripping over the supine men scattered about the hall floor.

"We have men to tend," she said calmly. "Jess, you must not forget your duties."

Lady Jessamyn de la Roarke would not be soothed by her outrageously composed sister. "But the enemy knights will kill us!"

"I do not believe they will do that. Why should they? It was not we who fought against them."

Jessamyn wasn't so convinced. She looked around, seeing the enemy soldiers already moving into the hall, swarming over the wounded. "Where is my husband?" she gasped. "Where is Brey that he might protect us from these men?"

Emera looked at the entry to the hall where the enemy was, indeed, starting to filter in. "Hopefully, he is dead," she muttered.

Jessamyn looked at her sister in shock. "You will not say such things!"

Emera focused on the woman who was eighteen months older than she was. "I will say what I please," she said. "Your husband is a vile excuse for a man. I have been telling you that since you married him. He handled this siege horribly and now he is nowhere to be found. Have you even *seen* him in the past week, Jess?"

Jessamyn turned red in the face. "He has been busy commanding the battle."

Emera wiped at her forehead with the back of her hand. "He has been making a mockery of everything he is supposed to stand for," she said. "When he is not beating his men or robbing travelers, he is in his personal retreat in the gatehouse bedding the servants. I have told you this before."

Jessamyn hissed at her, sharply. "Enough," she said. "I will not hear you. He is my husband and may do as he pleases."

"Including beat your own sister?"

"You should not have said things to displease him!"

"I refused to let him bed me, Jess!"

Jessamyn turned away from her sister, terrified at what was happening, confused and directionless. The old argument between her and Emera only heightened her sense of angst. Unless her husband was telling her what to do and where to go, she truly had no idea how to make a decision for herself. It had been that way for the past four years, ever since she had married Brey de la Roarke. He'd taken a lively young girl and turned her into something dependent and indecisive. When his wife's sister had come to live with them two years later, he'd tried to do the same thing to her, too, but Emera had been stronger than her sister.

Smarter, too.

But the result with Jessamyn was that the woman could hardly make a move without her husband because that was the way Brey wanted it. Even now, with the enemy overtaking the keep of Bowes, the only decision Jessamyn could make was to run away, but she was incapable of acting on it.

"What shall we do?" Jessamyn finally said, fearful that knights had now entered the keep. She watched them near the entry, wide-eyed. "Where is my husband? Will he leave us to the mercy of these… these barbarians?"

Emera could see the knights entering as well; big, battle-worn men in well-used protection. They were carrying weapons that had seen a good deal of service. She had to admit that she felt some apprehension but that was nothing new in her world. It was part of her everyday existence, ever since she'd been forced to come and live with her sister and the woman's husband.

Every breath she'd taken at Bowes for the past two years had been filled with apprehension over Brey de la Roarke and his constant harassment. A man that was supposed to protect her in a fatherly way had become a predator. Therefore, dealing with de la Roarke's enemies made her feel as if they'd saved her.

She intended to thank them profusely.

But the truth was that they were now the conquerors of Bowes. Three weeks of a nasty siege had delivered to them the prize of the mighty fortress. Standing tall, she set aside the cold rag she had been using to dress the burn wounds. Smoothing at her hair, she moved up beside her sister.

"They are in command of Bowes now," she said quietly. "We must greet them and offer our fealty."

Jessamyn looked at her as if she'd lost her mind. "I will do no such thing!"

Emera didn't answer. If her foolish sister was going to be stubborn about it, then so be it. Emera intended to be practical. She moved away from her sister, towards the men filling the entry. The sun had set early on this night and a cold winter's evening was settling, which meant it was dark in the world outside beyond the entry. Chill wind whistled in the open door, an unhealthy thing for the wounded that were lying near the entry.

The closer Emera came to the knights, the more her heart pounded. She didn't want to admit that her apprehension was gaining, but it was. Still, she felt she had little choice. If these men were now in charge of Bowes, then it would more than likely be much better for her if she simply showed them some respect. She drew close to a big man with dark hair and dark eyes, sporting a growth of beard on his weary face.

"My lord," she said, bowing her head respectfully. "I am Emera la Marche. I live here at Bowes and I am attending these wounded men. May I assume that the siege is over?"

The knight looked at her, as did his companions. All three of them eyed Emera with varied degrees of disinterest and suspicion.

"The commander of Bowes is dead," he said without emotion. "The castle is now held for the Count of Poitiers, Anjou, and Maine, Richard the Lionheart."

Emera had to admit she was shocked to hear those words. *The commander is dead.* Not shocked in a bad way, but in a way that bred utter astonishment. As big and powerful and brash as Brey de la Roarke was, there was something that suggested the man would never die. His particular brand of wickedness would go on forever. Therefore, she could hardly believe what she was hearing.

"Is it true?" she gasped. "Brey is... is dead?"

The knight nodded, now looking around the hall. "How many wounded?"

Emera looked around because he was. "I have seventy-nine wounded men, my lord."

"You will put them somewhere else."

She looked at him, somewhat confused by his statement. "But... there *is* nowhere else, my lord," she replied. "All of our outbuildings have been burned, so there is no shelter anywhere."

"Then you will move them into the bailey. I care not what you do with them, but remove them. My lord, de Royans, will require the use of this hall for his men."

It was a cruel command. Emera was beginning to feel the tendrils of desperation, realizing he meant to throw the wounded from the hall regardless of the fact they had no place to go.

"But these men are badly wounded, my lord," she said imploringly. "To move them outside into the freezing temperatures will surely kill them."

"Move them or I will."

Emera was struggling with her composure. The man meant to move the wounded no matter what she said. "Then you must give me time if that is your command," she said, sounding less respectful than she had been. "I must prepare a place to take them. Will you at least give me the night? Surely you can wait the night."

"De Royans waits for no man," the knight said, turning to his companions. "Send soldiers in here to remove the wounded."

"Wait!" Emera cried. "Surely you cannot show such inhumanity to wounded men. These are not animals to be cast aside. They are men who stood honorably against your flaming bombardment. Surely you will show them a small measure of respect."

The knight wasn't going to argue with her. Reaching out a big hand, he grabbed her by the arm, preparing to drag her away. But the moment he touched her, Emera's sense of self-protection kicked in, that same instinct that had been heightened and sharpened with Brey prowling the grounds of Bowes. Many a time, the man had tried to grab her or force himself on her, so Emera's reactions were stronger than most. The moment the knight grabbed her, she instinctively balled a fist and swung it at his face as hard as she could.

The strike was a brutal one, causing the knight's head to snap sideways, but he didn't lose his grip on her. He simply passed her off to the knight next to him, who threw her up over his shoulder as if she weighed no more than a child. Emera began to twist and fight, trying to dislodge his grip, but it was like fighting iron. He wasn't budging.

As the great hall deteriorated into bedlam as several de Royans soldiers moved in to cast out the wounded, Emera found herself hauled out of the keep over the shoulder of a man she could not fight. He held her tightly and her struggles were for naught. Somewhere behind her, she could hear Jessamyn screaming, too, a sure sign that she had also been captured by an enemy knight.

Gone were Emera's thoughts of thanking these men who had freed her from the tyranny of her brother-in-law. It seemed to her that she might have traded one kind of tyranny for another. Truthfully, she'd been idiotic to believe otherwise.

This was war. And she'd been a fool.

CHAPTER THREE

"RICHARD WILL BE pleased," Christopher said. "This was a great victory, Juston."

Given that it was evening on the day of the conquest of Bowes, there was a sense of jubilation among the men and Juston permitted his generals to address him informally. But it was also an evening of assessing the situation and securing the castle. They'd been doing that ever since de la Roarke had hit the ground and the gatehouse of Bowes had been claimed by Loxbeare, de Rhydian, and de Dere.

Now it was a matter of evaluating the state of the castle and the remains of de la Roarke's men. They had quite a job ahead of them as the cold dusk settled.

In fact, Christopher had just returned from a sweep of the castle as Juston remained in his tent. He wasn't a hands-on commander, instead, leaving the details to his trusted generals. He wasn't one to be bothered by little details that others could just as easily see to.

"It was a victory long in coming," Juston said, his tone between unhappiness and disgust. "It took far too long to secure the place. With my tactics, we should have had it secured in ten days or less."

"It was a great victory nonetheless."

"It was costly."

Juston drew out the last word and Christopher knew that it meant he was not to be argued with. Christopher was used to Juston's mood swings when it came to the end of a battle. He always felt the fight should have been a short one, as if a longer battle was a direct insult to his tactician skills. It was nearly the same thing every time, and all of the reasoning or praise in the world wouldn't change Juston's mood. Christopher didn't even try.

"David and Marcus are securing de la Roarke's men," he said, changing the subject. "Max and Achilles and Kress have been dealing with the keep and any surviving outbuildings."

"Where are Gart and Gillem?"

"They have command of the gatehouse."

Juston sat back on his portable bed, propped up with the pillows he carried around with him, pillows meant for his comfort alone. While most men weren't hugely concerned for their comfort in the field, Juston wasn't one of those. He demanded comfort. He poured himself a measure of the Malmsey wine on the table near his bed.

"I have been thinking, Chris," he said as he put the cup to his lips. "Bowes is a very important castle. The road it protects runs between Carlisle and Middlesbrough, to name a few. That's why Richard wanted to secure it; because it is so strategic."

Christopher nodded. "Indeed, it is."

Juston took a deep drink and smacked his lips. "So is Cotherstone Castle. It's about a half-day's ride north."

Christopher lifted his eyebrows curiously. "Are you thinking of confiscating that one, too?"

Juston nodded. "To have two castles in this area, not only securing the road but anchoring the area for Richard, would be ideal."

"Agreed."

Juston swirled the wine in his cup thoughtfully. "I am thinking about leaving you at Bowes and then sending David and Marcus to secure Cotherstone before I return to Netherghyll," he said. "I do not want to remain at either castle and I cannot imagine that Richard would expect me to. Once the walls are repaired sufficiently at Bowes and the castle secured, we will move on Cotherstone. I will then leave a contingent of men to guard both castles."

Christopher lifted a blonde eyebrow. "Do you expect trouble, then?"

Juston shook his head. "Nay," he replied. "Yet to leave either castle less than armed to the teeth would invite it. Hugh de Puiset is not far from here but he has wisely remained out of the siege of Bowes. He may reconsider that when I take Cotherstone, as well. He may very well try to reclaim the castles for Henry at some point."

Christopher couldn't disagree with him. "The Bishop of Durham has a few properties in this area," he said. "I believe Cotherstone belongs to him."

"It does."

"Yet he remains at his seat of Auckland Castle, which is a massive place," Christopher continued. "I've seen it. He has more than enough men to march on both castles to reclaim them."

"Yet he will not," Juston said confidently. "He does not wish to tangle with me, which is wise. I have an army as big as his and then some. Still, we have captured Bowes and I intend to move on Cotherstone once Bowes is secure. Therefore, I want you assessing the damage to the outer wall. We must estimate how long it will take to repair it sufficiently. More than that, tomorrow we move our army inside the walls. It is ours and we will occupy it."

"I believe Max is clearing out the hall."

"Clearing it of what?"

Christopher cleared his throat softly. "Wounded."

Juston could see that Christopher wasn't happy about that move, one he more than likely considered to be unmerciful. Christopher was a good man, the very best, but he tended to have a heart at times. That was both a good and a bad attribute. Juston took another drink of his wine.

"And you disapprove?"

Christopher didn't want to appear as if he was condemning another knight. "I did not mean to intimate that," he said. "Maxton is doing what he believes needs to be done, but there are dozens of wounded in that hall, so I've been told. What he is doing… it is cruel at best. There is nowhere else to put them but in the bailey, out in the elements. These are fellow Englishmen, not Scots or Welsh or even French. I do not look at them as a true enemy."

"You look at them as brothers-in-arms."

"In a sense, I do."

"And you believe we must show them mercy?"

"I believe we will be better men for it. You used to show mercy, years ago. I know you have not forgotten how, although you pretend to."

Juston shook his head reproachfully at the man although the corners of his mouth were tugging in a smile. Christopher was often his conscience in such matters because Juston had lost his conscience some time ago. Juston did what he wanted, when he wanted, and how he wanted. He'd been merciful years ago, before he became hardened to life and to men in general. Those were the days when he had genuinely cared about things. It seemed like a very long time ago, indeed.

Therefore, Juston seriously considered Christopher's suggestion and was about to ask him for alternatives to housing the wounded when there was suddenly a great commotion outside of his tent. By the time he and Christopher turned to the source, the flap slapped back and Maxton entered with a small figure slung up over his shoulder.

"An offering, my lord," Maxton announced. He suddenly shifted the burden on his shoulder, leaned forward, and dumped it onto the ground. "I found her and a second woman in the hall. Consider them spoils of war."

Sprawled on her buttocks, the woman pushed her black hair from her face and glared up at Maxton. She was clearly furious but showed surprising restraint in her response.

"The second woman you speak of is my sister," she said steadily. "We are clearly no threat to you and offer no resistance. Why do you treat us this way?"

Maxton's dark gaze lingered on her a moment. He wasn't going to lower himself to respond to a prisoner. His focus then moved to Juston. "The wounded are being moved out of the hall as we speak," he said. "I should have it completely cleared in an hour. I also have Achilles rounding up the servants. I will assume you will want a meal?"

Juston heard Maxton but he wasn't looking at the man. He was looking at the woman on the frozen earth in his tent. Her hair was as black as a raven's wing, somewhat curly and very messy, and her skin was the color of cream. He'd never seen such pale, perfect skin. When she brushed the hair out of her face, he could see that she had a pert little nose and enormous blue eyes the shade of a morning glory.

Truly, it was a shocking moment to be faced with such beauty. For the first time since Lizette's death, a woman actually had his attention. It was purely an aesthetic appeal, but an appeal nonetheless. Juston set aside his wine and quickly stood up, eyeing the woman with great curiosity while completely ignoring Maxton's question.

"What is your name, woman?" he asked.

The young woman's focus shifted to him and, for a brief moment, Juston felt a surge of awe bolt through him. *Wonder.* Those brilliant eyes had his attention, his curiosity, and he found himself inspecting her face as she replied.

"Emera la Marche, my lord" she said. "My sister is the wife of the garrison commander."

"De la Roarke?"

"Aye, my lord."

Juston's gaze lingered on her a moment. "He is dead."

"I have heard, my lord."

She said it quite emotionlessly, causing Juston to cock his head curiously. Her looks had captured his attention but now her behavior had his interest.

"I should think there would be more of a reaction, considering he is your kin."

She was precluded from answering when the tent flap was pushed aside and Kress entered with a second woman clutched against his chest. He held her awkwardly because she was trying to kick and fight, and he didn't want to lose his grip. He took two steps into the tent and let her fall to the ground roughly.

"Brute!" the woman hissed, seeing Emera and scrambling in her direction. "You fiend! My husband will have something to say about the way you have treated me!"

She practically crawled up over her sister. Emera put her arms around Jessamyn to comfort her. Together, they huddled on the floor, cold and shivering, looking up at their captors. While Jessamyn's expression was full of terror, Emera's was full of concern.

"My lord, as I have explained, my sister and I are no threat at all," she said. "We will obey your commands. We do not need to be treated as prisoners."

Juston looked at the pair. Emera was glorious while her sister was a somewhat paler version. He pointed at the sister.

"That is the wife of de la Roarke?" he asked.

Emera nodded. "Aye, my lord."

Juston spoke to the sister. "Your name?"

"Lady Jessamyn," she replied in a trembling voice as she clutched Emera. "Where is my husband?"

Juston looked at Emera, registering some surprise that evidently the woman didn't know of her husband's death. He saw no need to tactfully couch his reply.

"Dead," he said simply. "Bowes Castle now belongs to Richard. We will send you home to your family, should they agree to take you. We have no use for women at a military installation."

Jessamyn's face turned red and she buried her face in Emera's arm. "Then it is true," she gasped. "He *is* dead."

While Jessamyn made a good show of being devastated at her husband's death, for Emera knew it to be grief mostly borne of duty, the enemy knight had made a statement that had her singular focus – *we will send you home to your family*. That's not what she had wanted or even expected to hear. She found that she was now quite concerned for her immediate future.

"That would be quite impossible, my lord," Emera said. "We have no family. Bowes is our home."

Juston had absolutely no emotion as he responded to her. "I have no place for you here," he said. "If you have no family, then I will have my men escort you to the town of your choice."

It was a cold answer. He didn't wait for her to reply; he turned to the men who had brought the women into the tent and, with a quiet command, sent them on their way again. The two knights quit the tent, leaving Juston and Christopher with two women cowering at their feet.

Cowering was a good word. Recoiling was more like it, pulling away from a man who was intent on showing no regard for their well-being. Although Emera had not been afraid when Bowes had initially fallen, now she was growing increasingly fearful. It never occurred to her that she and Jessamyn would be left homeless as a result of the battle. She naively believed that those who defeated Brey would treat her as if she was not their enemy. Of course, that wasn't to be.

It was embarrassing to realize she'd been foolishly optimistic.

"My lord, I must again say that my sister and I have nowhere to go and no money even if we did," Emera said steadily, trying not to sound like she was begging. "Our father was a prosperous knight who retired to enjoy his estates, a cousin of the Lusignan family. Our family was small – it was just me, my sister, and our brother. Our mother died long ago. Brey married my sister four years ago and brought her to Bowes. When my father died two years ago, my brother did not want me to stay in the family home. He married, you see, and he had a wife and children and did not want his unmarried sister as a burden, so he sent me to live at Bowes. Now that you hold the castle, my sister and I cannot return home. We literally have nowhere to go."

Lusignan. Juston knew that name, a hated French family who was a great opposition to Richard. He'd fought against them many times in the past and that admission only served to make the lady even more of an enemy in his eyes.

Regardless of her beauty, his first reaction was to simply give the order that would see the frightened women carted out of his tent. He'd given that order many times. He didn't have time to argue with anyone, most especially a prisoner. But something had him holding back, biting off that order, because he was coming to think that two women with nowhere to go, and no male kin, might have use in his army after all. He could already think of a use for Emera – a humiliating use that would degrade a woman of the House of Lusignan.

He looked at Christopher.

"I am not in the habit of supporting prisoners like this," he said. "Can you think of a use for them? I suppose they could warm the men's beds."

Jessamyn gasped in shock as Christopher mulled over the situation. He was rather impressed that Juston hadn't ordered them thrown from the castle outright. *You used to show mercy, years ago,* he'd said. Perhaps this was Juston's way of presumably reclaiming an attribute that he'd been accused of losing. But it wasn't a very savory option. Thoughtfully, he made his way over to Juston.

"If you use them for the men, then you are sentencing them to a terrible fate simply for the crime of being kin to a man who supports Henry," Christopher said quietly so the women wouldn't hear. "They are women, after all. You do not want to be cruel to the weaker sex. That kind of reputation will haunt a man."

Juston lifted a dark eyebrow. "It would not bother me, nor do I care."

Christopher couldn't believe that. "They are *women,* Juston."

"They are Lusignan."

That brought an entirely new element to their fate. Christopher knew that name, as they all did, and it was a hated name, indeed. It was the women's misfortune to have been born into that family and Christopher couldn't argue with family ties. Without anything to say to the contrary with regards to the Lusignan relation, he simply lifted his eyebrows in resignation. Juston was going to do as he wished, regardless of what anyone else said.

Juston, sensing that Christopher had no more arguments, spoke softly. "They are fine looking women, Chris," he said. "At least, the one with the blue eyes is. I will mayhap take her for myself and you can give the other one over to the knights."

Christopher still wasn't happy with Juston's intention. "Do as you will, but I will again say that they are not concubines," he muttered. "Look at them; they are well formed and should not be treated like the dogs in heat that follow around the army. I know you believe that you are showing them some mercy by not banishing them from the castle, but believe me... they will not consider your suggestion merciful at all."

Juston eyed him. "You are getting soft in your old age," he said quietly. "The first rule of war is to let your enemies know that they have no meaning in the grand scheme of your life. No decision should be questioned and no decision should be reversed. When you divide this country up into enemy and ally, these women are the enemy no matter how you try to spin the truth. Men or women, it makes no difference and thinking the way you do, your compassion may cost you your life someday. Have I not taught you such things?"

"You have."

"Then take the uglier one out of here and see if the knights wish for her to warm their beds. I will keep the other one with me. These women are prisoners, loyalists to Henry, and shall be treated as such. And that will be the end of it."

Christopher didn't argue with him. There was some value in what he said, but Christopher still believed in mercy for the enemy. Perhaps that's because he'd never had one betray him as Juston had experienced. One of the many things the man had experienced over his lifetime so it was best to heed his knowledge.

Without another word, Christopher reached down and pulled Jessamyn from Emera's embrace. It was a swift and startling action, giving the women no time to resist. Soon, Jessamyn was being dragged out of the tent by a very big, blonde knight as Emera struggled to her feet and tried to follow. Juston grabbed her by the arm before she could move very far.

"Not you," he said. "You will stay with me."

The fear that Emera had tried so hard to keep at bay was coming on full-force. "Why?" she demanded as he pushed her back onto her knees. "Where is that knight taking her?"

Juston let her go and headed back over to the small table that held the Malmsey and cups. As he went to pour Emera some wine, hoping the liquor would shut her up and make her pliable to the demands he would soon be making, she scrambled to her feet again and bolted from the tent.

Juston was on her in a flash. Emera had hardly made it a few feet when he grabbed her, pulling her into a viselike hold. But instead of surrendering, she turned into a wildcat, struggling to pull herself from his grip, doing everything she could to release herself. She was in the grips of fear, causing her to kick and fight as she'd never done in her life. Still, Juston held her firm, dragging her back towards his tent when her struggles caused her to lose footing. Stumbling over herself, she fell into the frozen mud but Juston yanked her to her feet so sharply that he nearly pulled her arms from their sockets.

"Stop fighting," he commanded in a voice that left no room for doubt. "Are you listening to me? Cease your struggles, lady, or things will go very badly for you. Is this in any way unclear?"

When she refused to acknowledge him, now nearly out of her head with panic, he slapped her across the face simply to get her attention. It wasn't terribly hard but it was enough to sting, and it certainly got her attention. But instead of ceasing her struggles as he'd commanded, she did something very unexpected. One slap was met by another as Emera swung her open palm at him, slapping him across the face as swiftly and as sharply as he had slapped her.

He'd hit her and she'd hit him right back.

The sounds reverberated in the cold air, two sharp strikes – *plap,*

plap! Juston's eyes widened in surprise, looking into Emera's wide eyes when she realized what she had done. All of her struggling came to an instant halt and her mouth fell open in horror.

"Oh... my lord...," she gasped, terrified that he was going to beat her for striking him. "I... forgive me, please. I... I did not think... I only... well, it was much like it was with my sister's husband and... oh, God, please do not hurt me. I acted before I could think."

Juston gazed into her pale face a moment longer before dragging her back into his tent in a most undignified manner. He had her by the arm but he also had some of her hair in his grasp, which meant she was walking beside him most awkwardly as he pulled her back into his tent. There was utter misery on her face, as if going to her execution.

For all Emera knew, she was.

Once inside the dim confines of the tent, Juston roughly threw her to her knees again and, this time, Emera didn't try to rise. She remained there, on her knees, trembling with fear. She knew she'd done something terrible and she knew she was going to pay for it. Terror filled her like never before, even more than when she was terrorized by Brey. At least he was a known evil, something she'd been able to fight off for the past two years. But this man... she knew she couldn't fight him off.

In her terror, she'd dug her own grave.

CHAPTER FOUR

"WHAT DO YOU mean it was much like your sister's husband?" The question hung in the air between them as Emera cowered on the cold ground, her head lowered. Juston wasn't even sure why he asked the question, only that the look in Emera's eyes when she'd said it had him very curious. Was he angry about the slap? Oddly enough, he wasn't. Truthfully, he didn't even care. It had been a very long time since someone had swung back at him, someone who wasn't groveling at his feet, telling him how great he was and how magnificent. Someone who wasn't feeding that enormous sense of pride he had.

Truthfully, he didn't know *why* he wasn't angry at the slap. There was something in the woman's expression that cooled any anger he might have felt. Maybe he was simply getting foolish in his old age. Or maybe that mercy Christopher had spoken of was confusing him.

Now, he found himself asking the first question that came to his mind and he expected an answer. As he watched the meaning of his words sink in, Emera's head came up, her eyes turning to him with confusion.

"My… my sister's….?" she stammered.

"Tell me what you meant by that."

Emera swallowed hard. "I meant…," she stopped, swallowed again, and continued. "He… he is the commander of Bowes. *Was* the commander of Bowes, I mean. He could do as he pleased, or at least he thought he could."

"I know what a commander's rights are. Answer my question. I will not ask again."

His tone frightened her. "He... he thought that when he married my sister, I was part of that bargain," she said, her voice trembling. "For two years, I have told him that I was not. Simply because I came to live with my sister did not mean I became his property."

Juston had no idea why this woman's plight, or the dynamics between her and de la Roarke, should interest him. But he was interested nonetheless. Perhaps it was because his own life was so colorless and devoid of anything beautiful or pleasant that he found other lives more interesting. Or perhaps it was simply because the woman herself interested him. All he knew was that she had his focus more than she should have.

"But he was your liege," he pointed out. "He clothed you and fed you."

"That does not mean that I am his property."

"You are of marriageable age. He made no attempt to marry you off?"

Her pale cheeks reddened and she lowered her head. "He tried."

"What happened?"

She shook her head. "I do not make a pleasing prospect."

He frowned. "Ridiculous," he said. "Any man would consider you purely based on your physical appearance."

She looked at him, then. "The only men he chose were men to whom he owed a debt," she said, the strength returning to her voice as she spoke on a subject that both infuriated and sickened her. "Old men, sickly men, but all of them had one thing in common – they were wealthy and he owed them money or business dealings. If you've not heard, my lord, Brey de la Roarke was a thief. He treated the road that runs alongside this castle like his own personal property, exacting heavy tolls from travelers or even murdering men for their wealth. I cannot tell you how many wealthy travelers he simply killed and stole from.

Why do you think this siege went on for so long? Not only did he not want you to have the castle, but he did not want you to have the wealth it harbors."

Juston regarded her in the weak light for a moment, mulling over her words as he once again turned for the wine on the table. He'd already known most of the reputation of Brey de la Roarke but this was the first time he'd heard anything first-hand.

"You are divulging quite a bit of information to the enemy, lady," he said.

She snorted softly. "I have nothing to protect, my lord," she said frankly. "If Brey is dead, then there is nothing to fear. The vaults below the keep are full of his ill-gotten gains. I must presume that you commanded this siege against Bowes."

He poured his wine. "Why would you say that?"

"Because my sister and I were delivered to you as spoils of war."

"Then that was a clever deduction."

Emera couldn't tell if he was insulting her or not. "Then as the commander, you are now in possession of a great treasure courtesy of Brey's thievery. He would be furious to know all of his wealth went to his enemy."

He turned to look at her, wine in hand. "And you show absolutely no loyalty to the man who fed and clothed you," he said. "I find that very curious, indeed."

There was rebuke in that statement and she looked at him a moment; *really* looked at him. He was an older knight with shoulder-length blonde hair, wavy and dirty, half of it tucked behind one ear. His features were big and masculine, with a granite-square jaw and a big dimple in his chin. He was very tall as well as very muscular. Everything about him was big and booming and powerful, as if she was a little bug to be quashed up against his sheer size. The man had an aura about him that was palpable.

But the most noticeable thing about him was his eyes – they were a pale green color that was as vibrant as a green amethyst gemstone she'd seen once. They were also intense and intelligent, and a bit wild-eyed to tell the truth. When he looked at her, it was almost as if his eyes were burning right through her. Those eyes spoke of untold strength but they also spoke to her of something strangely tumultuous, as if he, too, had some upheaval in his life.

"He made my life miserable, my lord," she said after a moment. "Every day was a day trying to stay clear of him, every meal was a lesson in how to avoid his seeking hands, and every night I felt like a prisoner, locking myself into my chamber and ignoring him when he came pounding on my door. Do you not understand? I lived in terror of him. I am, therefore, as disloyal to him as one can be. In fact, when your men entered the hall earlier, I had a mind to thank them for freeing me of Brey's tyranny. But I think that was a foolish notion."

"Why?"

"Because I fear I am in a worse situation than before."

Juston couldn't disagree with that statement. He regarded her before taking a long drink of his wine. Then, he just looked at her, pondering what she had told him. In truth, she made perfect sense as to why she held no loyalty to de la Roarke. She was well-spoken and articulate, with a voice that sounded sweet and melodious.

"So you refused his marital contracts and you refused his advances," he said.

She nodded. "Aye."

He finished the last of his wine. "Are you so precious and pious that you are too good for a man's touch?" he finally spat. "You eat the man's food, allow him to clothe you, and you show absolutely no gratitude for that? Great Bleeding Christ, I would have thrown you to the wolves the first chance I had if you'd behaved so poorly with me. Woman, in case you have not yet realized it, you are at a man's mercy. You have no right to speak up for yourself; you will only do as you are told. Now you are at *my* mercy. Pray you do not behave so irrationally with me."

Emera was back to being terrified of him. "What do you mean?" she asked. "What are you going to do?"

He shook his head, his blonde hair waving back and forth. "It is what *you* are going to do," he said. "You belong to me now. You will do as I say."

She didn't like the sound of that in the least. "What... what would you have me do?"

He began to untie the heavy padded tunic that hung over his mail coat. "What a woman does best."

"What is that?"

"You will service me."

Those were horrifying words to Emera. Oh, she knew what he meant. She had no doubt. But she'd spent the past two years fighting off Brey de la Roarke and she had no intention of losing her carefully-guarded maidenhood to this brusque knight.

"Surely you cannot mean...," she gasped.

"I can and I do. Remove your clothing."

Her mouth popped open in shock and dismay. "I will *not*," she said, backing away from him, still on her knees. "I... I have never known the touch of a man, my lord. I would have no idea how to... to service you."

"You will learn."

She shook her head, recoiling from him yet again, only more strongly than before. What he was suggesting had panic filling her chest and tears were threatening as hard as she tried to stave them off.

"I will *not* service you," she hissed. "You can throw me to the wolves or worse and, still, I will not willingly touch you."

He pulled the heavy tunic over his head. "I do not care if it is willingly or not," he said. "You will do what I tell you to do."

"I will die before I do!"

His eyes flicked up to her as he went to work on the mail he was wearing. Usually, Gart helped him with it but Gart was in command of the gatehouse so there was no one to help him except a woman who swore she wouldn't do anything he told her to do. He'd not had that kind of refusal in a very long time and, to be truthful, wasn't quite sure how to deal with it. Perhaps if he ignored it, she'd forget all about her rebellion and simply give in.

"Stand up," he told her.

On her knees, inching away from him, Emera shook her head. "I will not."

He frowned. "I am growing weary of hearing those words come out of your mouth. I told you to stand up. I require your assistance."

She was looking at him, having no idea what he meant. One moment, he was speaking of her servicing him and in the next, he was asking for her assistance. She had no idea what he was trying to accomplish.

Was he trying to trick her somehow?

"Assistance for what?" she asked fearfully.

Juston sighed heavily. Now, her resistance to him was becoming annoying. "I require assistance with my mail," he said. "Stand up and help me."

Emera shook her head hesitantly. "I will not help you undress so you can then force me to… to do whatever it is you want me to do. I will not do it!"

He'd had enough of her refusal. Whatever patience he'd had snapped and he was on her in two big strides, grabbing her by the arms and yanking her to her feet. He then pulled her up against his broad chest, forcing her into contact with him, her warm body against his hard mail. They came together with so much force that he heard her grunt.

In truth, it had been a brutal action designed to frighten her. When Juston found himself staring down into Emera's terrified face, he was pleased to see that she was quite frightened.

It was time to show the woman who was in charge.

"I grow weary of your refusals," he snarled, his hot breath blowing tendrils of hair about her face. "If you think I am asking for your cooperation or permission, you are gravely mistaken. This is conquest, lady, and I take what I want. You have no say in the matter. Now, help me off with my mail and let's get on with it."

So his intentions had not changed. He wanted her to help him with his mail so he could continue with his lustful plans. Emera's eyes were wide with fear as she gazed up at him, a very large and very virile man who had her trapped against him. She'd never been this close to a man before and she could feel the heat from his hands as he gripped her. But his heated breath on her face was causing her to tremble for more reasons than simply fright.

Aye, he'd put a good scare into her but there was something more, something she didn't understand. All she knew was that the smell and feel of him was overwhelming her in a manner she'd never before known. Her heart was racing and her breathing was coming in uneven gasps. But in spite of her confusing reaction to him, one thing was clear – she would not obey him. She would not submit. She would not surrender herself to him in any fashion. That being the case, she could only give him one answer, the only answer that came to mind.

An answer, she knew, that would cost her.

"Nay," she breathed. "I will not."

Juston wasn't surprised to hear her answer. As much as it infuriated him, it also impressed him. He had the woman overwhelmed with his strength, snarling threats in her face, and she still refused. Either she was very brave or very stupid. He couldn't decide which. Now, it was becoming a game.

A game he intended to win.

Abruptly, he slanted his lips over hers, suckling her mouth and feeling her stiffen in his grip. He'd only meant to jar her, to frighten her further, but the moment he tasted her was the moment the tables turned on him completely. She was soft and sweet, like warm honey upon his tongue, and her flesh was delectable and tender. He suckled her lips, forcing them apart only to plunge his tongue into her mouth as if to gorge himself. There wasn't anything about her that wasn't wildly arousing, calling out to the potent male inside of him. But this wildly arousing creature had refused him. She hadn't thought him nearly as attractive as he thought her.

She had insulted him.

Abruptly, he released his grip on her and dragged her over to the tent opening. Throwing back the fabric panel, he was met with several soldiers on guard but no knights. Infuriated, he tossed her at the nearest soldier.

"Find Chris," he demanded. "Have him throw the woman in the vault. She is not to be released until I give the word."

The soldier, a seasoned man clad in a full array of well-used armor, reached down and grabbed Emera, who had essentially fallen at his feet. When she started to fight him, he motioned to another soldier to come and help him.

"Aye, my lord," the soldier said as he hauled Emera to her feet.

Juston jabbed a finger at him. "She is not to be touched, by anyone," he said. "If any man so much as touches a hair on her head, my justice shall be swift. Lock her up but she is not to be punished beyond that."

"Aye, my lord."

"And send Burton to me once you've delivered her to de Lohr."

"Aye, my lord."

Juston's focus shifted from the soldier to Emera, who was disheveled and struggling not to weep. He could see that she was completely, utterly rattled. He looked her in the eye.

"Mayhap a night in the vault will convince you to change your mind," he said. "For your sake, I hope it does."

With that, he flicked a wrist at the soldiers, indicating for them to remove the prisoner. As Juston turned for his tent, he could hear Emera's struggles as she was led away. Doubt mingled with his fury and he turned, briefly, to see that she was giving the two soldiers quite a fight, so much so that she was trying to kick one of them in the knees.

Somehow, he didn't like to see her fighting like that, as if fighting for her very life. He almost called them back but he had no idea what that would accomplish other than it would simply feed his anger – she was terrified and reacting in kind, and he suspected that they would only be back where they started if he took her back into the tent with him – him demanding her services and her refusing. Of course, he could take what he wanted from her but he'd never needed to. Women naturally fell at his feet, the revered feet of the great Juston de Royans.

But not Emera la Marche. She clearly wanted nothing to do with him and the fact that he'd shown her a morsel of attention had no effect on her whatsoever. Most women would have killed for such a thing. Was it possible there was actually a woman unwilling to submit to England's greatest warrior?

Not only was it possible, it was probable.

Humiliated, Juston retreated to his tent to drown that humiliation in more Malmsey. When Marcus showed up some time later, he was almost too far gone with the wine to effectively speak with him and he could only hope his humiliation didn't show. It wouldn't do if anyone else knew how Emera la Marche had treated him.

CHAPTER FIVE

"LOOK AT DAVID," Gart muttered. "See how disturbed he looks."

In the gatehouse of Bowes, it was well after sunset and torches lit both the inner and outer wards. They were quite vast, both of them, and after the battle, quite a mess of charred wood and debris. Everything smelled of smoke and damp, for between the burned buildings and the freezing rain, the sights and smells were brutal to the senses.

Gart was standing at the entrance to the outer ward, watching David de Lohr emerge from the inner ward, his young face pinched with cold and annoyance. Knowing him as well as he did, Gart could tell that all was not well with him. His words, low and quiet, were spoken to the knight who had command of the gatehouse alongside him.

Gillem d'Evereux was a broad knight with shoulder-length red hair, a color that many a woman had envied. He was pale-cheeked and reasonably handsome, and his brown eyes watched David as the man crossed from the inner bailey in a marching cadence that suggested to him what it had suggested to Gart – David was disturbed. Gillem grunted.

"He and Max have probably gone to blows again," he said. "Maxton has charge of the keep and he's been moving the wounded out into the open exposure of the inner bailey. That is not something I would do, personally, but I am also not foolish enough to express that opinion to him. David, however, is."

Gart shook his head. "David is not foolish," he said. "He says what he is thinking and he has the sword-hand to back it up."

Gillem shook his head. "Against Max?" He lifted his eyebrows. "Not many men have challenged him and lived to tell the tale. The only reason Max will not move against David is because Chris would get involved and no man wants to take him on in a sword fight. It is fear of the older brother that keeps Maxton away from his sword when it comes to David de Lohr."

Gart looked at him, his eyes glimmering with some humor. "You act as if David cannot handle himself in a fight," he said. "He is one of the best knights in all of England and you know it."

"Even against Maxton of Loxbeare?"

"Even against Maxton of Loxbeare."

"But Maxton has an edge of madness about him. Everyone knows that."

"David has the de Lohr speed and skill. I would put that against madness any day."

Gillem shook his head and turned away from the sight of David stomping his way across the inner bailey. "Why would Juston let Max move the wounded out of the hall?" he wondered aloud, although it was a rhetorical question. He didn't really expect an answer. "That is an exceptionally brutal move, considering the wounded have nowhere to go."

Gart leaned against the cold stones of the gatehouse, arms folded across his chest as he watched the activity in the outer ward.

"Juston is not in the habit of being concerned for the enemy," Gart said. "He lets the knights do as they please in most aspects. He trusts them to make the decisions they feel are best."

Gillem nodded. "You and I have spoken of his attitude before," he said quietly, unwilling for his opinion to be heard by any of the soldiers also occupying the gatehouse. "I have known Juston for almost ten years. Back in those days, he had an abundance of compassion and dedication. He was the first man into the battle and the last one to leave. He cared about the wounded and showed mercy to the enemy. But after his wife and children were killed at Taillebourg, he changed. Since then, it is as if his body goes through the motions of fighting battles but his heart isn't there. Great Bleeding Christ, if you could have seen the man back in those days, Gart. It was like watching a god descended. He never made a poor move in battle or made a bad decision. Men could depend on Juston de Royans to lead them to victory."

Gart looked at him. "They still can," he said. "Did you see his move with de la Roarke?"

Gillem nodded firmly. "That was like the Juston of old," he said. "Every day, he would make brilliant moves like that. What you saw today... that was something I've not seen in a long time."

Gart lifted his eyebrows. "Mayhap that is a good sign, a sign that the Juston of old is still inside of him, somewhere. Mayhap we will see that great knight again someday."

Gillem sighed heavily as he, too, leaned back against the cold stone of the gatehouse. "I cannot believe that. Whatever greatness inside of him that made him who he was died that day those years ago when his family was murdered. The heart of him is gone. But I tried to help him reclaim it; you know I did."

Gart looked at the man as he slumped against the frozen wall, his feet half-buried in the sludge of the gatehouse floor. It was a touchy subject Gillem had wandered into, something he wandered into quite often. When Gart didn't reply, unsure what to say to the man, Gillem simply continued the conversation himself.

"I tried to provide him with the legacy he lost," he pushed. "A bastard son, but a son nonetheless. The boy could be a great tribute to him if he would only do what is right by him."

Gart didn't particularly want to speak on the subject. "Mayhap he will," he said after a moment. "The boy is only three years of age. There is still time."

Gillem looked down at his feet as he spoke. "There is time for the boy, but what of my sister?" he said, finally lifting his head to look in the direction of the encampment outside of the walls. "My sister lives in shame on a daily basis. Bearing Juston de Royans' child has not given her the prestige or security she had hoped. It has only made her a whore who bore the child of a legendary man. There is no respect in that and time is growing short for her. Soon, she will be past her prime and her beauty will fade. De Royans will not want to marry her."

Gart came away from the wall, rubbing at his hands because the temperature was dropping as night descended. He had a few things on the tip of his tongue to say about Gillem's sister but he wasn't going to bring up the fact that Gillem and the woman had practically trapped Juston into bedding her, taking advantage of him one night when he had been drunk and miserable, and looking for a woman to warm his bed.

Gillem's sister, Sybilla d'Evereux, had stepped into that position readily, a virginal young woman who was hoping to trap a husband in the greatest knight in the land. But it didn't work out as she had hoped and Juston barely even acknowledged that the child was his, mostly because he couldn't really deny it. The child looked just like him. But the pregnancy had been Sybilla's fault as far as he was concerned and he'd refused to claim any responsibility for it.

He didn't want another legacy *or* another wife.

Which put Gillem in an awkward position. Gart knew, as the other knights knew, that Gillem had been trying to place his sister in a position of power as Juston's wife. He said he'd only been trying to help the man move on after the death of his family, but that wasn't the truth. Both he and his sister had been trying to take advantage of the man's misery. When Gillem's scheme had ultimately failed, he had no choice but to remain with the man he'd tried to manipulate simply because to leave him would have been to admit his guilt in the failed scheme and he couldn't do that.

The knights suspected that Juston knew that Gillem had tried to trap him into marriage, but he'd never said anything about it and he hadn't dismissed the man; he simply kept Gillem in his service, a rather miserable soul with a sister who had born a bastard. It was rather hellish at times but perhaps that had been Juston's plan all along. But the longer Gillem remained, the less respect and attention Juston showed him.

Perhaps *that* had been his plan all along, to punish the man for a scheme gone wrong.

Juston was both clever and vindictive that way.

"I would not worry about that right now," Gart finally said because he wasn't sure what else to say on an exhaustive subject. "As I said, the boy is still young. Who is to say what Juston will do in the future?"

Gillem shrugged restlessly. "That is a legitimate question," he said. "All I know is that he is not the same man I swore to serve those years ago. It seems as if there is no honor with him any longer, as if he cares for nothing but himself."

The humor faded from Gart's eyes. "I will never hear that from your mouth again."

"What?"

"That Juston is without honor."

Gillem flicked his eyes at Gart, perhaps guiltily. "I simply meant he cares for nothing these days."

Gart shook his head, his gaze intense. "That is not what you said," he rumbled. "Juston de Royans is a man of great honor. He is a man of legend. If I hear you say again he has no honor, I will challenge you myself. Do you understand me?"

Gillem waved him off even though he was intimidated by Gart Forbes. The man was young, but he was vastly strong and skilled, and he had a streak of bloodlust in him in the heat of battle that would scare even the most seasoned warrior. They'd all seen it. Squire or no, Gart was not one to be trifled with.

"I did not mean it," Gillem stressed, looking at Gart as if to empha-size his point. "Satisfied? I did not mean what I said. I am simply weary.

I do not know what I am saying."

Gart eyed the man as he headed for the mouth of the gatehouse. He knew that Gillem did, indeed, mean what he'd said and it had been a comment borne of frustration and a twisted sense of what was right and wrong. Juston refused to marry the mother of his child and, in Gillem's mind, that was a man without honor regardless of the fact that Gillem was, in fact, without honor himself for having tried to trap Juston in the first place.

But Gillem didn't see it that way and it wasn't the first time over the past three years that Gart or any of the other knights had heard Gillem speak poorly of Juston. One of these days, one of the knights was going to challenge Gillem about it or, better still, Juston would.

Gart hoped he was around to see that battle. He hoped he was around to see Gillem's day of reckoning.

IT WAS COLDER than Emera had ever known it to be. Even though some very big, very blonde knight with a trim beard had brought her a mound of blankets and a brazier for warmth, still, none of that was strong enough to stave off the cold of the room she'd been locked in.

She'd never been so cold in her entire life.

She'd ended up in one of the tower rooms on the outer wall, locked into a tiny chamber beneath the spiral stairs, a chamber with no ventilation or light except the glowing peat from the brazier. With the tiny chamber and the heat from the peat, one would have thought the room would warm up quickly, but it didn't. Moreover, with very little ventilation, the fumes from the fire had built up and her eyes were burning. The fumes also irritated her lungs so she'd been coughing fairly steadily for the past few hours. Or was it the past few days? She felt as if she'd been locked away for an eternity.

The big knight with the green eyes....

He'd locked her away. This was all his fault. She didn't even know who he was, for he'd never given her his name, but he was the man in command. That had been made clear, especially the way the knights behaved around him. And he'd kissed her... Sweet Mary, he'd kissed her in a way she'd never been kissed in her life. It was all moist heat and lips and tongue, an act of domination that terrified her at first... *at first...* she was loath to admit that something about his heat and intimacy had quickly transformed her fear into something else.

... but *what* else?

There was confusion in her mind as to why the brutal commander's kiss had made her feel something other than sheer terror, but along with those thoughts were other pressing matters as well – most of all, where was Jessamyn? She'd asked the big blonde knight who had tended to her needs but he didn't have an answer for her. He'd simply given her the blankets and stoked the brazier, and then went about his way. He hadn't said a bloody word about Jessamyn and the not knowing was eating away at Emera.

Through the night, fear gave way to frustration, and frustration to despair. The little room had no windows so she couldn't tell if it was day or night. There was no way of knowing what time it was except that she was becoming hungry. That told her that it was at least getting near dawn. She'd not eaten since early the previous night, before the keep had been taken, so it had been a long while since she'd eaten.

She wasn't even sure they would feed her. Certainly, she'd been given blankets and heat, but there was so much going on at the castle that, perhaps, they would forget to feed her. Perhaps, she might even starve to death in that tiny room, alone and forgotten, and that thought caused Emera to reflect on her life.

She was fairly certain that she was going to die in this place.

As the youngest child of three – an older brother and sister – she'd not accomplished much in her time on this earth. While her father was alive, she had been dedicated to the poor in the area she had lived in, making sure the sick were tended and the hungry fed. It was a mission she'd carried on from her late mother.

Her mother, Lady Iris, had been a kind and giving woman, so much so that she'd ended up contracting a malady from a poor woman she'd tended; a malady that ended up killing her. That had caused Emera's father to show particular disdain for the poor and needy. Emera had carried on her mother's work in secret, although Jessamyn had known about it. So had their brother, Payne, although he'd never cared much about what she did. He was a man of his own world and only cared for those things in it. Even though he'd never given her away to their father, that changed with the man died and Payne suddenly turned into a tyrant who accused her of trying to give away all of the family's assets to the poor. That was when Emera had been forced to live with Jessamyn and the constant flight from Brey had begun.

That had been the true beginning of hell.

For two years, she'd spent all of her time escaping her brother-in-law and trying to help her sister run an efficient house and hold. But all the while, she felt useless and restless, until one evening she'd heard a passing monk speak of a charity hospital near Sherburn that fed and clothed and even educated the needy.

Bowes sometimes housed travelers, at least those who paid Brey enough for him not to kill them, and Emera had sat in awed conversation one evening with a monk who was traveling back to a place he'd called Christ's Hospital of Sherburn. Since the man had virtually nothing to steal, and being that he was a man of God, Brey had left him alone and the man had slept on the floor of the hall before departing early the next morning. But Emera had brought him some food the evening he'd arrived and that was when they'd struck up their conversation.

Christ's Hospital sounded like a place she wanted to go to, to help with the poor and needy. It was relatively new, a place established by the Bishop of Durham and dedicated to the Blessed Virgin, among others. It was a true charity hospital that, according to the monk, housed lepers. Emera wasn't afraid of hard work and she wasn't particularly afraid of lepers. She could only believe her mother would have approved of her dedicating her life to charity work. Now, with Bowes fallen and no future in sight for her, she was coming to think that going to Christ's Hospital was the best option for her.

What was it the knight in charge had said? *I will have my men escort you to the town of your choice.* Now, she had a destination. She had a plan.

If only they'd let her out of this blasted little room!

At some point, she fell asleep in her cramped prison, coughing from the fumes from the peat and listening to her stomach rumble. She wasn't entirely sure how long she'd been asleep when the door suddenly rattled. Startled, she sat up so fast that she ended up hitting her head on the stone. Grunting in pain and seeing stars, she put a hand to her head just as the old oak and iron door lurched open.

It was evidently still dark outside, as evidenced by very little light filtering in through the open door. She could see a very big man, silhouetted against that light, and she suspected it was the same knight who had brought her here. He was about the same size. The moment he stuck his head inside the tiny room, however, he hissed unhappily.

"Christ," he said. "The air is unbreathable in here. Come out before you suffocate."

He had her by the arm, pulling her out of the room and into the cold, dark tower where the air was clean. She inhaled a big lungful of it as she stumbled out on stiff legs, her hand still to her head.

"If you are going to hold me prisoner, why can I not retreat to my own chamber?" she asked. "You can bolt the door from the outside. I will not escape. I told you that before."

The knight eyed her. "Where is your chamber?"

She pointed to the keep. "On the top level."

He shook his head. "The chambers in the keep are being used by the knights."

Emera sighed, feeling exhausted and frustrated. So the knights had every part of this place, including her bedchamber where her personal possessions were. Perhaps those possessions weren't even hers anymore, stolen by thieving knights. This entire siege had worn her down as much as she'd tried to keep busy and be helpful, but now at siege's end, she found her patience was gone. Her treatment tonight had properly demoralized her.

"Sir Knight, I will admit that I know nothing of siege etiquette," she said, rather snappishly. "I have never been part of one before so I am unclear as to my role in all of this, but when I was first brought to the knight I can only assume is your commander, I told him that I would be obedient. I have no intention of rebelling. Still, I am treated poorly and I have no idea where my sister is. Did you really give her over to the men as a… a whore?"

The knight still had a grip on her arm. "I do not know where she is," he said honestly. "I was charged with you and that is my duty."

Emera wasn't satisfied by his answer. "Will you at least find out? Please?"

He didn't respond other than to look around, outside of the tower door and into the inner bailey beyond. "Since I am not entirely sure where else to keep you, I suppose it is possible that your chamber can be cleared of any men that might be inside of it," he said. "I do not think this tower room is suitable to your needs. If you stay in here any longer, you will die."

He still wasn't really answering her. Greatly frustrated, Emera yanked her arm from his grasp and faced him.

"Please," she begged softly. "Let us not be enemies. I am not your enemy, or anyone else's. My name is Emera la Marche. My sister is Lady de la Roarke, wife of the garrison commander. Even though it is true that he is my sister's husband, I have no loyalty to him or anything about him. Since I have told you my name, will you please tell me yours?"

The knight looked at her and she could tell that he was debating how to respond to her. He wasn't an unhandsome man. In fact, he was quite comely with his blonde hair and neatly trimmed beard. But he was stiff and formal, like the rest of them had been, and just when she thought he was going to ignore her yet again, his answer changed her mind.

"De Lohr," he said after a moment. "Sir Christopher de Lohr."

"And your commander's name?"

"He did not tell you his name?"

"Nay. Is it a secret?"

A flash of a smile tugged at the corner of his mouth. "It is not," he said. "Mayhap he thought you should simply know it."

"How?"

"Because of who he is."

"*Who* is he?"

De Lohr fought of a smile again. "His name is Sir Juston de Royans. If you have not heard of him, then you should have. He is the greatest knight in England and he is now in command of Bowes."

Juston de Royans. Now the big warrior with the piercing eyes had a name. "I admit, I have not heard of him," she said. "But I do not travel much in war circles so that is not surprising."

"You have never heard of the man they call the Lord of Winter?"

"I have not."

He seemed either miffed or surprised; Emera couldn't tell which. "Then you have missed much, lady."

That was probably very true and Emera simply nodded. "I will not dispute that," she said. "Thank you for answering my questions. You have been very polite, but you seem to be the only one of your brethren who *is* polite."

He cocked a well-shaped eyebrow. "A battle is not a party," he said wryly. "There is no need for manners where swords and captives are concerned. Surely you have figured that part out by now."

He had a point. Now it was her turn to gaze at him, almost appraisingly. He had her curiosity now that he was talking. "De Royans," she said. "What makes him the greatest knight in England?"

She was back to asking questions again and Christopher saw no harm in telling her. Perhaps it would make her less apt to question the situation as she seemed inclined to do if he informed her of who, exactly, she was now a prisoner of.

"The list of his accomplishments is too great to tell," he said. "Suffice it to say that the man has spent a good deal of time at the side of Richard the Lionheart in France, fighting against Henry's tyranny. There is no battle too great for him to overcome and no man more talented than he is. He is clever in ways you would not begin to understand and has a greatness that eclipses even Richard at times. So if I were you, I would simply do as he says in all cases. You do not want to anger him."

Emera was listening seriously, coming to understand the man who was now in control of Bowes. "I am not trying to disobey him," she said. "But I do not believe it is right he should treat women so poorly. That does not speak of a great man to me."

Christopher had much the same conversation with Juston earlier so he couldn't disagree with the woman. "You are his prisoner," he said simply. "More than that, you are a woman. He may do with you as he wishes."

"But *I* was not fighting against him. I never lifted weapon."

Christopher refused to be sucked into the semantics of the battle. He was coming to understand what she'd confessed earlier; she really had no concept of battle etiquette. He had no time to explain the obvious. Reaching out, he took her arm again, this time more firmly so she couldn't pull free.

"Let us head into the keep," he said. "Once you are secured in your chamber, I will see what has become of your sister."

His statement both surprised and excited her. "Will you truly?"

"I said I would."

That was the kindest thing that had happened since the fall of Bowes. Emera looked at the big knight as he pulled her from the tower, trying to meet his eye but noticing he wouldn't be bothered with looking at her. Still, she felt a certain amount of gratitude towards him.

"Thank you," she said sincerely. "I will stay to my chamber and I will not cause any problems if you will only show common courtesy. I… I have not eaten in some time, either. Do you suppose I could have some bread or cheese?"

"That is entirely possible."

He was still pulling her along, still not looking at her, as they crossed the inner bailey towards the looming keep. Emera could see faint shades of pink on the eastern horizon, signaling the onset of a new day. It would be a day without siege and a day where the situation at Bowes had changed markedly. She tried not to be too terribly disheartened by it. After all, de Lohr had promised to bring her food and her sister. She was grateful for that.

But her struggle not to let depression swamp her was dashed when they passed around the side of the keep and straight into a gathering of the wounded from the hall. They had been lying out all night and they'd been rained on. Wounded men were laying there, freezing in the frigid temperatures while servants rushed about trying to light fires and dry them off and erect makeshift shelters. There was a good deal of chaos going on, by directionless servants now that both ladies had been taken away. The situation was dire.

Shocked at the sight of bleeding, miserable men, Emera came to a halt in spite of de Lohr's grip on her. Her horrified gaze moved across the clusters of wounded, freezing men right before her very eyes.

"Sweet Mary," she whispered. "Are you such soulless creatures that you cast the wounded out into the elements simply because they chose to pick up a sword against you because they were commanded to? You treat your animals better than you treat them!"

In a fit of rage and disgust, she jerked her arm free of Christopher's grip and ran to the wounded. The servants, seeing at least one of their mistresses returned, rushed to her like a moth to flame, loudly lamenting the situation. Female servants were weeping while the male servants hovered nervously, begging for help and direction.

Emera immediately began instructing them, pointing to the men, pointing to the kitchens, which were on the north side of the keep and clustered there along with the bakery and buttery. The only reason those buildings hadn't burned was because the roofs were heavy sod, not thatch that had been on the other buildings. Flaming arrows had hit the roofs but due to the soil of the sod, they'd not burned for long. Now, Emera had the servants running for the kitchens and still other men, wounded soldiers that could still walk, moving the wounded closer to the keep to use the exterior walls as shelter.

Christopher had followed her as she'd rushed towards the wounded but he'd stopped short of grabbing her again and hauling her into the keep as he'd intended. He'd been against Maxton's decision to move the wounded from the beginning and, truth was, he was as unsettled with it as Emera was. Something clearly needed to be done to help the poor men in dire circumstances so he simply let her do it. The woman wasn't going anywhere and he knew she wouldn't try to run; she'd made that clear. Therefore, he didn't stop her as she began to order the servants and other wounded about. He let her do it because it needed to be done.

"What goes on?"

The question came from behind and he turned to see Marcus Burton approaching. The man was without his helm, his hauberk bunched around his neck and his black hair unkempt. Christopher eyed him as the man came to a stop beside him.

"Lady Emera is moving the wounded," Christopher said simply. "Honestly, Maxton was wrong to throw them out of the hall, putting them out in the elements like this. She is trying to make them comfortable and I am not going to prevent her. It needs to be done."

Marcus didn't much care what Lady Emera was doing. He hadn't had any contact with her, anyway, so he had no feelings on the matter one way or the other. The wounded, however, were another matter – he agreed with Christopher that what Maxton had done was unsavory but he'd kept his opinion to himself. It was an unspoken rule amongst the knights that singular decisions were not questioned. With nothing much to say on the subject, he changed the focus of the conversation.

"Juston told me about Cotherstone Castle late last night," he said.

"He wants us to ride to Cotherstone today and assess her strength. David is having the horses saddled."

Christopher nodded. "Very well," he said, his gaze moving from Emera to the sky above. "Then let us depart. The weather is holding for now but by the looks of the clouds to the south, that may not be the case much longer."

He started to move away but Marcus stopped him. "What about the lady?" he asked. "Will you not secure her before we depart?"

Christopher looked over his shoulder at the woman, now dragging a wounded man into the shadow of the keep. He shook his head. "Nay," he replied. "She does not need to be secured. Her duty is to tend these men and she will not leave them. Do you know what happened to her sister?"

Marcus yawned, scratching his black head. "I did not know there was a sister."

Christopher had duties to attend to but found it perturbing that he'd told Emera he'd locate her sister. He felt an obligation to do that before he left to assess Cotherstone purely based on the fact that he told the woman he would. Giving his word meant something to him, even if it was his word to a prisoner. He was honorable that way.

Therefore, leaving Emera in the cold bailey trying desperately to secure the wounded, he headed off across the compound with Marcus beside him, tracking down the lady of the keep, the one married to the knight Juston had so brutally killed. Maybe it was weak of him to do it, or perhaps it showed good character. Either way, he was annoyed with himself as he followed the trail of Lady Emera's missing sister.

When he got to the end of his quest, just as the sun began to peek over the eastern horizon, he wasn't particularly surprised with what he'd found. Truth be told, he was relieved. Lady Jessamyn de la Roarke was found in the vaults in the sublevel below the keep, bottled up in a tiny cell with an old iron grate. She was cold and weepy, but she was safe and untouched. As it turned out, none of the knights wanted any part of her and it had been Maxton who had locked the woman away, unsure what else to do with her. It had been another one of Maxton's cold moves.

Christopher released the woman and sent her back to her sister, hoping Maxton would hear of it and confront him. Somehow, at some point, he was fairly certain he and Maxton would have a moment where one was going to have to deal a brutal beating to the other for it was something that had been coming to a head for some months.

Christopher was certain of one thing – he wouldn't be the one to submit.

CHAPTER SIX

H E HADN'T SLEPT.
Oh, he'd pretended to. He made a good show of it because he didn't want anyone bothering him, but the truth was that he hadn't slept much. That blue-eyed vixen had him fidgeting and tossing on his cushioned cot.

The tent was cold and damp near dawn, his brazier having burned out almost completely until Gart snuck in at some point and filled it with peat again. Using kindling, he'd ignited it and the blue flame flickered in the brazier, staving off the freezing temperatures in the tent.

Gart had left as silently as he'd come in but Juston had been awake, watching his squire move around in the darkness. He had always appreciated Gart but he knew he didn't tell the man that nearly enough. He'd taken his efficiency for granted for years and kept promising himself he'd do something about it someday. Gart wasn't due to be knighted yet for at least a couple of years, but it wasn't unheard of for a man to be knighted before he turned twenty years of age. Juston was thinking he might just knight the man and get it over with. He already fought as good as the knights and then some.

But his thoughts rolled back to the la Marche woman after Gart had departed. Bright-eyed and stunningly beautiful, he still wasn't over the fact that she hadn't fallen all over herself to please him. He didn't understand her apathetic attitude towards him, something no woman had ever shown towards him. Ever. That was the only reason she was on his mind, he told himself. Her apathy had him intrigued. If she'd done as he told her to do, perhaps he wouldn't be giving her a second thought. It was her refusal that had his interest.

... *wasn't it?*

Sitting up in bed, he ran his fingers through his thick, curly mane before reaching for the last of the Malmsey wine. There wasn't much left and he downed it, rising from his pallet to dress in the darkness. Outside, he could hear his men stirring about so he thought he'd better head into the castle to see what the current situation was. Maybe he'd even ask Christopher where the la Marche woman had been secured. Maybe he'd give her a second chance at pleasing him. He wondered if she'd be smart enough to do as he wished this time.

Something told him she wouldn't be.

Considering the freezing temperatures, he pulled on a couple of heavy woolen tunics before pulling on a fur-lined leather robe that was heavy and durable, with a big collar and fur-cuffed sleeves, trailing all the way to his feet. It was an impressive piece of wardrobe that Lizette had commissioned for him years ago when he'd been fighting with Richard in the Aquitaine. Richard had even tried to steal it from him, twice, telling him that it was too regal to be worn by anyone other than a king. When Juston pointed out that Richard wasn't the king yet, Richard didn't speak to him for an entire month.

The thought of that argument still made Juston smile.

Wearing the robe these days didn't hurt him like it used to. The garment reminded him so much of Lizette that it had been at least three years before he could even look at the thing. But these days, he looked upon the garment with fond memories of his worrying wife and her demands that he take care of his health. She had always been so concerned for him, something that had amused him at the time but something he found he'd missed greatly once she was gone.

It had been nice to have someone care for him so much.

In truth, his heart didn't ache for her now like it used to but there were times when he missed her and his daughters greatly. It was just easier to push it aside as time went on as he steeled himself against any kind of emotion for anyone or anything else.

The Lord of Winter's heart was a frozen thing, indeed.

With thoughts of Lizette, Richard, and fighting days in the Aquitaine on his mind, Juston quit the tent and headed out into the freezing dawn. The air was heavy with moisture and a layer of smoke from the early morning fires blanketed the desolate land. With the sunrise behind the clouds, everything was a cold shade of gray as he headed towards the castle, noting that men were already beginning repairs on the outer wall he'd so effectively bombarded with his siege engines. He was proud of his handiwork and found it a shame they had to build the walls back up again. But it was necessary.

He was nearing what was left of the drawbridge when he caught sight of three big chargers approaching. He recognized Christopher, David, and Marcus right away, coming to a halt when they came upon him. A perusal of the three knights showed they were dressed for battle in heavy armor and weapons. Aware of the drunken discussion he'd had with Burton the night before, Juston was pleased to see they were carrying out his wishes as the sun rose.

"Watch the road as you head to Cotherstone," he told them. "De Puiset is undoubtedly aware of our siege of Bowes so he may have men watching the roads. Do not engage in any fighting if you see any of his men; return to Bowes immediately. Is that clear?"

The three knights, astride their hairy and excitable chargers, nodded. "It is, my lord," Christopher replied. "We are not taking any soldiers with us so as not to attract attention. It will just be the three of us."

Juston was satisfied. "Be on your way, then," he said. "I will expect you back before nightfall."

The three knights spurred their horses onward, heading to the main road that would lead them to a smaller road north. Juston watched them go, wondering what they would discover this day at Cotherstone, before finally turning for the gatehouse once more. He glanced up at the sky as he moved, noticing the increase in dark clouds heading in their direction. He was fairly certain they were in for another storm and from the speed in which the men repairing the wall were moving, he was fairly certain they knew it, too. Men were cutting damaged stone and hauling it up with a makeshift pulley system, moving quickly.

The gatehouse passage to the outer bailey was dark and icy, and remarkably undamaged from the siege. Since the gatehouse was so big, with a double portcullis system, Juston's strategy had been to bombard the interior of the castle to force a surrender rather than trying to break down the impenetrable gatehouse. As soon as he entered the gatehouse, Gart and Gillem were there to greet him.

"My lord," Gart said, his nose pinched red from the cold. "I can give you a report of the status of the castle unless you'd rather see for yourself."

Juston eyed him, the dark circles around his eyes. "Did you sleep last night?"

"I did, my lord."

"Liar."

Gart gave him a half-smile. "I *think* I did."

Juston rolled his eyes. "You are no good to me if you are sleep deprived," he said. "Where are Maxton and Achilles?"

Gart rubbed his hands together, trying desperately to warm his fingers. "Maxton is in the keep, I believe, as is Kress. I saw Achilles heading to the outer wall repair before dawn."

Juston digested the information before turning to Gillem. "Double the number of soldiers in the gatehouse to relieve you and Gart for a short time," he said. "Meanwhile, I am taking Gart with me."

Gillem nodded smartly. "Aye, my lord."

With Gillem under orders, Juston and Gart headed out of the gatehouse and into the inner bailey, a vast thing. Bowes Castle was built on an ancient Roman fort and part of the fort walls were incorporated into the outer walls of the castle, but there were also berms and a ditch to add to the defenses. It was one of the features that made it so difficult to breach.

Once inside the bailey, Juston could see for himself the damage his siege had caused with the burned outbuildings and wandering animals from a stable that had been destroyed. There was a large group of men working on the damaged wall and still others who were cleaning up and organizing the outer bailey. Animals were being corralled for the most part and the outbuildings were being sifted through. There was a good deal of activity.

"There is a storm coming in from the south," Juston said as he watched the work on the damaged wall. "Mortar will not set in weather such as this. It will slow the repairs down considerably."

Gart nodded, pointing to the battlements. "Several of the wooden shutters in the battlements were damaged as well," he said. "Christopher has been supervising the repairs for the most part. He told the men not to worry about replacing the defensive shutters right now. He wants them to focus on the wall."

Juston approved of that decision. De Lohr and Burton usually took charge in situations like this and he knew how they thought, how they operated. With them riding north to Cotherstone, however, that left Achilles in charge and Juston could see him over by the broken wall, directing the men. Seeing that everything was well in-hand in the destroyed outer bailey, he and Gart proceeded to the half-burned bridge that crossed the moat surrounding the inner bailey.

The inner bailey was big, housing the keep and kitchens, among other structures. The first thing Juston saw as he crossed into the ward was a collection of wounded against the southern wall. There were rows of them, closely packed together, while servants struggled to erect some kind of shelter over their heads. They had driven poles into the ground, scrap wood from some of the structures that had burned, while still other servants were hammering together more pieces of half-charred wood to place on top of the poles to provide some shelter from the angry sky.

It was a very busy operation and servants were moving quite swiftly. They didn't have the proper tools or materials, or even the strength to do such things, but they were working valiantly. The first thing Juston saw, other than the men on the ground, were two women moving among the wounded, offering what comfort they could. He was immediately drawn to Emera, kneeling on the ground near a man who had his legs splinted. His eyebrows lifted at the sight.

"What are the women doing out here?" he demanded. Then, he pointed to Emera. "I told de Lohr to lock her up."

Gart could see the woman Juston was referring to. Even though there were two de Lohr brothers, Gart knew he meant Christopher. He was the only brother Juston ever called by his last name.

"I do not know, my lord," he said honestly. "I have been in the gatehouse all night. But if the lady is out here… surely Christopher had a good reason."

Juston was building up a righteous anger. "He disobeyed me," he grumbled. "I told him to lock her up."

Gart wasn't sure what more he could say. "There are many Bowes men that were wounded, my lord," he said. "Maxton moved them out of the keep last night and almost a quarter of them perished in the freezing temperatures. I know that Christopher did not agree with Maxton's decision so mayhap he brought the lady here to help them. It is clear that they needed help."

Juston jaw was ticking angrily. His gaze lingered on the collection of wounded and the women moving among them. "Find Maxton for me," he growled. "Send him to me."

Gart nodded and headed towards the keep as Juston headed towards the Bowes wounded.

And Emera.

He wasn't entirely sure what he was going to say to her. It wasn't her fault that Christopher disobeyed him, but Gart made a good deal of sense. Christopher hadn't agreed with Maxton's decision and he'd been clear on that, so it made perfect sense that he'd direct the lady to help her own wounded. There was that mercy they'd spoken of the night before; Juston's lack of it and Christopher's overabundance of it. Juston wasn't sure which was the better trait, to be truthful. An excess of compassion could cause trouble. He knew that better than most.

"My lord de Royans?"

Juston felt something on his right leg, looking down to see that one of the wounded men had reached out to touch him. More than that, the man had called him by name. Considering these were all Bowes wounded, he thought that rather odd that a soldier should know him but he came to a halt, peering down at the older man who was lying on a pathetic bed of wet rushes and frozen woolen blankets. The man was ghostly pale as he gazed up at him, eyes sunken in his pasty face.

"Who are you?" Juston asked. "How do you know me?"

The man smiled weakly, his blue lips quivering with cold. "I served beneath you at Taillebourg," he said. "You were brilliant in that action, my lord. I should have known it 'twas you who laid siege to Bowes. You managed to take down the castle that could not be taken."

Juston's anger at Christopher, at Emera, was doused like a water to flame. He crouched down beside the old soldier, looking at him seriously.

"Taillebourg," he muttered. "That was several years ago. What is your name?"

"Cowling, my lord."

"And you now fight for Henry?"

Cowling blue lips twisted wryly. "I served de Cieto, Baron Belthorn. Do you remember him, my lord?"

Juston nodded, warming to the conversation in spite of himself. "Of course I do," he said. "He is a strong ally of Richard's."

Cowling nodded. "He was, but his son was not," he said. "De Cieto died three years ago and his son came into power. Young Edwin, if you will recall. He swore fealty to Henry, who rewarded him well. De la Roarke was a friend of young Edwin and when de la Roarke called on his allies to reinforce Bowes, I was sent north with about three hundred de Cieto men."

That was a surprising statement. Juston hadn't known that de la Roarke had support from other Henry allies. "I see," he said. "So the de la Roarke men are not all his own?"

Cowling tried to shake his head, made difficult because of the cold. "Nay, my lord," he said. "He did not have many of his own men so he sought help from allies to reinforce his ranks. That is why... my lord, you've heard of the crimes de la Roarke has committed? Against travelers, I mean. Men he would rob and murder?"

Juston nodded. "I know if it," he said. "Why do you ask?"

"Because he was not alone in his crimes. He did it to pay tribute to the other allies who supported him. There were many men involved in his crimes. He would send riches and coinage to his friends and allies."

An even more surprising statement. Juston hadn't known any of this. "Is that so?" he asked, but it was a rhetorical question. He was simply astonished to hear such things. "A network of men involved in his dirty dealings?"

The soldier nodded. "He would distribute some of the stolen items," he said. "They would supply him with men and other things."

"Allies in here in the north?"

"Mostly, my lord."

A surprising network of thievery going on in the name of Henry. With that thought, something else came to mind, something that could be significant. "And de Puiset?" Juston asked. "He is the lord over this land. Is he involved?"

"Heavily, my lord."

It was a serious revelation. Truth be told, Juston wasn't all that surprised to hear such things, but the conversation was very enlightening. Things were starting to make more sense to him now, especially in the sense that Henry's supporters in the north seemed to be quite well supplied with wealth. They seemed to have an unlimited supply of coinage to support Henry's armies, which was something Juston had always wondered about.

But the revelation also underscored the fact that when Juston captured Bowes and killed many men, it was the men of several of Henry's allies he killed in the process, not simply de la Roarke men. And that made him a bigger target than ever for those seeking revenge on his actions – not only had he taken away a source of wealth for Henry's allies, but he'd killed their men as well.

No wonder de Puiset hadn't rushed to Bowes' aid… it could possibly mean he was gathering strength, and allies of de la Roarke, to lay a counter-siege to Bowes in revenge. If money and riches were involved, then it might not even have anything to do with Richard or Henry – and everything to do with a revenue stream that had been cut off when de Royans had taken the castle.

It was certainly something to think about.

In an uncharacteristic display of camaraderie, Juston put his hand on the old soldier's shoulder. "Thank you for your honesty," he said. "I am grateful for your information."

Cowling nodded. "Serving you at Taillebourg has been my greatest honor, my lord," he said, lowering his voice. "But watch yourself. Many of these wounded do not feel the same way. If they know you are the commander, wounded or not, they may try to move against you."

Juston looked around at the dozens and dozens of wounded, men lying on the frozen ground, half-frozen themselves.

"Are there any more like you, men who have served with me at some point?" he asked.

Cowling reflected back on the men he knew who were wounded, too weak to actually turn his head to look at them.

"A few," he said. "I do not know if they survived the night, though."

That comment caused Juston to look and see just how horrible the conditions were. Men were lying in mud, their wet blankets frozen to their bodies as another storm approached. He knew they couldn't survive another bout of freezing rain out in the open like this. As much as he hated to make what he considered a trivial decision, as his decisions were confined to battle and life or death situations, he was about to override Maxton's directive to move the wounded into the bailey. Men like Cowling deserved better.

Removing his hand from Cowling's shoulder, he stood up, looking around the wounded only to come face to face with Emera. She was now only a few feet away from him. Somehow, she had moved within close proximity of him and he hadn't even noticed. She was staring at him, studying him, digesting him....

Those eyes, he thought. The purest blue looking at him – half in fear, half in curiosity, but all-consuming. Before he could say anything, he heard Cowling at his feet.

"My lord?" the man rasped.

Juston tore his eyes from Emera and knelt back down beside the old soldier again. "Take heart," he said, putting his hand on the man's shoulder again. "I will have you moved someplace warm and safe. You shall not endure these terrible conditions much longer."

Cowling grasped at him. "It is of little matter, my lord," he said, his freezing fingers digging into Juston's arm. "I am old. It is my time. But that is not what I was going to say... the lady, the sister of Lady de la Roarke... has anyone told you?"

"Told me what?"

"Her father... he is a Lusignan."

Juston's manner hardened. "I have been informed."

"I heard rumor that her father was at Taillebourg."

That news, in and of itself, wasn't a great revelation. Many men had been at Taillebourg. Juston simply patted the man on the shoulder again and stood up, just in time to face Emera as she took another step towards him. In fact, she was rather close and he found himself oddly unnerved by it.

"Sir Juston," she said before he could speak. "May I speak with you?"

He eyed her. "You know my name."

"Sir Christopher told me."

Juston cocked an eyebrow at her, a gesture that suggested he wasn't quite pleased about that. "I see," he said. Then, he looked her up and down. "What else did he tell you? And what are you doing out here? I distinctly ordered you to be locked up."

Emera could see that he wasn't being much friendlier than he had been the night before. Even so, the sight of him in her midst had caused her heart to stir in a way she'd never experienced before. It had been a curious sensation, one that took a dousing at his snappish manner.

"I was," she said. "Sir Christopher locked me up but when he came to me this morning, the small room he'd put me in was full of bad air from the fire in the brazier. He said if I remained in there any longer it would kill me. So in the process of taking me to the keep to find somewhere else to put me, we came across the wounded that one of your knights so callously purged from the keep. I insisted that I be allowed to tend them and Sir Christopher agreed."

Juston was even more displeased after her speech. "Do you always go about insisting you be allowed to do whatever you wish?"

Emera shook her head. "Of course not. But look around you; these men are dying from exposure. I am simply trying to make them more comfortable although it seems like an impossible task. They simply do not deserve to be treated this way, my lord. Please allow me to continue to aid them as best I can."

Juston didn't want to admit she was right. He glanced down at Cowling, still at his feet, and he could see the blue shade of the man's lips and the even bluer cast of his hands. This was a good soldier who had served with him, years ago, now left out to die by Maxton's orders. But he was afraid that if he agreed with her, it might be perceived as weak in her eyes. She was a strong woman, *too* strong. He didn't want her to think that he was pliable to her wishes. But he also couldn't allow these men to freeze to death out in the elements. Now that he'd seen the reality for himself, he agreed with Christopher's assessment of it completely.

Perhaps it was time for him to show some of that mercy again.

"You cannot make them more comfortable out here," he said.

"Shelter must be provided. Is there any other shelter other than the hall?"

Emera was vastly surprised he should ask her such a question and she took it very seriously. Last night he'd seemed too cold-hearted about everything but this morning, his manner was different.

"We put the wounded in the hall simply because it was the most protected place we could put them at the time, my lord," she said, sounding very respectful since he seemed to be inclined to agree with her about the wounded. "But since you will be occupying the hall, mayhap we could move them to the vaults below the hall, on the ground level of the keep. Due to the siege, most of our stores are gone, anyway, so there is room for them there. The only problem would be keeping them warm. There are no hearths and I fear if we bring in braziers, then there would not be proper ventilation. It would turn the air bad again."

It was a rather astute suggestion coming from a woman, something that made Juston think she wasn't as empty-headed as some. He glanced up at the sky, with more dark clouds moving in. Time was growing short. He scratched his head thoughtfully.

"Are the kitchens intact?"

"Aye, my lord."

"Then boil all the water you can. Since we have an abundance of it, let us put it to good use. Make hot compresses with rags and cover the wounded with them. That will keep them warm for the time being."

It was a simple yet brilliant plan. Emera was very pleased that Juston should show such mercy to the wounded of Bowes.

"We will, my lord," she said quickly. "May we start moving them inside?"

He nodded. "Show me where you plan to take them, first," he said. "And I would see your stores to see what you have left."

He meant to confiscate them, or so she thought. Emera's relief in the situation with the wounded was tempered somewhat. "We do not have much," she said. "It was a long siege, my lord. We have mostly oats and grains left. The men have been living on porridge."

"Show me."

She did. Leaving Jessamyn with the servants, she gathered her muddy, dirty skirts and headed towards the keep to show Juston the great storage vaults. Just as they were approaching the stone forebuilding that housed the staircase leading to the first floor entrance, they were met by Maxton emerging from the keep with Gart. Maxton's attention was on Juston.

"My lord?" Maxton greeted Juston. "Gart said you wished to speak with me."

Juston nodded. "You moved the wounded out of the hall," he said. "I cannot believe many of them survived the night, being left out in the freezing weather."

Maxton's expression hardened. He looked straight at Emera, thinking all sorts of things at that moment – that perhaps she'd used her female wiles to convince Juston that Maxton had made a terrible decision in removing the wounded from the hall and that these men, these prisoners, were to be treated fairly. He could just hear the woman complaining. Although Maxton had never known Juston to be seduced by a woman, there was always a first time. He felt as if he had to defend his decision, something he wasn't used to doing.

"The keep is secured for Richard," he said firmly. "The hall has been cleaned out and scrubbed, and last night about three hundred of our men slept inside by a warm fire for the first time in weeks. They've had little shelter and comfort in all that time, as you know. There are three big chambers in the keep; one on the first level and two on the second level, and they are all comfortably appointed. They will make excellent quarters for the knights."

He made sense and Juston knew that Maxton was only doing his job, harsh as his stance had been. He crooked a finger at the man, pulling him away from Gart and Emera. When they were out of earshot, he turned to him.

"Among the wounded is a man who fought with me at Taillebourg," he said quietly. "He has already provided me with a great deal of information and he says there are others among the wounded that are loyal to Richard as well. I realize that you did not know this when you ordered them cleared from the hall, but now that you know, I want you to move all of the wounded down into the vault where the lady and her sister will tend them. I intend to speak with these men who are still loyal to Richard to find out what they can tell us of Henry's movements in the north. Already, I have been informed of quite a bit of information with regards to those loyal to Henry. I think it will behoove us to keep the wounded comfortable for now. Comfortable men might speak of more than what we currently know, if you understand my meaning."

Maxton was listening quite seriously. "I do," he said. "That being the case, I will move them into the storage vault at once. But you should know that I have already perused the vault and found it quite empty of anything we can use."

"I suspected as much."

"What I did find, however, was an entire chamber filled with what looks like money and valuables."

That bit of information caught Juston's attention. "Did you secure the room?"

"I did. I have four men guarding it until you have a chance to assess it."

Juston nodded. "Excellent," he said. "I have been told that de la Roarke robbed and murdered travelers for their valuables and that he kept his ill-gotten gains in the vault. It seems that you have found his treasure room."

Maxton lifted his eyebrows in surprise. "If that is the case, then there is a great deal of wealth to be had."

"Did you find any prisoners in the keep?"

"What do you mean?"

"The murdered or imprisoned travelers de la Roarke stole from."

Maxton scratched his head thoughtfully. "There is a sublevel below the vault with two cells," he said. "I found a corpse in one of them. It could have been one of de la Roarke's victims but we shall never know that for certain. I had it removed and tossed into the pile of bodies that are being burned outside of the walls."

Juston grunted unhappily. "The church will have something to say about burning bodies, Max."

"We have no choice. The ground is too frozen to bury them."

Juston knew that but he still didn't want the added burden of the church being unhappy with his actions. They didn't like bodies turned into charcoal. He sighed heavily. "Then make sure the ashes are gathered so they can be buried when the weather permits," he said. "And try not to be obvious about the pyres."

"Did you know about it?"

"Nay."

"Then I am not being obvious."

Juston had to grin at the man, who grinned back. Maxton could be glib at times, but it was never in bad humor. At least, Juston never thought so. Maxton was a no-nonsense knight with that odd dark streak in him, but Juston wanted to believe he wasn't truly evil. He was simply darker than most, fearless in decision and actions.

"Then I will say no more," Juston said. "I will see to the treasure room now but meanwhile, begin the transfer of the wounded. The lady and her sister will continue to tend them. I cannot spare men for the job, so let them do as they will. For now, they are serving a purpose and will be treated as such. But watch them… they are the opposition."

Maxton nodded. "I understand."

He headed off to find men to help move the wounded. Juston was particularly pleased at how the conversation had gone. He didn't condemn Maxton for his decision to move the wounded out of the hall, instead, making it clear why it was a good idea to find them a comfortable place inside to be tended. Maxton was not humiliated by his initial decision and Juston got what he wanted. Such was the brilliance of a man who truly knew how to lead men. It was one of the traits that made

Juston such an indispensable commander.

As Maxton walked away, Juston's attention returned to Emera. She was standing politely near Gart, who was looking at Juston as if there wasn't a lady nearby. Gart was much more focused on his duties than any woman and he watched Juston closely, waiting for a command to come forth. Juston made his way back over to the pair.

"Maxton is going to start moving men down into the vault," he told Gart. "Go with him and help. We need to get them into shelter before this storm hits."

Gart nodded smartly and was gone, moving swiftly after Maxton. As he turned to look at the collection of wounded, wondering how long it would be before the storm let loose above them, he heard Emera's soft voice.

"Thank you, my lord," she said quietly. "You have shown great mercy to these wounded men."

He looked at her, then. "How many did you lose last night?"

Emera turned to look at the wounded clustered in the mud. "We had seventy-nine last night," she said. "Thirty did not survive the night."

That was a lot of men. Juston simply nodded his head. "Hopefully, you will lose no more," he said. "My knights will see to moving the men down into the vault. You might do well to have the cooks begin boiling all of the water they can before going to the vault to prepare a place for the wounded."

Emera nodded. "I will, my lord," she said. "But did you not wish for me to show you the vault?"

He shook his head. "I can find it. Go about your duties."

Emera didn't argue with him. Still, there was something more on her mind, something she was careful to speak of.

"Before I go, my lord," she began hesitantly. "I was wondering... my sister and I have need of some of our possessions. As I told you, I do not know the etiquette of conquest, but I am hoping we may have our clothing and other personal items returned to us."

"Where are they?"

"Top floor of the keep."

"I will make arrangements to have them delivered to you in the vault with the wounded."

That was not the immediate answer she had been expecting and great relief flooded her. So did courage. "Thank you, my lord. And… well, there is something else."

He wondered if she was about to turn demanding on him since he had agreed to move the wounded and return her belongings. He wasn't so apt to give in to her every wish.

"What is that?"

He sounded impatient now and Emera cleared her throat softy. "Last night, you said that you would escort my sister and me to a town of our choice," she said. "There is, in fact, a place I would like to go to. I am hoping you would be so kind as to still provide an escort."

For some reason, he wasn't entirely happy that she was asking to leave Bowes. "You said you had nowhere to go," he pointed out. "Now you have changed your mind?"

She seemed rather nervous now, an odd manner for the lady who had shown nothing but bravery since he'd known her. "There is a charity hospital in Sherburn," she said. "You see, I have followed in my mother's footsteps of tending the sick and injured. Even when I lived at my father's house, I helped the needy. It was something my mother felt strongly about and she imparted upon me the importance of helping others. I would like to go to the charity hospital if it is not too much trouble. I am sure they would accept my help."

That beautiful creature in a charity hospital? It was his first thought and he struggled not to belittle her request. In no fashion did this exquisite beauty belong in a charity – anything. More than that, he realized that he didn't want her to go. He wasn't over his interest in her yet. He wasn't sure what was feeding his attraction, but he wasn't ready to let it go. He could only remember feeling such interest one other time in his life and that had been when he'd first met his beautiful

Lizette.

Now, he was feeling something awaken in him again.

He should have run from it at the very least. He should let her go to the charity hospital this very day simply to get her away from him, but he couldn't seem to do it. Against his better judgment, he was going to force her to stay, at least until he could get over his attraction to her.

You are intrigued with her beauty and nothing more, he told himself.

But it was a fact that he wasn't really sure was the truth.

"We shall discuss your future after the wounded have been tended," he told her. "Right now, you have a good deal of work before you right here at Bowes. Last night, you begged to remain, so I am going to grant your request. I will keep you here until you are no longer required."

Emera wasn't distressed that he would not permit her to leave, mostly because she knew what he said was true – there were a great many wounded that required help and here was where she was very much needed. Nay, she wasn't sorry to remain at Bowes in the least. She was having her way in the situation, ultimately, and that was tending Bowes' injured and dying.

The charity hospital could wait.

"Thank you, my lord," she said. "And my sister may remain as well?"

He nodded. "I am assuming she was chatelaine. Her services will be useful."

It seemed that from the uncertainty and fear of the previous night, the day had dawned considerably brighter. Emera found a great deal of relief in that. It didn't matter that she was still a captive of de Royans; he was allowing her to do what she wanted to do. She had a place to live, a roof over her head, and Jessamyn was still with her. All things considered, she counted herself extremely fortunate.

"Thank you for your generosity, my lord," she said. "I am most grateful."

Juston simply nodded his head, watching her as she turned for the kitchens to relay the orders of boiling water. He watched her go, a rather curvy woman in a dark and dirty dress, something that was completely uncomplimentary to her. A woman like that deserved to be dressed in silks and jewels, not wool and leather. But as he watched her walk away, one predominant thought came to mind...

... just *how* grateful was she?

He intended to find out.

CHAPTER SEVEN

B Y EARLY AFTERNOON, Juston's tent had been broken down and his possessions had been moved to the keep, into the large second floor chamber with the massive bed. It had been rightly assumed that the chamber had belonged to de la Roarke because the bed was unnaturally big and de la Roarke had been an enormous man. It was also very comfortable and the linens were surprisingly clean, Juston suspected, because a woman also shared de la Roarke's bed.

It was the perfect place for him to sleep while he was at Bowes and he was looking forward to sleeping in that big bed, getting his stink all over it. It was akin to dogs pissing to mark their territories; Juston had triumphed over de la Roarke and he was staking his claim and marking his territory by sleeping in the man's bed. It would be his smell in the bed now.

As rebuilding and organizing went on around him, Juston had no interest in partaking of any of it. He hadn't in years. Therefore, he began to remove his soiled, wet clothing, hanging them to dry on the pegs that jutted out from the hearth. There was a roaring blaze in the fireplace and half of the smoke was billowing out into the chamber, lingering up by the ceiling. Juston didn't particularly care but he noticed that the hearth had no back, meaning that it opened up into the small chamber next to his. One hearth serviced two chambers.

Sticking his head into the smaller chamber, he could see that it had a decidedly feminine look to it. Looms were neatly tucked into the corner and a frame with a half-finished piece of embroidery was pushed back against the wall near the hearth. It was warm and smoky in here, too.

Juston was coming to think that the chamber might have very well been occupied by Emera because there was really nowhere else she could have been housed. Next to her sister in the master's chamber would have been logical and as he realized that, he went into the chamber and began to seriously look around it.

Damn my interest in the woman! He thought with some frustration. He actually found himself looking at the bed, at the neatly made coverlet with embroidered stitching around the edges. He touched it; it was soft. The same softness that touched her body when she slept, all curled up and warm and....

That thought caused him to rip his hand away from the coverlet and nearly run from the chamber. He shouldn't be thinking such thoughts; thoughts to soften that rock in his chest where his heart used to be. The last time he entertained such thoughts was the last time he permitted his heart to feel anything at all.

That had ended very badly for him.

Back in the main chamber, he took a deep breath, trying to force thoughts of Emera from his mind. Or was she even a noble woman? She hadn't introduced herself as such; she'd simply introduced herself as Emera, without the proper address before it of "lady". So her father had been a knight who'd fought at Taillebourg. That didn't make her a noble woman, simply a knight's daughter.

But the last name... la Marche... that was related to Lusignan, one of the most powerful families in France. She was surely from noble blood. A knight named Dorian Lusignan had made himself judge, jury, and executioner for his family those years ago and Juston had spent a solid year hunting for the man, who seemed to have disappeared without a trace. Juston knew that the French were hiding his trail, unwilling to deliver him to a vengeful English knight. He really couldn't even find out much more about the man other than his name. There-fore, Juston couldn't even hear the name Lusignan without feeling an inordinate amount of hatred. To this very day, that was his reaction.

He was rather thankful that Emera's last name wasn't Lusignan.

Thoughts of his days in France faded as the chamber door opened and Gart entered, carrying the last of Juston's gear. He set it all down next to the door.

"My lord," he said. "Riders have been sighted coming from the south. A patrol just returned and says there are two riders heading in our direction."

Juston nodded, grateful for the distraction as he shook off dark memories of Lusignan. "Colors?" he asked.

"None."

"How far away are they?"

"Less than an hour. I thought you would want to know."

"I do. Tell me when they arrive."

Gart nodded. "I will," he replied. Then, his gaze moved about the large, comfortable chamber. "This is very nice. De la Roarke lived like a king."

Juston looked around, too, because Gart was. "Indeed, he did," he said, "and I intend to sleep on his bed in the comfort he has provided for me. Now *I* shall live like a king. By the way – the items in the treasure vault?"

"Aye?"

"I will personally divide up the cache between the knights. I want no one in that room until I have had a chance to do that."

Gart nodded. "*Just* the knights, my lord?"

Juston gave him a half-grin. "You know I mean you, too," he said, "although I supposed I should give some to the men as well."

"There is a good deal of silver in that room, enough so that each soldier under your command could have a few coins," Gart said helpfully.

"How many men survived the battle?"

"Christopher assessed it at thirteen hundred and forty-three."

"And you believe there is enough silver coinage to give to the men?"

"I believe so, my lord."

Juston nodded. "Then it shall be done," he said. "For the three weeks it took to breach this place, they deserve something. But tomorrow. For now, I intend to take a hot bath to warm my bones. And do we have anything other than pork to eat?"

Gart knew he was sick of it; they were all sick of it. "You ordered many pigs slaughtered for their fat," he reminded him. "We will be eating pork for quite some time."

Juston made a face. "Then bring me a meal with whatever we have," he said. "And speak to Lady de la Roarke and see where there is a tub. I require a bath."

Gart nodded and fled the chamber while Juston pulled off the last of his dirty, damp clothing and put it all by the hearth to dry off. His boots came off, followed by his leather breeches. Even though it was in the middle of the day, he felt a weariness to his bones that compelled him to climb into that big, comfortable bed. He'd spent the last twenty-five years of his life in one battle or another, sleeping in horrific conditions and fighting in the same. At his age, he deserved some comfort. While the younger knights were putting in their time, working themselves into exhaustion, Juston had done too much of that. He didn't want to do it anymore. So, he climbed into bed and fell asleep nearly the moment his head hit the pillow.

A heavy, blissful sleep.

"Juston!"

Someone was hissing in his ear and he sat up so quickly that he hit Gart, who had been leaning over him. He'd plugged Gart right in the jaw with his head and the squire stumbled back, hand on his face, as Juston saw stars. He rubbed at the contact point between his skull and Gart's face.

"Great Bleeding Christ," he hissed. "You know better than to startle me like that."

Gart was moving his jaw back and forth to make sure nothing had been broken. "My apologies," he said. "I called your name twice but you did not respond. Next time, I'll simply throw something at you."

Juston snorted, seeing some humor in the fact that he hadn't been easily awakened. That was unusual for him. "In the future, that would be the wiser choice, aye," he said. "What is so important that you nearly had your head taken off?"

Gart was still moving his jaw around. "The riders are here, my lord," he said. "You wanted me to tell you when they arrived."

"I did. Who are they?"

"Erik de Russe has brought a boy with him," he said. "He would tell me no more. He says he comes to you with a message from Eleanor."

Eleanor of Aquitaine. Juston's eyebrows lifted in surprise. There was only one Eleanor in their world and the mention of her name alone had Juston leaping from the bed and going in search of his breeches. He found them, warmed before the hearth, and he began to hastily pull them on.

"Eleanor," he repeated, disbelief in his tone. "How on earth did your good friend Erik have any contact with her? Last I had heard, she was still being held prisoner at Sarum."

Erik de Russe was yet another of Richard's knights who had served with Juston. He and Gart had grown up together and were nearly the same age, although Erik had been knighted the year before. Mostly, Erik remained with Richard as one of his most dependable knights so the fact that the man had arrived at Bowes was astonishing to say the least. Richard was rarely without the powerful de Russe knight. As Juston pulled a warm, dried tunic over his head, Gart went to collect the man's boots.

"It is possible she has been moved," Gart said as he handed a boot to Juston, who yanked it on his foot. "Henry moves her around with regularity, so it's possible she has been moved. How Erik came into contact with her, I do not know. He would not tell me any more than what I told you."

Juston yanked on the second boot and grabbed the heavy fur-lined robe. "Then it must be secretive, indeed."

"Aye, it must."

Where is he?"

"In the hall."

Juston was already in the stairwell, taking the spiral stairs down to the next level where the hall was. It was quite warm on this level from an overworked hearth, as servants had it full of peat, trying to stave off the icy weather outside. The hall was relatively empty of fighting men, however, with most of them either repairing the wall or tending other necessary things. Juston had very few wounded from the siege but he could see those men who had been injured were tucked into one corner of the hall and he could see his physic, an old man with very bad teeth, moving among them. But two figures by the hearth had his attention most of all. He moved quickly in their direction as Gart trailed after him.

Erik de Russe was a young knight with deep blue eyes, dark blonde hair, and a muscular build. He was as serious and dedicated as a knight could be, deeply devoted to his king. Richard saw greatness in the young warrior, which is why he kept him close, but Richard was in France at this point in time… and Erik was not. Juston was, therefore, greatly concerned with the man's appearance. Whatever it was must be important, indeed.

"Erik?" his voice reflected his concern. "What are you doing here? How did you find us?"

Erik's handsome face was pale from exhaustion and the cold. "It has been a long trip, my lord," he admitted. Then, he lowered his voice. "Is there somewhere we may speak privately?"

Juston simply nodded, indicating for Erik to follow him but not before Erik looked at Gart and pointed to the boy, indicating that Gart keep the boy in his custody. While Gart took up position next to the trembling child who was trying desperately to warm himself by the fire, Juston took Erik into the smaller chamber next to the hall, cold and dark. In the empty room, Juston faced Richard's knight.

"What is happening?" he muttered. "Who is the boy?"

Erik sighed heavily, a sign of his level of exhaustion. "We have been riding for weeks," he said. "It all started a few months ago when Richard received a missive from Eleanor. She is at Sarum, you know."

"Still?"

"Aye."

"Go on."

"Her missive to Richard was that he must send his most trusted knight to her on a matter of vital importance, so he sent me to Sarum. She has custodians, you know, but because I had a written request from Richard, I was allowed to see her privately."

"And?"

Erik pulled off his helm, peeling back the coif beneath it and running his fingers through his short blonde hair. "And, she had something of an astonishing message to deliver," he mumbled, his dark-circled eyes finding Juston. "It would seem that Lady Ida de Tosny, wife of the Earl of Norfolk, had some information for Eleanor that she would only deliver in person. When Eleanor asked for and was granted her visit, Lady Ida proceeded to inform Eleanor of something very shocking – that she'd heard her husband discussing the whereabouts of a certain child. She had come to provide Eleanor with the location of said child."

Juston's brow furrowed in confusion. "What child could possibly be so important to Eleanor?"

Erik sighed heavily. "A child who was the son of Henry and Princess Alys," he said, his voice barely above a whisper. "You know that it has been rumored that King Philip of France's sister, Alys, who is Richard's betrothed, bore a child for Henry. We have all heard that rumor and we have all known that Henry took the young woman as his mistress. Now, the rumors of a bastard have proven to be true. Lady Ida gave the location of the child to Eleanor, who in turn sent a missive to Richard. She wanted the boy extracted from his location and hidden away. That is where I came in; Richard sent me to Canterbury where the boy was a page to Baldwin of Forde, the Archbishop of Canterbury."

Juston's eyes were wide with astonishment as he listened to the fantastic story. "And the archbishop turned the lad over you?"

Erik shook his head. "Nay," he said, "but one of the priests pointed him out to me. I had to bring the priest a young woman, if you know what I mean, before he'd tell me anything. But he finally revealed the identity of the boy and I was able to take the child from Canterbury. Richard told me that once I had him, I was to take him to you for safekeeping. He wants that lad with an army to protect him. And that, my lord, is why I am here."

Juston could hardly believe what he was hearing. Without a word, he marched over to the doorway between the great hall and the smaller chamber, his focus fixed on the young man by the hearth with Gart standing guard beside him. He was still staring at the lad when Erik walked up beside him.

"*That* is the son of Henry and Alys?" Juston asked. "Are you certain?"

Erik nodded. "As certain as I can be," he said. "You will be certain, too, when you look at him – he resembles Henry to a fault. There is no denying who his father is."

Juston could already see the boy's profile and it was familiar, indeed. It was all quite overwhelming. "Great Bleeding Christ... so the rumors of a royal bastard were true."

Erik's gaze was on the boy as well. "Indeed," he muttered. "We speculated for years about it, that Alys bore Henry a son, and now we know that it is true. His name is Philip Alexander Tristan, but he goes by Tristan. He's actually a polite lad, well mannered. He gave me no trouble."

Juston's focus was still on the boy. "Does he know his royal lineage?"

Erik shook his head. "I do not believe so," he said. "From what I gather, Alys gave birth and sent the boy to live with servants, who in turn put him in the cloister for his education. I'm assuming they thought it was the safest place for him. His identity has been kept secret for years, even from him, so he does not know that his father is the King of England. And he has no idea why I took him from Canterbury. He is upset, as you can imagine."

Juston let out a pent-up sigh, a sound of frustration. "So what does Richard want me to do with the boy?"

Erik gave him a knowing look. "As I said, he wants an army to protect him," he said. "That boy unites two kingdoms. I do not need to tell you how valuable that makes him."

No, he didn't need to tell Juston just how valuable the lad was. The son of the King of England and the King of France's sister made him a hugely valuable commodity to many different people.

"Is Eleanor or Richard planning on using the lad against Henry?" Juston asked the obvious question. "Did Eleanor tell you anything to that regard?"

Erik shook his head. "She did not," he said. "But you know that is on her mind. It is an opportunity far too good to waste, now that Henry and Alys' son is in her custody."

Juston could only imagine the greater implications of that. Being that Eleanor had custody of him, there was something very ominous about that. The boy was caught up in a deadly game, something bigger than he could possibly imagine. But men like Juston and Erik knew the stakes. They knew Eleanor and Richard.

The game could become deadly, indeed.

"Then no one is to know who the boy is," Juston said. "I will tell my knights, of course, but no one else must know. He will be watched and protected. You will tell Richard that."

Erik shook his head. "I am to remain here, under your command," he replied. "Richard wants me to personally watch the boy."

"Then he shall be your charge."

"My new squire."

They understood one another. That would be what they told every-one else. A new squire from a good family. But nothing more than that. Resigned to the new element in his midst, Juston put a hand on Erik' shoulder.

"I can only imagine what great lengths you went through in order to find me," he said. "You must be exhausted."

Erik nodded. "I went to Netherghyll and they told me you were seeing action at Bowes," he said. "That is how I found you. How long have you been here?"

"Over three weeks," Juston said. "Richard sent word a few months ago that he wanted Bowes secured in his name, so here we are. I've not had a chance to send word to him about it yet. In fact, it seems that there is a good deal going on here, far more than we realized. Eat and rest and I shall tell you more when you have taken time for yourself. Meanwhile, I will take young Master Tristan in-hand. I think I should like to come to know this boy."

Erik thought a meal and a bed sounded very good. "He has already eaten this morning," he said. "He also slept like the dead last night. I do not recall the days of youth when I could sleep like that. I am envious."

The corners of Juston's mouth twitched. "As am I," he agreed. "A three-week siege has left me believing I will never sleep again. Go, now. I will tend to the lad."

Erik nodded and wandered off while Juston headed to the hearth where Gart and the boy were. When he came upon them, he sent Gart away to continue his duties of securing food and a hot bath for his liege while Juston faced the young lad sitting by the fire.

It was an interesting moment for him as he gazed upon the face of someone he was never really sure existed. It was like looking at a ghost. Once the boy looked up at him and Juston saw that he, indeed, had the shape of Henry's eyes and mouth, there was no doubt in his mind who Philip Alexander Tristan really was. Truth be told, it was a bit of a shocking realization.

"I am Sir Juston de Royans," he told the boy. "I am told your name is Tristan."

The child stood up, a mannerly gesture. "Aye, my lord," he said timidly.

"How old are you?"

"I have seen nine summers, my lord," the child said.

Juston studied the lad. He had red hair and freckles, much as his father did, and he was rather short. But the brown eyes were wide and curious, if not slightly fearful. Juston scratched his chin in a thoughtful gesture.

"Well," he said. "I understand that you are to be Sir Erik's squire, but there is more you should know. Now that you are here, understand that this is a military installation. You must stay very close to the knights who will be watching out for you. Do not wander off and do what you are told. Is that understood?"

The boy nodded apprehensively. "Aye, my lord," he said. "But why... why am I here?"

"I told you. You are to be Sir Erik's squire."

"But why?"

It was clear the child was very confused, as Erik had stated. Pulled from Canterbury and probably given very little information as to why, his confusion was understandable. Juston proceeded carefully.

"What did Sir Erik tell you?"

The boy looked like he was trying very hard not to cry. "That I was to learn to be a knight."

Juston nodded. "It is part of your education," he said. "Don't you want to learn to be a knight?"

"I want to be a priest."

Juston resisted rolling his eyes, knowing how much that statement would have displeased Henry. "Mayhap when you grow older, you can make that decision," he said. "But for now, it is important that your education is well-rounded. All young men must learn to fight. Sir Erik will be a good teacher."

Tristan blinked rapidly, trying to blink away his fear. He was trying to be brave. "Then what shall I do, my lord?"

"What do you mean?"

"I… I had duties at Canterbury. Will you not give me duties here? I can work. I like to work."

That gave Juston a moment of pause. Work? He couldn't exactly send the child out into the elements, out where men were repairing walls or dealing with prisoners. And there wasn't much to teach him today about being a knight; that could wait for another time. But he could send the child to the vault to help with the wounded of Bowes. He thought perhaps it was a very good idea to send the boy down to assist Emera and Lady de la Roarke.

Besides… it would give him the opportunity to see Emera again, that woman he was trying so hard not to linger on. With that thought, he put his big hand on the boy's skinny shoulder.

"Come with me."

SPENDING THE NIGHT in freezing temperatures had brought more woes for the wounded than Emera could have imagined.

That became evident when they'd managed to move the men back into the keep, forty-nine of them in all as the survivors of the venture out into the elements. All of the men were half-frozen but those who had touchy wounds, like belly or lower abdomen wounds, seemed to be holding their own better than they should have.

Emera had seen belly injuries before and they were almost always fatal, but she was coming to think that somehow the cold had slowed down the progression of the wounds. Those with penetrating wounds to the torso seemed to be surprisingly stable until they moved them back inside and began covering them with hot compresses to warm them up.

That was when the situation changed markedly.

By late afternoon on the second day of conquest, she'd already lost two men with serious bowel injuries. For some of the men, moving them inside and warming them up had been a very positive thing, indeed, but to others, it had hastened death. It was difficult to know just who was benefitting from the warmth of the compresses and who wasn't, so she and Jessamyn continued to work diligently through the day, keeping warm compresses on the men with the help of most of Bowes' servants. There were eleven of them in all, those who had survived the siege, and they made an attentive workforce on the men who had been wounded.

Somewhere towards the end of the afternoon, one of Juston's men had brought down her possessions as well as her sister's, clothing taken from their top-floor chambers that had all been shoved into two satchels, now overflowing with items. It looked as if someone had taken the bags and shoved everything they could into them without any thought of organization, but it didn't matter. They had their things returned, including combs, two hand mirrors of polished bronze, and soap that smelled of rosemary. That was all that concerned them, that they had their things now, possessions that were important to them.

The first thing Emera did when the clothing was brought down was seek out a place in the vault for her and Jessamyn to sleep. Neither one of them had slept much in the past few weeks, ever since the siege had started, so it had come to the point where exhaustion was playing a major role in their thought processes. They were slower to react, sometimes more emotional about things than they should have been.

Emera discovered just how exhausted she was when she'd made a pallet for her and her sister to share, tucked into a secluded corner of the vault, and had promptly fallen asleep right on top of it. She'd only intended to close her eyes for a brief moment, but that had been her downfall. Next thing she realized, Jessamyn was shaking her awake.

"Em," she hissed. "Em, wake up. The commander is here to see you!"

Emera sat up, groggy and still half-asleep. "How long have I been asleep?"

"I have not seen you for the last hour."

She'd fallen asleep for a mere hour. She felt worse now than she had before she'd fallen asleep. With an aching head, she struggled to her feet and staggered after her sister.

The vault of Bowes was mostly one wide open space, lit by a few scant torches shoved into iron sconces, and it had a few alcoves built into it to keep the stores separate. There were two full alcoves filled with turnips they'd recently harvested from one of the fields, turnips that were meant for a winter market. Since the goods were meant for sale, they had not counted it among their food stores. Had the siege lasted any longer, however, they would have had to dip into them.

As soon as Emera emerged from her little alcove, stumbling past the mounds of turnips, she could see Juston standing over near the stairwell that led to the floor above. She kept her focus on him as she made her way through the minefield of wounded, stepping around men, her gaze on the knight with the shoulder-length hair. And she saw, very distinctly, when he caught sight of her.

A little jolt popped through her, a curious leap of her heart that she was wholly unfamiliar with although ever since the commander had kissed her, she had been feeling that strange little sensation whenever he was around. She'd felt that same jolt earlier in the muddy ward. As she drew close to the knight, she noticed a boy standing behind him.

The child couldn't have been more than nine or ten years of age. Emera was curious but she couldn't seem to tear her eyes away from Juston.

That jolt....

"My lord," she greeted politely. "How may I be of service?"

Juston almost choked on his reply because he immediately thought of that moment in his tent the previous night when he'd told her to service him. Demanded it, really. She's refused and he'd been humiliated. Now, she was asking that question which he very much wanted to answer with what, exactly, she could do for him. But he knew she hadn't meant that. Unfortunately for him, he couldn't quite keep his pride out of it.

"I told you how you would be of service to me last night but you refused," he said, watching her face turn red. "Yet you ask me again today. Do you think to taunt me, lady?"

Emera was mortified. "Nay, my lord," she said, realizing the boy was listening to their conversation. "I simply meant… I meant to ask if…."

He waved her off, feeling even more embarrassed now because she hadn't thrown herself at his feet to beg his forgiveness. "I know what you meant," he said. Then, he pointed to the boy beside him. "This is Tristan. He has just come from Canterbury, where he was a page. He has asked to help and I thought you could use him. Can you?"

Emera looked at the lad, standing next to Juston. He looked so very frightened. "Certainly," she said hesitantly. "I suppose he can help with the compresses. We are still applying them, my lord. For the most part, they are doing a great deal of good with the men. Thank you for your suggestion."

Juston motioned in the general direction of the wounded. "Then give him over to your sister or another servant so they can show him what to do," he said. "I wish to speak with you."

He really didn't have anything to speak with her about but he didn't want the conversation to end. He didn't want to walk away from her again and then spend the rest of the day thinking about her until he could come up with another excuse to speak with her. So he watched as she took the frightened young boy with her, leading him over to her sister, who was bent over one of the wounded and applying the hot compresses. He could see the steam rising into the cold of the vault. After a few exchanged words, the sister smiled at the boy and immediately began to show him what she was doing, encouraging him to do the same.

The young lad jumped right in, helping with the compresses. Juston felt some relief that he'd found something for the child to do in order to occupy his time. He was still rather shocked with the turn of events for the day, the appearance of the lad, but his shock was of no consequence. He'd had a serious duty assigned to him and he intended to fulfill it flawlessly.

Henry's bastard son was now under his protection.

With the boy busy tending the wounded, he could focus on his infatuation with Emera. Aye, it *was* infatuation, he'd decided. He was convinced it was only because she'd denied his advances. Surely such a woman would be intriguing to him, a challenge. She was heading in his direction now, returning to him as she'd been told to do, and all he could think of was taking her back to his new bedchamber and forcing her to service him. He would not take no for an answer. But he knew, instinctively, that he'd have a fight on his hands – again – and that wasn't exactly the mood he wanted to set. He needed relaxation and a warm female body after weeks of battle, and he wanted all of that with a calm and attentive woman at his side. Forcing Emera to his will wouldn't accomplish that.

But perhaps being kind to her would.

Aye, he could be kind when he wanted to be. And generous. He knew women responded better to sweetness than to force; any fool knew that. It had been a long time since he'd had to work for what he wanted but he supposed he hadn't forgotten how. He knew he could be quite persuasive when the situation called for it. Therefore, he already had a plan in mind as Emera approached. If he couldn't force her to his will, then he'd have his wants fulfilled another way. It might take more time, but he was willing to try.

For those brilliant blue eyes, he was willing.

"You wished to speak with me, my lord?" Emera asked as she reached him.

He couldn't help but notice she didn't ask if she could be of service again. Nay, that unfortunate choice of words had only caused her embarrassment. He simply nodded to her question.

"My men were supposed to collect your possessions and bring them to you," he said. "Did they?"

Emera nodded. "They brought down two satchels," she said. "To be truthful, I am not exactly sure what is in them but I did manage to pull out a few things that we needed, like a comb and soap. But…"

She seemed hesitant. He lifted his eyebrows expectantly. "But *what?*"

Emera cleared her throat softly. "I do not wish to be a bother, but we were only given two blankets, and not very warm ones at that," she said. "I have fashioned a bed for my sister and me, but we could use more blankets. It is quite cold down here."

Juston's gaze lingered on her a moment. Then, he crooked his finger at her, silently asking her to follow. She did.

Up the spiral stairs they went, past the first level great hall to the second level above. It was very warm on this level because the hearth was still burning brightly, a haze of smoke in the room. Juston pointed to the chamber.

"I would assume that this was the master's chamber," he said.

Emera nodded. "My sister and her husband slept here."

"And that small room beyond is yours?"

Again, she nodded. "Aye, my lord."

He began to walk through the bigger chamber to the smaller one beyond. He unlatched the door, opening up the very warm and smoky bower. Emera was still beside him, watching him because she was uncertain of his motives. Juston knew that by just looking at her; she had no idea why he had brought her up here.

Truth was, he really didn't either.

"If you see anything in your chamber that you would like to take with you, then you may do so," he told her, his tone rather quiet. "Soon, there will be filthy knights sleeping upon this bed and if they see any trinkets, they make collect them. Make a sweep of your chamber and make sure you have everything you wish to keep."

Emera's gaze lingered on him a moment, perhaps in some confusion, before she entered the chamber. It was her own comfortable room, a room she'd had for two years. She was grateful for Juston's show of benevolence but saddened when she realized there was so much in this chamber she wanted to take. The more she looked around, the heavier her heart.

"This is everything I have in the world," she said softly. She pointed to the frame that contained the half-finished embroidery. "My mother gave me that frame. I do not wish to leave it to be smashed or stolen. It is virtually all I have left of her. And the looms... those were hers as well. My sister and I use them to refine wool to make fabric. Everything in this chamber means something to me. It is very difficult to choose."

He could hear the sorrow in her tone. Certainly, he'd heard sorrow before, countless times, but he had the ability to ignore it in favor of his own wishes. Let no man – or woman – play upon his sensitivity. But hearing the sadness in Emera's voice brought him to a pause. He sighed.

"Take what you can carry," he said quietly. "If you truly are determined to go to a charity house once your duties at Bowes are complete, they will not let you bring your possessions, at least not things like looms and sewing frames."

She turned to look at him. "I realize that," she said. Interestingly enough, he didn't appear hardened to her plight. In truth, he almost seemed sympathetic to it. "I am sorry to sound sentimental. But I suppose my possessions do mean something to me, especially where my mother was concerned."

He was being sucked into those eyes. "Then mayhap it was a mistake to bring you here to choose what you wished to keep," he said. "Mayhap it would have been easier not to give you the choice at all."

Quickly, Emera shook her head. "I did not mean to sound ungrateful or as if I was trying to coerce you into letting me keep everything," she said. "I simply meant that choosing what to keep is like trying to choose between your children. Each item means something to me. Do you not have possessions like that? Things that are of sentimental value?"

He tore his gaze away from her. He was uncomfortable with the way she was looking at him, as if she could look into his very soul, yet at the same time, there was something about her presence that he wanted to bask in. It was a very strange feeling that swept him.

"We are speaking of you," he said, clearing his throat softly. "Take what you can carry, what you do not want to be taken from you."

He sounded cold now, his manner freezing up. Emera realized asking him about sentimental value had been a mistake.

"I am sorry," she said timidly. "I did not mean to ask you a question of a personal nature. I have always been that way, I suppose, wanting to know people, know what they are thinking and feeling. That is why I like to tend those who are sick or injured. There is something in me that demands to be helpful. I cannot sit about and complete delicate tasks like most ladies. I must *do* something. What is broken, I must fix."

He was back to looking at her again; he couldn't help it. "Fine ladies are taught to sing and paint and sew," he said. "At least, when I was fostering, that is what the female pledges did. I cannot recall them being taught to fix things."

She grinned, a reluctant gesture. "Unfortunately, I am not a fine lady," she said. "My mother believed our best education was in the church and in working at our home. I did not foster."

He leaned against the doorjamb. "But your father was a knight."

She nodded. "He was, but he was born in France. He did not have many allies here in England other than, at one time, King Henry. My father served Henry in France, so I suppose that makes me more of your enemy than you realized."

Juston's gaze lingered on her. "Your father was at Taillebourg."

She looked at him, surprised. "How did you know that?"

He was evasive, but not in a negative way. He simply didn't want to reveal his sources. "There is much I know," he said. "There is also much I do not. But I will discover it, eventually."

She could help but smile, reluctantly, at the way he said it. He wasn't cold any longer, back to being rather neutral about the conversation. More than that, she realized she rather liked talking to him when he wasn't intimidating her. He seemed excruciatingly arrogant, but there was some charm in that. She didn't mind male pride, at least not really. Confidence was a good quality in a man and a man of Juston's caliber had an abundance of it out of necessity and experience. She turned back to her bed, considering the coverlet she wanted to take with her.

"May I ask where you fostered?" she asked.

He saw no harm in telling her. "Winchester Castle," he said. "Then I went to East Anglia for a time, to Thunderbey Castle, seat of the Earls of East Anglia. I fostered under du Reims. I finished my fostering at Warwick Castle under de Vini."

She pulled the coverlet off the bed and lay it upon the wooden floor, spreading it out. "Is your family from East Anglia?"

"Nay," he said. He was talking more than he should have but, quite honestly, he didn't particularly care. "My home is Netherghyll Castle in Yorkshire. If you have not yet been told, I am the High Sheriff of Yorkshire, Baron Cononley by title. I have more men and more allies in the north than Henry does. And now I have Bowes Castle."

Emera was listening to him with interest. He was announcing his title like it was something she needed to be very impressed with. She began to place things in the center of the coverlet, her meager jewelry collection, for instance, and more combs and a few phials of precious oil from a trunk next to the bed.

"You have a great deal," she said, stroking his pride because it seemed that was the right thing to do with him. "Do you have brothers to share it with?"

"A younger brother who serves with Richard in France."

"What is his name?"

"Quinton."

"Is he a great knight, too?"

Juston couldn't help but notice she was putting a great many things in the center of the coverlet. "Of course he is," he said. "You mentioned that you also have a brother. What is his name?"

"Payne la Marche."

"Is he a knight?"

She shook her head. "He trained as one but it was not a vocation he enjoys," she said. "With my family contacts in France, my brother has become a wine importer. He imports wine to most of the south of England."

"Is that where your family home is?"

"Aye, in Dorset."

"That is a long way from Durham."

"A very long way, indeed."

He stopped talking because he was finding more interest watching her load possessions into her coverlet. It seemed that she was loading everything she could from the trunk and from a wardrobe against the wall onto the coverlet, arranging things carefully so they wouldn't smash one another. She seemed to have a purpose although he couldn't figure out what that purpose was. Finally, his curiosity got the better of him.

"What *are* you doing?" he asked.

With everything piled into the center of the coverlet, she carefully folded up the ends to make what essentially looked like a giant sack. Taking a satin hair ribbon, because she had no rope, she tried to tie up the four ends together.

"You said I could take whatever I could carry," she said, pulling tight the ribbon. "I can carry this coverlet."

Juston fought off a grin. "You cannot be serious."

She turned those big eyes to him. "You said I could take whatever I could carry."

Fact was, that was exactly what he said. He couldn't dispute that. He should have been annoyed that she took advantage of his generosity like that but he found he wasn't irritated in the least. He rather appreciated her ingenuity and her bravery. He pushed himself off of the doorjamb.

"You are correct," he said. "I did say that."

"Then you will not stop me?"

"I will not stop you."

He stood aside and she began to drag the coverlet across the floor. When she reached the doorway, however, the width of the giant sack she was dragging was too broad and it got stuck in the doorway. She tugged and tugged, and tried to shift the load around, but still, it stuck. Juston stood there and watched the entire circumstance without lifting a finger to help her. Part of him wanted her to fail, but part of him was very curious about how she would figure it all out.

A narrow doorway didn't stop Emera. She was creative as well as logical. She shifted the load inside of the coverlet enough so that she could pull it through the door. Once through, she dragged it across the floor, grunting under the weight of it, for it was quite heavy with all of the clothing and personal effects she loaded into it. Still, she was determined to follow through on her plan. She was not about to admit she may have taken on too heavy a burden. She wouldn't give de Royans the satisfaction of knowing he had been right and she had been wrong. She was only wrong if she failed.

In fact, Juston strolled casually behind her as she heaved the coverlet across the floor. He hadn't said a word about the difficulty of her task. He knew once she hit the stairwell that she was going to run into a problem, but he didn't say a word. He rather liked watching her work it all out. She was not only beautiful to watch, she was smart and determined. More and more, he found great interest in watching her.

More and more, he was drawn to her.

Finally, Emera reached the most difficult part of her task. She came to a halt at the top of the steps, looking down the narrow spiral stairs and knowing, much as Juston did, that she was going to have a difficult time dragging the sack down three stories. But she refused to ask for help or even pretend there was an issue. She'd come this far and she had to see it through.

Stepping into the stairwell, she thought it would be best to simply drag the thing behind her and try to keep it from tumbling down the stairs using her body weight to block it. But once she started to pull, the weight of the sack tumbled forward and she lost her balance, falling down a couple of steps before ending up on her bottom, wedged against the wall. But she didn't fall far. When Juston realized she was falling, he rushed forward and grabbed both her and the sack, preventing them both from rolling all the way to the level below. Trapped in the stairwell with the sack on her legs and lap, Emera pulled her arm from Juston's grip.

"Thank you, my lord," she said crisply. "I did not need your help. I was able to catch myself."

He stood back as she tried to stand up, saddled by the weight of the sack. "Not much, you were," he muttered. "Lady Emera, as much as I admire your determination, dragging most of your possessions down to the vault is not practical. You are going to break your neck falling down these stairs. It is simply too heavy for you."

She looked at him, those big eyes sucking him in once more. "But you said I could take whatever I could carry!"

He nodded. "Aye, I did, but you are not carrying anything. It is carrying *you*, and it will do so all the way to the bottom. You are going to kill yourself."

Emera was feeling some desperation. She didn't like to admit failure. "Please," she said softly. "I do not have great titles or lands as you do. I only have those things you saw in that small chamber. These are my things and I want them. Please let me try."

He shook his head and yanked on the sack, pulling it up off of her and carrying it with ease back into the big chamber. Emera scrambled after him.

"Where are you taking my things?"

Juston hauled them back into the smaller chamber and set the sack on the floor. When he saw the panicked look on her face, he held up a hand to ease her.

"You can keep them all," he said. "I dare not deny a woman who so cleverly used my words against me. On the contrary... if I do not let you keep everything, you are going to kill yourself trying to take it down those stairs and then your death would be on my conscience. I will not be made to feel guilty for your stubbornness."

Emera's face lit up. "You… you will let me keep my possessions?"

"I will."

"Even if I cannot carry them?"

"Even if you cannot carry them."

It was clear that she was quite surprised. "Oh, my lord," she breathed. "I cannot tell you how grateful I am. With all of my heart, thank you!"

He simply stood there and looked at her. *Here she is, telling me she is, once again, grateful.* Grateful women could be most pliable, in his experience. Perhaps now was the time to push his advantage.

Not being a man with much restraint when it came to that which he wanted, Juston reached out and grabbed her by the arm, whipping her against his chest so hard that she grunted. Before he even realized what he was doing, his lips slanted over hers, hungrily. Now he was tasting her again and he'd never felt a greater sense of contentment.

In his arms is where she belonged.

CHAPTER EIGHT

I T WAS UNFORTUNATE for Juston that Emera still didn't feel the same way.

He began to suspect that when he felt slapping to his face. He ignored it. He was enjoying a deep and lusty kiss with the woman when a fist suddenly hit in him the throat. That forced him to release his hold on her, grabbing his throat as he struggled to breathe. In the process of her fight, however, Emera ended up on her bum. As Juston drew in a great gasping breath, she scrambled to her feet, ran for the smaller chamber, and slammed the door. The sound of the bolt being thrown filled the chamber.

Juston could hardly believe she'd run from him. Infuriated, he went to the door, hand still on his throat, and rattled the latch with his free hand. It was clearly bolted, but instead of yelling at her through the door, he was going to show that he was resourceful, too. He went to the hearth, which was smoking heavily and giving off a great deal of heat, and used one of the big ash shovels to move the peat aside, enough so that he could create a passageway through the hearth and into her chamber on the other side.

Emera, seeing what he was doing from the other side, grabbed her own ash shovel. As much as he would shovel the peat away, she would shovel it back again. That went on two or three times until he took his ash shovel and hit hers, causing her to drop it. She shrieked but pick the shovel back up again, in time to smack his shovel as he tried to move the peat aside again. Soon enough, they were dueling through the flaming peat, each one trying to hit the shovel out of the other's hand.

Juston had managed to hit her hands a couple of times, undoubtedly bruising her, but she wasn't giving up. It was a trait he'd admired in her but now found tiresome. Finally, he stopped battling her all together and scowled at her through the flames.

"This is how you treat the man who holds your life in his very hands?" he demanded. "What is the matter with you, woman? Are you completely daft?"

Emera still had the shovel in her hands, terrified he was going to charge through the hearth, flames and all. "I will not let you degrade me," she hissed. "I told you I have never known a man's touch but, still, you force yourself upon me. I will not let you!"

Juston sighed heavily. "Do you ever wish to marry?"

She faltered, confused by his question in the midst of their argument. "I... I do not know. Why does that matter?"

"Because the way you behave, you will never know a man's touch because no man will *want* to touch you. You have the beauty of an angel but the disposition of a shrew!"

She was incensed. "And you have the manners of a barbarian!"

He jabbed a finger at her. "If you were more agreeable, there is no telling what I would do for you. I might even give you your chamber back. I might even let you and your sister sleep in comfortable beds. You understand that you belong to me, do you not? I do not have to ask your permission for anything. I can just as easily take it!"

Her insults turned to fear. "If you try, I... I shall kill myself!"

He threw up his hands. "Good!" he boomed. "Then I will no longer have to deal with your foolishness. Did you not stop to think that I want to kiss you not because I'm trying to rob you of your innocence, but simply because you are beautiful? Because I find you alluring and desirable?"

Emera came to a sudden halt, her eyes suddenly wide at him. She'd never heard such words spoken to her, at least not honestly spoken to her. She could tell, simply from his tone, that he was being completely truthful. She was astonished.

"Me... *desirable?*" she stammered.

When Juston realized what he'd said, he felt like a fool. He'd spoken thoughts he had only intended to keep to himself, ever. He certainly hadn't meant to shout them at her. But something had compelled him to spit them out, shouting at her across a smoking hearth, and he'd angrily yelled things he shouldn't have yelled.

Vastly embarrassed, he abruptly stood up and threw the ash shovel to the floor. He had to get out of there, to get clear of her overwhelming presence. Something about the woman made him lose his control and he didn't like that in the least. He was almost to the stairwell when the door to the smaller chamber flew open.

"Wait!" Emera called after him. "Please... please do not leave."

"I must."

"Nay," she begged. "Please... you must understand... please, do not go. I do not mean to be ungrateful but I cannot allow you to grab me whenever you please."

He came to an unsteady halt, facing her with much anger in his expression. "You do understand that I do not have to ask you if I want to touch you."

"But I will not allow you to treat me like a... a *whore.*"

"You are what I say you are," he snapped. "If I want you to be my whore, then you shall be."

"Is that what you want?"

Now, it was his turn to falter. Her question had been soft, nearly painful. It shook him. "I did not say that!"

He was yelling at her but he wasn't leaving the corridor, at least not yet. He lingered there as if they had unfinished business, unspoken words hanging in the air between them. Emera sensed that the great conqueror of Bowes, the man whose word was obeyed without question, had something more to say to her. He was still intimidating and imposing, but there was something more there... something softer, perhaps perplexed and seeking.

Was it possible he was bewildered somehow? It was as if he didn't even know what he wanted or how he wanted to treat her. He was trying to be kind, but kindness wasn't in his nature. It was completely alien to him. In that moment, something told Emera that there was far more going on in the man's mind than she could understand. Something that had to do with her. She could tell that simply by the way he was looking at her.

At that moment, she started to look at him a bit differently as well.

"I have spent the past two years fighting off Brey de la Roarke," she said, her voice considerably softer. "It is simply the way I have become accustomed to reacting to a man who tries to grab me as you have done. I have spent two years fending off unwanted advances and... do you *really* think I am beautiful?"

She asked the question as if she could hardly believe he meant what he said. But Juston was ashamed, feeling terribly uncomfortable as he stood at the top of the stairs. Nearly everything within him was willing him down those stairs to get away from her, but something – a very small but powerful something – was holding him back. He cleared his throat softly.

"Do you not even know that?" he asked quietly.

Emera shook her head even though he couldn't see her. "I... I do not," she said, taking a step towards him. Her heart was racing and she could hardly breathe. She had no idea why she was feeling this way. All she knew was that it had everything to do with what Juston had said to her. "My father told me I was. Brey told me I was, but coming from them... I am sure my father told me that because I was his daughter and Brey simply wanted to... well, I have told you what he wanted to do. I have never had anyone other than my family tell me I was pleasing to look at."

Juston turned to look at her. Her black hair was mussed, her face pale, but the blue eyes were alive. Looking at her did something to his soul.

"You are more than pleasing," he said simply. "You *are* beautiful." He turned back around, facing the stairwell. "I have duties to attend to and you should return to the wounded. You may leave your possessions in that room, for I will tell the knights they are not to use that chamber. You and your sister may sleep in that chamber instead of in the cold vault."

Emera was truly astonished. "But why would you do this? You told me your men were to take the chambers in the keep. I do not understand why...."

He cut her off. "Why must you question everything I say?"

Emera shut her mouth, realizing he was correct. She had, indeed, questioned nearly everything he said to her since the beginning of their association. Moreover, she didn't want him to change his mind. Juston sounded like he was defeated somehow. He appeared to relent his stance of a captor to a captive. It was so very strange coming from a man who had shown nothing but arrogant disregard for her since the moment they had first met. Now, he was showing some compassion, far more than she'd ever expected.

Emera didn't say a word as he descended the stairs and disappeared from her view, wondering why he was suddenly so subdued and wondering why she felt guilty about it.

Giving him time to descend the stairs and get clear of them, in pensive silence, she followed.

BY NOON, THE clouds had bunched up overhead and by early afternoon, freezing rain was, once again, pummeling the land. It made for genuinely slow and miserable travel as Christopher, David, and Marcus had made their way north to Cotherstone Castle.

The village of Cotherstone was set to the southwest of the castle, which sat on a rise overlooking the small Balder River, a tributary of the

River Tees. It was a bustling village with a good coach inn that was popular with travelers called The Lion and the Lamb. Christopher, David, and Marcus had been to the inn before, at various times, since it was on a major road through the Pennines from Scotland. In fact, many a knight coming down from the north had stopped at the inn which was famous for its collection of "talented" wenches.

The castle was secondary to the fame of the inn, to be truthful. The castle was nothing more than a garrison for the Bishop of Durham, holding the road from the north. At any given time, it housed no more than two or three hundred men. It was really rather small as garrisons went. But it was a strategic location and that was why Juston wanted it. The more of a foothold he had in Durham, the less of a foothold Henry had.

Traveling through the morning in freezing rain had been a miserable experience for the knights. A trip that should have taken an hour at the most took far more than that. The rain had turned their mail into sheets of ice, heavy and frozen, and the horses were spent, exhausted from the cold weather and terrible traveling conditions. The main road they were traveling on was flooded out and they'd had to find a detour which took them far out of their way. The conditions of travel were, simply, awful.

The wind was picking up now, whipping the freezing rain straight at them. As the trio neared Cotherstone, Marcus, who had been in the lead, pulled his horse to a halt and waited for Christopher and David to catch up with him.

"Do you know what I have been thinking?" he asked, his gaze on the town ahead, visible through the heavy foliage that lined the road. "I have been thinking that we must be smart about our reconnaissance of Cotherstone Castle. In truth, on a day like today, with the weather as it is, do we believe they will have patrols out? We've not seen evidence of any patrols. Only a fool would be out in weather like this."

Christopher, with ice forming on his trim beard, looked off to the west where the dead landscape gently rolled. "Then count us among the foolish," he muttered. "Cotherstone Castle is nothing more than a pele tower surrounded by a wall. There is no moat but there is a river to the north. I am not sure what we will see of the castle or her level of alert considering what happened at Bowes, but we have come this far. Let us separate here and converge on the castle from different directions to see what we can see."

Marcus shook his head. "I have a better idea."

David was interested, mostly because he didn't want to be crawling through the frozen tundra, spying on Cotherstone from icy trees. "I am listening," he said.

Marcus pushed his helm up on his head, scratching at his forehead. "We all know of The Lion and the Lamb," he said. "It is a popular place with travelers as well as knights. I have been there a few times myself. I would be willing to wager that since it is well known, and many travelers stop there, then mayhap the men of Cotherstone populate it as well."

Christopher looked at him, quickly understanding what he was leading to. "Exactly," he agreed. "The men of Cotherstone more than likely haunt the place on a regular basis and it is well known that The Lion and the Lamb has a selection of women for a man's comfort."

David caught on as well. "Then we find a woman that knows something of the men at Cotherstone," he said as if he'd just had a great epiphany. "Women cannot keep their mouths shut. They will speak freely of what they know of the men of Cotherstone."

Marcus nodded. "I suspect we might find out much more of Cotherstone from the tavern wenches than from trying to gather intelligence ourselves," he said. "In fact, if we hang around the inn long enough, men from Cotherstone might even come in. We can pretend to be Henry supporters and there is no telling what they will discuss with us."

While David liked that idea a great deal, Christopher wasn't so sure. "If they have heard of the siege of Bowes, then it is possible the garrison commander has bottled up the castle and is not letting anyone in or out," he said. "But I do think visiting the inn and seeing what we can extract from the women is an excellent idea. Besides… I'm cold and hungry. I have no desire to remain out in this weather any longer."

The decision was made. The knights spurred the horses onward, entering the village of Cotherstone. They rode past closed businesses and homes, heading to the heart of the town where the popular inn was. As they sighted the two-storied stone structure, with two heavily smoking chimneys, the first thing they did was locate shelter for the horses, in this case in a livery across the street. It was a long, rather slender stone building with a low ceiling, smelling strongly of hay and animals.

The old man and his son who ran the livery were more than happy to tend the heavy-boned horses with the generous coinage Christopher paid them. The knights collected their saddlebags, waiting until the tack was removed from the horses and they were bedded down with plenty of grass and grain before leaving because the horses could be excitable at times. The horses were fed oats, usually reserved for sheep, which they loved. The knights quit the livery to the sounds of munching, happy horses.

The rain had picked up as they crossed the road and entered the smoky, warm establishment that smelled heavily of sweating bodies. It was not particularly crowded at midday and they easily found a table near the hearth that gave them a prime view of the entire common room. They settled down for a good, long stay, slinging saddlebags across other chairs, and pulling the table closer to the hearth. Their commotion attracted attention. Like a moth to the flame, the serving wenches began gravitating in their direction.

There were worse looking knights in England but between Marcus, David, and Christopher, there were few that could be considered more handsome. With Marcus' black hair and deep blue eyes, he was an exceptionally attractive man and the first wench to the table focused on him. Big-breasted, with curly dark hair, she smiled openly at Marcus as if no one else in the room existed.

"Stopping to rest on this dreadful day, m'lord?" she asked, leaning in to him. "I've got several things to keep you warm. Anything you like at all."

It was a hugely leading question because she clearly meant herself. Marcus, who could handle an aggressive woman quite ably, smoothly handled her proposal.

"Warmed wine will do for now," he said. "But do not go far. I may require something more."

Her smile brightened. "My pleasure, m'lord."

"And send some of your friends over here. My comrades require warmth as well."

As she sashayed away from the table, Marcus looked at Christopher and lifted his eyebrows in a rather suggestive manner. Christopher bit off a grin but David couldn't quite hide his; he lowered his head with a smile on his face, focusing on removing his gloves as three more women approached the table.

It was open season on knights.

David suddenly found himself with a petite blonde hanging over him, her long hair tickling his face. "Welcome to The Lion and the Lamb, m'lord," she said in a squeaky little voice. "Can I bring you anything? Anything at all?"

David had to pull back to look at the woman because she was literally hanging over him. She was a cute little thing. He was immediately interested.

"My friend has ordered warmed wine," he said. "What else do you have for us back in the kitchen that is hot and satisfying?"

It was a sexually charged question and the young woman giggled. "There is plenty in this place that is hot and satisfying, m'lord. You need only ask."

"I'll take food for now. We'll speak of the rest afterwards."

She nodded, enticed with the thought of spending some time with her naked flesh against his. "There is some excellent stew and fresh bread," she said. "I will bring you some."

David grinned, reaching up to touch her cheek as she giggled again and ran off. Meanwhile, there were two fairly curvy wenches who were on either side of Christopher as he removed his gloves. He wasn't much interested in being smooth or glib with women. Usually, he was quite serious and focused on his knightly duties, which made him something of a challenge for a woman trying to attract him. As he pulled off a glove, one of the women took hold of it and yanked while he extracted his hand.

"My thanks," he muttered as she set the glove on the table. When he saw that she was trying to help him with the other one, he simply let her. That was the extent of his flirting at the moment. "Again, my thanks."

The woman smiled as she took the gloves and set them on the hearth to warm. "It is a pleasure, m'lord," she said. "Your friends are having warmed wine and food brought to them. What can we do for you, m'lord?"

Christopher looked at the pair; they weren't unattractive, but he simply wasn't one to arbitrarily bed women. He was far more selective with the women he pursued. Still, they had come to this inn for a purpose. He forced himself to play the game.

"You can bring me warmed wine as well and some food," he told them. "And then you can sit and talk to me. It has been a long time since I've had such lovely companionship."

That was enough for the women. They dashed away, hissing at each other, arguing as to who would bring him what, and who would sit by his right hand. He watched them disappear into the rear of the inn.

"Now," he lowered his voice once they were free of the wenches. "I suggest we divide and conquer. David, take the blonde and do whatever you want to do with her. But whatever it is, do not take long. I want to make it back to Bowes before nightfall. Marcus, work your magic. I've seen what you can do."

Marcus laughed softly. "It will be a pleasure. What will you do?"

Christopher cocked an eyebrow. "I am the only one of the three of

us who had two women approach him," he pointed out arrogantly.
"Whatever I do, it will be in pairs."

David and Marcus snorted, quieting down by the time the women
began flooding back in their direction. Wine and food was presented in
copious amounts and soon, they were downing hot wine with cloves
and big bowls of mutton stew. It was thick and hearty, full of carrots
and turnips, and they ate several bowls of the stuff while the women
fawned over them, chatting and trying to engage them, doing everything but laying in their laps in order to gain their attention.

While Marcus and David were somewhat attentive to the wenches,
Christopher was more interested in his food. He would have been
happier had they left him alone so, once again, he forced himself to
make the effort. They filled his cup before he'd barely even had a sip of
the wine and then they would bring him more fresh bread. He spent a
good deal of time kissing dirty hands in thanks. The games went on and
on, the three men and the five women, for at least an hour.

Then, things became interesting.

David was fairly drunk on the hot wine and jiggling flesh at that
point. He'd had too much of one and hadn't had enough lately of the
other. He wasn't really sure how much wine he'd had, but the little
blonde wench, named Edith – or Edie – had ended up in his lap about
halfway through his meal. Still, she sat there, laughing with David and
feeding him pieces of bread. He'd pretend to gobble up her fingers and
she would squeal. Then he progressed from nibbling her fingers to
nibbling on her neck. Marcus and Christopher, who weren't quite as
drunk, hoped he'd have enough sense to take the woman someplace
private before ravaging her. They could see it was coming to that.

But they'd come here with a purpose. As David nibbled and Marcus
flirted, Christopher decided to take the lead.

It was time.

"This place is not as busy as I had remembered," Christopher said
to the two women sitting on either side of him. "I suppose it's the
weather, but I thought you'd have more patrons."

The women beside him nodded. "It will be busy tonight," the busty redhead replied from his right side. "When travelers are looking for a place to come in from the cold, we'll be full enough to bursting."

Christopher took a drink of his cooling wine. "It has been fearsome weather to travel in," he said. "I shall be glad when we reach our destination."

"Where have you come from, m'lord?" the woman on his left spoke.

Christopher threw a thumb in a general southerly direction. "South," he said. "We were passing near Bowes Castle, but the place was under siege. We quickly made our way around it for I have no desire to be caught up in whatever was happening there. Have you heard of the trouble?"

"Aye," the woman on his left answered quickly, before the other woman could because she didn't want to be left out of the conversation. "We heard about the battle but we don't know what the trouble is about. Do you?"

Christopher shook his head, playing dumb. "I could not tell you," he said. "I thought mayhap the garrison at Cotherstone would know. My comrades and I were thinking of seeking shelter there for the night, but I find your company much more pleasing than a gaggle of soldiers. Haven't any of the soldiers spoken of the trouble at Bowes?"

The woman hanging over Marcus slid into his lap, toying with his black hair as he sat there and let her. "They haven't come to see us as of late," she said, grinning at Marcus when he winked at her. "They usually come every night but we haven't seen them the past few weeks. One of the men came over here yesterday, though, because he can't stand to be away from us. He snuck out through the postern gate. He told us the commander ordered all of the soldiers to stay inside and be vigilant."

"Vigilant for what?" Christopher asked.

The woman shrugged her shoulders, the tattered remnant of her clothing sliding off one arm. Before she could answer, David suddenly stood up with Edie in his arms and, with both of then snickering, carried her away from the table and up a flight of unsteady stairs that led to the upper floor. They could hear Edie laughing as David proceeded into a narrow, low-ceilinged corridor and then they heard a door slam.

Once the door slammed, the other women began to laugh. "Your friend should pray her husband does not come soon to seek her," the redhead on Christopher's right said. "He does not like to share!"

Christopher and Marcus looked at each other in alarm. "She is married?" Christopher asked.

The redhead nodded, snaking her arm casually around Christopher's shoulders. "Aye," she said. "But I'm not. There's no chance of an angry husband with me, m'lord."

Christopher was trying not to get off-focus. He wasn't finished interrogating the women about Cotherstone Castle but he was concerned for his brother bedding a married woman. Taking advantage of the wenches in the inn didn't cover that particular scenario. His brother's welfare finally won over.

"What husband allows his wife to work in a tavern?" he asked to anyone who could answer him. "Why would he even permit it? And where *is* the husband?"

The women were still giggling, evidently unconcerned. "The money she makes is far better than the money he makes," the redhead said. "She tells him that she simply serves food, but she serves far more than that."

More giggles sounded at the implication of that statement. Christopher was not amused. "Where is her husband?" he repeated.

The redhead now had both arms around his shoulders, pulling herself closer to him. "He is a smithy," she said. "His stall is at the edge of town, near the river, and he does work for the castle because they lost their smithy last year to illness. He will be here soon to take her home. Whatever your friend is doing, he had better hurry before he comes. Edie's husband often brings his hammer with him to keep the customers away from his wife."

That statement cemented Christopher's concern for his brother as something very pressing. He looked at Marcus and they both shared the same expression of disbelief. A jealous husband carrying a hammer? They knew immediately what they had to do; finish their business and get the hell out of there. There was a great sense of urgency now but they endeavored to keep it from their manner.

"Then we should probably tell him to finish his business quickly," Christopher said, sounding calm enough. "Knowing him, he will not take long. Meanwhile, let us speak more on the battle at Bowes. Had I known there was a battle going on there, I would have avoided it. I hope there will be no battle at Cotherstone before we get clear of the town."

The redhead was practically in his lap now. "It's hard to say, love," she said, foregoing the "my lord" form of address. She was willing to tell him everything she could as long as he let her get close to him. "Before they bottled up the soldiers, they sent messengers away."

He put his hands on hers, stilling her caressing fingers. "How would you know that?"

She shrugged. "We've seen the dispatch messengers before, coming in and out of the castle," she said. "People don't think we know much at 'tall, but we do. We know soldiers and we've seen enough of them. Mayhap there will be more soldiers coming because of the messengers, but I don't care about them so long as I have you."

He released her hands and they started to wander, rubbing his chest. All Christopher could think about, however, was riders being sent out. *Before they bottled up the soldiers*... that was a few weeks ago, according to her, which was right around the time they started the siege at Bowes. Time enough to send out messengers for reinforcements which, if men and material moved with any speed at all, would not be far away. Even in this weather, they'd had three weeks to plan and move. He struggled to maintain his calm, slightly disinterested manner.

"Where more soldiers are, trouble follows," he said, draining the last of his wine. "I cannot say I will remain here if more soldiers are coming. I wonder where they could be coming from."

He was trying to draw more out of her, whatever she might know or have heard. She seemed to know quite a bit. He let her snake her hands under his tunic, hoping she'd not really give thought to answering his probing question.

"Are you not from around here, love?" she asked.

Christopher shook his head. "Nay," he said. "I am from Gloucester."

She had found his skin, now scratching at his warm chest, tickling him. "The riders went south that we saw," she said. "We saw them pass by, four of them, as the rains fell. We thought it strange because they were riding so fast in the terrible weather, but Bousey – he's the man that owns this place – he said they were soldiers riding off to tell Lord de Puiset that his castle was under siege. Bousey has lived here many years and he knows much of what goes on in Henry's wars. Aren't you fighting Henry's wars against his son?"

"I am trying to stay out of it."

She believed him, a heavily armed knight, which made her something of a fool. "As I said, Bousey says he thinks the riders were going to Auckland and to Richmond. So there may be more wars around here soon enough. Where are you heading, love? Mayhap I should come with you to avoid the fighting that's coming."

She was chattering on, rubbing the bare skin of his chest, having no idea that with every word, Christopher was growing more and more interested. *Auckland… Richmond…* aye, he was most interested in what she was saying. And he knew that Juston would be, too.

"Will you fetch me more hot wine?" he abruptly asked her, holding up his cup. He gestured to Marcus, who had been listening to everything said quite intently. "And my friend needs more hot wine as well. I want it so hot that I can barely drink it. Go, now. Fetch it for me."

The two women left his side, reluctantly, the redhead snatching the cup away from the other woman who was just about to take it. As they scurried off, arguing with each other angrily, the woman draped all over Marcus took his cup as well. She left him with a kiss on the nose as she went off to fetch him more hot wine.

The hot wine had only been an excuse. Christopher wanted the women gone so he could speak with Marcus. When the wenches were out of earshot, he leaned forward on the table and lowered his voice.

"Word has been sent to Auckland and to Richmond," he whispered urgently. "Richmond carries a massive army, dedicated to Henry. If they march north and Auckland comes in from the east, the convergence of those two armies on Bowes will be catastrophic. The castle will not be able to withstand it."

Marcus nodded. "My thoughts exactly," he hissed. "Middleham Castle is not far beyond Richmond. If they draw support from that castle, then they will overrun us with no trouble."

"The messengers went out three weeks ago."

"So I heard."

Christopher cocked an eyebrow. "That means they've had time to mobilize," he said. "We must return… *now*. Juston must know."

Marcus was in complete agreement. "He will need to seek reinforcements from Netherghyll as well as Brough Castle," he said. "That is the closest castle loyal to Richard that I know of. Stephen St. John is in command."

"You know him?"

"I do."

Christopher stood up. "I will retrieve David," he said. "You will go and collect the horses. And hurry."

Marcus was on his feet. The sense of urgency was tremendous now that the situation had been made clear – Cotherstone, informed of the siege on Bowes, had sent word to Auckland Castle and, possibly, Richmond, a massive royal property. Worse still, both castles were enormous and had been given time to mobilize. Juston had to know immediately because it was he, and he alone, who had to determine just how strategic Bowes was to Richard's cause. It could be a massive battle should Brough Castle be pulled into a conflict with Richmond and Auckland.

The situation was far more volatile than they realized.

Marcus was already heading to the entry of the inn as Christopher dug into the purse at his belt and drew forth a few coins, tossing them onto the table. Just as Marcus reached the door, it suddenly flew open and, in a flurry of wind and freezing rain, a big, burly man in heavy wool and very worn leather entered. He slammed the door behind him, grumbling, and shook off the water. But there was no denying the man's state; he was dirty and smelled of cinder. Shaking off what he could of the rain, he stomped past Marcus without noticing him and began to look around the common room as if searching for someone. His movements were edgy, jerky.

"Edie!" he boomed.

Christopher, who hadn't much noticed the man, suddenly looked at him when he began to shout. Edie was the name of the woman David was with. It took Christopher a split second to make the connection between this barbaric-looking man, dirty and ragged, and that lovely blonde creature that had enchanted David. The first thing he did was look to see if the man had a hammer in his hand. He didn't see one but that didn't mean one wasn't buried somewhere in the layers of clothing he wore.

Christopher's gaze flicked to Marcus, who bolted from the entry door, undoubtedly heading for the stables to collect the horses. They both understood the need for haste in this matter. The wenches, emerging from the kitchen with their hands full of hot wine, scattered when they saw the burly smithy. The redhead darted over to Christopher, spilling the wine as she went.

"'Tis him!" she whispered fearfully. "'Tis her husband!"

That was confirmation of what Christopher already knew. He knew he could dispatch the man, easily, if it came to it. But he'd much rather simply extract his brother from his illicit tryst and spirit the man away. No bloodshed, no fuss. Simply grab David and leave that place. He wasn't looking for a fight, especially in this case – the husband would have every reason to be furious with David.

"Hold him here as long as you can," Christopher muttered to the wench. "Give me time to get my brother away from that man's wife."

The redhead was clearly frightened. "How shall I do that?"

Christopher pointed to the wine in her hand. "Give that to him," he said. "Tell him that I have purchased the drink for him. Keep him busy for a minute or two."

"I am not sure if I can!"

"Try!"

To punctuate his demand, he leaned over and kissed her on the cheek, which was enough to feed her bravery. She would have walked through fire for a kiss from the handsome knight. Fortified, the wench headed over to the fat, slovenly smithy while Christopher grabbed their saddlebags and slipped from the inn, back out into the freezing rain.

The storm had let up a bit but it was still an icy mist as he raced around the side of the inn, over to the side he presumed David was in one of the upstairs rooms. He had no way of knowing, of course. It was purely a guess from the direction he'd last seen his brother heading in. But he had to get to the man before the smithy did.

Standing in the mud and mist, he emitted a shrill whistle from between his teeth, his focus on the two upstairs windows shuttered against the cold. By the third whistle and no movement, he began to call up to the windows, trying not to shout. He didn't want to attract the wrong kind of attention from a certain smithy who was inside the establishment, too.

Where in the hell was his brother?

"David!" he called. "*David!*"

No response. He was preparing to climb the wall when one of the shutters finally pushed open and his brother appeared, naked from the waist up. He was clearly perturbed.

"What do you want?" he demanded.

Christopher held his hands up to quiet the man because his voice was loud. "Your companion's husband is in the common room looking for her," he said as quietly as he could and still be heard. "He is big and mean and probably carrying a hammer. You cannot get past him. You must jump from the window!"

The frustrated expression on David's face dissolved into shock. "*Husband?*"

Edie suddenly appeared in the window, a coverlet wrapped around what was clearly her naked chest. "My husband is here?"

She was in a panic. As David stood there, an astonished expression on his face, the door to the chamber must have rattled because both he and Edie turned inward, as if hearing a sharp sound. The next thing Christopher realized, his brother was throwing his legs over the windowsill, now hanging out of it as naked as the day he was born. He didn't have a stitch of clothing on. Christopher raced up to the man, able to catch him around the legs. David let go of the sill, falling into his brother's embrace just as the door to the chamber overhead splintered open.

Wood from the broken door went flying from the open window as Christopher stumbled with his brother's weight nearly falling atop him. But he managed to keep his balance as his naked brother landed on his feet. Above them, they could hear Edie screaming and her husband bellowing. Not waiting to see the outcome of that particular family argument, Christopher and David raced to the front of the inn just as Marcus came across the road with the horses.

The animals were hastily tacked, with straps hanging from saddles that hadn't been fully secured, but it didn't much matter. They had to leave, and leave in a hurry, and both David and Christopher jumped onto their steeds just as Edie's husband stuck his head from the second-floor window, bellowing threats to the three knights as they took off down the road.

David would have frozen to death had Marcus not tossed him a woolen tunic that was hanging from one of his hastily-secured saddlebags, because they weren't stopping any time soon. David had to dress on the run. There was the chance that the enraged smithy would come after them, so they continued down the road, through the freezing rain, heading south until David began to turn blue and they knew they had to make a hasty stop to let the man put more clothing on. At this point, there was little choice.

Having left his clothing, including his mail, back at the inn, David dressed in Marcus' heavy tunic and a spare pair of leather breeches from his own saddlebags, but his boots were also back at the inn and there was no way he was going back to retrieve them. But he had his sword and what was in his saddlebags, and that was all he really cared about.

He also had his life.

The tale of the wench's smithy husband would make for a funny story someday, but for the first half-hour after leaving Cotherstone, no one was laughing. That soon changed, however, when they realized they weren't being followed.

There was relief in the realization they'd escaped the wrath of the angry husband. Marcus and Christopher, reflecting on the memory of a naked knight with a fully-erect manhood trying to ride a horse, began to snort with both humor and relief. Within a half-hour of leaving Cotherstone, they were howling with laughter until they cried.

David, eventually, had to admit that it was humorous, too.

CHAPTER NINE

Bowes Castle

"TRULY, EMMY, YOU are exhausted." Jessamyn's voice was soft. "You must try to sleep a little. I can tend the men while you do. We have plenty of help."

It was early evening as Emera sat beside a dying man, watching him breathe heavily and unsteadily, knowing there was nothing more she could do to help him. He was another man with a belly wound who was succumbing to a raging fever. He was an older man and Emera had seen him around the castle for the past two years as he went about his duty. He had always been kind to her.

She was sitting on the ground, her knees folded up. A bent arm rested on her knee, holding her head up. She glanced at her sister in the dim light.

"I will not leave him until he passes," she said quietly. "He is not long for this earth. No man should have to die alone."

Jessamyn understood. Her sister was more tender-hearted than most, to the point of sacrificing herself for the sake of another. She wasn't happy about her sister's stance, but she didn't fight her on it.

"You did not eat much for sup," she said. "May I bring you something to eat?"

Emera shook her head. "I am not hungry," she said, "although I will admit, the pork and beans that de Royans' men provided is a vast improvement over the porridge we have been relegated to."

Jessamyn smiled. "I agree." She sobered, looking around the dark, quiet vault. "Still, we are prisoners even if they have been fair to us."

Emera's gaze lingered on her sister. "We were prisoners before, only you were married to our jailor."

Jessamyn didn't flare to the comment as she usually did. In fact, she seemed rather thoughtful. "You can say what you like about Brey," she said. "I know you were not fond of him."

"*Fond* of him? Jess, are you serious?"

Jessamyn held up a hand. She didn't want to get into an argument. "He was my husband," she said. "He was not yours, he was *mine*. What I feel… it does not matter. But for you, I would understand your dislike of him. But for all of his faults, as least we had a home and food and a place where we belonged. Now, we do not even have that. Did you ever think of it that way? Last night, you told that… that terrible knight that we had nowhere to go and we do not. Now, we are worse off than you thought we were before."

Emera thought on her sister's words. She was correct for the most part. But Emera didn't agree with her completely.

"The commander's name is de Royans," she said quietly. "Sir Juston de Royans. He is from Netherghyll Castle, which is not far from here, so he says. He was somewhat rigid and cold last night. But today I was able to speak with him and he did not seem quite so cold and terrible. He allowed us to take the wounded into the vault, did he not? He allowed us to keep our possessions. I would say that we are not as bad off as we could be."

She didn't tell her sister about the two attempts he'd made to kiss her; somehow, she didn't want to. She wasn't sure if she was ashamed of it or not. Brey had chased her for two years and had never managed to kiss her the way de Royans had after only being around a short amount of time. She didn't want her sister to think she was giving herself over to the enemy, so confusion kept her silent because one thing was for certain – she wasn't nearly as resistant to de Royans' advances as she was to Brey's.

"I suppose we have been treated better than most prisoners," Jessamyn conceded. "But the fact remains that we *are* prisoners. What will become of us?"

Emera had already planned out what her future would entail. She wasn't so sure about Jessamyn. "When the wounded no longer need us, I have asked de Royans if he will provide me with an escort to a charity hospital in Sherburn," she said. "I do not know what your future will be, Jess, but I wish to go to the charity hospital. You know that I have followed Mother's path of helping the sick and needy. I have no desire to do anything else. You…mayhap you wish to marry again, and that is fine for you. But I have no desire to be the mistress of my own home."

Jessamyn was looking at her with doubt in her expression. "A charity hospital?" she repeated. "But… Emmy, those are terrible places filled with disease. It will kill you to work and live in one of those places."

"It will not kill me."

"It killed Mother!"

Jessamyn was starting to raise her voice. Knowing her sister could become agitated quite easily, Emera simply lifted her hand to quiet her. "Do not trouble yourself," she said. "It will not happen for quite some time, I am sure. Meanwhile, we must take care of Bowes as best we can. In fact, I was thinking of the turnips we have stored in the northwest corner. Those were intended for the winter market in Gainford. If we do not move those vegetables, they will rot."

She was changing the subject. Jessamyn, who was easily manipulated, shifted her focus from the charity hospital to the turnips. She even turned around, craning her neck and trying to see back to the area were the turnips were stored.

"We cannot move them," she said. "We have no means."

Emera thought of de Royans and his endless wealth of men and animals. She was certain the man had wagons, too. He had to, considering the size of the army he had to move.

"Mayhap we do not, but de Royans might," she said. "The crop is now his, after all, and all of those serfs who worked the land to harvest it are his vassals. He must understand that taking the crop to the winter market is his responsibility."

"What of the money he will get from selling them?"

"He must understand that it should be put back into seed for next year's crops."

"Are you going to tell him that?"

"Of course I am."

Jessamyn simply shrugged, not entirely convinced de Royans would listen to her bold sister. Emera's attention was diverted from more conversation about turnips as the man beside her suddenly took a deep breath and then blew that breath out.

Emera leaned over him, feeling for his pulse and finding nothing. Sadly, he was gone and she quietly called over to a pair of male servants to take the body away. Once the dead man was being carried out of the vault, Emera rose stiffly to her feet.

"I must have a breath of fresh air," she said, rubbing her neck and feeling some sorrow over the loss of yet another wounded man. "I do not even know how long I have been down here."

Jessamyn stood up as well. "Since before the nooning meal, at least. You have been by that man's side for hours, Emmy."

Emera simply nodded, taking a deep breath. "Let me go up and stretch my legs a bit," she said. "I will return."

She needed a change of scenery for a few moments, away from dying men, and Jessamyn understood. She followed Emera as the woman moved towards the spiral stairs that led up to the levels above. But they both paused when they came upon the young child de Royans had left in their charge.

The lad was curled up on an old blanket near the stairwell, sleeping like the dead. He had been sleeping that way since practically inhaling two bowls of the pork and beans they'd been provided for sup. The food and exhaustion had rendered the child unconscious and they'd simply let him sleep.

"He has been a great help today," Emera said, her gaze on the boy. "But he seems rather fearful, doesn't he?"

Jessamyn nodded. "He's a polite lad," she said. "He is a hard worker and very helpful. But you are correct. He seems… timid. I feel sorry for him. I wonder who his parents are."

Emera shrugged, not giving the child much more thought. It wasn't her concern who his parents were but she was concerned that he seemed too frightened and nervous. She felt some pity for the child but she didn't feel it was her place to ask de Royans about him. She pointed to a spare blanket, left behind when the man who had used it had been taken away.

"You had better cover him up," she told her sister. "It is quite cold down here. We do not want him to catch his death."

As Jessamyn went to tend to the lad, Emera made her way up the stairs and into the hall above.

The hall had a great many men in it, all de Royans men. Since it was well into the night and their duties for the day were finished for the most part, they were crowded around the two big feasting tables that filled the room while groups of them lingered about, playing games or singing. Over in one corner, several men were gathered together, singing loudly and drinking. They all seemed rather happy, perhaps happy they were out of the freezing weather and into some solid shelter for a change.

But to Emera, it seemed odd seeing men other than Bowes soldiers inhabiting the hall. She paused at the top of the stairs, watching the men through the smoke, seeing that they'd brought dogs with them as several big mutts roamed the hall, trailing after some of the men and hunting for scraps. Emera didn't much like dogs. She was afraid of them, so she stayed close to the wall, heading for the keep entry.

About the time she reached the doorway, she caught sight of de Royans at one of the tables. He had his head down, eating something from a trencher as his knights crowded around him, eating and drinking also. They were talking loudly, pointing, gesturing. Whatever they said must have been very important because they seemed very adamant about their conversation. All of those armed men intimidated her, men she remembered from the night before, so she quickly slipped from the hall and into the forebuilding that led out into the ward.

It was brisk and icy outside, but the storm that had pounded for most of the day had rolled out, leaving a crisp dark sky above with a brilliant half-moon in the middle of it. A blanket of stars slashed across the heavens and Emera took a moment to gaze up, appreciating the beauty of it. But the clear skies meant bitterly cold temperatures; already, she could feel it plummeting. She was clad only in her durable wool shift and surcoat, the same ones she had been wearing for days. It wasn't much protection against the cold.

"How do your wounded fare?"

The voice came from behind. Startled, Emera whirled around to see Juston standing behind her. Clad in heavy clothing, including a luxurious leather robe that was lined with gray fur, he looked every inch the conquering battle lord. But the sight of him made her heart leap strangely and that odd buzzing filled her limbs again. She was coming to think the man had cast a spell over her because every time he came around, she started to tremble.

"Good eve, my lord," she said. "I saw you in the hall but you were with your men and I did not wish to disturb you. I was not trying to escape by coming out here."

"I did not think that you were."

"I simply needed some fresh air."

"I believe you."

An awkward silence settled. The last time they had faced each other, he called her beautiful and then he'd simply walked away as if regretting he'd said such a thing. Emera was, therefore, feeling nervous and uncomfortable. But she was also glad he had come to talk to her because when she thought of what he'd said to her earlier in the day, the memory made her smile. So he thought she was beautiful; there were worse things he could think of her.

"We lost two more men this afternoon," she suddenly said as if only just remembering his question. "I believe the others are stable but time will tell."

He simply nodded. "I have a physic I can offer you if needed," he said. "I did not suffer many wounded during the siege. I am sure your men are much worse off."

It was a very kind offer. "That would be gratefully accepted, my lord," she said. "Although I have experience tending the sick and wounded, some of the wounded are beyond my experience. It would be a blessing to have a physic look at them and give guidance."

His eyes lingered on her, glittering in the cold moonlight. "I shall send him to the vault."

"Thank you, my lord."

It seemed there wasn't much more to say. Although from the expression on Juston's face, it appeared that he wanted to say more. Still, perhaps he was reluctant to after their last conversation had ended with his embarrassment. Before the silence became awkward again, he simply turned and walked away.

Emera watched him go, thinking the man seemed to be in a generous mood tonight. That thought brought about the subject she and Jessamyn had been discussing only moments earlier, the turnips that very badly needed to be taken to market. Before Juston moved too far away, she called after him.

"My lord?" she called out, watching him pause and turn to her. Quickly, she closed the gap between them. "I was hoping to ask your permission for something that very much needs to be done. You see, Bowes has a vast farming system and many serfs to work the land. I am not sure if you noticed the many cultivated fields we have to the south, but that is where our farming takes place."

Juston shook his head, folding his big arms across his chest. "I did not pay any attention to the area, to be truthful," he said. "My concern when I came to Bowes was not the agriculture."

She smiled, an ironic gesture. "I realize that," she said, "but I am attempting to make a point. We currently have at least three wagon-loads of turnips in the vault right now. It is an early winter crop that we must take to market or it will rot. We will use the money to buy seed for next year's crops. We were preparing to take the produce to market when the siege happened and now we no longer have the wagons to haul the turnips into town. I was hoping you could spare a few wagons to complete this task."

He cocked his head. "What do you need the money for? De la Roarke has an entire treasure room in the vault."

She nodded. "I know, but that was his and his alone. It is not meant for the castle or those who work the land. The crops are all the peasants have; all they are *allowed* to have. Won't you please help them, my lord?"

Juston scratched his head, pondering the situation. "That crop belongs to me now."

"Aye, it does. But if you are now lord of Bowes, then there are about three hundred serfs you are responsible for, who depend on the castle to live. These turnips are all they have to see them through the winter. That is *your* responsibility."

She had a point. If he was now the lord of Bowes, indeed, that meant he was responsible for those dependent on the castle. He was a military man but he understood there were duties that went along with his command and one of those duties was to his vassals. She also made sense about the money aspect of it; the money from the food would be returned to the serfs to a certain extent, for both seed and labor.

"I can see that there is more to this bastion than meets the eye," he said. "Treasure rooms, great agricultural stores. I have a feeling there is even more that I am not yet aware of."

Emera sensed some humor to his statement. "With a big place like this, there will always be things to do and things to know," she said. "You already know that my sister is chatelaine. She will help you navigate the difficulties when it comes to managing the functions of the castle."

"You seem to be far more of an efficient chatelaine than she is."

"You've not had much contact with her."

"True enough. But I intend to."

"Why?"

He cocked an eyebrow. "You are asking questions again."

Emera was properly contrite, although she seriously wondered why he'd said he intended to have more contact with Jessamyn. Was it because she had been Brey's wife? Did de Royans think she might know all of Brey's dark secrets? They were his subjects now. It wouldn't be unheard of for him to interrogate the wife of an enemy. Emera was pondering that distressing idea when Juston spoke, interrupting her thoughts.

"When does the produce need to be taken to town?"

They were back to the turnips. "As soon as possible," Emera replied. "There is a winter market every Saturday in Gainford. If the weather is good two days from now, it would be wise to move it then. I am not entirely sure it can wait any longer."

Turnips. They were talking about turnips. Juston should have agreed with her statement and then walked away from the exchange, but the truth was that he was keeping the conversation going simply because he wanted to talk to her again.

An entire afternoon of feeling confused and embarrassed brought him to the conclusion that he was simply being foolish. He didn't like that feeling, not in the least, especially with a woman he'd barely known a day. This time yesterday, he was telling her that she was his prisoner and trying to force her to his will. But tonight saw a different dynamic, something he was both intrigued with and confused by.

Lady Emera la Marche was unlike any woman he'd ever met before. Beautiful, intelligent, and brave, she was unafraid to speak her mind or stand up for herself. The battle with ash shovels in the pass-through hearth had opened his eyes to a woman who was remarkably courageous against a man twice her size. But more than that, he could see deep and abiding compassion in her. He could see that as she dealt with the wounded. She was concerned for everyone and everything. That depth of kindness intrigued him.

She intrigued him. And that was exactly why he had followed her out on this cold and dark night. The woman bloody well intrigued him.

"Very well," he said. "If I am able to spare the men and wagons, then you shall have your escort to Gainford. In fact, I...."

He was cut off by a shout from the outer ward. Cries were echoing off the icy stone walls. There seemed to be a good deal of activity by the gatehouse, men relaying calls to open the portcullis. Suddenly, men on horses were charging into the outer ward. Juston could see them from where he stood. He recognized Christopher and Marcus and David right away but before he could make his way to them, they charged into the inner bailey, heading straight for him.

The horses thundered into the bailey, coming too close, frothing and excited. Juston had to reach out and pull Emera away as frozen earth was kicked up by sharp hooves. Christopher yanked off his helm.

"We've just come from Cotherstone," he said, sounding breathless. "Gather the knights, Juston. They must hear this."

Juston's brow furrowed in concern. "What has happened?"

Christopher threw a leg over his horse, dismounting as soldiers came to take the horses away. As Marcus and David dismounted, Christopher took a few steps towards Juston and lowered his voice.

"Much more than we anticipated," he said. "Let us retreat inside. Marcus and I are famished while David is freezing. I thought we were going to lose my little brother on the ride south."

It was then that Juston noticed that David was without his mail and boots. In fact, he was dressed rather lightly for such cold weather.

"What happened to David?" Juston demanded. "Where are his boots?"

Christopher glanced at his younger brother as Marcus grinned. "Inside," Christopher said. "Everyone is going to want to hear this."

Juston went with the knights back into the keep, all but forgetting about Emera, still standing out in the ward. But she was very concerned with the knights' behavior as well as very curious. Well, the man had said everyone would want to hear what he had to say. She was "everyone", wasn't she?

Knowing full well she wasn't, she followed them inside, anyway.

CHAPTER TEN

"I BELIEVE WE may have a very serious problem on the horizon, Juston."

Christopher was speaking to all of the knights in the smaller chamber next to the great hall. They had been congregated in the great hall as it was, so it was no great feat to move them into a more private room. This smaller chamber, too, had the same pass-through hearth that the floor above had, so the great hall and this smaller chamber shared a very large hearth. It was blazing brightly and smoking heavily as David sat on the hot stones in front of it, trying to warm his chilled body.

Meanwhile, servants had brought food and drink for Christopher and Marcus, but Emera was among those servants. She was busying herself serving the men, pretending she was oblivious to the fact that they had returned to Bowes bearing some kind of serious news. She poured hot wine into cups, wanting to hear what they had to say. If Juston noticed her, he didn't say anything. He seemed to be solely focused on Christopher.

"Tell me what has happened," Juston asked. "What did you see at Cotherstone?"

Christopher had his helm and his gloves off, with Gart taking them away and putting them near the hearth to dry off. In fact, Gart was efficiently helping both Christopher and Marcus undress, for both men seemed harried and exhausted.

"It was not what we saw at Cotherstone but what we heard," Christopher said as someone shoved a cup of hot wine into his hand. "The weather was horrendous for most of the day, as you know, and it took us some time to arrive. There is an inn at Cotherstone – mayhap some of you have heard of it – The Lion and the Lamb." A few of the knights nodded and Christopher continued. "We went there seeking the wenches that work there, wenches who would know the men of Cotherstone and would, mayhap, be able to provide us with information on Cotherstone and her movements, her strengths."

Juston was listening intently. "A wise plan," he said. "What did they tell you?"

Christopher was gulping his hot wine so Marcus spoke. "One of the wenches told us that a few weeks ago, about the time our siege of Bowes began, Cotherstone sent out riders," he said. "She was positive they were dispatch riders, messengers, and she said they were traveling south. After that, the garrison commander at Cotherstone bottled up the garrison and no one has been in or out since. Juston, if dispatch riders were sent out around the time we began our siege at Bowes, then they have had time to reach Auckland and Richmond Castles. They may have even gone so far as to reach Middleham or Helmsley. In any case, it is quite possible that de Puiset is not afraid to engage you. He could simply be biding his time and building an enormous army to purge you from Bowes. If that is the case, then they have had much time to mobilize. They could be on our doorstep tomorrow."

Juston's expression didn't change but the men who were hearing this information for the first time – Maxton, Kress, Achilles, Gart, Gillem, and even Erik de Russe, who had joined the feast that evening after a day of sleep from his travels, glanced at each other in various stages of concern. If what Marcus said was correct, there was much to be concerned over. After a moment of digesting the information, Juston grunted.

"That is indeed troubling," he said, almost casually. "It would behoove us to send our own patrols out this very night. It is a clear night and, providing the weather holds, our men would have the opportunity to see far into the distance to note if anyone is approaching. I would suggest we send patrols south and east, and then send our own messengers to Brough Castle and also to Appleby. Richard holds those castles and we can summon reinforcements. We need to hold Bowes at all costs. We must also send word to Netherghyll to send a thousand men to reinforce us."

Marcus frowned. "If you do that, you'll leave Netherghyll with a very small army to protect her."

"The walls of Netherghyll can hold back God himself. I am not worried about her should some fool decide to attack her while she is down on manpower. Besides… anyone who would do that is more than likely heading for Bowes. There *isn't* anyone else."

He had a point. Marcus simply shrugged, returning to his hot drink. Juston, his mind working furiously with the possibility of Bowes soon being under siege, turned to Maxton.

"Max, will you see to sending out patrols?" he asked. "Move them out quickly. There is no time to waste."

Maxton nodded. "Indeed," he said. He looked at Christopher who, most times, was his chief nemesis. He didn't have to like the man, but Maxton respected him as a very astute tactician and commander. "Is there anything else the patrols should know before I send them out? Did the wenches mention riders heading to the north?"

Christopher shook his head, smacking his lips of the hot wine. "Riders to the north or even to the west were not mentioned, but I would think it would be wise of us to send a patrol north just to make sure we are not in for a surprise."

"Carlisle is north. She can raise a mighty army against us."

"Exactly."

Maxton sighed heavily. "If Carlisle enters this fight, then we may as well abandon Bowes now," he said. "We cannot stand against her armies."

Christopher could only lift his eyebrows in mute agreement. For once, Christopher and Maxton were thinking alike. Maxton swiftly departed, taking Achilles with him, heading out to form patrols. Meanwhile, trenchers were brought in, steaming pork and beans, cheese and bread. It was enough to get David off the floor and heading to the table, where he began to wolf down his food. Christopher and Marcus, equally hungry, also began to eat.

As the knights shoveled food into their mouths, Juston remained seated, silently pondering the information from Cotherstone. To say it was distressing was an understatement, but one thing was certain – he had to hold Bowes. He'd fought too hard to let her go so easily. Brough Castle wasn't far and it was quite a large fortress, so he knew he could expect heavy reinforcements from Brough and also from Appleby Castle, which was a half-day's ride from Brough to the north. It wasn't as if he couldn't reinforce his ranks with high numbers, but the fact remained that if Richmond Castle and Auckland Castle were coming for him, they would, indeed, bring thousands.

Then it would be a hell of a fight.

"Kress." He turned to the knight standing off to his right. "I have not seen the damaged wall. You and Achilles were in charge of repairs. How goes it?"

Kress' expression didn't suggest much enthusiasm. "Are you asking if we can withstand a siege so soon?" He shook his head. "We cannot. The mortar is not setting in this freezing temperature. The western wall is very weak."

Juston sat forward on the table, his hands folded in thought. After a moment, he spoke. "If we cannot reinforce that wall, then we will need to keep attackers away from it," he said. "We can sink spiked poles into the berms around the moat and then again on the other side of it against the walls. Dig holes, set traps, and fill the moat with the bodies of the dead. Did we burn all of them?"

Kress shook his head. "Not all of them," he said. "We have another pyre we are building for tomorrow."

Juston leaned back, giving the man a deliberate look. "Do not burn them," he said. "Throw them into the moat. Get every bit of rotted flesh and disgusting slop into that moat. We have to keep any attackers away from the weakened walls."

Kress nodded wearily. "Indeed, we do," he said. "I will put the men on the pikes and moat in shifts."

"Starting tonight."

"Starting tonight."

"See to it."

Kress set down his cup of wine and quit the small chamber, orders in hand. When Maxton, Achilles, and Kress were gone, it was just Christopher, Marcus, David, Gart, Gillem, and Erik sitting around the small table with Juston. As the fire in the hearth snapped softly, the men ate and drank in silence, but there was a cloud of apprehension hanging over the room. They could all feel it. Taking the castle had been one thing; now, it seemed that holding it would be another.

"Do you still want us to try and take Cotherstone, Juston?" Christopher asked. "That was your original plan. If we take the garrison, then that gives us two castles to hold against Henry. If Bowes falls, then we will have Cotherstone to fall back to."

Juston was still deep in thought. "It is not big enough to hold all of us," he said. "It is a very small outpost."

"We could fall back to Brough," Marcus put in. "That place is enormous."

Juston toyed with his half-full cup of wine. "I would prefer not to fall back at all," he said. "Bowes is mine. I intend to keep it."

It was a simple statement but a powerful one. Juston had made his wishes known and they would not argue with him. Moreover, they all understood that keeping Bowes was not only a strategic move, but a prideful one. No one wanted to be perceived as weak, least of all Juston.

He would stay with Bowes until the last stone fell.

"I must say that I am quite interested to know why David is without his mail and his boots," Juston finally said, changing the subject away from the possible doom facing them. "Care to enlighten me?"

The mood of the table changed as everyone looked to David, who was on his second trencher of pork and beans. But he didn't seem apt to answer the question so Christopher answered for him.

"Suffice it to say that David's boots and mail were lost during the course of his duties," Christopher said tactfully. "He was trying to obtain information from a wench and we were forced to leave in a hurry, which meant leaving his possession behind."

Juston's brow furrowed. "Why did you have to leave in a hurry?"

"Because the wench's husband discovered them."

Gart, Gillem, and Erik, seated across the table from David, burst into snickers, younger men who still had some humor in life. Marcus was fighting off a grin and Christopher was struggling greatly as well. Juston simply shook his head reproachfully.

"God's Bones," he hissed. "David, is this true?"

David moved his head but didn't go so far as to actually nod. "In my defense, I did not know that she was married," he said wryly. "She failed to mention it."

"David was forced to flee the inn, jumping from a second-story window as naked as a babe and fleeing, equally naked, on a horse," Christopher said. "He nearly froze to death."

Now, Marcus burst into soft giggles but Gart and Gillem and Erik weren't so discreet; their laughter grew. Juston eyed David seriously.

"Did you lose anything vital?" he asked, poking fun at the man. "Weather like this will snap a man's ballocks right off his body."

Christopher lost the battle to giggles at that point, amused at his brother's embarrassment.

"I did *not* lose anything vital," David clarified. "But it was rather painful riding. Worse still, my privates smell like a horse now. I am sure that is a wonderful smell to any mare in season, but I've no interest in bedding horses."

Gart and Erik were howling with laughter at the mental image of David riding with his manhood naked against horse flesh. Even Juston was grinning. He simply shook his head again, drinking his wine as he tried to sober up.

"Mayhap a bath is in order, then, for I do not want you attracting randy horses into the keep," he said. Then, he looked to the three knights seated across from him. "In fact, I would say that all three of you have earned a hot bath and some rest. Mayhap you should retire for a few hours, as I intend to do. It has been a long day for us all."

The three knights couldn't disagree. David went so far as to take his food with him as he quit the room, wandering out into the bigger hall beyond as Christopher and then Marcus eventually followed, all of them off to find a warm bed for the night. Juston finished his wine and bid Gart, Gillem, and Erik a good evening as he, too, had thoughts of that giant bed on the floor above. He was very much looking forward to a night in a real bed rather than his travel cot.

But just as he moved away from the table, he caught sight of Emera as she moved out of the shadows, going to the table to collect the cups that had been left behind. He hadn't even realized she'd been in the room.

"Lady Emera," he said. "Have you been here the entire time?"

Emera had her hands full of cups, looking at him with a mixture of guilt and feigned innocence. "Not too long, my lord."

"*How* long?"

She shrugged. "I… I helped bring the meals," she said. "Why do you ask?"

His expression suggested he was not pleased. He crooked a finger at her. "Put the cups down," he said. "Come with me."

Emera was coming to think that listening in on his meeting with his knights had not been a wise move on her part. Clearly, he didn't sound pleased. Truthfully, she wasn't sure why – it wasn't as if she was going to run off and tell the men of Auckland or Richmond what she'd heard. She'd wanted to listen simply because whatever the fate of Bowes was her fate as well. She wanted to know what was coming.

But Juston evidently didn't see it that way. Reluctantly setting the cups down, she followed the man as he led her from the smaller chamber and out into the hall beyond.

When Juston and Emera were gone, Gart, Gillem, and Erik remained at the table, the three of them left in the chamber that seemed oddly quiet now. Even with the spillover noise from the great hall, still, the smaller chamber seemed quiet. The mood was gloomy as a result of the conversation that had taken place there.

"Well," Erik said, "it seems that I should have remained with Richard. At least the man is knowing peace at the moment. It seems I have walked into a coming storm."

Gart sat next to his friend, draining the last of his drink. "So it would appear," he said, setting his cup down. "Now that you have delivered your message to Juston, will you tell me why you have come? Who is the boy you've brought with you?"

Erik sat back in his seat, putting a hand on Gart's head. "I have missed you, my friend. How long has it been since we have seen one another?"

"Almost a year. Answer my question."

"I will answer it but you cannot tell de Royans I told you."

"I will not."

Erik looked at Gillem, seated down the table from Gart. "You, either, d'Evereux."

Gillem, who had already had three cups of the hot, spicy wine, shook his head. "I will not."

Erik's gaze lingered on Gillem a moment, as if he didn't quite trust him, before proceeding. He knew if word got out by way of Gillem's mouth that Gart would take care of the man.

"That lad is the son of Henry and Alys of France," he said quietly. "He is now the prisoner of Richard and Eleanor. They wanted me to bring him to Juston for safekeeping. Eleanor wants an army surrounding the boy to protect him from Henry; Juston's army. But after what I've heard here this evening, I am thinking on taking the boy to Brough. It is a bigger castle and will protect him from whatever storm is moving in Juston's direction. I cannot imagine what would happen should the boy fall into Auckland's or Richmond's possession."

Gart was shocked by the news. "That boy is Henry's son?"

Erik nodded. "You may address him as Tristan. And no one is to know."

Gart shook his head. "Of course not," he said. "God's Bones... so the rumors were true. Alys really did bear Henry a son."

"She did."

"What are your orders once you have delivered him to Juston?"

Erik went about looking at the other cups on the table, looking for one that still had wine in it. "I am to stay with the lad as his personal protector, at least for the time being," he said. "That means you are going to be seeing my ugly face for quite a while. I wonder what kind of mischief we can get into."

Gart grinned. "I believe David has already taken that crown."

Erik found a cup with wine and downed it. "That is the truth," he laughed. "But there is more foolery out there for us to get tangled up in. And more wenches."

Gart simply grinned. "Unless Juston sends us out on errands, I'm afraid our activities will be confined to Bowes," he said. "There are no wenches here."

"There are two that I've seen," Gillem spoke up. "One was just here, the one Juston removed from the chamber when he left. I would not be surprised if she ended up in his bed."

Erik and Gart looked at Gillem, who was slurring his words as the result of too much wine. In fact, Gillem had been sitting in silence, not really listening to the banter between Erik and Gart. His attention was elsewhere, lingering on the expression Juston had given the woman who had been serving them, one of the women who had been somehow associated with de la Roarke. He wasn't sure if it was the man's wife or not, as he'd heard she'd been captured, but the way Juston had looked at the woman... he hadn't liked it at all.

"That is the sister to the lady of the keep," Gart told him. "She has been giving Juston some trouble, I think."

Gillem looked at him. "Did you not see the way he looked at her?" he asked. "I have seen that look on his face before when it comes to a woman. She will end up in his bed."

Gart shrugged. "It is his privilege."

Gillem didn't like that answer. "So he can beget another woman with a bastard?" he snapped. "He already has one. He does not need any more!"

Gart frowned. "God's Bones, Gillem," he grunted. "Keep your mouth shut or it will get you into trouble. Go to bed. You are drunk."

Gillem wouldn't leave. "He should not be looking at another woman," he said. "He has my sister, but he ignores her!"

Gart thumped Erik on the arm, indicating for the man to stand up. Erik, having heard of the situation between Gillem's sister and de Royans before, didn't want to hear anything more about it. He didn't care, much as Gart didn't. As he and Gart stood up, Gart turned to Gillem.

"Go to bed," he repeated. "And what Juston does is his own business. It is not up to you to tell him what he can and cannot do."

Gillem, grumpy and drunk, pretended to ignore him. But once Gart and Erik left the chamber, Gillem sat alone and stewed in his own resentment. Juston had no right to show attention to any woman considering what he'd done to Sybilla. Sybilla, in fact, had lived a chaste and modest life since bearing Juston's bastard, raising the boy lovingly, hoping that Juston would come to his senses and marry her.

It was true that Juston was the master of his own destiny. No one could tell him what to do and what not to do. But, as Gillem saw it, perhaps he needed a little help.

Perhaps temptation needed to be removed from him.

Temptation in the form of one of his female prisoners.

CHAPTER ELEVEN

"I WAS *NOT* deliberately eavesdropping," Emera said firmly. "I was simply helping serve your men. Our servants are stretched thin as it is and with all of the men in the hall, I simply sought to help. That is all."

Standing in the master's chamber, Juston faced Emera with his hands on his hips. The expression on his face was one of suspicion.

"I left you in the inner bailey," he said. "You were there when my knights arrived. You heard that they had something important to tell me. The next I realized, you were in the chamber where we had our private discussion and you were there the entire time."

He was right, essentially, but Emera wasn't sure she could explain that she was eavesdropping out of curiosity and not malicious intent. In fact, she didn't want to discuss it with him at all.

"I told you why I was there, my lord," she said. "It is your choice whether or not you believe me. May I have your permission to leave now?"

He eyed her, trying to determine if she was, in fact, telling the truth. Having only known her a short amount of time, he was concerned that his attraction to her had caused him to overlook any character flaws. A liar, perhaps, or even a betrayer. She had sworn that she would not escape and he said he believed her. Now he wasn't so sure.

Was she up to something?

"Go where?" he asked.

Emera was frustrated; it showed in her manner. "Down to the vault," she said. "Down to where the other prisoners are. I will go down there and remain down there since trying to resume my duties is evidently upsetting to you."

Juston frowned. "It is not upsetting to me," he said. "But you heard some privileged information whilst serving my men. How do I know you are not going to run off and divulge it to Henry's loyalists?"

"I do not know any of Henry's loyalists!"

"Your father was a la Marche. You are embedded in Henry's cause whether or not you have made the conscious choice to do so."

Emera was coming to understand what he meant and it infuriated her. "You mean that no matter what I say, no matter how much I tell you that I have no loyalties, you will not believe me when I tell you I was not serving your men to gain information?"

He looked at her with an expression that told her far more than words could. Now, embarrassment joined her rage and she turned away from him, unable to look him in the face any longer.

"I am not a liar and I do not go back on my word," she said. "I told you that you needn't worry about me but you do not believe me. I told you yesterday that I am ignorant of war etiquette. Even if I did have information to give to Henry's loyalists, I would not know how to go about it. Think what you will, my lord, but I am not the devious maid you evidently think I am. Now, I am going to go back to the vault where I belong."

She started to move towards the spiral stairs but he stopped her. "Hold, lady," he said. "I have not given you permission to leave yet."

She paused, cocked her head slightly as if listening to him, and then continued on just as she pleased. Enraged that she should disobey him so, but not particularly surprised, he charged after her and caught her when she was about halfway down. Once he grabbed her, she turned into a wildcat, hissing and slapping at him, throwing herself down on the stairs as he dragged her up, step by step.

When they finally reached the master's chamber, he continued dragging her into the smaller chamber beyond. Once inside, he tossed her onto the small bed and slammed the door, bolting it so she could not escape. He stood there on the inside of the room, by the door, and scowled.

"You are a wholly disagreeable female and if I had any sense, I would lock you up in the gaol down below and melt down the key," he snapped. "You are headstrong and stubborn and a fickle inch from a sound thrashing if you do that again. Do you understand?"

Frowning deeply and quite upset, Emera sat up on the bed, pushing her hair from her eyes. "I was simply going down where I belonged," she said. "You have no further use of me, I am sure, unless you simply wish to berate me some more."

"What I do is none of your concern."

"I have heard everything you have said. Bellowing it at me is not going to make any difference!"

His eyes narrowed. He was coming to realize that she walked a very fine line between courage and stubbornness. And stupidity as far as he was concerned. He held up a finger.

"It might," he said. "It might do a world of difference to bellow it at you so I can impart some wisdom into your thick head. I never told you I did not believe you. I simply questioned your presence in the smaller chamber when I was having the private conversation with my men. As commander of an enemy installation, and with you as my prisoner, it is my duty to question your presence in order to keep my men safe. I would be a poor commander if that was not my priority."

Emera understood, somewhat, but she was still offended. "And it is my priority to keep *me* safe," she said. "Whatever happens to Bowes happens to me. Aye, I heard what your men said. Messengers have been sent out to Henry's loyalists. I can tell you that the garrison commander at Richmond was an ally of Brey's. His name is Dev de Winter and his family hails from Norfolk. I know this because he has come to visit Bowes and he has brought his wife with him. She is very nice but she is also sickly. The last I heard, she was with child and not faring at all well. Had you asked me any of this, I would have told you. Even if Richmond had received word of Bowes' siege, Deverell de Winter is very attached to his wife and if she has passed, then it might make putting duty before his grief difficult."

Juston listened with great interest and great astonishment. "How would you know any of this?"

She cocked an eyebrow. "Because I served the men at Bowes, including Brey, much as I served your men this evening," she said. "I have heard Brey discussing de Winter and Richmond."

Juston's anger with her was quickly evaporating. "What else do you know?"

Emera, too, was forgetting her irritation with the man. Odd how she was willing to so quickly overlook his insults. "I have heard Brey speak of de Puiset in unfavorable terms," she said. "He did not like him. He felt him ineffectual and weak. He has sided with Richard in the past."

"I know."

"He sides with Henry now. Brey says that he is a faithless woman, supporting one man and then another."

"What else did he say?"

She shrugged. "That the bishop does not like to winter in Durham," she said. "I have heard Brey say that de Puiset is unreliable because he takes his army and winters to the south."

That bit of news drew a reaction. "Where in the south?"

She shook her head. "I do not know," she said. "I never asked. But it seems to me that if he has gone south, then he was not at Auckland when the messengers arrived."

It was an astonishing bit of news. Juston was fed by the possibilities of it but, in the same breath, he wasn't entirely sure he could believe her. She was the enemy, after all.

... wasn't she?

"God help you if you are not being honest with me," he said. "Do you swear upon your mother's grave that this is the truth?"

"Of course I do."

"Will your sister tell me the same thing?"

"If she heard Brey say such things, then I am sure she will."

"You will not mind if I ask her?"

"I would encourage you to."

That gave her a bit more credibility as far as he was concerned. A liar would not be so quick to have her lies discounted. But he hadn't lived this long giving utter faith to people he didn't know. After a moment, he shook his head in wonder.

"You freely give me information that is strategic to my command," he said. "Why?"

Emera averted her gaze. "I am not entirely sure of that myself," she said. "All I know is that when you took Bowes from Brey, you freed me from a terrible prison I had been living in for two years. My sister seems to think we are worse off than we were before, but I do not think so. You have been kinder and more fair to me than Brey ever was. In a sense, you saved me from him. You even called me beautiful. Mayhap I am a fool, but I feel gratitude towards you."

Either she was a very smooth liar or she was being openly truthful. In fact, she reeked of sincerity. Any anger or frustration Juston had been feeling towards her vanished as that word was introduced between them again – *gratitude*. The last time she'd expressed that sentiment, he wondered if she would willingly demonstrate that sense of thanks. As he'd mulled over before, a thankful woman might be willing to express that gratitude.

Tonight, he needed such a display of thanks. He needed it from her.

His first reaction was to pull her to him. Surely she would not refuse him this time. But he'd tried that tactic with her twice before and it hadn't worked. It had simply made both of them angry. He had no idea why he was not forcing the woman to his will as he'd done others. He'd done it before and never hesitated. But with Emera, it was different. He didn't want to force her.

He wanted her to come willingly. But, God help him, he had little patience for such things.

"Very well," he said. "If that is true and you genuinely have no subversive intentions, as you have indicated, then I will permit you to demonstrate your gratitude."

Emera looked at him as if she truly had no idea what he meant. She had a rather blank expression on her face. "Demonstrate…?"

He began to remove his heavy leather robe, the elaborate one with the fur lining. "You will please me."

Emera's blank expression held for a moment longer before she realized, exactly, what he meant. Her eyes widened.

"*Demonstrate?*" she repeated, aghast. Then, she shook her head in disbelief. "Are we back to that again?"

He laid the leather robe across a chair, very carefully. "We have never left it."

Emera's frustration was returning. She'd foolishly opened herself up to the man, just a little, and he'd taken advantage of her. "Instead of grabbing me and forcing yourself upon me, you are using this… this incident to make demands."

He began to loosen the belt of his tunic. "I am making no demands," he said steadily. "You said you are grateful. I am giving you the opportunity to demonstrate that gratitude."

Emera was about to explode at him, in all directions. The situation between them, since the beginning of their association, had been extraordinarily volatile. They set each other off quite easily. But Emera didn't want to snap at him again. She was growing weary of fighting the man who was surprisingly kind one moment and outrageous the next. He kept making inappropriate demands, as if they were commonplace in his world, and that led Emera to believe that, perhaps, was all he'd ever known. He was a warlord, after all – perhaps in his world, there was nothing else but commanding people to do what he wanted them to do.

"Is that how it has always been with you?" she finally asked. "Rather than have a woman come to you willingly, you simply command her to your will?"

His belt was off. He tossed it onto the bed. "Once again, you do not understand the etiquette of being a prisoner. I give the command and you obey. It is a simple system."

Emera didn't move. She was watching him as he pulled off a heavy woolen tunic only to reveal another tunic beneath. There was something in what he'd just said that caught her attention.

"That is correct," she said. "I am a prisoner and I must obey your command. But as you've said repeatedly, you can simply take what you want. Why give me a command if you can simply take me?"

He looked at her, then. "Is that what you want?"

"I do not want any of it."

"Then you have a choice – either I take what I want or you come to me willingly."

"If that is my choice, then you will have to take it. But know I will not give up so easily."

He sighed heavily, bracing both fists against his hips again. "You are wrought with trouble, woman."

"I am sure you see it that way."

"It is the only way *to* see it."

Emera didn't respond. She simply stood there, staring at him. "Is that how women have always come to you?" she asked. "Because you demand it?"

He wasn't going to give in to her questions. His own men didn't even ask him such questions. "Tread carefully," he warned her. "You do not know why I do what I do. It is not your business."

For once, she heeded his warning. There was something in his tone that suggested she should. She didn't say another word as he removed three tunics, finally revealing a magnificent muscular torso and arms. But that's when things changed. The sight of all that flesh was shocking to Emera because she'd never truly seen a man stripped down like that before. Juston was clad only in leather breeches and heavy leather boots that went to mid-calf, tied up with strips of thick leather to keep the elements out and his feet dry.

Her mouth went dry and her heart raced at the sight of nude man flesh. But the moment of shock faded and something else took hold, something she'd never experienced before. It was as if something deep in her belly was quivering, made worse as she watched Juston lay his tunics out before the hearth to dry them. With the firelight reflecting off of his naked torso, she could see the muscles flexing. It was mesmerizing for a woman who had never seen such things before. She was still staring at him when he finally turned around to look at her.

"Well?" he asked. "Why are you standing there? Take off your clothing and get into bed."

It was difficult to tear her eyes from his muscular chest and look him in the eye. "I will not," she said. "When I said I was grateful, I did not mean you should take advantage of that."

One minute he was standing by the hearth and the next minute, he had her by the wrist, pulling her towards the big bed. Startled, not to mention frightened, Emera dug her heels in and strongly resisted.

"If you think this is the way a woman wants to be treated, then you are wrong," she grunted through clenched teeth. "Have you only bedded whores and slaves? Do you not know that a fine woman will not be thrown around like this?"

He could easily pull her but she was giving him a fight. He hadn't wanted to take her by force but she'd tried his patience. Picking her up by her slender waist, he tossed her onto the bed. Unfortunately, she rolled right off and fell onto the other side, coming up swiftly, her black hair hanging askew.

"Get on that bed," he said, pointing to it. "I will not tell you again."

Infuriated, and increasingly terrified, Emera fell to the floor once more and crawled under the bed to escape him.

"I will not!" she said, seeing his booted feet move around the bed in her direction. "I will not let you steal what I have tried so hard to protect!"

He went down on his knees, snaking a big arm underneath the bed and grabbing her by the ankle. She kicked at him, barely missing his face.

"If you strike me in the face, know that my punishment against you shall be swift and painful," he said menacingly. "Try to kick me again and I will throw you to the men and let them take you to sport. Is that what you want? You can fight off hundreds of them instead of only one. With God as my witness, I will throw you to them and ignore your screams. Are you listening?"

He was pulling her by the ankle but she had hold of one of the bed legs. She knew it was her last hope to hold out against him. If she let go of the leg, her anchor would be gone and he would yank her out from underneath the bed and probably have his way with her right on the floor. Therefore, she held on for dear life.

"You are a barbarian!" she grunted, holding on to the bed fiercely. "That you could do this to a woman! That you could be so callous! So – so brutal! What if someone was doing this to your daughter? How would you feel if someone brutalized your daughter? Pretend I am your child and then think about what you are doing! You are wicked and heartless and you have no feelings whatsoever!"

He yanked for a split second longer before suddenly letting her go. Panting, and startled by the swiftness of his release, Emera scampered back underneath the bed, tucking her legs up to keep them away from his long arms. She could see his boots, simply standing next to the bed. Oddly enough, he didn't say anything. The boots simply remained stationery for several long moments. Then, they began to walk around the side of the bed.

"Get out of here," he told her. "Get out from beneath the bed and go. I do not want to see your face again."

He said it in a tone that didn't sound like him at all. Emera had never heard that voice come from his lips. Something deep and dark and... dull. Definitely dull, as if there was something unspeakable behind it. When she didn't move fast enough, he kicked the bed and she yelped.

"Get *out*!" he boomed. "I said leave!"

Strangely enough, Emera was more frightened now than she'd ever been. There was something incredibly sharp in his voice, like daggers being thrown at her. But she wormed her way out from underneath the bed, afraid of what would happen if she didn't. All the while, however, she was wondering why his manner had changed so abruptly. What had she said to him other than the usual?

I will not let you...

Have you only bedded whores...

What if someone was doing this to your daughter...

... daughter?

Emera came out from beneath the bed, her eyes searching warily for Juston only to find him over by the hearth, pulling his tunics back on. He was getting dressed, pulling tunics over his head, his movements sharp and jerky. They were the movements of a man with a great deal on his mind and the more she watched, the more concerned and curious she became.

It was true that Emera had a good deal of compassion and that she was inquisitive about people in general. She was a woman of deep feeling. Something told her that Juston was a man of deep feeling as well. A powerful warlord, a man who commanded thousands, and a man with arrogance greater than any she had ever seen, but as he threw on the heavy woolen tunic, something told her that all of that posturing was to cover up something soft and damaged deep inside him.

She was willing to take that chance.

"I apologize if I insulted you, my lord," she said softly.

"I told you to get out."

She stood up but she didn't leave. He was just reaching for his big leather robe when she spoke again.

"What happened to your daughter?"

It was a soft question, like a gentle breeze across his ears. But for as soft and gentle as it was, somehow, it was the most painful question he'd ever heard. He couldn't even answer her. Jaw ticking, he quit the chamber and disappeared down the stairs.

Emera stood there a moment, thinking this situation was much like the situation earlier in the day when he'd left after telling her she was beautiful. But this moment was so much different; that moment had been shame because she'd sensed it. But this moment...

... it was pain.

CHAPTER TWELVE

Two days later

THE POINTED PIKES had been shaped and planted all around the outer walls of Bowes, holes dug in the frozen ground by weary soldiers who were fed by the anticipation of half of England bearing down upon them in Henry's name.

The patrols sent out two days before had yet to return and there was anticipation in the air, a kind of brittleness that had the men on the battlements watching the horizon every second of the day, waiting and watching for the little specks that represented their patrols to appear.

Men who, quite possibly, could come bearing life-altering news.

Meanwhile, the weary soldiers under de Royans' command continued to work like Trojans, digging holes, planting sharp-edged logs cut down from the local groves, and filling the moat with the bodies of the dead that hadn't yet been burned. Even in the cold, the smell of greasy human rot was heavy in the air, made worse when the smoke from the cooking fires would mingle with it and turn it into a slick layer that settled on both man and beast. The rains had not returned and the skies had remained clear, but still, the mood and the stench of Bowes were increasingly foul.

The damaged wall of the castle had seen some progress due to the shift in weather. The sun, although weak, nonetheless provided some manner of faint warmth to the stones so that the mortar was beginning to set somewhat. Maxton, Achilles, and Kress had been overseeing the repairs, driving the exhausted men with a heavy hand. As the morning dawned on the third day of the conquest of Bowes, the three knights and hundreds of men were already at work on the dusty, destroyed wall.

"I think we might actually be able to repair this wall," Maxton said to Kress as he gazed up at the work going on. "Perhaps the weather gods will favor us with sun for the next few days so the mortar can finally set. It would be a blessing."

Kress was looking up at the busy workers as well. "But let us hope that any attending army does not try to batter the wall. I am not entirely sure how well it will hold against bombardment."

"They will not be able to get past de Lohr's ring of pikes all around the perimeter of the moat."

Kress nodded. "Most impressive," he said. "The de Lohr brothers packed them in close together and are now stringing them with rope, which will make it cumbersome to try and penetrate."

Maxton lifted his eyebrows. "Far be it from me to give Christopher a compliment, but he did a fine job."

Kress looked at him, his eyes twinkling. "We are all on the same side, Max. I have told you that before."

Maxton grunted. "Tell de Lohr that," he said. "The man vexes me at every turn."

Kress held up a hand, not wanting to hear the same argument again. They'd had it many times in the past. "And he has been doing it for years, so I would think you would simply accept things the way they are," he said. "Moreover, he does not vex you. He simply has a different way of doing things."

Maxton shrugged. "Mayhap," he said. The conflict between him and Christopher was an old story. "In any case, the wall should be completed by the time the de Lohr brothers and Burton finish the perimeter barriers. We shall be ready for any army that comes to attack us."

Up above, they were distracted by Achilles yelling to the men who were using a pulley system to haul up the stones. The men had been working like mad to repair the wall. For three days and nights, the work had gone on uninterrupted for the most part. Maxton and Kress watched Achilles instruct the men on some particular portion of the wall before using a rope to slide down to the ground. Brushing off his hands, he made his way over to Maxton and Kress.

"Some of the sentries think they see a patrol returning from the south," he told Maxton. "I could see the excitement from my perch on the wall."

That bit of news brought interest to Maxton and Kress. "Could you see what had their attention?" Kress asked.

Achilles shook his head. "Nay," he replied. "But it has been two days. I was becoming nervous that our patrols might have been captured."

Achilles was the voice of doom in all things, something that Maxton and Kress had learned to brush off for the most part. Maxton began to walk, motioning his colleagues with him.

"Then let us see to them," he said.

The three of them headed towards the gatehouse, moving through the outer bailey that was busy with men going about their duties. Beneath the weak sunlight, men built and hammered, cleaned up and mended. The gatehouse loomed ahead, a big structure of pale granite, and they could see Gart, Erik, and Gillem milling about at the mouth of it. As the keep came into view off to the left, Maxton's gaze trailed off towards it.

"Has anyone seen Juston today?" he asked.

Kress shook his head. "Nay," he said quietly. "I asked Gart about him earlier today and Gart said that he is down with another sick headache."

"He has had the headache for two days," Achilles muttered.

No one said much about the headache after that, mostly because there wasn't much to say on the matter. Juston was known to have frequent and terrible headaches that could, at times, keep him down for days. It was unfortunate with the threat of Henry's armies on the horizon to have their commanding officer down, but such was the way of things at times. They had learned to adjust.

"His headache came on rather suddenly," Kress commented. "Right after he told us what the sister of Lady de la Roarke had said about de Puiset wintering to the south. It seemed that he gave us the news and then took to his chamber and we've not seen him since. Gart said he will not even open the chamber door."

They were nearing the gatehouse, drawing close to Gart and Erik, who had seen them coming and were turning to greet them. Maxton spoke quietly.

"Am I the only one who has noticed Juston has spent an inordinate amount of time with Lady de la Roarke's sister?" he asked. "She is a beautiful thing, no doubt, but with his history with women, it is mayhap not the safest thing for him to do."

"Do not say anything to Gart about it," Kress muttered. "He is fiercely protective over Juston. You do not want to unleash that squire's sword hand."

Maxton gave him a half-grin. "It was merely an observation."

"Let it *only* be an observation."

Maxton chuckled, holding up a hand to indicate he would keep his mouth shut where Juston was concerned, at least in front of Gart. They were all colleagues and comrades, fighting for one another and killing for one another, but that didn't mean they all got on like a tight-knit brotherhood. They had their differences as well as their common ground. But one thing they all knew was to tread carefully around Gart when it came to Juston.

"Forbes," Maxton greeted evenly. "It seems there may be a patrol returning."

Gart nodded. "One of the men on the wall told me," he said. "I suppose we shall soon find out if your repaired wall is about to get knocked down again."

Maxton cast him a wry glance. "Let us hope not," he said. Then, he looked at de Russe, standing next to Gart. "And you. Why are you still here? Even if we are about to be sieged, that does not mean you must stay and die alongside us. We do not expect you to be a martyr. In fact, it might take the glory away from the rest of us."

Erik grinned. "Richard disagrees with you," he said. "I have been ordered to remain until such time as Juston grows weary of seeing my handsome face and sends me away."

"Handsome face?" Achilles snorted. "I've seen better asses on a dog."

Erik cocked an eyebrow at the man as the others snorted at his expense. "You will be sorry for saying that to me when we are in the heat of combat and I am the only one available to save your miserable hide," he warned, although he was clearly jesting. "Be kind to those you may need, de Dere. Didn't anyone ever tell you that?"

Achilles waved him off as the commotion in the gatehouse distracted the knights. The soldiers on duty were growing increasingly excited as the patrol drew close. Now, their fate might be determined by men who had seen the countryside and had, perhaps, assessed the threats.

No one was more aware of that than the knights as they entered the gatehouse as a group, coming out of the other side and watching the road as a party of four scouts thundered towards them. They could only pray that the news was in their favor, for surely, there was much against them at the moment. They could taste anticipation, perhaps even nervousness, on their tongues as the patrol drew close to the gatehouse and slowed their pace. Now, the moment was upon them.

Soon they would know what they were potentially facing.

HIS HEAD WAS killing him.

Literally, or so he thought. Surely death would be less painless than the headache he was currently experiencing. It had started two days before and hadn't eased up no matter what he'd done. The physic had given him a potion of white willow to drink and he'd spent two days with a pack of lavender and sage on his head, trying to draw out the pain. But nothing was working, made worse by the fact that his mind had been wandering at times.

More accurately, people were wandering through it. Little girls, ages four and three, who would have been young women by now. Lady Blossom, his eldest, and Lady Cedrica, his youngest. They'd had his hair, his eyes, and he wondered if they would have continued to look like him into adulthood. He'd always wondered that. He'd spent years avoiding thinking of his girls who had been denied the chance to grow into young women but Emera's words the other night had opened the door to those thoughts, thoughts he'd tried so hard to avoid.

What if someone was doing this to your daughter?

He knew that Emera had no idea what kind of question she had been asking him. She'd been frightened because he had been terrorizing her. The problem was not in the question but in the answer – someone *had* brutalized his daughters and his wife, as well. They'd nailed shut the doors to Annepont's manse and sealed tight the shutters. Then, they'd launched great urns of burning oil onto the roof, which quickly caught fire. When Lord Annepont tried to help his family escape through a rear door, men with arrows were waiting and cut Annepont down. Somehow, Lizette and the girls, and several servants, had been corralled back inside the house to die.

And he'd been unable to protect them.

He hadn't tasted that guilt in years but now it was back, more bitter than he'd ever known it to be. With it, his headache had returned and his sense of failure with it. For two days, he'd had visions of Blossom and Cedrica as they might have been in adulthood. What would he have done to a man who had tried to do to them what he tried to do to Emera? It was that answer, above all, that sent daggers into his heart.

He would have killed them.

So Lady Emera did not find him attractive. She did not want to kiss him and she certainly didn't want to bed the man. That was no great crime. But it was a blow to his ego and to the attraction he was feeling towards her, attraction towards a woman he'd not felt since Lizette. He'd loved his wife and he knew what it was to love a woman. He was certain he could never feel that way again. In fact, he didn't *want* to feel that way again because those emotions had nearly killed him when he had lost her. But the event of Lady Emera had stirred something within him that he couldn't seem to fight off.

Hence, the headache.

A soft knock at the chamber door jolted him from his thoughts. Lying flat on his back with the lavender-sage poultice across his eyes to block out the light, he grunted.

"Go away!"

A soft voice came from the other side. "My lord, a patrol has returned. I thought you would want to know."

It was Gart. Frustrated and in pain, Juston threw off the compress and struggled to his feet, his vision blurred from the pain. He staggered to the door, throwing it open.

"What?" he barked.

Gart had a cup of wine in his hand. "Here," he said, thrusting the cup at Juston. "You have not ingested anything in two days. The physic says you should drink the wine."

Juston snatched it from him and downed the contents. He made a face, smacking his lips. "He put white willow in there, didn't he?"

Gart took the cup back. "I do not know," he said. "I have come to tell you that a patrol has returned from the south. They went as far south as Richmond and have reported that there are no signs from Richmond that an army is amassing. That patrol stated that the castle appeared to be business as usual."

Juston leaned against the doorjamb, rubbing at his eyes as he pondered the information. "How many patrols did we send south?"

"Two, my lord."

"And the second one has not returned?"

"Nay."

Juston sighed heavily and stopped rubbing his eyes. "Let us see what the second patrol has to say before we assume anything," he said. "Men were sent to Brough Castle, were they not?"

"Aye," Gart replied. "We have not yet heard back from them."

So the patrols and messengers were still out, but Juston was relieved to hear that there wasn't an army nearly to their doorstep. He moved away from the doorjamb, staggering back into the chamber as Gart hesitantly followed.

"Keep me informed," Juston said as he picked up his lavender compress and threw himself back onto the bed. "And you should probably send me something to eat or it shall be a contest as to what will kill me first – my aching head or starvation."

"Aye, my lord," Gart said. "Do you require anything else?"

Flat on his back, Juston put the compress over his eyes. "Nay," he said. Then, quickly: "Wait – there is something you can do. There is a store of turnips down in the vault that needs to be taken to market. I have been asked to provide wagons and men to do so. The ladies of the keep wished to take the produce to market tomorrow, so will you please see to it?"

Gart frowned. "Market?" he repeated. "You want me to leave the castle with the possibility of Henry's army lurking?"

"Aye, I want you to leave the castle with the possibility of Henry's army lurking," Juston said, annoyed. "We've already had one patrol return and tell us there were no immediate threats. The produce in the vault represents a good deal of money to the people of Bowes and I do not wish to waste it. So take it to town tomorrow and be done with it. Is that clear?"

Gart thought it was a ridiculous order to leave the fortress when they were under alert, but he didn't say anything more. Where money was concerned, he could somewhat see Juston's point.

"It is," he said. "I will make sure it is taken to market."

"You and Erik and Gillem can ride escort. In fact, take the de Lohr brothers with you. I want the other knights here at the fortress should we need them."

"Aye, my lord."

"And send the bloody physic back to me. Nothing he has done for me is working."

"Aye, my lord."

Gart left the chamber after that, quietly shutting the door and taking the spiral stairs down to the great hall level. At this time of day, men were in the hall seeking some warmth and shelter from the brisk day and there were several dozen men in the hall, eating warmed over pork and drinking boiled wine. His gaze moved over the smoky room simply to see who was in the hall when his eyes fell upon the physic that traveled with Juston's army. The man, usually quite competent, had a taste for drink. And in the middle of the day, he now sat in a chair, slumped and asleep.

So much for getting the man's help. Gart shook his head at the sight, both disgusted and resigned with the physic's drunken behavior. But that left Juston without any help for his aching head. That was a rather critical issue. But it soon occurred to Gart that there were others who might help Juston, including the ladies of the keep who were down in the vault tending Bowes' wounded. Surely they might have something to help the man. On a hunch, and with little choice at this point, he continued down the spiral stairs to the vault below.

It was cold down in the lower recesses of the keep. It was also dark, with very little light other than the smoking torches wedged into iron sconces on the walls and a few oil lamps. But it was quiet down here, with men grouped into neat rows and bundled tightly against the cold.

They'd stopped the hot compresses the day before, instead choosing to bundle the men up with warm blankets. They had a rotating stock of them – while some would heat up outside by the massive cooking fire next to the kitchens, they would then bring the heated blankets in and exchange them for cooled blankets. It was an exhausting ritual and one that had kept the servants very busy, but it was necessary. With no direct heat source in the vault, they'd had to be resourceful and, truth be told, it was a rather clever solution.

As Gart's eyes adjusted to the dim light, the first thing he saw was a small boy. Tristan was seated next to a wounded man, carefully spooning mashed beans into the man's mouth. He was being very precise about it, spilling nothing, as the hungry man slowly ate. The boy was so dedicated to his duty that he failed to see Gart for several long seconds and only then because Gart cleared his throat. Startled, the boy looked up.

"M-my lord?" he said, a fearful expression instantly on his face. "Am I wanted?"

Gart shook his head. "Not that I am aware of," he said. He lifted his chin at the lad, to indicate his situation. "What are you doing?"

Tristan looked at the bowl in his hand. "I am feeding this man," he said. "He cannot eat. He needs help."

"You like to help."

"I do, my lord."

Gart's gaze lingered on the lad who, the more he looked at him, very much looked like Henry. He had Henry's eyes. He wondered if anyone else would notice for as far as Gart knew, only Juston, Erik and Gillem and perhaps one or two others knew who the lad really was. Truthfully, the boy had been kept out of sight down in the vault so it was possible no one even really remembered he'd come. But Gart remembered; he remembered everything.

"Where is Lady Emera or Lady de la Roarke?" he asked.

Tristan stood up, looking into the bowels of the vault. "Look over there," he said, pointing to the far end of this row of men. "There is Lady Emera."

Gart simply nodded, silently thanking the boy, before proceeding on. He looked at the men as he went, noticing that they seemed, on the whole, much better than they had the last time he saw them. All bundled up with warm blankets, some of them were looking back at him rather suspiciously. Not that he blamed them; he was, essentially, the enemy.

Emera caught sight of Gart as he approached in the darkness. It was rather hard to miss him for the size of the young man. She, too, had been feeding a man so she set the bowl aside, wiping off her hands as she rose to her feet. She faced Gart politely.

"Sir Gart," she said. "How may I help you?"

Gart's gaze lingered on her a moment before speaking. She was certainly a beautiful woman with her black hair and pale skin, and he knew that Juston thought so as well. Not in so many words, perhaps, but definitely in his actions. He hadn't paid so much attention to a woman since Gart had known him. He wasn't sure how Lady Emera felt about Juston but he hoped she was inclined to help him.

"Lord de Royans is suffering a bout with a blinding headache," he said. "His physic has provided him with wine and white willow, but it has been two days now and my lord is still not seeing improvement. I have gone to fetch the physic again but the man is drunk. I was wondering if you had anything that could help my lord."

At the mention of Juston, Emera's heart did that strange fluttering thing again. She was coming to associate that feeling with Juston in general. But she hadn't seen the man in two days, ever since he had tried to attack her and then threw her from his chamber. She'd remained down in the vault, wanting to stay clear of his anger with her, but every moment of those two days, she'd thought about Juston to some degree.

As the hours dragged on, and one day turned into another, she was coming to feel some depression about the entire situation. She wasn't hard pressed to admit that she was attracted to the man. Why? She didn't really know. He'd tried to force himself on her and he'd been generally rude at times, but there were moments when the man had a kindness to him that touched her. Moreover, there was something in his eyes that begged for her to be kind to him in return, as if he was a man pretending to be a hardened soul but he really wasn't.

Juston de Royans was a puzzling enigma, indeed.

"I am sorry to hear of his troubles," she said, genuinely concerned. "I have acquired some knowledge of healing over the years and there are ways to ease an aching head. What has caused it?"

Gart shook his head. "He has suffered from terrible headaches since I have known him," he said. "Sometimes they are so bad that he must lie still in a darkened room, for even light will hurt his head. They have been most terrible at times."

Emera pondered that for a moment. Then, she held up her hand as if to beg a moment of patience from Gart and she went back to the corner where she and her sister had their possessions. It was where they had been sleeping for the past two days, when they were fortunate to have the time for sleep. In the satchels that Juston's men had packed for them with items from their chamber, there was a small bag containing some medicinal things that they had been using on the wounded.

Most of the medicaments they had been using had been in the great hall but she had no idea what had happened to them after Juston's men had thrown the wounded from the chamber. However, those medicaments were part of a larger collection she and Jessamyn had assembled over the past two years, medicaments from the apothecary in Gainford when they had enough money to purchase such things. The expensive poppy powder to ease the pain of the wounded was nearly gone but there was a tiny amount still in a small leather envelope that they'd hoarded away. There were other things in this bag that would help Juston's head so Emera collected the leather bag and returned to Gart.

"Take me to him," she told the squire. "I will do what I can."

Gart was grateful that she seemed so willing. He took her back up the dark spiral stairs to the master's chamber. Before they entered, Emera stopped him.

"I will need hot water and a cup," she told him quietly. "I will also need linen rags, clean, if you can get them for me, and a bowl."

Gart was listening intently. "Aye, my lady."

"And hurry."

Gart nodded quickly and pushed the chamber door open, revealing

Juston spread out across the bed exactly where Gart had left him. The fire in the hearth was burning low as a result of not being stoked and there was probably more smoke in the room than heat. But for now, the conditions were right for a man whose eyes hurt with light that was any brighter. As Gart went on the hunt for the things she had asked for, Emera set the medicament bag on a table and went straight to the bed.

"My lord?" she said softly. "I understand your head is hurting you. I have come to help."

Juston had heard the door open and footsteps in the chamber, but he'd assumed they were Gart's steps. He was startled to see Emera bent over him as he lay flat on his back. His bloodshot eyes gazed up at her.

"It will pass," he said hoarsely. "Where is the physic?"

"Drunk, I am told," she said, taking the poultice from his hand and sniffing it to see what was in it. "I realize that I am probably the last person you wish to see, but I believe I can help you if you will let me try."

Juston nearly sent her away. He wasn't ready to face her yet but he couldn't quite bring the words to his lips. *Leave! Get out!* Nay, the words wouldn't come. So, he watched her as she walked back to the table where her small bag sat, setting aside the compress he'd had over his eyes while she dug around in her bag. As he watched curiously, she began to pull out small envelopes and at least two glass phials with some kind of liquid in them. He really couldn't see what it was. He watched her curiously as she sparingly poured one of the liquids onto her hands and, heading back over to the bed, rubbed her hands together.

"Gart is fetching me some things that I need. Meanwhile, I will try to rub the pain away a bit," she said. "Lay your head down on the bed, once more, please."

He eyed her. "What are you going to do?"

For a big, powerful man, he sounded mildly frightened of a small woman with oil on her hands. She cocked an impatient eyebrow. "Nothing to cause you pain, I assure you," she said. "Put your head back down. Do it now."

She was giving him a command. Frowning, Juston did as he was told, wondering what she was going to do. And what was that liquid she'd put on her hands? Poison, perhaps? Fortunately, he didn't have to wait long to find out – Emera's hands descended on his head and, almost immediately, Juston fell victim to a gentle massage of his head using lavender oil.

The heady scent overwhelmed him, filling his nostrils as her soft hands began to very gently rub at his forehead and scalp. His suspicion of her motives instantly vanished. *God's Bones...* it was heavenly.

Very quickly, he succumbed to her expert touch as she rubbed at his head. Her fingers applied gentle pressure as she smoothed his forehead, tending him more carefully than he'd ever been tended in his life. Was it really true that such gentleness existed in the world? His head hurt, that was true, but her massage was so incredibly relaxing that it transported him into another state of consciousness. There was bliss here, bliss that only Emera was capable of inducing. He was half-asleep almost immediately, for sleep had been somewhat elusive during this painful episode, and the more she rubbed, the more limp and relaxed he became. He didn't even realize when he fell asleep.

Emera realized it, however. The man began to snore like an old bear and she grinned. She was also quite touched that he had relaxed enough under her attentions that sleep came easily. Perhaps it was indicative of his pain level that he had allowed her to touch him at all.

As she gently rubbed, she found herself admiring his square jaw and the color of his hair, because it was a lovely color if not quite dirty. The man needed a bath. But that was of no matter; being this close to him, gently tending a man who had probably known very little tenderness in his life, brought her a certain kind of peace.

Being with him brought her another kind of peace.

When they weren't fighting or chasing each other around, there was something about Juston that overwhelmed her. It was difficult to describe. It was as if he filled up the entire room and she could hear nor see anything else but him. She wanted to rub his head; she wanted to give the man peace in a world where there wasn't any. She didn't know his history or why he was who he was, but she had a feeling he'd been through much hardship in his life. Something in his manner told her so.

She continued to rub as he continued to snore. Her gaze moved down his body, inspecting his impossibly big arms and hands, his trim torso, and long, muscular legs that hung off the end of the bed. He was easily more than a head taller than she was, for when standing next to him, she barely came to his chest. Juston de Royans was simply a very big man, bred for battle and responsibility in this volatile world they lived in. She had to admit that when he wasn't trying to force himself on her, she was very curious about him.

Drawn to him.

The minutes ticked away as she continued to rub his head, her thoughts drifting to her future once the wounded didn't require her any longer. They were getting better by the day and she was coming to think that, soon, she would no longer be needed. She would again ask de Royans for an escort to the charity hospital in Sherburn. But the longer she remained at Bowes and in the presence of de Royans, the more she was starting to question wanting to go to the charity hospital at all. It was foolish and she knew that, but it didn't stop her from vacillating on the subject now. Perhaps de Royans wouldn't mind if she remained, after all. Provided he would stop trying to force himself on her.

One of these days, she just might give in.

The thought made her grin; a naughty, giddy grin. She continued to think of that possibility as she massaged him, the scent of lavender filling her nostrils. The oil on her hands was calendula oil that she and Jessamyn had made over the summer when the calendula flowers bloomed. It was an oil used to soothe and soften skin, but adding lavender blossoms to it gave it a strong, heady, lavender scent. It was something her mother had taught her to do with the lavender and with the oil, because the lavender was quite common and it had many medicinal uses, including helping an aching head.

But the oil was eventually absorbed by the skin and she removed her hands from Juston and headed back over to the table to pour more on her hands. Just as she reached the table, however, Gart appeared with a small iron pot of steaming water, a cup, a bowl, and the rags she had requested.

"Put them here," she said softly. "Thank you for bringing this so promptly."

Gart sat the pot of water on the table along with the other things, watching Emera curiously as she immediately took the cup, dipped it in the water, and then sprinkled what looked like dried leaves in it. She set that aside to steep as she then took the bowl and also dipped it into the hot water, filling the bowl half-full. Taking one of the phials with liquid, she poured a generous amount into the bowl and the smell of lavender filled the air.

"Is there anything more I can do?" Gart asked.

Emera turned to look at Juston, no longer snoring on the bed although his eyes were still closed. "I am reluctant to wake him," she said, "but it is important that he drink this tonic. It will help his head tremendously."

"I am not asleep," Juston mumbled. "What would you have me drink?"

Emera motioned to Gart to help Juston sit up. Gart went to the bed, pulling the exhausted, sick man up into a sitting position. His dirty hair was askew from Emera having rubbed oil into his scalp, giving him a bit of a wild-looking appearance. Emera approached the bed with the cup of steaming tea.

"This is a tonic made from dried featherfew leaves," she told him. "If you do not know what that is, it is a flower that grows wild in many places and the leaves have healing properties. My mother swore by this for an aching head, so drink it down. It should help."

Juston didn't even make a fuss. After her soothing lavender massage, he was willing to do anything she told him to do, so he gulped down the hot, bitter tea, making a face as he handed the cup back to her. Emera smiled at his nasty expression.

"I know it does not taste very good, but it should help," she said.

Juston grunted. "Are you certain you did not just have me drink the water that Gart has washed his dirty hose in?"

Emera laughed as she went back over to the table, setting the cup down and picking up the bowl with the lavender oil in it.

"Nay, I swear to you that I did not."

"It tasted like it."

Gart entered the conversation. "How would you know that?"

Juston grunted. "Because that water tasted the way you smell."

Gart rolled his eyes as Emera brought over the bowl of hot water. She had also brought a few rags with her, clean ones, and she set one on Juston's lap before putting the bowl on it. He gripped the bowl so it would not spill.

"Now," she said. "I want you to inhale the lavender steam. Hold your face to it and breathe deeply."

Juston did. Holding the bowl up to his face, he drew in several long, deep breaths, inhaling the strong lavender scent. He continued to do it until the steam started to fade. By that time, he was a little woozy from having taken so many deep breaths. Emera took the bowl away and set it on the table.

"You may lie back down again," she told him, watching him fall backwards onto the mattress with his feet still on the floor. "Between the lavender oil and the tea, hopefully you will feel some improvement soon."

Gart picked up Juston's legs and swung them onto the bed. "Your efforts are appreciated," Juston said wearily. "You were kind to leave the wounded to tend to me since my own physic seems to be unreliable. I shall whip the man for not giving me rotten tea and a head massage."

Gart grinned and looked at Emera, who was also smiling. There was humor in Juston's voice, the reflections of a grateful man.

Gart eventually cleared the chamber, leaving Emera to resume rubbing Juston's scalp with more of her oil. She felt as if she had accomplished something today, helping a man who very badly needed it. And by doing so, she had hopefully eased any animosity or hard feelings between them. She sincerely hoped so. That was really why she'd jumped at the chance to help Juston; perhaps she wanted to ease over the difficulties that seemed to have been between them since the beginning.

"You did not have to tend me."

Juston's quiet voice broke into her train of thought. Emera wasn't entirely sure what he meant. "Gart asked me to," she said. "You are in pain. I could not refuse to help you."

He was greatly soothed as she rubbed his forehead. "I would not have blamed you if you had refused," he said. "All I have done is harass you and make demands. That you would be kind to me after all of that speaks well of your character."

It sounded suspiciously like an apology. Because he was willing to admit his boorish behavior, she was more than willing to forget about it.

"I am your prisoner," she said simply. "You are only doing what comes naturally to you."

"What is that?"

"Taking command of a situation and ensuring those beneath you carry out your will."

"Mayhap that is true, but you were correct when you said my behavior was… unacceptable."

She smiled faintly. "I do not believe I used those words. You have not always been unacceptable. Right now, you are quite acceptable."

She saw a flicker of a smile cross his lips. "Nay."

His answer confused her. "What do you mean by that?"

He sighed faintly. "Nay, I would not be very happy if someone was brutalizing my daughter," he muttered. "In fact, I had two. They did not survive past early childhood."

His words brought instant melancholy. Emera heard her own words in his unexpected reply followed by something quite startling – *I had two daughters*. Now, that pain she had sensed from the man was suddenly starting to make some sense.

"Oh… my lord, I am so very sorry to hear that," she said softly. "I did not know."

"I know you did not," he replied. "But you made me think about them the other night when you said that. I had not thought about them in many years but you brought those memories back to me. I do not welcome them. But know that I do not blame you for the fact that they have returned. You made me think of my children again and how I would feel if a man, a man of conquest, was attempting to brutalize them. It is a helpless feeling, you see, because my daughters, along with my wife, were murdered and I was not there to protect them. In your quest to stop me from brutalizing you, you forced me to understand your perspective by putting it into context. Now, I understand."

Emera closed her eyes tightly, briefly, against the horror of his admission. *Murder!* Most definitely the feeling of pain was making a great deal of sense.

"Forgive me," she murmured. "I was callous in what I said. I did not mean to be cruel and cause you to relive a terrible memory."

He opened his eyes, looking up at her as she stood over him. "In truth, the remembrance of their deaths is a terrible memory but I found myself wondering what they would have looked like at this age," he said. "Blossom was four years of age and Cedrica was three years of age. That was about nine years ago which means they would have been thirteen years and twelve years, respectively. They would have been young women. I wonder what they would have loved and what they would have dreamt of. What did you dream of at that age? I have never been in conversation with a woman long enough to ask."

Emera could sense that his guard was down. That staunch and powerful shield that he kept up in front of himself all of the time had fractured somehow, fading away and leaving him vulnerable. She was quite certain it was the medicine causing it, but it was still an astonishing thing to see. It would seem that Juston de Royans had a bit of a philosopher's soul within him, something deeper than she could have imagined.

"I am not entirely sure," Emera said thoughtfully. "It seems like such a long time ago."

"How long ago was it?"

"Six years."

"You are nineteen years of age and have yet to marry?"

She gave him a wry expression. "We have already discussed that, if you recall."

He blinked. "We did. I called you foolish for refusing to let de la Roarke wed you off."

"I know you did."

"I was wrong."

"Why would you say that?"

"Because a woman like you is exceptional. Not any husband will do."

It was a flattering thing to say. First he'd called her beautiful, now he was telling her that she was exceptional. A faint mottle crept into her cheeks.

"I am glad you see my point," she said quietly. "I could not marry simply any man Brey thrust at me. Besides... I do not think I shall ever wed."

"Ridiculous. Every woman should wed."

She shook her head. "Unlike most girls, I did not dream of marriage and a family when I was younger," she said. "You have asked me what I dreamt of as a young girl. I dreamt of helping the poor and tending the sickly. I believe that it is what God wants me to do. He has given me a talent for such things. I cannot use it if I have a husband who demands all of my time or children who hang upon my apron strings."

He watched her for a moment before his eyes slowly closed. "If you feel that way, why not become a nun?"

She thought on that. "I suppose because I do not want anyone telling me what to do and when to eat and how to dress or what to think," she said. "I do not need a nasty Mother Superior ordering me about."

He did grin, then. "You are a strange and unusual woman, Emera la Marche. You think too freely for my taste."

"Do I offend thee, my lord?"

He could hear a slightly mocking tone and it made him grin. "Nay," he replied. "But you are very unusual. Who do you get that particular trait from?"

Emera was smoothing his forehead, enjoying the feel of his skin beneath her fingers very much. "My mother, I am sure," she said. "She was English, you know, but she married my father, who was French, yet she refused to move to France. She insisted on raising her children as English. My father spent most of his time in France fighting Henry's wars, but you already knew that. To be truthful, I had, mayhap, seen him ten times in my entire life before he died. When he passed away, it was as if I had lost a distant relative. I did not even really know him."

"Your family is related to Lusignan?"

Emera nodded. "It is."

Juston fell silent for a few moments, lulled by her rubbing hands. But the medicine she had given him was making him a bit giddy, a bit sleepy, and it was loosening his tongue as Emera had suspected. That carefully-held control he employed was drugged.

"I do not know why I should tell you this, but I shall," he said, sounding very sleepy now. "I have sworn to hate the House of Lusignan. Even though I knew you were Lusignan from the beginning, I supposed I thought I was being quite benevolent by not throwing you out of Bowes on your ear, or worse. Now that I have come to know you over the past few days, you are not like any Lusignan I have ever known. You are compassionate and kind. It was a Lusignan who killed my family."

Emera gasped and her hands came away from his forehead. "Is it true?" she breathed. "I... I do not know what to say!"

Juston's eyes were open now and he was struggling to sit up, reaching out to grab her hands before she moved too far away.

"There is nothing to say," he assured her, holding on to one of her oily hands. "As I said, I do not know why I should tell you that. I suppose… I suppose because I wanted you to know that you have changed my mind about the family somewhat. I have never met a kind Lusignan. It may not seem like an important revelation, but from someone who has hated the mention of the name for the past nine years, I feel as if something in me has been healed, if only in the slightest. It is difficult to describe… I fear I am only sounding foolish as I make the attempt."

Emera was looking at him, greatly distressed by what he'd told her and struggling not to feel that way. He was trying to pay her a compliment and she endeavored to focus on that.

"You are not sounding foolish," she said. "But if I could apologize for what happened on behalf of every Lusignan and la Marche, I would. We are not a bad family, my lord, but there are those who bear the name that have done some unsavory things, I am sure. From the bottom of my heart, I am truly sorry for your loss."

Juston could see the sincerity in her eyes. As he'd come to see, she was a woman of deep feeling. He smiled faintly and pulled her back towards the bed.

"It was not your fault," he said quietly. "But I thank you for your gesture. It means a great deal."

"Does it? I am glad."

He was lying back down again, realizing the throbbing in his head was lessening. He thought he might actually be able to sleep a bit now. So much about his body and spirit had been eased that he truly felt more relaxed and at peace than he had in a very long time. Perhaps it was the drug, perhaps not. Perhaps it was simply Emera and her soothing presence. He laid his head back onto the mattress, flat.

"If you would not mind continuing to rub my head with the oil, I would be grateful," he said softly. "I think I may be able to sleep now."

Emera simply nodded and resumed rubbing his forehead, smoothing it, feeling as if this entire conversation had been some sort of milestone between them. Juston had been more open with her than he'd ever been and her attraction to him was beginning to grow. She'd been fearful of it before, reluctant even, but at this moment, she wasn't fearful or reluctant at all. When he began to snore again, she dropped a tender kiss on his forehead simply because it seemed like the thing to do. She *wanted* to do it. The man had been through so much; it was the very least she could do.

Juston thought he'd dreamt the kiss.

CHAPTER THIRTEEN

AT DAWN, THE wind was blowing and fat clouds scattered across the sky, but there was no rain or snow in sight, fortunately. The weather was clear as three big wagons were brought around to the inner ward of Bowes, next to the keep, so the loading of turnips could begin.

Emera had to admit, it was both an impressive and intimidating sight to see several soldiers, as well as a few knights, bringing basket after basket of turnips from the vault and dumping them into the wagon beds. She and Jessamyn had already been up, tending the wounded, when Juston's men started filtering into the vault with baskets, loading them up and taking them to the waiting wagons.

Leaving Jessamyn with the wounded, surprise and curiosity prompted Emera to follow the men up the spiral staircase, through the hall, and back down into the inner bailey where there was quite a bit of activity surrounding the wagons. She stood there, watching the activity, thrilled and relieved that Juston had kept his word. After everything that had happened, she was certain he'd forgotten about it.

"Good morn to you, my lady."

Emera turned to see Christopher standing next to her, dressed in heavy layers against the cold weather. She smiled politely.

"Good morn to you, my lord," she said. "Are you in charge of our trip to the market this morning?"

"Aye," he said, running an eye over the loading that was going on.

"I will be your escort along with my brother, Sir Gillem, Sir Erik, and Gart. By my estimation, it should not take more than an hour to reach town if the weather holds."

Emera nodded. "Indeed," she agreed. "I hope the road is passable. Sometimes it becomes great hills and valleys that are impossible to get a wagon through."

Christopher's gaze moved off to the east. "Having considered that, I have already sent a few men out to see to the condition of the road. They've taken shovels with them should they need to fill in holes."

"That was excellent thinking."

He gave her a humorless smile. "One does not succeed within de Royans' ranks if one does not think excellently."

She laughed softly simply from the way he had said it; there was humor in his manner. In fact, the past few days had seen these knights, her initial enemies, relax their harsh stance around her tremendously. It was almost as if they were on the same side these days, united English instead of men for Richard and men for Henry. As Christopher walked away to supervise the situation, a smaller figure took his place.

"Lady Emera!" It was Tristan, who had run all the way up from the vault. Having not been outside for several days, the boy winced in the sunlight. "Lady Jessamyn says to tell you not to forget the apot... apotic...."

Emera grinned. "Apothecary?"

"Aye!"

She laughed softly as the boy grinned, embarrassed. "I will not forget," she said. "There are things we need for the wounded now that we are able to go outside of the castle walls. It should be a short trip today but I intend to see to the apothecary before we leave town."

Tristan nodded, standing close to her as knights and soldiers moved all around him. He could see Erik, the man who had brought him to Bowes, as the man tried to right the weight load on one of the wagons. The sight of Erik gave him an idea.

"Can I come to town, too?" he asked. "I promise I will be no trouble. I should like to go and see the market. I have never seen one before."

Emera knew there was a hierarchy with Tristan when it came to his well-being. It had been made clear to her that Sir Erik was his guardian. She, too, could see Erik over on one of the wagon beds.

"Ask Sir Erik," she said. "If he agrees, then you may come."

Thrilled, Tristan ran off towards the wagon that held Erik, nearly getting run over by men bearing baskets of turnips in the process. Emera smiled as she watched him dodge the men. He was a cute little fellow, extremely helpful and wanting to please. She had enjoyed having him assist with the wounded over the past few days because he'd truly been a help. He was not afraid of work.

Emera saw as Tristan approached Erik, asked the question, and she saw clearly when Erik frowned and shook his head. But Tristan didn't give up; he continued to ask, finally pointing at Emera, who nodded her head to Erik's dubious expression. She wanted him to know that she was in favor of the boy going along. Finally, Erik rolled his eyes and waved the boy away, but Tristan was very gleeful. He came running back over to Emera.

"He says that I may go!" he said excitedly.

Emera nodded. "I am happy for you," she said. "But you must dress warmly. Go and put on your traveling clothes and tell Lady Jessamyn that you will be going with me to town."

The happy boy raced off, dashing into the forebuilding of the keep and plowing into Juston in the process. Juston was just emerging from the forebuilding as the boy was running in and the child bounced off the big knight, nearly losing his balance. But Juston set the boy to rights, looking at him with some curiosity as the child then raced past him and disappeared into the keep.

Emera was surprised to see that Juston was up and about. She'd stayed with him long into the previous night as he slept, rubbing his head with lavender oil until her fingers hurt. Somehow, she just couldn't bring herself to leave him. So she remained until she was exhausted herself before retreating down into the cold vaults and climbing into the pallet beside her sleeping sister. When she finally slept, fitfully, it was with dreams of a long-haired knight.

He'd never been out of her mind and now here he was, not only out of bed but evidently dressed against the cold weather as if resuming his normal duties. As he approached Emera, she could even see that it was possible the man had combed his hair and even shaved. He appeared cleaned up and shiny, like a new coin.

Her heart began to flutter, just a little.

"My lady," he greeted as he approached. "The weather gods have smiled upon us for this morning's trip."

His voice, smooth and deep, flowed over her like warm honey. The fluttering in her chest turned into a mad frenzy. "Indeed, they have," she said, struggling not to sound breathless. "I would thank you again for doing this for us but, truthfully, you do not need so many knights with us. A few men, perhaps armed, and we can make this trip just as well."

Juston shook his head. "My men have purchases to make in town as well," he said. "In truth, this is a fortuitous venture. I have an army to feed so there may be things in the market that we can purchase – grains, staples for the horses, things of that nature."

Emera grinned. "I can sell you wagonloads of turnips very cheaply."

Juston smiled, a lopsided grin, but it was especially important because it was the first time Emera had ever seen him openly smile at her. "I was going to speak to you about that, in fact," he said. "I would discuss keeping at least one wagonload. How much will you charge me?"

Emera had been jesting with him but now she saw a business opportunity. The man's army needed food and she had it. She didn't know why she didn't think of it before. She turned to look at the last wagon that Erik was still fussing over.

"It is usually sold by weight," she said. "In the winter market, if the crop is good, it is usually a shilling for five pounds."

Juston glanced at the wagon she was looking at as Erik tried to even out the load so the imbalance of weight wouldn't harm the axles. "Is the crop good?"

"I believe it is."

"Then a shilling for five pounds would be reasonable."

"I believe it is very reasonable, my lord."

He headed over to the wagon and Emera followed, sensing a deal in the air. For the past two years, she had been a very good saleswoman for the goods from Bowes, mostly because Brey didn't care and Jessamyn didn't have business sense. So she'd stepped in and filled the void. She watched closely as Juston picked up a big turnip, dirty, and looked it over. Then, he looked at Erik, who was standing in the wagon bed amidst the turnips.

"How much would you say this produce weighs?" Juston asked him.

Erik was looking at his feet. "Each basket of turnips the men have dumped into this wagon weighs close to ten pounds and they've dumped thirty or forty baskets in here."

"Be more precise. Is it thirty or forty baskets?"

"I would have to say forty."

Juston cocked an eyebrow thoughtfully. "Forty baskets at ten pounds each," he said. "That is four hundred pounds. If you charge me one shilling for every five pounds of turnips, then that would be four pounds, as there are twenty shillings to a pound. Are my mathematics correct?"

Emera knew how to do sums thanks to her mother. The woman had made sure to educate her daughters in things like writing, sums, reading, as well as in the healing arts. Jessamyn didn't have the mind for sums and writing, but Emera had. Therefore, she, too, could do sums in her head as Juston had just done. She nodded.

"That is four pounds, indeed," she said.

"Will you sell me these turnips, then?"

"I will do so happily, my lord."

He flashed her a hint of a smile before turning to Erik. "Get out of that wagon," he said. "Have the men take everything in this wagon back to the vault. I have just purchased this produce from Lady Emera. The other two wagons we will take with us into town."

Erik looked at the man as if he'd lost his mind. Christopher, who had been standing nearby, also heard him. Christopher walked up to the other side of the wagon, peering at Juston most curiously.

"You *bought* these turnips?" Christopher clarified.

Juston nodded. "I did, indeed. Make sure they are taken back to the vault."

Christopher lifted his eyebrows. "But that is where they have just come from," he said, puzzled. "These turnips already belonged to you. Why did you buy them?"

Juston realized that he must look like an idiot in front of his men. He looked between Christopher and Erik, seeing the bewilderment on their faces, and cleared his throat softly. He was going to have to find a way to explain this to them without sounding like he hadn't gone daft.

"This crop is part of the money crop that the peasants of Bowes have grown," he said. "They expect to be paid for it. If they do not make money, then we will have starving peasants on our hands and I will have to spend money to feed them, anyway. Since the lady was going to sell the crop at market today, and we are heading in to town with her to purchase goods of our own, I have done away with the need to take one of these wagons to town. The peasants get their money and we get our food. And this is the last time I will explain anything like this to you again."

He made sense but there was also a definitive warning in his explanation. Christopher simply nodded his head while Erik, frustrated that he would now have to remove all of the turnips he'd been fussing with, barked at a few soldiers nearby to bring the baskets. When he explained to them that the turnips were to go back to the vault, they looked at him as if he was the one who had lost his mind but Erik began bellowing and the men began moving. Back the turnips went into the cold, dark vault of Bowes.

After that, the focus was put on the remaining two wagons as Erik and Christopher were joined by Gart, David, and Gillem. The knights were dressed in battle attire, with a full array of weapons, and their scarred war horses were brought out from the makeshift stable. As the men were getting ready, Juston excused himself back to the keep and Emera followed a short time later. In her case, it was to retrieve her cloak and her purse, which she had found at the bottom of one of the satchels that Juston's men had packed with her belongings. Surprisingly enough, the contents were still intact.

Ready to take the turnips to market, Emera and Tristan finally made their way back out to the wagons and climbed onto the single-plank seat of the first one. It was usually only meant for the driver, but Emera didn't intend to walk all the way to town. So she and the boy took up positions and waited for the escort to assemble.

It wasn't long in coming. Six knights bearing colors of blue and silver, astride very big and very mean war horses, assembled with two wagon drivers and about twenty men-at-arms, all heavily armed, and the two wagons left the safety of Bowes and headed to the main road.

There was a sense of excitement in the air as they moved forward beneath blue skies and brisk winds. Juston rode at the head of the party, in a position of command, clad in a coat of mail but no helm. Instead, he had secured it to the side of the saddle. Emera watched the man as if nothing else in the world existed. She watched him relay orders to the others, making sure the escort was properly positioned around the two wagons.

As Emera watched, she realized she'd never really seen Juston in command mode before and he was truly something to behold – he was quiet with his command, relaying orders to his senior knights and then trusting them to carrying them out. It was clear by the way the knights hung on his every word that there was a great deal of respect there, something that was impressive to witness.

Out here in the world, away from the confines of Bowes Castle, Emera felt as if she was truly seeing Juston for the first time. Here he was, in his element, unhindered by battles and broken castles and searing headaches. Watching him as he sat, tall and proud astride his horse, it was as if she was looking at an entirely new man.

But he wouldn't look at her as they rode along, nor would he talk to her. He kept his manner professional, alert to the surrounding area, speaking to his knights only when necessary. It was a little disappointing that he wouldn't look at her, but she supposed she understood. He wasn't here to socialize.

At one point, she heard him say something to Erik about Tristan as the boy rode alongside Emera on the wagon bench, but she couldn't quite hear everything that was said. Erik evidently gave an adequate explanation for the lad's company because Juston didn't mention the boy, or look at him, again.

Tristan, however, must have heard his name. He inched close to Emera as if she could protect him from the big, nasty-looking knight riding point.

"He will not make me go back to the castle, will he?" Tristan asked fearfully.

Emera looked down at the boy. "Who?"

Tristan gripped her sleeve as he pointed to Juston. "*Him.*"

Emera fought off a grin. "Do you not know who that is? You have been at Bowes for a few days. You should know who the commander of Bowes is."

Tristan eyed Juston several feet ahead of them. "It is Lord de Royans."

"That is correct."

"Sir Erik told me that he is a great knight."

"I am sure he is."

"Sir Erik said that he fought in France. Sir Erik fought in France, too."

Emera found herself staring at Juston's back as he rode on ahead. Not that she hadn't been staring at it for most of the trip. "Lord de Royans told me he fought in France but I did not know that Sir Erik did, too," she said.

Tristan nodded his head. "When we left Canterbury and traveled north, Sir Erik told me many things," he said. "He talked mostly at night when he had too much wine to drink. He likes to drink a lot of wine, you know. He told me that Lord de Royans fought many battles and did great things. He said that Lord de Royans did things that no other knights would do because he was so brave."

Now the conversation was getting a bit interesting as the boy spoke of Juston and his accomplishments. "Is that so?" Emera said. "I would believe that. He seems very brave."

Tristan nodded. "He said that Lord de Royans has killed men with his bare hands, ripping their heads from their bodies!"

Emera frowned at the sudden morbid turn. "He told you that?"

Tristan nodded. "Aye," he said. "That is why Lord de Royans is so scary."

Emera shook her head, disapproving of what Erik de Russe had told a small boy. "He should not be scary to you," she said. "He only kills his enemies. You are not his enemy."

That made some sense to the nine-year-old boy's mind. "Nay, I am not," he said. "I am glad I am not. He is vengeful with his enemies. Sir Erik said that Lord de Royans spent an entire year searching for the man who killed his family. Did you know his family was killed? Lord de Royans looked for the man for a whole year and killed people who would not tell him where he was."

Now he was gossiping, speaking of darker things that should not be voiced. Emera cast the boy a long look. "You should not tell people that," she said. "It is impolite to speak of others and their troubles. Poor Lord de Royans lost his wife and children. It is right that he should seek vengeance against those who killed them, don't you think?"

Tristan was too caught up in the conversation to realize he'd been rebuked. "Aye," he said. "Sir Erik said that a man named Lusignan killed Lord de Royans' family."

Emera was unhappy the lad hadn't taken her advice and shut his mouth. "Sir Erik told you all of this? He should not have done that."

Tristan nodded firmly. "He had too much to drink and he would talk too much."

"*You* are talking too much."

"He said the man's name was Dorian Lusignan. He said if I ever come across a man named Dorian Lusignan, then I am to tell him immediately."

It took a moment for that name to sink in to her brain. She was, truthfully, trying to shut out the child's chatter, hoping if she didn't respond that he would shut his little mouth. But the moment he mentioned the name Dorian Lusignan, Emera looked to the boy with such horror that she could barely draw in a breath. The world began to rock unsteadily and she gripped the bench to keep from falling off of it.

Dorian Lusignan!

"That name," she gasped. "He... he said *that*?"

Tristan nodded eagerly. "You should tell him, too, if you ever meet a man with that name. Sir Erik said that Lord de Royans will pay a reward for anyone who finds the man."

Emera simply stared at the child, her mind whirling, laboring with every bit of strength she had to keep her composure. It was a sickening, horrible revelation, for she had an uncle of the exact same name.

Sweet Mary, is it possible it is the same man?

Dorian Lusignan was her father's older brother, a man who lived on the family properties in France while her father, the younger brother with no property, had fought in France for men who would pay him for his services. When her father had finally married his English wife, he had forsaken the name Lusignan and taken la Marche instead. It was a name associated with Lusignan but la Marche was a name that attracted far less attention. House of Lusignan was well known and, at times, well-hated. Her father had never given his reasons for changing the name and Emera had never asked, but now she wished she had.

Perhaps her father had known something that she had not.

On her right, Tristan was still chattering, now about his travels with

Erik, but Emera wasn't listening. Her thoughts were wrapped up with the murderer of Juston's family and feeling horror that she could, in fact, be related to the man who had caused Juston such grief. It was a horrific realization. As she watched the man ride up ahead, cutting a powerful and impressive figure, she vowed at that moment never to mention what she knew. She could only imagine what horrors it would strike for Juston, not to mention the fact that it could very well end whatever attraction or attention he might be feeling towards her. Since last night, when she had rubbed his head and they'd shared a pleasant conversation, she was almost certain he had some interest in her. She could tell by the look in his eye. But knowing her uncle was Dorian Lusignan, perhaps the same man who had killed his family, would surely end it.

He might even hate her, too.

With thoughts of Juston and her Uncle Dorian on her mind, Emera sat in silence for the rest of the trip. Fortunately, the rest of the journey was uneventful. The road wasn't too bad, thanks to the men that had been sent out earlier to fill the holes, so the party made it to town in a little over an hour. Because the weather was good, many people were out. By the time they reached the town, it was quite busy with those going about their business. Once they reached the edge of town, Juston brought the party to a halt. He turned to Emera.

"My lady, I am unfamiliar with the market of this town," he said. "Where is it?"

They were at the bridge that spanned the River Tees. On the opposite side of the river sat Barnard Castle, a large stone bastion that sat on a rise overlooking both the river and the town. Emera, sitting straight as he addressed her, pushed aside her depressed mood and pointed in the general direction of the town.

"We must cross the bridge and when the street forks, we proceed north and pass in front of the castle," she said. "It will take us around the wall to the gate that will lead us directly to the market."

Juston nodded, waving a big arm to motion the wagons. If he noticed anything odd about Emera's manner, he didn't say so. He didn't give her a second look. He was focused on making their way into the town. In fact, he'd spent the trip deliberately not looking at her, afraid his expression would belie the confusion he felt in his heart. Already this morning, he'd made a fool out of himself by purchasing her turnips. His men had thought he was daft. He wasn't about to cement that opinion by passing her appreciative glances, knowing that the lovely Lady Emera had somehow turned his head.

To be honest, turning his head was putting it mildly. Last night, she had been kinder and gentler to him than anyone had ever been with the exception of Lizette. Sweet, tiny Lizette had been delicate and sweet, and that was something he'd missed from his life terribly. He missed it so much that he blocked it out and pushed it into a hole, burying it so he could never think about it again. But Emera... she had the same sweetness and gentleness, but with her, there was more. She had a fire and a strength Lizette had never possessed, something that had initially repulsed him but now it was something he rather liked. Properly handled, he was sure he could learn to appreciate it.

Already, he appreciated *her*... very much.

The party lurched forward across the bridge, distracting him from thoughts of Emera. As he was trying very hard not to look at her, he was startled when Christopher rode up alongside him. The man flipped up his visor, his blue eyes fixed to the enormous castle perched on a hill overlooking the river.

"I have not been to Gainford for several years," he said. "The castle was not like this the last I saw."

Juston's gaze also found the imposing castle, the shadows cast by the rising sun to the east turning the entire west side facing them a dark and gloomy gray. "It has been built up over the past few years," he said. "Bernard de Balliol is now in command and he is neither for Henry nor for Richard. He has his own trouble with the Scots and also with de Puiset. The man is like an island unto himself."

Christopher knew the name and the family Juston spoke of. "I was rather curious why we did not see de Balliol when we laid siege to Bowes," he said. "Much like de Puiset, he remained safe in his castle and did not venture out to get involved, which was wise of him."

Juston shook his head as if baffled by the dealings of de Balliol. "He does not involve himself with anything that has to do with Henry," he said. "If anything, he is sympathetic to Richard, but he has never publicly supported him."

Christopher's gaze lingered on the castle for a moment longer before turning away, refocusing on the bustling town in front of them. "As long as he does not try to impede us in any way while we are here, I am at peace with the man," he said. "If he does not bother me, I will not bother him."

Juston agreed. "My thoughts exactly," he said. "And I have no intention of announcing myself to him while we are here, which would have been good manners under normal circumstances. I would prefer to conduct my business without making a fanfare of it and quietly leave. Pass the word down the line that all of the men are to behave in the same fashion. We do not want to attract attention to ourselves."

Christopher reined his horse around, heading back to where his brother and Gart were riding. After telling the pair of his discussion with Juston, David and Gart moved down the line, informing the men what was expected of them.

Meanwhile, Tristan had stopped talking and now sat quietly next to Emera, his eyes wide at the city gate they were approaching. There didn't seem to be any guards on it, which was a good thing, and once they passed through the massive stone gate built into the city wall, the bustling town spread out before them. Children were running in the streets, dogs barking, evidently happy to be out and about on this rare mild winter day. Farmers with great loads of hay moved down the street with their oxen carts and, somewhere, bread was being baked because the rich odor filled the air. Tristan sniffed it hungrily. He turned to Emera.

"I have not eaten, my lady," he said. "Will we stop and eat soon?"

Truth be told, the smell of bread was making Emera nauseous. She had not broken her fast before they left Bowes and the stress of the conversation with Tristan had left her mouth dry and her stomach in knots. Juston was up ahead of her by several feet and she called to him hesitantly, not wanting to shout and sound demanding. By the third call, he heard her and turned around.

"My lady?" he reined his horse back so the wagon could catch up to him. "Do you require something?"

Emera nodded. "I am afraid so," she said. "In the excitement of loading the wagons this morning, Tristan did not break his fast. Would it be too much trouble to find something to eat?"

Juston nodded his head. "I am sure there are a dozen vendors around here willing to sell us all manner of food," he said. "What is your wish?

Emera looked over towards the marketplace, which was off to their left. She could see it from where they were. It was crowded with men and merchants, buyers and sellers, and it was next to a wide open field in the middle of the town that held some of the overflow from the market. To the north of the markets was the street of the bakers, although it was really just an alleyway where several bakers shared one large oven. Emera pointed in the direction of the bakers.

"The smell of bread is coming from over there," she told Juston. "I am sure we can find something there."

Juston turned his attention in the direction she was indicating. "Let us settle the wagons first, if you can wait that long," he said. "It would be better to take them into the market than parade them all over town."

Emera agreed. Then, she climbed off the wagon with the driver helping her to drop to the ground. Gathering her skirts so they wouldn't drag in the mud, she began to walk.

"Follow me," she said to Juston and to the drivers. "I will show you where to take the wagons."

They followed, like obedient boys following their mother. Juston reined his horse up behind her, close enough to provide a silent statement to any man foolish enough to look at her that he was her protection. Her long black hair was braided, draped over the shoulder of her rather worn-looking cloak, but to him, she walked and looked like a queen. He was quite sure that he wasn't the only one who thought so, either, because she was attracting some attention from the curious males he passed. Juston made sure to narrow his eyes appropriately to any man who looked at her and then caught sight of him right behind her. Many a male went scurrying on his way.

The market was a wide area with brokers lining the fringe of it, with even more brokers and farmers bunched up in the middle doing business with customers. Emera found the man in charge, one of the merchants in town who had graduated from selling his wares to coordinating the Saturday winter market and taking a cut from the merchants and other brokers who were there. He was given this appointment by the mayor of the town, who also took a cut of the money.

The man in charge, named Ilsby, was pleasantly surprised to see Emera, whom he knew from doing business with her for the past two years. As Juston and the knights hung back with the wagons, Emera and Ilsby had a rather lively conversation and she kept pointing to the wagons, obviously explaining her needs. The conversation dragged on for a little while, causing boredom with some of the knights, but Juston wasn't bored in the least. He was watching Emera as she spoke with the man in charge, noting every fluid movement of her lovely hands, every smile and every laugh. God's Bones, she was an exquisite creature. The more he watched, the more enchanted he became.

Finally, Emera finished her business and returned to Juston and his men. She pointed to the west side of the market where it seemed to be less crowded.

"Ilsby has asked us to park the wagons over there," she said. "He believes he already has buyers for the product, so this may go very quickly."

Juston emitted a whistle between his teeth, motioning the men to the area Emera had indicated when they all looked to him expectantly. Slowly, the party began to move and they positioned the wagons out of the path of travel, uncoupling the teams so they could be moved to an area with the other horses and rested. As some of the soldiers took the teams away to a large, bare-branched tree in the field beyond, Juston turned to Emera.

"Now," he said, "we can go to the bakers and get some food to break your fast."

Emera shook her head. "I must be here to negotiate with any potential buyers," she said. "But you may take Tristan. He is very hungry."

Juston had no intention of going anywhere without her. He turned to the de Lohr brothers and to Erik. "Take Master Tristan and find food," he said. "Gillem, go with them. I will remain here with Lady Emera. And do not be overlong; I am famished as well."

Christopher and David were already reining their horses for the main road beyond the market as Gillem followed. Not far behind was Erik, who directed his horse close to Tristan, still sitting on the wagon seat. Grabbing a skinny arm, he pulled the boy onto his horse and spurred the animal after the other knights.

That left Gart and Juston and about fifteen men-at-arms to linger in the market, protecting the product and just generally being bored about it. A market was no place for fighting men. As Gart wandered away to inspect some of the other merchants around the market, Juston dismounted his charger and handed the horse over to a soldier to tend.

"Do you do this often?" he asked Emera.

She was rather giddy that everyone had departed, leaving her essentially alone with Juston. "Fairly often," she said. "We sell produce at least three times a year but I am here as a buyer at least once a month."

"Why?" he asked. "Does Bowes not supply everything you need?"

She shrugged. "For the most part. We have crops and we have a herd of sheep for food. We are self-sufficient for the most part except we lost our smithy last year and it has been difficult to replace him. We do not grow grain, either, so we must purchase that regularly, and although we have cows for milk and cheese, sometimes they do not produce enough, especially when the weather grows cold. Jessamyn and I have been saving money to purchase two more cows."

Juston listened, all the while thinking of Brey de la Roarke and his thievery. "De la Roarke had an entire room full of stolen goods and he could not supply you with money to purchase more cows?" he asked, incredulous. "That is an extraordinarily selfish man."

Emera knew that. "You may as well know that all of that treasure was not his and his alone," she said. "I was not going to say anything, because it is purely speculation on my part, but I believe he gave some of the things he stole to allies of his. I do not know this for sure, but Brey would invite his friends and allies to feast, and men would leave with things that did not belong to them. I have been wondering…."

"What?"

She looked at him. "If these men will come to you and demand their due," she said quietly. "Just because Brey is dead, that does not mean they should not demand from you what they demanded from him."

Juston had already heard of this tidy arrangement from the wounded soldier who used to serve with him, so this wasn't any great shock to hear it from her. Furthermore, he wasn't surprised Emera knew of the change of hands with de la Roarke's stolen booty. She was a smart woman; it didn't seem that she would be ignorant to anything like that.

"Who are these allies?" he asked. "Do you know them?"

Emera was thoughtful. "The commander of Cotherstone was one," she said. "He came to Bowes quite frequently. Once, I saw him ride out in a very fine fortified carriage that Brey had brought home a few days before. There was blood inside of it and I saw them drag the body of a man out of it. I do not know what happened to the man, but Brey gave the carriage to the garrison commander."

Juston was coming to think that it was probably a good thing Christopher and David and Marcus hadn't made contact with the garrison commander at Cotherstone when visiting the village those days ago. He had a suspicion the commander wouldn't have been too happy to make their acquaintance since he was evidently thick as thieves with de la Roarke.

"Well," he said after a moment, "I should not worry. I am sure if any of these allies show up at Bowes, you will identify them for me so I know."

"I will, my lord."

"Will you do something for me?"

"Of course, my lord."

"When we are in private, like we are at this moment, you will call me Juston."

Emera looked at him in surprise. "I... I would be honored."

"May I call you Emera?"

She stared at him a moment before a smile spread across her lips. "You may."

"Thank you."

They looked at each other a moment longer before she broke away, flushing with delight. Her heart was beating so forcefully against her ribs that she was positive he could hear it.

"Emera?"

"Aye, Juston?"

He grinned at the sound of his name coming from her lips, but it wasn't just any grin – it was one of satisfaction. He liked hearing her say his name. "Are you still thinking of leaving Bowes for the charity hospital?"

"Why do you ask?"

He shrugged, unwilling to answer the question because the answer would surely embarrass him. "'Tis only that you serve a vital function at Bowes," he said. "It seems to me, in the short time I have been at Bowes, that you are the one who sees to the daily operations of the place. It is you who took charge of taking the turnips to market and you who have helped serve the men and work in the kitchens. I have not seen your sister at all."

What he said was true and Emera was well aware. "Jessamyn is still grieving the loss of her husband."

"Is she?"

Emera nodded. Then, she shook her head. "Nay, she is not," she said flatly. "That is a lie. Although she has not told me, I believe she hated him as I hated him. The man was a pig, in every sense of the word. I should personally like to thank the man who killed him because he did us a tremendous favor. Mayhap it is crude to say such a thing, but it is the truth. Was it one of your knights?"

She sounded embittered, even angry. And based on everything she'd said about the man, he knew her bitterness to be genuine. "Nay," he said softly. "It was not one of my knights."

She looked at him, then. "You never did tell me how Brey died," she said. "Did he catch an arrow? Did one of your soldiers kill him?"

Juston shook his head faintly. He was looking off across the market as he spoke. "After three weeks of battle, de la Roarke proposed that I should pit my best warrior against his best warrior," he said. "As it so happens, I am my best warrior so I met de la Roarke in one-on-one combat. I won."

By this time, she was looking at him in astonishment. "It was *you*?"

He looked at her, then. "Aye."

Emera wasn't sure what more to say other than to express her gratitude. She had said she'd wanted to thank the man who had freed her from Brey's tyranny. But in this case, she took it a step further simply because she wanted to. Without a word, she stood on her tiptoes and very gently deposited a kiss on Juston's right cheek. It was his turn to look surprised, but all she did was smile.

"Thank you," she murmured sincerely. "You have my undying gratitude, always."

There was that word again – *gratitude*. Only this time, he didn't grab her and try to kiss her so she could show him just how thankful she was. This time, she had kissed him, instead.

It was the best kiss he'd ever had.

God's Bones, he was close to blushing. What an idiot he was! His eyes were riveted to Emera as she smiled shyly and looked away, resisting the urge to grab her as he'd done before. In spite of the fact that she'd kissed him, he knew she wouldn't react well to him trying to assert himself on her. That's just not the way Emera liked things. She was not to be pushed around, grabbed, or trifled with. Juston was starting to understand that now.

"Emera?"

"Aye, Juston?"

"Do not go to the charity hospital."

She looked at him, over her shoulder. "Why not?"

"Because I do not want you to. I cannot tell you any more than that."

Emera couldn't help the smile now; her face was nearly split in two with it. She looked away from him, quickly, so he wouldn't see how utterly delighted she was with his statement. If she'd had any doubt that the man was attracted to her, his simple statement had dashed it.

"If you do not want me to go, then I will not."

"Good."

"What will you have me do if I remain at Bowes?"

"Why… you shall be my chatelaine, of course. You are invaluable to me."

That didn't sound quite as romantic as she'd hoped, but she was willing to accept it. If they kept going as they were going, perhaps she would mean more to him in the days and weeks and months to come. She'd told her sister that she'd never dreamed of running her own home and having her own children, but the advent of Juston de Royans had changed that opinion. Still, she couldn't help but goad him a bit. Something in her feminine vanity demanded it.

"So it would be like a business arrangement, would it?" she asked innocently. "Or did you have something else in mind?"

"Like what?"

That wasn't the answer she had been looking for. In fact, he sounded rather puzzled as he'd asked it. He'd turned the situation around on her quickly and she was immediately embarrassed. Obviously, this had been a bad ideal. She'd jumped to conclusions.

"I do not know," she said. "That is why I asked. You do not have any... expectations of me?"

It was a very leading question and Juston was feeling cornered. Certainly he had expectations of her, only he wasn't so sure what those were. All he knew was that he didn't want to be without her but, beyond that, his intentions were a little muddled. Confusion made him defensive.

"My expectations are that you run Bowes efficiently," he said. "Beyond that, I have no expectations."

Emera was crushed. He only had a business arrangement in mind, after all. That was worse than him chasing her around and trying to force himself on her as far as she was concerned. She had feelings for the man but if he wasn't going to admit anything, then neither was she. Perhaps she'd been wrong all along about his attraction to her. Perhaps it was all in her mind. Feeling increasingly embarrassed and upset, Emera simply nodded her head.

"It is good to know where I stand," she said, realizing she was verging on tears. "Please... please excuse me for a moment."

She dashed off before he could say anything, squeezing back between the wagons and disappearing through the merchants that had taken up position behind them. She thought she might have heard Juston shout her name but she didn't stop. She kept going, pushing through the marketplace before emerging on the other side. Then, she began to run.

Foolish, ridiculous emotions swelled up within her. She was feeling despondent when she should not be feeling so, aching for something she'd foolishly placed some hopes in. It wasn't Juston who had expectations but *her*, silly expectations of a woman who had never been attracted to a man in her life. She had no idea how to deal with those feelings. It pained her greatly to think that the only tender contact she'd ever have with the man had happened the night before. Now, all of that was dashed.

Racing down an alley, she emerged onto a main street and continued across it, knowing that behind the houses and shops lining the street were an open field and a stream. Perhaps she needed to sit calmly for a few minutes to regain her composure. She was feeling so utterly foolish at the moment, uncharacteristic of her, that she simply needed some time alone to gather herself.

Heart pumping, tears blinding her, she squeezed between the homes and entered the dead-grass field. There was a line of frozen trees cutting through it and Emera knew that was where the stream was. Skirts hiked up against the mud and dead grass, she scurried across the field and into the shielding canopy. Once she reached the trees, she felt as if she was hidden for the moment, as if she now had some privacy to make a fool of herself.

It was icy cold amongst the frozen trees and the creek had partially frozen over as well. Beneath a thin layer of ice, she could see the water flowing. Away from the bustle of the marketplace, it was peaceful. Emera wallowed in self-pity for a few moments without an audience. Wiping the tears from her eyes, she took a few deep breaths to steady herself. How could she have been so foolish to think there was any potential between her and Juston? He was a powerful knight, the High Sheriff of Yorkshire, so naturally he could command a very wealthy and refined bride. She was neither of those things, barely more than a servant herself.

He wanted her to stay at Bowes and become his chatelaine without any further commitment than that. It was a fine offer, in fact. She had to look at it that way. It would ensure she had a position of importance and guarantee a roof over her head in the years to come. Perhaps it was better than scraping by an existence at the charity hospital. Perhaps she simply needed to be grateful for what he was willing to provide and forget about what he wasn't willing to provide.

"What did I say?"

It was Juston. He had followed her as she'd fled the market and was now standing behind her, beneath the canopy of frozen branches. Emera gasped with fright when she heard his voice, turning to see him as he entered the thicket. She wished he would go away but, then again, she was glad he'd come. She was so confused she didn't know what she was feeling. She backed away from him as he came close.

"N-nothing," she tried to assure him but she didn't do a very good job. "You did not say anything. I... I simply needed a moment to myself. Sometimes women need moments to themselves."

The fallen twigs snapped under his big boots as he came closer still. "I know," he said. "I was married once. She would chase me away constantly for things I said or things I did not say, so I know what it means when a woman wants a moment of privacy. I will, therefore, ask again – *what* did I say that made you run off?"

Emera was near tears again. She wished he hadn't asked that question. Taking a deep breath, she shook her head. "It is of no matter," she said quietly. "I am a foolish woman and fits of confusion simply go along with that particular personality trait. I am grateful you have asked me to be the chatelaine of Bowes and I will conduct my duties to the best of my abilities. You can depend on me."

"I know I can," he said, coming to a halt. He looked down at her as she stared at the stream. He couldn't help but notice she wouldn't look at him. "Emera, I am a bright man. I understand that I said something to upset you. What I am not is a man of tact, so I will come to the point. You ran off when you asked me if I had any future expectations of you. I cannot tell you if I do or not. I have only known you a few days at most, so to have expectations at this point would be foolish and premature. Do you not think so?"

He sounded so reasonable and that only made her feel worse. "Aye," she nearly whispered. "I do."

He eyed her lowered head. "But let us presume that I am foolish for a moment," he said. "If you ever repeat that, I will deny saying it and I will whip you soundly for lying. But, for argument's sake, let us say I am foolish. A few days ago, I met the most beautiful woman I have ever seen. She is stubborn and rigid and frustrating. She refuses to do what I ask. If she had been a man, I would have bound her up and thrown her in the river. Because she is a woman, however, I did not. I have come to discover that along with those annoying traits, she is also brilliant and compassionate and brave. I have never seen such a brave woman. Do you understand what I am saying?"

By this time, Emera had turned to face him, astonishment on her features. The brilliant blue eyes were wide with shock at words she never thought she would hear from him. In fact, she was so surprised that she wasn't quite following what he was saying.

"I… I do not know," she said honestly. "You think I am annoying?"

He frowned at her. "You are not listening to me," he said. "Let us try this another way – you tell me what *you* think of me. And be honest, for I have been honest with you."

Now, the focus was on her and her innermost thoughts, ideas and feelings she had kept carefully guarded. At least, she had kept them guarded until she had run from him. Now, she knew he suspected how she felt. Only a fool would not have figured that out and, as he'd said, he was no fool. Since he had been brave in speaking his mind, she decided she might as well be, too. But it was difficult to bring forth what was in her heart.

Did she even dare try?

"I have told you that I never intend to marry," she said hesitantly, swallowing hard because her mouth was dry. "I have only wanted to help others, never thinking of myself and my own personal happiness. But… but I met you and even though we have had moments of frustration as you have called it, I have also seen moments of generosity and warmth from you that makes me feel… I suppose it makes me feel things I have never felt before. I have never known anyone like you. Do you understand what *I* am saying?"

He did. But he wanted to hear it from her. "I do. But I asked you first. Tell me everything."

He was being deliberately stubborn but she could see an impish gleam in his eye. He knew he was being difficult and he didn't care. Some of her nervousness left her and she sighed heavily, now irritated by the fact that he seemed to be toying with her.

"I mean that I have never wanted to marry," she repeated, snappish. "But if I were to meet a man like you, and he felt for me as I feel for him, then I would, mayhap, change my mind. Now, you tell me what *you* meant."

The corners of his mouth twitched in a way that greatly frustrated her. He *was* toying with her!

"I lost my wife and children years ago," he said. "You already know that. I have no intention of remarrying, ever. Now that I know how you feel about me, it will make you the perfect chatelaine, for if you love me, you will never leave me."

That wasn't what Emera had expected to hear from him and her eyes opened wide. "And that is all you have to say about that?"

"That is all."

She grunted loudly, hugely frustrated that he had coerced her into confessing her thoughts without reciprocating other than to make a hugely boastful statement. Enraged, she gathered her skirts and pushed around him.

"I will leave you," she growled. "I will leave you right now and you shall never see me again. Of all the arrogant things to say! If I *love* you? Who says I love you? I did *not* say that!"

He reached out to grab her before she could get away and Emera could hear him laughing softly, low in his throat. Suddenly, she was trapped up against him, his face in hers, and all she could see was that smug, seductive smile on his lips. Outraged, she tried to bring her hands up to smack that smarmy look off of his face but he trapped her arms, rendering her unable to move. He continued to laugh.

"You spark to anger faster than anyone I have ever seen," he murmured. "But I rather like that. You only anger because I mean something to you."

"Nay!"

"Admit it."

"I will *not!*"

His laughter continued and he suddenly dipped his head down, nuzzling her cheek, her neck. His breath against her flesh was causing her entire body to quiver, now overheating because of his tender attentions. She could feel his lips, tenderly kissing her neck, and it was enough to suck the fight right out of her. She'd never had a man touch her in such a way and the effects were nearly paralyzing. Her struggles slowed but they didn't cease completely.

"Stop, Juston," she commanded, trying to sound firm but failing miserably. "Stop this right now. I do not want you to do this."

He nipped at her neck and her entire body shuddered with excitement. "Liar," he whispered. "You want me to do this. You have wanted me to do this for quite some time."

Her eyes were starting to roll back in her head and she was quickly giving up the fight. Everything in her body was turning molten, as if her limbs had no more shape or form. Everything was melting. She struggled to retain the last scraps of her sanity.

"Please, Juston," she whispered. "Please stop."

He lifted his head from her neck, looking her in the eye. It was all hot breath and trembling flesh between them, swept up in the roaring blaze that had ignited. Juston had been singed by such a blaze before and he knew how to quench it. He asked her what was inarguably the most important question he had ever asked.

"Do you really want me to?"

Emera started to nod her head. At least, that was what her reasoning mind told her. But everything in her body was screaming for him to continue and that was the call she heeded. She couldn't even muster the strength or will to feel like a fallen woman for doing so.

"Nay," she whispered. "I do not."

Juston latched on to her mouth, claiming her in the most forceful way possible. He swooped in over her, bending her head back at the same time he crushed her body against his and, at that moment, he knew he'd lost control. He'd tried to kiss her before but it had always been in lust, in the heat of the moment, but this… this was different.

This fire was fed by a different source.

As Juston overwhelmed her with his presence, Emera had absolutely no control over herself. Juston's scent, his power, quickly consumed her. Every method of self-protection she had ever employed was smashed as he held her against him, sucking the life from her. Her hands, usually slapping at him, were on his face, tangled in his long hair, as he backed her up against a frozen tree trunk, bracing her body against it as his hands began to roam.

Emera could feel his fingers fumbling with her cloak, loosening it so he could get to her body beneath. Did she care? The sensible part of her did. That part of her that knew what he wanted to do, instinctively, and that part of her which wanted to protect her maidenhood. But the part of her that was weak and willing to Juston and his desires did not resist. It was the stronger part of her at the moment for not only did she want the man to touch her, she liked it as well. She liked everything he was doing to her. She wanted him to do more.

More….

A big hand closed over a warm breast, the woolen fabric of her surcoat and shift between them. Emera flinched at his touch and tried to pull away, uncomfortable with it, but Juston's kisses softened and he held her fast, his fingers caressing her breast, brushing against it, feeling the nipple tighten. He wanted her to become accustomed to his touch, to like what he was doing to her. When he pinched it through the fabric, she flinched and he laughed low, in his throat. That laugh, that deeply male rumble, caused her knees to tremble. It was like fuel on the fire.

The hand on her breast wandered away and his mouth moved from her lips to her neck, leaving Emera gasping for air. He had been suffocating her and she hardly realized it until now. As he suckled on her neck, Emera could feel him tugging at her skirts. She was starting to come out of her haze now, realizing he was trying to lift them, but the moment his bare flesh touched the heated skin of her thigh, her intention to resist him fled. She rather liked his hand on her leg. She liked it even more when he moved it up her thigh, to the inside.

Something was happening to her, something she'd never before experienced. Her entire body was quivering strangely as Juston dragged his hand up her thigh, to her private core, an area she only touched when necessity required it. She'd never lingered on herself any more than that. But the moment Juston touched the smattering of dark curls between her legs, something let loose. Her body bucked against his and she could hear him muttering something about God, or bloody God, or something of that nature. It sounded like a prayer. Emera gasped as he stroked her, his touch gentle but sure, and Emera hips instinctively pushed against his hand. That primal gesture, the inherent gesture of all women seeking a man's seed between their legs. To the scent of Juston's silent mating call, Emera was responding without reserve.

"De Royans?"

It was a distant voice, filtered through the frozen trees, and Juston's head came up immediately. It sounded like Gart but he couldn't be sure and, for the lady's sake, he didn't want Gart to wander into the trees and find the lady in an unflattering position. Normally, he wouldn't have cared about such things but with Emera, he did. He didn't want his men to think of her in a negative light. Quickly, he removed his hand from her skirts and let her go, carefully, so she wouldn't fall. He only realized then how firmly he'd had her backed up against the tree. He smoothed at her cloak, brushing off the tree bark, as Emera struggled to catch her breath.

Juston moved away from her, towards the opening in the trees that he had come through, knowing he had a raging erection but thankful that his mail and tunics covered it. It was a little painful, but nothing he couldn't manage. He'd been in this position before. Emerging from the trees, he could clearly see Gart standing about ten feet away.

"The men said you had come in this direction," Gart said. "Is everything well?"

Juston nodded. "Aye," he said, not elaborating. "What do you require?"

Gart gestured back to the market area. "There are some buyers for the produce," he said. "I was looking for the lady and some of the men said that she had run off and that you had gone after her. Did you find her?"

There was no use denying what men had seen. Juston nodded his head but before he could speak, Emera emerged from the trees looking utterly disheveled. Her lovely hair was askew, her clothing twisted, but she was apparently unaware because she looked at Gart and Juston quite innocently. Juston cringed inwardly, however, when he saw how red the woman's mouth and chin were as the result of his beard stubble scraping against her. She also had a love bite on her chin. The woman looked as if she'd been mauled.

If Gart noticed, which he would have been a blind man not to, he didn't say a word about it. He kept a straight face and looked her in the eye.

"My lady, there are some men who wish to buy your produce," he said. "Will you come?"

Emera nodded. "Aye," she said. "Do you know who they are? Did they give a name?"

"Stainton, my lady."

That brought a bit of a reaction. "I see," she said. She glanced at Juston. "The Stainton family has a big manse to the north of Gainford. They are quite wealthy."

She started to walk with the men following. But Juston hung back, waiting until Gart passed them both, before tugging on her arm and making silent hand gestures about her hair and clothing. Chagrinned, Emera quickly smoothed at her hair, trying to tame it, but she couldn't see the back of it so Juston licked his hand and smoothed down the back of her hair, trying to help her. He felt rather responsible for her slovenly appearance.

Not strangely, however, if given the chance again, he would have done it all over again. And given another opportunity like that, he would surely take it.

CHAPTER FOURTEEN

"**D**O YOU SEE them?" Christopher asked.

David, his eyes riveted to the quarry his brother spoke of, nodded slowly. "I did."

"De Puiset men."

"I know. I see their colors."

Lingering near the Church of St. Mary where there was a great deal of traffic on this day, the de Lohr brothers had seen the de Puiset knights near the church, which made sense considering the town was part of the Bishop of Durham's properties. They had been searching out additional food vendors while Erik and Gillem and Tristan were at the bakers, but the de Puiset knights saw the de Lohr brothers through the crowd and a staring contest of sorts began.

Juston purposely had his knights leave their tunics behind with the identifiable de Royans blue for a situation just like this. As he'd said, he didn't want to announce his presence in town so it was best to try and stay as unrecognizable as possible. Therefore, de Puiset's men had no idea who the de Lohr brothers were but from the way they were dressed, heavy armor and well used weapons, it was clear they were seasoned knights. Seasoned knights without heraldry were a mystery, and not a good one.

Christopher and David knew that they could not run, for the bishop's men would only chase them, so they held their ground and didn't move, even when Erik began shouting at them from over by the bakers. Christopher and David ignored the knight, so much so that Erik finally had to make his way over to them.

"Chris!" Erik called. "Did you not hear me? We are ready to leave."

Christopher and David didn't look at him. They were still looking at the church. "I heard you," Christopher said steadily. "We have company, Erik."

Erik had no idea what Chris was talking about until he looked to see what had them so riveted. Immediately, he saw the de Puiset knights and his entire manner changed. No longer irritated, his demeanor cooled dramatically.

"Indeed, we do," he said, also staring down the bishop's men from across the wide intersection. "The Bishop of Durham's knights."

"Where is Tristan?" Christopher asked without looking.

"He is with Gillem."

"Instruct Gillem to return the boy to Juston immediately. Go with him and tell Juston that the bishop's men are here. He must take all due care."

Erik wasn't keen on leaving Christopher or David but someone had to warn Juston so, very casually, he reined his horse back in the direction of the bakers where Gillem and Tristan were. As he fled, Christopher and David maintained their gazes on the distant knights, who were beginning to stir.

"What do we tell them?" David asked. "They will want to know who we are and where we are going. That is normal protocol."

Christopher didn't hesitate. "We are from Lohrham Forest," he said. "We serve our uncle, Philip de Lohr, and we are going north to Scotland where our mother's family lives."

"But our mother wasn't Scottish. She was the sister to the Earl of East Anglia."

"I know that. But those knights do not."

David memorized the story. A lie to prevent battle and bloodshed was understandable, especially since Tristan, son of Henry, was among their group. They couldn't let the boy fall into Durham's hands. Soon enough, the four Durham knights began to move, heading in their direction, casually moving through the crowd. Christopher spurred his horse forward, going to meet them, and David followed. They came together somewhere in the middle of the wide, muddy street.

"Who are you?" a knight with a bushy, dirty beard demanded. "What is your business here?"

Christopher looked the man in the eye. "We were looking for something to eat as we passed through town," he said. "We are heading north, into Galloway, to visit our mother's kin. We only wish to eat and then we shall be gone."

The knight's gaze lingered on them, trying to determine if they were telling the truth. "Who was that other man you were talking to? The one that went away?"

"One of our comrades. He means you no harm, I assure you. None of us do."

The Durham knight studied Christopher and David. They were very big knights, well-armed and on seasoned horses. It was clear they had seen a battle or two in their time. He was suspicious.

"Who do you serve?" he asked.

"Sir Philip de Lohr of Lohrham Forest," Christopher replied. "In Derbyshire. He is my uncle, in fact. We do not serve anyone so grand as the Bishop of Durham."

The knight's eyes narrowed. "How would you know that?"

Christopher gestured to the man's tunic. "Everyone knows that," he said. "His standards are very recognizable."

The knight looked at his tunic purely out of reflex when Christopher pointed. Then, he looked at his men, the other three knights at his side, as if to read their minds. Did they believe the strange knights? Did they not? The Durham knights had noticed the two big warriors near the bakers, threatened by the size and appearance of them. They didn't like strange knights, especially given what had just happened at Bowes Castle. Because of that, all of Durham was on edge. The knight with the dirty beard leaned forward on his saddle.

"How long have you been here?" he asked.

Christopher replied. "Not long."

"How did you come?"

"North from Richmond."

"Then you saw what happened at Bowes. It is right along the road you traveled."

Christopher nodded. "I saw the siege," he said. "It was big and nasty."

That made him more interesting to talk to as far as the Durham knights were concerned. "Did you see who it was?" the bearded man asked anxiously.

Christopher nodded. "De Royans," he said. "Have you heard of him?"

The four Durham knights all expressed various degrees of surprise. "De Royans?" the knight with the dirty beard hissed. "The High Sheriff of Yorkshire? Are you for certain?'

"I could see his banners."

"What is he doing so far north?"

Christopher was on tricky ground at this point. He knew whatever he said would make it back to the bishop. So he wanted to convey the futility of trying to take back Bowes Castle without looking like he was siding with those who captured it.

"I would not know," he said. "But even if I had not seen his standards, no one brings more siege engines and tactics to a battle than de Royans. If you are a fighting man, it is impressive to watch. But we did not linger, fearful we might be pulled into it somehow."

The knight scratched at his bushy beard. Christopher and David watched as crumbs fell out of it.

"God's Bones," the knight muttered, both awed and puzzled. "We have de Royans on our doorstep. I wonder if he's coming for Auckland next?"

Christopher could see the apprehension in the man's eyes, which was exactly what he wanted. Now, it would get back to the bishop. Rather pleased with himself and the way the conversation was going, he was caught off-guard when a fifth knight, bearing the colors of Durham, suddenly rushed up to the group of four.

"There is a party from Bowes Castle in the market!" he said. "Ilsby just told me! He knows the woman from Bowes but not the knights. They must be from the army that laid siege!"

Suddenly, the situation turned in an unfavorable direction. The knight with the dirty beard went from relatively calm to the makings of a madman as he heard the news.

"Here?" he boomed. "Are you sure?"

The fifth soldier nodded his head. "They came with several knights, Ilsby said. At least six!"

All eyes suddenly turned to Christopher and David, who continued to maintain their calm demeanor in spite of the fact that they were caught in a landslide of their own making. Everything was rolling downhill and they knew that they wouldn't be able to maintain their web of lies for much longer.

The knight with the dirty beard narrowed his eyes. "*Who* did you say you were, again?" he asked dubiously.

It was a pivotal question. Christopher looked at David, who merely shrugged. He then returned his focus to the Durham knight. At this point, there was no use in denying the obvious. To continue the lie would be futile because, eventually, the truth would have to come out, especially now.

There was no use in refuting it.

"My name is Christopher de Lohr and I serve Juston de Royans," he said. "We have brought six knights with us so unless you have a stable of fifty knights somewhere nearby, I suggest you let us leave in peace. If not, you will leave your share of blood on the ground. Is this in any way unclear?"

The knight with the dirty beard stared hard and his eyebrows flew up in both shock and outrage. "You – you are with de Royans?"

"I said I was. Are you hard of hearing?"

The knight shut his agape mouth. "You bastard," he hissed. "I should kill you right now!"

Christopher put his hand on the hilt of his broadsword, sheathed on the left side of his saddle. "As I said, let us leave in peace," he said, his voice low, "or you will be the first one to die."

The Durham knights began to back up, as did David, but Christopher remained where he was. The knight with the dirty beard was backing up as well but he was also unsheathing his broadsword. The weapon came out, gleaming in the weak winter sunlight, but he stopped short of actually engaging Christopher. Still, he wielded the sword in a threatening manner.

"The bishop shall hear of this," he declared. "Do not get too comfortable at Bowes for it shall soon be back in our hands!"

Christopher watched the Durham knights as they continued to back away, with two of them suddenly whirling around and charging off down the road that headed out of town. The rest of them were huddled together as if waiting for the fight to begin.

"Bowes is now held for Richard, Count of Poitiers, also known as the Lionheart," Christopher announced. "It is my suggestion you tell the bishop who, exactly, holds Bowes. It is my sense that he will not want to tangle with de Royans. He would do well to understand that Bowes is lost."

"Not for long!"

"That remains to be seen."

The knight with the dirty beard glared at Christopher but he didn't reply. It was apparent that he had no intention of actually engaging the de Royans men in a fight, mostly because he'd heard that de Royans knights drank the blood of their enemies. At least, that was what some fool had once told him. He didn't want to take the chance that it was actually true. Swiftly, he swung his mount about and followed the rest of his men as they tore out of town, heading back to Auckland Castle.

As the bishop's men raced off, David reined his horse next to his

215

brother. "I thought we were going to have a fight on our hands," he said, his gaze on the fleeing knights. "You know they are going to run right back to the bishop and tell him what you told them."

"I hope they do."

"They'll come. You know they will."

Christopher nodded. "I know," he said, finally looking away from the running knights and looking at his brother. "We need to get out of here, quickly."

David nodded, following his brother as the man spurred his horse back the way they had come. He, too, was thinking they needed to leave town quickly because he suspected the bishop's army would come to Bowes sooner rather than later.

And they needed to be prepared.

CHAPTER FIFTEEN

*D*URHAM IS COMING.
A siege is coming.

Gillem heard the discussions among the men as the party from Bowes quickly left Gainford and headed back home at a clipped pace. The knights were on alert, helms on, visors down, weapons ready to be drawn from their sheaths at any moment. The problem was that they were traveling with two wagons, empty wagons since the lady had managed to sell her produce to the Stainton buyer, so the wagons now carried the men-at-arms so they could move more swiftly.

And they were heading back to Bowes with a vengeance.

Gillem was covering their retreat along with the de Lohr brothers, while Gart and Erik were at point with Juston. The only reason Juston was at point was because he wanted to be near that la Marche woman, that black-haired vixen he was increasingly interested in.

As Gillem cantered along the road behind the wagons, he kept his eyes on the woman seated in the first wagon. When they'd first arrived at the market, she had been groomed and lovely, but when Gillem saw her later after he'd returned from the baker, her hair had been askew as if someone had run their fingers through it and de Royans had lingered quite close to her as she negotiated with a buyer. Gillem had seen that look on de Royans' face before.

He'd had the same look before he'd bedded Sybilla.

De Royans wasn't merely tempted by the lady – he was lured by her, hearing her siren's song. Whether or not the lady was deliberately tempting him wasn't the issue – the fact was that the attraction de Royans had shown towards the lady was obviously growing. Gillem had thought once to remove that temptation, or blur it somehow, but he hadn't been given the opportunity to do anything about it. He'd had his duties at Bowes and he'd never crossed the lady's path, not once. His only thought now was that he had to remove the woman completely because when de Royans was on a scent, he didn't give up. If Sybilla and her son had any chance of having de Royans return to their fold, then the la Marche woman had to be removed.

Unfortunately, this wasn't an infatuation that was going to pass, at least from what Gillem had come to understand. What he'd heard from the other knights, purely by eavesdropping on their conversations, had proven to him that de Royans had some manner of serious intentions towards Lady Emera. Therefore, there was no more time for him to delay.

He had to formulate a plan.

Gillem worked on that plan as the party made its way back to Bowes, bumping over the muddy winter road, concocting how he was going to get rid of Lady Emera. He kept thinking of his sister, of the scheme she'd had for de Royans that had ultimately left her with an illegitimate child. Sybilla wasn't a bad girl; she was actually quite kind and thoughtful. But she was also desperate for a prestigious husband and she was a social climber, so she'd set her cap for de Royans. The unfortunate part was that de Royans had no use for a wife and child. Now, Sybilla's chances of finding a prestigious husband were dashed as she harbored the stigma of having a child out of wedlock.

Which meant de Royans, somehow, had to see his way to doing the right thing with her and he could only do that if temptation was removed. Gillem was fairly certain he couldn't force the woman away. He didn't particularly want to kill her, but if need be, he would. But it stood to reason that it would be easier for all of them if she left of her own free will. If he could convince her that de Royans was merely a predator, then perhaps she would choose to leave on her own. That meant that he would have to convince her that remaining at Bowes and under de Royans' command would not be in her best interests.

Beware, lady – de Royans will make a whore out of you as he did my sister!

As Gillem plotted and stewed, Emera was oblivious to his intentions. She sat on the wagon bench beside the driver, holding tight to the bench because she was being bounced around so. Beside her, Tristan was doing the same thing, gripping the seat as the wagon lurched and rolled, both of them fearful because the knights were on battle alert and the men-at-arms in the wagon beds had their weapons in-hand.

There was a great deal of apprehension surrounding the party, fleeing because the Bishop of Durham's men had been sighted in town. Considering Gainford was part of his bishopric, it wasn't surprising. But the fact that the man was an enemy made it concerning on principle alone. Although the bishop hadn't interfered with the siege of Bowes, that could change when he found out the knights who had captured Bowes were now bold enough to stray into one of his villages. If the bishop felt threatened enough, then he would retaliate. That was where the apprehension came from.

A siege is coming.

Emera had heard Christopher as he'd relayed his encounter with the Durham knights to Juston and she'd been forced to conduct and conclude her business with Stainton very quickly because of it. She didn't exactly get the price she'd wanted for the turnips – de Royans had paid more, in fact – but that couldn't be helped. As soon as the price was agreed upon, Juston's men had offloaded the turnips very quickly, dumping them right out onto the dirt of the marketplace for the Stainton men to collect. They couldn't even bother to take the wagons, full of produce, over to the Stainton wagons. They simply took the money and dumped everything, fleeing Gainford as if they had a price on their heads.

It wasn't far from the truth, in reality. They were the enemy in an enemy's town. Therefore, it had been a harried and somewhat frightening flight home. From the way the knights were behaving, Emera was wondering if they weren't about to have a legion of angry Henry supporters coming down on them at any moment.

Other than Brey, she'd really never been around fighting men and once she overcame her trepidation of the situation, she began to watch the knights and the way they reacted to a crisis. They were professional and collected for the most part, but more specifically, she began to watch Juston.

His heated touch and searing lips were still burning her. She could still feel them. Looking at the man only made it worse, now feeling some deeper connection to him. It was so very strange, really – other than her sister, she'd never really had anyone she was close to, someone with whom she shared a deeper level of communication or understanding. But now, Juston seemed to be entering that inner circle because she shared with him something she had never shared with anyone. He'd kissed her in a way she'd never been kissed before and he'd touched her only where she had touched herself. She should have been embarrassed about that but, in truth, she had liked it a great deal and she was eager to feel that sensation again.

Something told her that her experience near the frozen trees would not be her last one with him. In fact, she was looking forward to the next time.

Shameless! She scolded herself, but that was her self-defense kicking in, that sense of self-preservation that had kept up her resistance to Brey and his disgusting attempts. With Juston, there was no sense of self-preservation. She wanted him to touch her and if that made her shameless, then so be it.

With racing thoughts of Juston de Royans, Emera was hardly aware when Bowes Castle came into view. In fact, she had been watching Juston, so caught up in the sight of him that she was startled when one of the knights bellowed something about home. Only then did she look over to the southwest to see Bowes looming in the distance, perched upon the rolling, winter-dead fields like a great sentinel surveying the land. But the first things they saw were horses pouring from the gatehouse, heading in their direction.

The group from Bowes drew closer and closer. Soon, they were surrounded by three more knights and several men-at-arms, all of them heavily armed. Emera recognized the other knights – Maxton, Kress, and Marcus, men who had been left behind to man the fortress while the commanding officer was out. There was still one more knight, Achilles, who hadn't ridden out to meet them, and Emera watched curiously as Maxton and Marcus had a serious discussion with Juston and Christopher. There was some shouting going on, mainly to hear each other clearly, and the pace was increased as the wagons and the men made it back inside the safety of the castle.

The ropes and pulleys groaned as the portcullises were lowered behind the incoming party. The familiar sights and smells of Bowes greeted Emera as the wagons came to a halt in the outer bailey and the men-at-arms climbed out of the wagon beds. Tristan leapt off of the wagon bench, falling into the mud as he did so, but Emera was a bit more careful in gathering her cloak and her purse, helped from the wagon by Gillem, who happened to be there. She smiled gratefully at him as she lifted her skirts and marched off across the outer bailey, heading for the inner bailey and eventually the keep.

Tristan was running on ahead of her, the entire left side of his breeches muddy from where he fell, but he didn't seem to care. The two of them crossed the wooden bridge in tandem across the secondary moat, through the opening in the inner wall, and into the inner bailey just as Jessamyn emerged from the keep, bundled up against the cold. Tristan ran past her and Jessamyn turned to watch the dirty child race into the keep.

"Where is he off to?" Jessamyn asked. "And why is he so dirty?"

Emera approached her sister. "He fell as we were exiting the wagons."

Jessamyn's interest in Tristan's dirty clothing didn't extend beyond the inquiry. She returned her attention to her sister. "Were you able to sell the produce?"

Emera nodded, patting her purse. "Indeed, I did," she replied. "The Stainton family was there. They bought most of it. Lord de Royans purchased the rest, so we have sold everything. We can count the money and distribute it to the farmers tomorrow so they have something for the next few months to live off of."

Jessamyn put her hands on the purse, feeling the weight of the coin. "I am glad to hear that," she said. "Did you get what we needed from the apothecary?"

Emera frowned. "I did not," she said. "Knights sworn to the Hugh de Puiset were in town and Lord de Royans felt that it would be wise to return home as soon as possible. In fact, de Royans' men seemed quite concerned about it. From what I gather, they believe that de Puiset will come and try to regain the castle."

Jessamyn didn't seem as concerned over a potential attack as she was about the absence of the items from the apothecary. She frowned. "I am disappointed to hear that you were unable to make it to the apothecary," she said unhappily. "We have very few things left. No lavender? Featherfew? Meadwort? You did not get any of those things?"

Emera could see that her sister was more focused on the missing ingredients than any impending battle. "There is nothing I can do about it," she said, pushing on and heading to the keep with Jessamyn following. "We will have to try another time. Meanwhile, how are the wounded faring today? Have there been any changes since I left this morning?"

Jessamyn shook her head. "Nay," she replied. "In fact, a few of them feel well enough to move about. One of them – Cowling – has been helping me with the others. You remember him, do you not? An older warrior. He says he knows de Royans. Did you know that?"

Emera shook her head. "I did not," she said. "But I am glad to know the men are feeling better. Still, that brings about the question of what de Royans will do with the wounded once they are healed. They are still the enemy, you know. I wonder if he will want to keep them imprisoned in the vault."

Jessamyn eyed her sister. "You would know that more than I would," she said. "'Tis you who have de Royans' ear, so I have heard."

Emera looked at her sister sharply. "Who has told you that?"

Jessamyn gave the woman a long look. "Do you not think the men have been speaking of such things?" she asked. "Why did I have to hear it from them? You are my sister, Emera. You should have told me that there is something occurring between you and de Royans."

They had just entered the forebuilding that led into the keep and Emera came to a halt, facing her sister in the dimness.

"There is nothing to tell," she said, although she was lying. She simply wasn't sure what to tell her sister – yet – so it was best to tell Jessamyn nothing lest her sister become agitated about it. She had no desire to listen to her sister condemn her. "I have had to have dealings with the man, you know. How do you think I was able to have the wounded moved into the vault? How do you think I was able to have the turnips moved into town? Someone has to speak to him and since you will not, I have taken the duty."

Jessamyn wasn't entirely happy with what she was hearing. "You have spent a great deal of time with him."

Emera threw up her hands in frustration. "Aye, I have," she said. She began storming up the stairs. "Out of necessity, I assure you. Stop listening to gossip, you silly wench. That is all it is – *gossip*."

Jessamyn still wasn't satisfied with her sister's answer. She harped away at her as they crossed the great hall and headed to the spiral stairs that would take them down to the vault. Once down in the cold, darkened vault where the wounded were grouped, Jessamyn continued to pick at her, following her into the little alcove they shared. Emera had finally had enough of the woman, putting up a hand to silence her as she put her purse away, burying it for safety in one of the two satchels.

"Enough, Jessamyn," she hissed. "If something was occurring between me and any man, I would tell you. I have told you that I spend time with de Royans out of necessity and you will do me the courtesy of believing me. I do not want to hear any more about it!"

Jessamyn frowned but she kept her mouth shut. It was difficult, but she did. She had spent the morning alone, listening to the wounded gossip, and then heading into the hall to hear de Royans' men doing the same. Rumors were flying fast and furious that de Royans had his eye on her sister and she was frustrated that she hadn't seen it before. Emera had never said a word about it. Even in Emera's denial, she knew there was a grain of truth. She knew her sister too well not to see it.

But she didn't press, at least for the moment, because Emera's relationship with de Royans had, indeed, provided them with privileges that they probably wouldn't have had otherwise. Perhaps in some way, she was jealous. She was the lady of the castle, wasn't she? Surely de Royans should have looked at her first, but that was the story of her life – men always looked to her beauteous younger sister before they ever looked at her.

Such had been her curse, always.

As Jessamyn pondered her lot in life, Emera finished securing the money and removed her cloak. She intended to check on the wounded personally and then head to the kitchens to see about the plans for the next meal. She knew her sister wouldn't have done it because Jessamyn didn't normally see about things like that, so Emera left their little alcove and began to check on the men, making sure they were warm and healing, taking the time to speak with them.

She noticed one thing right away – that, indeed, some of the wounded seemed to have recovered well enough to sit up and even move about. It was gratifying to see that they were healing, giving her a sense of satisfaction in that everything that had happened to them since the arrival of de Royans – namely, putting them out in the icy weather on that first terrible night – had not had overwhelmingly horrific consequences. Certainly, they'd lost some, but most had survived. She felt very good about that.

But she also noticed something else – either men would smile rather knowingly at her or they would not look at her at all. Remembering what Jessamyn had said about the men gossiping about her and Juston, she struggled not to be embarrassed by their reactions. It simply made her move faster among them, eager to be away from the leering, sneering men.

Once she'd made the rounds, she stopped to speak with Tristan and the older soldier Jessamyn had indicated, Cowling, as they sat huddled near the spiral stairs. Tristan was telling the man all about their flight from town. With Cowling now saddled with the chatty child, she continued back up the spiral stairs and into the great hall.

As she entered the vast chamber above, she found herself hoping she would see Juston. Perhaps that's why she had really come back into the hall and why she was planning on going to the kitchens – she was hoping she would see Juston at some point. The man was heavier on her mind than he'd ever been, especially after hearing that the soldiers were gossiping about her. She simply couldn't tell Jessamyn what had happened at Gainford, the kissing and the touching, because Jessamyn would condemn her and probably rightly so. Therefore, she would keep that information to herself, memories that made her heart race with excitement.

Kisses that made her tremble.

Passing through the great hall, she could see that Juston wasn't there and she was disappointed. She didn't want to look as if she was obviously seeking him out, so she tried not to look around too much or look too anxious as she continued through the hall and into the forebuilding.

Once in the inner bailey, she had to fight off the urge to look about anxiously again, seeking out Juston. She knew he was out here, somewhere, so she merely pretended as if she was focused on her duties, which meant heading to the kitchen. If rumors were already flying about that Juston had his eye on her, then she didn't want to give those rumors more fuel. Heading around the north side of the keep where the well and the kitchens were located, she caught sight of Gillem and Erik as they went about their duties.

Emera's gaze lingered on the pair, just for a moment. Erik was very young, perhaps just a little older than she was, but he was very handsome and seemed pleasant enough. Gillem was a little older, with lovely red hair, but she thought had had kind of a nervous energy about him. But she forgot all about the knights as soon as she saw the cook and discussed the coming meal with the old woman. According to the one-eyed cook, they were nearly down to the last of the pork that de Royans' army had brought with them. No other meat was on the horizon, at least not for the day, and Emera left the kitchen, disappointed with the idea of more pork. She was nearing the keep once again when she heard someone call her name. Turning in the direction of the hail, she lifted her hand to shield her eyes from the weak sun.

Gillem was heading in her direction and he held up a hand when he saw he had her attention, calling her name again. Emera paused, waiting for him to catch up to her since he clearly wanted to speak with her. She even smiled politely.

"Sir Gillem," she said. "I believe that is your name, is it not?"

Gillem nodded. "It is," he said. "We have not been formally introduced, but these are peculiar circumstances. I hope you will make allowances."

"Of course."

"I also hope you will forgive me for boldly addressing you, my lady."

"There is no need to apologize. May I help you with something?"

Gillem was looking at her rather strangely, and Emera sensed that nervous energy from him again. There was something edgy in his eyes.

"I… I was wondering if I might have a word with you, my lady," he said. "In private, if that is possible."

Emera didn't sense anything odd other than his edginess. She nodded. "Where would you like to speak?"

Gillem scratched his head, looking around. "I suppose there really isn't anywhere that could be considered private," he said, "and I suppose it would not be proper, anyway. 'Tis simply that I have something very important that I need to speak with you about and I pray you will not be offended."

Emera cocked her head. "Why should I be offended? You may speak your mind to me, my lord."

Gillem ran his fingers through his hair. This was the moment he'd been contemplating, that very moment where he would rid de Royans of his temptation. When he saw the lady moving from the kitchens to the keep, alone, he knew he had to take the chance. It had been an unexpected opportunity, really, but one he would grasp. However, if de Royans saw them together, he knew the man would wonder what was being discussed and he didn't want to explain himself, so he knew that whatever he said would have to be swift. But he had to ensure he made some sort of an impact. Therefore, he spoke quickly and, he hoped, sincerely.

"I am not entirely sure how to approach this subject so I will simply come out with it," he said. "My lady, I have a sister, Sybilla, whom I love dearly. She is a good lady, kind to the poor and generous to the church. It is because of my sister that I must speak to you about Lord de Royans."

Emera wasn't sure what he was driving at so she kept her manner neutral. "As you wish," she said. "I am not entirely sure why such a conversation would affect me, but you may continue."

Gillem was very serious. "But it *does* affect you, my lady," he said. "Has... has Lord de Royans made you any promises? Has he tried to lure you in any way?"

Now, Emera was feeling somewhat defensive, shocked at his questions. "You will forgive me, my lord, but that is none of your affair. I am sure you understand."

Gillem sighed impatiently. "That is not what I mean," he said. "I only ask because he made promises to my sister also. My lady, forgive me for being blunt, but he has a child with my sister and he refuses to marry her. I would not wish to see you fall into the same despair that my sister has fallen in to. Lord de Royans, while he is a fine knight and a great commander, has a less than savory reputation where women are concerned. He will tell you things you wish to hear and when he has had his way with you, he will refuse to marry you. Please, my lady… learn from my sister's mistakes. Do not fall prey to de Royans. And please do not tell him that I told you these things, for he will only take it out on my sister and their child. I only seek to warn you about him, I swear it."

Emera stood there, looking at the man in astonishment. Nay, *more* than astonishment; shock. She was shocked to the bone. Her mouth became dry and she realized it was because her mouth was hanging open. Closing her mouth, she swallowed hard.

"He… he has a child with your sister?" she repeated, her voice sounding weak. "How old is the child?"

"He is three years of age, my lady," Gillem replied. Then, he looked around. "Lord de Royans must not see us together because he will know that I have warned you. Be wise, my lady – stay away from Lord de Royans before he ruins you as he has ruined my sister. If I were you, I would leave Bowes. I would return to wherever you were born or wherever your family lives. If you stay here, you will end up like my sister – with a child to support and no husband. That is not how you should end up."

With that, he slipped away, heading back in the direction he'd come from and leaving Emera standing, stunned, where he'd left her. Like a statue, she simply stood there, digesting what he'd just told her. She couldn't even summon the will to move. Was it a lie?

Was it truth?

Sweet Mary… she couldn't think straight. Her mind was overwhelmed with the idea that de Royans had done this kind of thing before… sweet and kind to a maiden until she gives herself over to him, and then he moves on after he has his way with her.

Oh, God... was it really possible?

An avalanche of emotion suddenly spilled over her, breaking her from her unmoving stance. Unsteady, she turned for the keep, feeling shame and embarrassment that cut deep, deep enough to bleed. Had she been so foolish that she hadn't realized de Royans was simply playing a game? Having no experience with men, she wouldn't have even known what to look for. That was the truth. De Royans could tell her anything and, because she was attracted to him, she would believe him.

She *had* believed him.

Now, she felt like a fool.

The keep loomed before her and she disappeared into the fore-building, taking the stairs up to the great hall and emerging into the stale warmth of the chamber. She started to go down to the vault where the wounded were but something stopped her. Perhaps, it was knowing that those men had been discussing her, speaking of her and de Royans in the same breath. They knew she'd been a fool. Evidently, everyone knew she'd been a fool by allowing de Royans to charm her. Nay, she couldn't go down to the vault and face those men. She was too embarrassed to do that.

The spiral stairs led up to the second floor of Bowes where her old bedchamber was. It was still there, as she'd left it, because de Royans hadn't let any of his knights sleep there. He'd kept it just the way it was and she entered the chamber, shutting the chamber door and bolting it. She needed to be alone in her chamber, surrounded by her beloved possessions. She was too ashamed to face anyone at the moment and, in particular, her sister. She couldn't even tell Jessamyn what a fool she'd made of herself.

Depressed, despondent, she went to the dark hearth, with just a few glowing embers at the bottom, and put a few pieces of wood into the ashes and piled some dead rushes around them. Using a flint and stone, she lit the rushes and, soon, a nice blaze was developing. An iron arm jutted out from the side of the hearth, used to hang pots so water could be heated, and that was exactly what she did – put a few ladlefuls of water from a bucket in the chamber into a small stone pot and then hung that on the arm to boil the water. She wanted some hot water to wash her hands and face and, perhaps, even use a rag on her body if she could find a bit of soap. She was going through the motions of being busy, trying to work through the heaviness of what was on her mind.

The water heated and she managed to locate a small piece of soap in her trunk that smelled of rosemary. Using the scrap of soap and a rag, she stripped down to her shift and proceeded to wash her arms, feet, hands, neck, and face. The heated water felt wonderful, soothing her body and her mind, just a bit, because all the while she considered what the knight had told her about Juston. He had asked her not to tell Juston what he'd said, but Emera was a forthright person. She spoke the truth and she wanted the truth. Juston had led her to believe that he was very interested in her but if it was an act, she wanted to confront him with it. Perhaps he would be truthful about it, perhaps not. There was only one way to find out.

There were still some of her garments and things left in her trunk that Juston's men hadn't packed up in the satchels she'd been given. A fresh shift was rolled up at the bottom, made of lamb's wool, and she put that on. Over it went a dark blue wool surcoat that had what were known as angel's wing sleeves – long sleeves that draped over the hands, keeping them warm. She put another surcoat over the blue one, this one green and with shorter sleeves, and the result was warm layers of clothing that looked quite fetching on her. Running a comb through her long, black hair, she braided it and tied it off at the bottom.

Warmed, and now with a sense of determination when it came to Juston, she left the chamber and returned to the vault. She knew that the soldiers would still be looking at her, knowing she'd made a fool of herself over de Royans, but she firmly decided to ignore them. She wouldn't give them the satisfaction of knowing that she knew *they* knew. Until she spoke with Juston and he explained his side of things, there was still hope she hadn't made a fool of herself, after all.

"Do you really believe he will come?"

The question came from Marcus, who hadn't been in town to see the encounter between Christopher, David, and the Durham knights. But it was clear that the encounter had concerned all of the knights who had gone into town and that was why he'd asked the question. It was Christopher who answered.

"If I were de Puiset, I would come," he said. "When an army lays siege to a fortress and manages to capture it, that is one thing. But when that same army sends men out into the neighboring towns and villages, that is a threat to everyone in Durham. De Puiset would be foolish if he did not act on this. The man needs to protect his bishopric."

Huddled at one end of a feasting table in the great hall, Juston and his men were in intense discussions about how they should react to the potential of a de Puiset attack. Marcus, as well as Maxton and Kress and Achilles, on the outside of what had happened in town, were trying to make sense of it.

"So he will come," Maxton said, leaning on his big arms as he faced the table. "It was only a matter of time, anyway. We had been expecting this since the messengers went out from Cotherstone. This is not any great shock, I would say. We will be prepared."

Juston, at the head of the table, listened to his knights go back and forth. Usually, they did all of the talking and he did all of the listening, only speaking to make the final decision. But in this instance, he had questions himself. He looked at Achilles.

"You have been overseeing the rebuild of the wall," he said. "Has the mortar set up sufficiently?"

Achilles shook his head. "It has not," he said. "There is too much moisture in the air still and the sun, although shining, has not been enough to help the mortar cure. I fear that wall will not hold should it be put to the test. However, the defenses are fortified with the pike sticks that de Lohr put up. The perimeter, I feel, is secure."

Juston sat at the table, hands folded, listening seriously. He began to shake his head. "This is not as I had hoped," he said. "I do not like being bottled up in a castle whose walls will tumble at the first bombardment."

Achilles lifted his big shoulders. "We have the moats to protect us," he said. "It will still be an extremely difficult task breaching the castle."

Juston sat on that statement for a few moments. It was clear that his mind was working. "Mayhap," he finally said. "Mayhap not. My instinct tells me to secure the fortress as best we can and then take the army out to meet de Puiset on open ground."

The knights were looking at him in various stages of puzzlement. "Leave the safety of the castle?" Kress repeated. "I must disagree, Juston. We remain inside and withstand de Puiset's attack. When he sees that he cannot breach the fortress, he will leave."

Juston looked at the man. "Keeping my army trapped within the walls of a compromised fortress would be foolish," he said. "Moreover, why should de Puiset leave when he is on the outside with unlimited resources? He will have the patience and the supplies to wait until the wall fails and the fortifications can be breached. He can be resupplied time and time again, while we remain inside with our supplies dwindling, simply waiting for that wall to crumble and for de Puiset to overrun us. Nay, I will not do that. If the walls were solid, that would be one thing, but they are not. If we remain here in a siege, it will be our deaths. We will meet the man on the field of battle."

Kress was in disagreement. He sighed faintly and sat back, unwilling to argue with Juston when the man seemed so convinced. A few of the other knights, Gillem and Erik included, seemed inclined to agree with Kress. It was Christopher finally who spoke up.

"I must agree with Juston," he said, directing his conversation not only to Juston but to the rest of the men. "We will have heavy patrols between us and Auckland. When they see the army approach, they will notify us and we will be prepared to move out. We'll secure the fortress and take most of the army out to fend off de Puiset. We'll chase the man away before he can reach Bowes."

"That is a foolish tactic, de Lohr," Maxton rumbled.

Christopher focused on him. "Why?" he asked. "Because we choose to give ourselves more of a fighting chance by meeting de Puiset out in the open? What Juston said is correct. This is a compromised fortress. If we have the opportunity to remove the army and set up a defensive line rather than remain inside walls that will surely fail, then why would we not take that chance? Moreover, de Puiset will have unlimited opportunity to resupply while we slowly starve to death and the walls give out under his bombardment. I do not plan to die here, Maxton."

Maxton gave Christopher a rather disapproving look, but when it came to those two, they were used to disparaging looks and remarks between them. It was simply the way of things between them and although no one had ever thrown a punch or, worse, raised a sword, everyone was aware of the contention. But Christopher and Maxton were too professional to let it go any further than that.

But Juston knew it was better not to take chances with them. Christopher could wipe out ten men in a sword fight and not even raise a sweat, while Maxton wouldn't be quite so noble about it. He would cut low and use tactics that some might consider unsavory. He would do whatever he needed to do in order to win. Therefore, it was simply better not to let things get out of hand.

"Nor do I intend to die here," Juston said. "When I die, it will be in a battle where I know I have done my best to survive it. That means we do not trap ourselves in this fortress that I spent three weeks battering. Therefore, my decision is as follows – we prepare to move our army out of Bowes and meet de Puiset somewhere between here and Gainford. We will set the lines and dare him to come over to us. Max, send several patrols out. I want them watching all roads leading in from Auckland and all river crossings. At the first sign of de Puiset and his army, they are to return to us with all due haste so we have time to move our army into position. Is that clear?"

Whether or not Maxton agreed was not at issue. He'd been given a direct command and he was sworn to obey it.

"It is," he said, resigned.

Satisfied, Juston turned to Christopher. "You and your brother and Burton will begin preparing the men to move out," he said. "This is no different than the situation a few days ago when we thought Richmond would be moving against us except that instead of waiting for them to come to us, we will go to them. We sent men to Brough and to Netherghyll, if you will recall, and I expect to hear from Brough very soon. We will continue on the assumption that they are still moving in to reinforce us."

Christopher nodded. "Aye, my lord."

With that settled, Juston turned to the rest of his men. "Kress, you and Achilles make ready the supplies to take with the army, leaving enough behind for those who remain in the castle," he said. "Erik and Gillem, you two will see to the wagons and the animals we will need. Anything we will take with us to an army encampment, you will also see to. Get with the quartermasters and make sure we are fully prepared. Are there any questions?"

The men shook their heads. Juston's gaze drifted across their faces, men he had served with for years, men he trusted with his life. He'd been in this position, many times, heading up a battle, preparing for it, knowing what lay ahead. He hadn't failed up to this point and he didn't intend to start now.

"And so, it comes," he said quietly. "This is a show of force, gentle knights. Make no mistake about it. We will defeat de Puiset and send him back to Auckland like a beaten child. This engagement will serve as a warning to anyone else who feels the need to move against us. After we meet de Puiset, we will take Cotherstone, as I had planned, and we will hold this road for Richard. With Brough Castle loyal to Richard, and Appleby, we will be the third and most valuable jewel in the crown along this road leading from the north into this part of England. With time, I would expect to move on Richmond and Auckland at some point. I will send word to Richard of our great victory here and our foothold, and he will be very proud of all of us. This is a glorious move for Richard and the future of England, so bear that in mind. We *must* triumph."

Juston's word meant a great deal. It was something that made him a great commander, the ability to put into context the value of certain situations. The men were fortified now, encouraged, and they had their orders. No longer were they waiting for an army to come to them. They, in fact, were going to rise to meet the incoming army and chase them back to where they came from.

As Juston had said, they must triumph.

Triumph or die trying.

CHAPTER SIXTEEN

EMERA MET JUSTON on the spiral stairs. She was going up just as he was coming down.

In fact, in the darkness and given the fact he was moving swiftly, he very nearly plowed into her and sent her tumbling. Only his quick reflexes saved her from falling back to the bottom of the stairs. She gasped in fright as he put his hands on her.

"Sweet Mary," she gasped, gripping the side of the stairwell. "I did not see you coming."

Juston let her go when he was sure she was stable. "I pray I did not injure you."

Emera shook her head. "You did not," she said, looking up at the man but not seeing much more than an outline in the darkness of the stairwell. "I am well."

"Where are you going?"

"I am going to the kitchen to see to the meal for the wounded."

He shifted direction, politely taking her elbow. "I will accompany you," he said. "I must speak with you."

And I must speak with you, she thought. But she didn't say what she was thinking. An afternoon down in the vault, focused on her duties, had helped calm her mind somewhat. At least now she could speak to him about Gillem's allegations without feeling an inordinate amount of resentment towards him. Even running into him unexpectedly in the stairwell didn't rattle her much to that regard.

In fact, as he took her elbow and helped her up the stairs, her heart began to flutter again and her palms began to sweat. It was the same reaction she'd always had to him as if there had been no terrible revelations from Gillem's lips. Still, she had to know the truth. As they emerged from the stairwell into the great hall, she spoke.

"What did you need to speak with me about?" she asked.

At this time of day, there was virtually no one in the great hall other than the servants. It was an hour or two away from meal time and Juston's men all had duties to attend to, even the lowliest soldier. Preparing for a coming battle would keep everyone busy. Therefore, Juston could answer her without fear of being overheard.

"I have just left a meeting with my men," he said, slowing his pace before eventually coming to a halt and facing her. It was then that he noticed she'd changed her clothing and combed her hair sometime over the course of the day. Never had he seen such a beautiful woman and it was difficult to stay on task. He would have much rather talked about her than of the subject he was about to broach. "As you know, we ran into a few of the Bishop of Durham's men in Gainford. That is why we returned to Bowes so quickly."

Emera nodded. "I know," she said. "At least, I heard Sir Christopher as he told you of his encounter with the bishop's knights. I understood that you did not want the bishop to try and attack our party before we could return to Bowes."

Juston nodded. "I apologize that I did not explain it to you fully at the time, but we were in a hurry," he said. "That is why I wanted to explain things to you now. There have been some… developments."

She was interested. "Oh?"

Thinking that perhaps they should sit for a few moments, he took her elbow and began leading her over to one of the big feasting tables, in fact, to the table he had so recently been sitting at with his knights.

"You are aware of the conversation I had with my men after the de Lohr brothers and Marcus Burton returned from Cotherstone," he said.

"You are aware that we believe messengers were sent out to Henry's supporters in the area when I began the siege at Bowes."

Emera remembered the great argument they'd had over that subject when he thought she'd been eavesdropping. She didn't want to enter into that discussion again, fearful to start another argument. "I recall," she said. "I did not run off and tell anyone if that is what you are wondering. I told you that I would not and I haven't."

He smiled thinly. "That is not what I was wondering," he said. "You have had no opportunity to leave the castle, so I know you've not run to tell anyone. I was simply bringing up that conversation to preface what I am about to tell you."

She wasn't sure that she believed him but she gave him the benefit of the doubt. "I see," she said. "Then in answer to your question, I remember all that was said. Why?"

He indicated for her to sit once they reached the table and she did. He sat down somewhat close to her. "Because that conversation ties in directly with what happened in Gainford today," he said. "We have been preparing for an assault by Henry's forces who want to reclaim the castle, but because de Puiset will know we have been in town this day, I fear it will hasten his response. He will think we are threatening all of Durham now, not just Bowes."

Emera considered that information. "I am not a fighting man so I do not know what, exactly, that means," she said. "Are you telling me you believe he will most certainly lay siege to Bowes now?"

Juston nodded. "That is exactly what I mean. But there is a problem – Bowes spent three weeks being bombarded by me. I damaged it severely. The western outer wall took a beating and we have been trying to repair it, but the mortar will not set because of the cold temperatures. That means it is very weak. If the castle is attacked, then I am not sure it could withstand it. It could be easily breached in spite of our precautions."

Emera thought that it all sounded rather frightening. "What will you do if de Puiset attacks, then?"

He sat forward in his seat, which coincidentally moved him closer to Emera. "I intend to take my army from Bowes and meet him on the field of battle somewhere away from here," he said, his voice softening. "I will take my army and form a defensive line he will not be able to pass. But that means that whoever is left here at Bowes risks remaining in a compromised fortress, with few men to protect it, should de Puiset overwhelm my army and make a run at the castle. It means... it means that I do not want you to remain here when I go to meet de Puiset. I want to send you and your sister south, to Netherghyll."

Emera looked at him in surprise. "Leave Bowes?"

"Aye."

She eyed him for a few long seconds and it was clear that she was deliberating his rather astonishing suggestion. "I am not sure...."

He cut her off. "Please, Emera. I am removing my entire army from Bowes. If it is attacked, it will fall. I do not want you here if that happens."

She was still clearly uncertain. "So you would send me to your home?"

He nodded. "Netherghyll is a vastly fortified castle and you would want for nothing," he said. "When de Puiset is tamed and Bowes is secure, I will come to you there."

It sounded as if he was suggesting that they could be together, or even that they *were* together, and that he had intentions that would lead to something permanent. Until the day she died, she would swear that both his manner and his words suggested such things. Gillem's words suddenly came back to her in an avalanche.

My sister bore his bastard... he is trying to do the same thing to you!

"Why?" she finally asked.

His brow furrowed. "What do you mean?"

She couldn't quite look him in the eye as she spoke; it was too upsetting, painful even. "Why would you return to me?" she asked. "All of those things we said to each other in Gainford... you told me you never had any intention of remarrying, Juston. You said many things that led me to believe there is to be no future between us. Why would you send me to Netherghyll? To become your concubine? You said that you found me beautiful and brilliant and brave. Did you only say that so I would bend to your will, so that I would agree to anything you demanded?"

He cleared his throat softly, almost nervously, and looked away from her. "I said them because they were true."

"Then all I can ever be to you is a concubine?"

"I never said you would be a concubine."

"Then *what*?"

He hung his head, sighing faintly. "I do not know yet."

"When will you know?"

"I told you – I do not know."

"Is this the same thing you told Gillem's sister before you took her to your bed?"

His head snapped to her, caught off-guard by a most unexpected question. The eyes flared for a moment, his mouth working, but he said nothing, at least not right away. But the spark of rage had ignited in the depths of his green eyes.

"Who told you that?" he finally asked.

She looked at him, then. "Does it matter?" she asked. "I have been told about Sybilla and the son you had with her. Did you tell her these things, too, and then when she became a burden, you discarded her?"

He stared at her, his eyes glittering with shock and outrage. He stood up, swiftly, and took a few stomping steps away from the table as if determined to leave her presence and not answer her question, but ultimately, he didn't leave. He raked his fingers through his hair angrily as he paced around, shaken.

"Gillem," he muttered. "He told you that, didn't he?"

Emera wasn't intimidated by his agitation in the least. By his reaction, she knew she hit on a vein of truth.

"It does not matter who told me," she said. "Is it the truth? That you had a child with Sybilla and refuse to marry her?"

Juston looked at her, his jaw ticking. "It is not your place to question my decisions or my motives."

"It is when you tell me you want to send me to Netherghyll and that you will come to me when the threat against Bowes is over," she pointed out. "Juston, you are behaving as if you want me to mean something to you. If you want the same behavior from me, then you must be honest with me."

"What I do and who I do it with is none of your affair."

Now, he was starting to rile her. He was being stubborn and defiant and, in her opinion, unreasonable. She had every right to defend herself from him if his motives were immoral. She was only trying to get to the truth of the matter but he refused to cooperate. The great and mighty Juston de Royans was being questioned, probably for the first time in his adult life, and he resented it. Standing up, Emera began to move away from the table.

"You are absolutely correct, it is none of my affair," she said crisply. "*You* are none of my affair. Therefore, I will remain at Bowes, come what may. I am not going anywhere regardless of the battles that might consume this place. I would rather stay here and be bombarded to death than go to Netherghyll to become your caged pet."

He snatched her by the arm before she could get away completely. "Stop," he commanded. "Stop before this gets out of control and we say things we do not mean. I do not wish to return to the first few days that we knew each other, Emera. I do not want to fight with you any longer."

She didn't struggle against him as he held her, but there was anger in the air. Breathing was coming heavily. "Then tell me the truth," she said. "That is all I require and I do not believe it is asking too much. Tell me why you did not marry Sybilla and tell me why you wish to send me to Netherghyll."

She was asking him to bare his soul, to discuss things with her he had never discussed with anyone. Juston de Royans' decisions were not to be questioned, ever, yet she was doing so. She was asking something of him. If he wanted something of her, then he knew he would have to answer her questions. Still, it was difficult. He wasn't sure he could do it.

"You ask too much," he muttered, letting her go. "I do not need to explain myself to you. Lest you forget, you are my prisoner. I can do with you as I wish."

She threw her hands in the air as if to wave all of that nonsense away. "We have been through all of that," she said snappishly. "Is that only what you want between us, Juston? I am your captive and you can do with me as you will? Or do you want something else, something that means something to us both? Would you have me come to you willingly or is it more gratifying for you to force me and feel my fear and hatred?"

He simply looked at her, his frustration mounting. Why did she have to be so difficult? Why couldn't she simply do as he asked?

"You ask about things that do not concern you," he repeated. "I have told you this before. You ask too many questions."

That only served to frustrate her further. "Where my life is concerned, I have every reason to. I have only heard one side of this story, Juston. I am asking to hear your side. Do you not trust me enough to tell me?"

Juston's jaw ticked furiously. Did he trust her? Oddly enough, he did. This had nothing to do with trust… did it? Was it possible that he was ashamed to tell her, ashamed that his lack of control beget a bastard? He didn't even know. But it was increasingly clear that he had to tell her something. He had to force it out.

"If you must know, I will tell you what happened so you do not believe me to be ignoble or careless," he said, his voice low. "Lady Sybilla and her brother attempted to trap me into marriage. She seduced me when I was drunk and conceived a child. Both she and her brother hoped I would marry her and when I refused, they went out of their way to tell people that I am a heartless bastard with no honor. Aye, I know what Gillem says about me. I am not a fool."

Some of Emera's anger faded as she listened to what turned out to be a rather terrible story. "That is dastardly!" she exclaimed softly. "Why do you permit him to serve you?"

Juston cocked an eyebrow. "Have you ever heard the old saying – keep your friends close and your enemies closer?"

"I have."

"I would rather have Gillem serve me than run off to an enemy and have him tell them all that he knows about me, my inner secrets, my tactics, and my men. Nay, it is better to keep Gillem close than let him run amok."

She understood, somewhat. "But he does not have good things to say about you."

"Then it was him who told you about Sybilla."

There was no use in denying it. "He attempted to warn me off."

"Did he?"

She sighed faintly, bewildered. "I do not know," she said. "All I know is that I will not be your concubine."

"I have never said you would be. I have never even used that word."

The air was calming between them now, enough so that their conversation was starting to have some meaning once again. Emera's expression was almost beseeching.

"Then *what*?" she begged. "You would not tell me earlier, when we were alone. You flattered me. You kissed me. You led me to believe you were attracted to me but in the same breath you told me you had no intention of marrying. If you want to send me to Netherghyll, then what else am I to be? A trophy from your conquest of Bowes?"

His gaze lingered on her a moment before looking away. He couldn't look into her eyes without feeling vastly confused. He knew what he wanted. Why couldn't he simply tell her?

"I do not know," he muttered. "All I know is that I want to protect you from what is to come. I would kill any man who would try to harm you. I want to send you to Netherghyll to keep you safe. Mayhap when the crisis is over and I return to Netherghyll, I will be able to think more clearly. Is that not a sufficient reason for you?"

Emera could see that he seemed depressed. Confused, even. The man had the weight of a prince of England on his shoulders and when that should have been his focus, he had a woman badgering him about his motives. Aye, she had been badgering him. She knew that. But she also knew she couldn't go to Netherghyll and wait for him. Once she went there, she was giving him permission to treat her however he wanted to. She wasn't going to be at his beck and call.

She would not let him do that to her. She would not let him break her heart.

"As much as I appreciate the fact that you wish to protect me, I must decline your gracious offer," she said. "Mayhap it is best that I simply go to the charity hospital as I had originally planned. Before you think me ungrateful or stubborn, please understand that is not my intention. The truth is that I am not your responsibility. As you have said, I am your prisoner. I will not go to your home where you would grow weary of having me as your burden. And what if, by chance, you do marry again? Do you believe your wife would allow you to keep a grown woman about her house? Of course she would not. I would rather not enter into a situation that could be uncomfortable for us both. I will remain here at Bowes until the threat of de Puiset has passed and then you may have a few of your men escort me to the charity hospital in Sherburn."

He didn't like what she was saying at all. "I do not view you as a burden."

"Not now, but you may."

His frustration was returning. "You do not seem to understand that Bowes will not be a safe place for you. Let me send you and your sister to Netherghyll and then when the threat has passed, we shall... speak on your desire to go to the charity hospital."

"Nay. I shall remain here. I will not go to Netherghyll."

His frustration grew. "Do you seriously not understand that I am attempting to protect you?"

They were starting to go in circles now and the conversation was becoming painful for her. He wouldn't admit to any feelings for her whatsoever. Therefore, Emera was coming to think he had none. It was all in her mind, as she'd reasoned before. She was finished discussing any of this with him because it was futile; he wanted something to play with. She would not allow that to happen. Already, it was tearing at her heart, like claws, knowing that she would have to distance herself from him. Anything else and she might possibly agree to go to Netherghyll simply to be near him. She wasn't going to be one of those women, so desperate to be with the man they loved that they would be with him under any condition, even the lack of a marriage.

The man they loved.

How could she possibly love him?

"As I said, I appreciate your concern, but it is not necessary," she said crisply, averting her gaze because she was certain she would burst into tears if she looked at him. "Thank you for informing me of what is to happen with de Puiset. I will set up the great hall so that if you need to evacuate your wounded, you may send them to me and I will tend them. If you will excuse me now, I must see to the meal for the wounded."

She moved away from him, heading for the keep entry, and this time he didn't try to stop her. He watched her walk away, hating himself for being unable to tell her what was in his heart. With every step she took away from him, he felt his resistance being beaten down further and further.

He wanted her with him. He couldn't stand the thought of her being away from him. He wanted to see her smile, hear her laughter, and, aye, even spar with her now and again. She was a most worthy sparring partner. Traits that had initially repulsed him were not traits he liked. Great Bleeding Christ, what was not to like about her? He wanted to send her back to Netherghyll because he wanted her safe, so she could be with him for always. Did that mean he loved her? Or he could potentially love her? Was it possible his frozen heart was thawing?

All he knew was that he couldn't let her go. If opening himself up to her was the only way to make her stay, then he would have to force himself. That mammoth pride that he carried around had to be pushed aside. If he didn't, he would lose her.

"Emera," he called after her. "Wait. Please… just wait."

Emera was nearly to the door. There were tears in her eyes but she dashed them away, unwilling for him to see how upset she was. "Aye?" she responded evenly.

Juston moved towards her, his gaze on her lowered head. His mouth was dry, his heart pounding, as he labored to bring forth the words.

"When my wife was alive, I told her that I loved her every day," he murmured. "I know what it is like to love someone, Emera. I also know what it is like to lose that. I swore I would never let myself feel those unbridled emotions ever again because it was too painful to deal with the loss. I can tell you that I care for you. Aye, I do. I want to learn to love you but I want you to give me that opportunity. I cannot do it in a day, a week, or mayhap even a month, but I *am* capable of such things. All I am asking is that you give me the chance to unfreeze that which has been frozen in me – that part of me that was a husband once, a father. If anyone was worthy of being loved again, by me, it would be you. But I beg your patience in this matter while I sort this all out in my mind. I have some healing and some growing to do. That is all I am asking – patience."

Emera kept her gaze averted as he spoke and the tears she'd so recently dashed away returned with a vengeance. She blinked and they splattered. By the time she turned around to look at him, they were rolling down her cheeks. A smile of the most radiant magnificence spread across her lips as she gazed into his uncertain expression.

"I am not asking you to love me tomorrow, Juston," she said hoarsely. "Because I, too, know I could love you given time. I am already very fond of you. If you believe we have a future and your intentions are honorable, then that is all I wish to hear. I will be patient as you have asked. And there is nothing I will not do to make you happy."

He smiled in return, with some relief in his expression now. "My intentions are honorable."

"I believe you."

"Then you will go to Netherghyll?"

Still smiling, she shook her head. "Nay," she said. "My place is with you. I must remain at Bowes in case you need me. I can tend wounded and I can help defend the castle. You need help and I intend to give it."

He could see there was no way around that. She was determined to remain. With a heavy sigh, he shook his head and went to her, wrapping his enormous arms around her and holding her close. He could feel her arms go around him as well and it was the most satisfying feeling he'd ever known. In fact, at this moment, he couldn't recall ever feeling so content and whole, as if Emera had been a piece of himself that he'd been searching for since the loss of Lizette.

Certainly, Lizette had been a piece of him as well, a piece that had been lost and, through time, gradually healed over. Emera represented something he never thought he'd feel again and the gratitude he felt, the sheer joy, was unimaginable. Rocking her gently, he planted a tender kiss on her forehead.

"You are by far the most frustrating and stubborn woman I have ever encountered," he said, kissing her forehead again. "But your bravery and your loyalty are truly humbling. Never did I imagine I would ever be so fortunate to have someone so devoted to me."

Wrapped up in his arms, Emera collapsed against him, feeling his warmth and strength. It was enough to cause her knees to weaken, her heart so alight with happiness that she never wanted the moment to end.

"Then you will let me stay?" she asked, muffled, against his tunic.

"Do I have a choice?"

"I do not believe so."

"Neither do I."

She giggled and she could hear Juston laughing, low in his throat. It was more of a rumble, really, something that shook his entire body. Lifting her head, she put her hands on his face, gazing up into his eyes.

"Please believe me when I say I am not trying to be stubborn," she said quietly. "I simply could not leave you in your hour of need. It is my duty to remain here and help. I would be miserable if you forced me away. I would find some way to return."

Juston had to admit that he was very flattered that she would be so determined to remain by his side. This proud, stubborn woman had given him her loyalty and affection. Surely there was nothing more he could want for.

Except *her.*

He wanted her.

Bending over, he picked her up, gazing deeply into her eyes as he did so. There was so much emotion in his heart that it was difficult for him to find the words, but his expression told Emera everything. Perhaps the man had difficulty speaking of his feelings, but they were there. All she wanted to hear was that they were there and that he felt for her as she felt for him. At this moment, she belonged to him completely and, come what may, she would remain by his side forever. He wanted very much for the opportunity to love her.

She would give him that chance.

Emera buried her face in his shoulder, arms around his neck, as he carried her up the spiral stairs to the master's chamber.

Entering the chamber, Juston shut the door behind him and when he put Emera onto the bed, this time, she didn't crawl away or try to hide. Her arms were still around his neck even as he put her onto the bed, as if she was unable to let him go. He was warm and musky, his powerful arms causing her to swoon, and even when he moved to remove her clothing, she didn't stop him. She couldn't. It was as if all of her resistance had fled and knowing the man had feelings for her made all of the difference in the world.

For once, she wanted to be touched and loved. She wanted Juston's hands upon her. If her taste of him earlier in the day was any indication, she knew that whatever he wanted to do to her, whatever he was planning, was meant to be.

It was meant to happen.

Juston was kissing her now, forcing her back onto the bed even as he unfastened the ties on her surcoat. She could feel his hands on her waist, yanking loose the ties as his kisses grew feverish. She might have actually though he was trembling. Was he? Or was she? She was breathing so heavily, trying to catch her breath between heated kisses, that it was difficult to tell. All she knew was that there was something building in her chest, a liquid fire of sorts, that she had no control over. Every time Juston kissed her, the fire grew.

Panting… gasping… the surcoat suddenly came over her head, followed by the second surcoat that was under it. Then there was nothing left between her and Juston but her lamb's wool shift, soft and delicate. His mouth left hers, seeking her neck, her collarbone, and points farther south. He was kissing the swell of her bosom with heated lips as his hands snaked under the shift, lifting it.

Well she remembered his hot hand to her thigh, his flesh against hers, and she was not disappointed with her second experience. It was something she could learn to crave. His lips left her bosom and she could feel him fumbling about, half of his monstrous weight on top of her, still mostly in his clothing. Then his head was underneath her shift, his heated mouth on her belly, kissing and suckling the flesh, and Emera heard herself groan in delight. He dragged his tongue over her rib cage, under her breasts, before finally capturing a tender nipple in his mouth.

Emera gasped and bucked beneath him, hardly realizing he had pulled her legs apart to settle some of his weight off of her and onto the bed. She had her hands on his head, buried beneath her shift, experiencing his mouth on her breasts with the utmost delight. *Sweet Mary, is this what I have run from all of these years? Is this what I was so afraid of, the touch of a man?* She felt shameless and wanton, but she didn't care. Legs spread wide open, she gave herself over to him completely.

It was a delirium from which there was no return.

Fingers were touching her private core again, that warm, moist junction between her legs. It was a sensation she had folded to the first time and this time was no exception except the fingers were stroking her, touching her in a way that made her entire body quiver. Juston suddenly bit down on her left breast, not hard enough to break the skin but hard enough to cause her some pleasure-pain and Emera felt a big finger as it entered her body, acquainting her with his intimate touch.

Instead of being afraid of it, she welcomed it. It filled a need in her, somehow, a need she never even knew she had. She rolled her pelvis forward, into his hand, and he put a second finger into her. It was an oddly full sensation but it didn't deter her. She was enjoying it.

More kisses, more suckling on her breasts followed as his fingers probed her. Eyes closed, Emera was adrift on a sea of lust when he removed his fingers and she immediately felt a strange sort of emptiness. She needed his touch, for whatever he was doing to her was causing more pleasure than she had ever known to exist. Gentle kisses, intimate fingers. But what came next was something she wasn't prepared for.

Her young, nubile body was primed for his body to mate with hers, her woman's center swollen and primed for his entry. The next Emera realized, his weight came down on hers and between her legs, she felt something full and hot and hard thrusting into her virginal body. She was so slick, and he was so eager, than one full thrust had him nearly halfway into her, breaching her maidenhead. Emera felt the sharp sting of possession but he didn't give her time to react. He drew back and thrust again, so hard that he drove himself to the hilt.

Emera was seized with the pain of his thrust and she cried out, her hands biting into his arms as he braced himself over her. But his mouth covered hers, suckling her, kissing her deeply, as he coiled his buttocks and thrust into her again and again, a steady rhythm building. The pain that Emera had felt was quickly dulled, replaced by a sensation she could hardly describe. Where their loins came together, a fire had ignited and she swore she felt the sparks every time they came together.

"Juston," she breathed. "Please… Sweet Mary, we cannot…."

Juston wouldn't let her talk. He continued to coil his buttocks, thrusting into her, as she clawed at him.

"This is how we were meant to be," he breathed, biting gently at her lower lip. "Give me a son, Emera, and I shall never deny him. I swear to you that I shall belong to you and only you, forever."

She groaned softly as he plunged deeply into her, grinding his pelvis against hers, causing sparks to fly in earnest. When he did it a second time, she felt an explosion in her loins the likes of which she had never experienced before, tremors radiating throughout her body and exploding through her mouth with a cry.

After that, she remembered little. Dazed, her body was rocked by Juston's continuing thrusts until he took one hard, final thrust and she heard him grunt as he released his seed deep into her womb. But Emera continued to lay there, in a stupor, her arms around his neck, holding on to him so tightly it was as if she was afraid to let him go. She could feel his body weight atop her, his lips by her ear. His steady breathing filled her brain. It was enough to lull her into a deep, exhausted sleep.

When she finally awoke some time later, it was to an empty bed, a stoked fire, and bread and cheese on the nearby table.

CHAPTER SEVENTEEN

Auckland Castle (manor house, seat of the Bishops of Durham)

T HE RECEPTION ROOM of Auckland Castle was a vast and lavish forum, resplendent with furs upon the floor, imported tapestries on the walls, and braziers placed around the room that not only burned peat to stave off the chill, but incense to give the room a smell like those in the bathhouses of Rome. Expensive myrrh and sandalwood filled the air which, combined with the smoke from the braziers and the open flame in the enormous hearth that serviced the chamber, created a nearly unbreathable layer that hung heavy in the room. It choked the throat and burned the eyes.

But it was meant to display the wealth of the owner. Auckland Castle was really a fortified manor, a very large and opulent residence, for the Bishopric of Durham and the reception room, or great hall, was the throne room. There was, in fact, a throne at one end of the chamber, a magnificent piece of carved wood that had been brought to Auckland all the way from Rome in the back of a wagon that had taken thirteen months to make the trek. It was the chair of the man who ruled the See of Durham with powers given to him by the pope and by God, and Hugh de Puiset took those powers very seriously. He used them for everything he could get his hands on.

But there were times when things did not go his way.

This was one of those times. Faced with five knights who had returned from Gainford with a concerning tale, de Puiset wasn't thrilled with what he was being told. It was bad enough that Bowes Castle had been taken by Richard's forces because de Puiset had lost a revenue stream in the tribute de la Roarke paid him from those he stole from, but now it was evident that the army who now held Bowes was filtering into nearby Gainford. Nay, he didn't like that news at all.

Obese, with a pug nose, very expensive robes embroidered with gold, and hair worn in the style of *tonsure*, or the shaving of most of his scalp, Hugh de Puiset was a man who was brilliant in some areas but not in others. One area he was not brilliant at was military might, or tactics, even though he commanded a fine army. He didn't like to use it, for various reasons, which is why he hadn't sent his men to counter the siege on Bowes. That would have meant spending money and losing resources, so he'd had to weigh the value of the lost revenue stream from Bowes against losing men and material. The latter had won over.

Yet, the news from Gainford described the army from Bowes becoming bold and expanding. The name behind that expansion was even more concerning – the High Sheriff of Yorkshire. Aye, de Puiset knew the man and his army. Everyone in England did. The *Lord of Winter*, Juston de Royans was called, and de Puiset wasn't happy in the least to hear that de Royans had made his way into his bishopric. Misery was reflected on his round face.

"De Royans," he muttered. "You are certain of this?"

The knight with the bushy beard nodded. "He was identified to me by one of his knights, Your Grace," he said. "Juston de Royans is now in possession of Bowes and we saw his men in Gainford."

De Puiset sighed heavily. "Then the man is becoming bold," he said. "First Bowes, now Gainford."

"Auckland may be next," the dirty-beard knight said anxiously. "Your Grace, we are all aware that you did not wish to aid Bowes during the siege, but if de Royans is becoming bold, then there is no telling what his next target will be. We *must* act."

De Puiset knew that. He wasn't thrilled with it, but he knew it. "We cannot have the man come to Auckland," he muttered. "Worse still, what if he chooses to invade all of Durham? We received word those weeks ago from Cotherstone regarding the siege of Bowes and the messenger told us that men had also been sent to Richmond and Carlisle. What of them? Do we know if Carlisle or Richmond have moved to regain Bowes?"

As usual, the bishop was looking for others to do his work, to protect him. The knight with the dirty beard shook his head. "There is no way of knowing, Your Grace, unless we send word to them," he said, trying to stress the urgency of the situation. "That will take time. We do not have much time if de Royans is expanding his reach."

De Puiset nodded reluctantly. He had truly hoped this moment would not come but it had. Ever since the siege of Bowes, he had been praying that would be the end of it, that whoever held Bowes would not become greedy and invade more of his territory. But his prayers to that regard had not been answered.

"I suppose you are correct," he said, clearly unhappy. "We must protect ourselves against Richard's invasion. Moreover, if I do not act, Henry will once again view me as weak, as he has in the past when I have failed to move swiftly enough against Scot raids. If I do not move to quell Richard and his servant, de Royans, then Henry would once again view me with disfavor. I have worked too hard over the years to rebuild the man's faith in me."

The knight with the dirty beard was greatly encouraged. "Then we move, Your Grace?"

De Puiset gave the command he'd been dreading. "We move. Gather my military advisors. We move immediately to Bowes and expel de Royans from her innards."

That was what the Durham knights wanted to hear. Finally, a favorable decision from de Puiset that would see him defending what belonged to him and purging Durham of Richard's surge against Henry's properties and loyalists. They weren't honestly sure if de Puiset would act, being that he tended to be reluctant to enter into any sort of military conflict, so this was a great and significant moment as far as they were concerned.

Finally, they could act.

After that, the Durham knights scattered, gathering the bishop's military advisor, men who were surprised to hear of the situation and of de Puiset's response. By night, the military council had convened and by morning, the bishop's army was being amassed. Men were outfitted, food and materials loaded into wagons, and there was a sense of purpose in the air. Richard had sent de Royans to destroy Henry's hold in Durham and it was time for the Bishop of Durham to hold his ground. It was time for him to purge de Royans from Bowes and take back the castle.

Something that was far easier said than done.

Bowes Castle

"BROUGH IS NOT coming."

It was a blustery and cloudy morning as Juston and his knights stood at the gatehouse of Bowes. One of their own messengers had just arrived, a man they'd sent to Brough Castle to ask for assistance. The words out of his mouth were not words that Juston had wanted to hear.

Having been roused from a warm, cozy bed with Emera sleeping soundly against him, Juston had been summoned by Gart with whisperings of the returned messenger. By the time he reached the gatehouse, all of the knights were there, lingering, hovering anxiously.

The news was not good.

"Why not?" Juston demanded. "Why will they not come?"

The messenger, heavily armed, was purposely not wearing de Royans colors. If the man was captured, it was to protect him against those who might be enemies of Richard and, subsequently, de Royans. He was a seasoned soldier and had ridden very hard for the past few days. Consequently, he was filthy, cold, and exhausted. He tried to explain his message without sounding as if he was miserable and whining.

"Because Brough is under attack, my lord," the messenger told him. "She was under attack when I reached her. I cannot be sure, but it looked to me as if it was Carlisle."

Juston's eyebrows flew up, as did Christopher's and nearly every other knight's. *Attack!* "Carlisle?" Juston hissed in disbelief as he turned to look at Christopher. "Great Bleeding Christ… why would Carlisle go after Brough?"

Christopher shook his head. "I can only speculate," he said. "It is entirely possible that Carlisle was alerted to the siege of Bowes and had come to aid them. We were told that Cotherstone had sent out messengers, several of them. We speculated that some had been sent north to Carlisle."

"It seems as if that was true."

"Carlisle's army would have to pass by Brough Castle on the way to defend Bowes."

"And Brough stopped them from going any further," David suggested what they were all thinking. "Brough guards the mouth of the pass where the road leads to Bowes. They would not let Carlisle pass."

It seemed like the most logical assumption. It was a stunning realization. "Then Brough saved us," Maxton said. "They saved us from facing Carlisle in battle."

Juston could only nod. "It would seem so," he said. "They held them there and prevented them from moving any further into the pass. Carlisle would have made a good attempt at destroying us, to be certain. They carry far more numbers than we do. But the fact remains that they are well south of Carlisle and have left the castle open to the Scots if they brought the bulk of their army south. That would not have been a smart move, which leads me to believe they did not bring their entire army."

"There were at least a thousand men or more doing battle at

Brough," the messenger said. "They had already established an encampment and the surrounding area had been picked clean. It looked as if they had been there a week or two at least."

Juston looked at the man. "A thousand men from Carlisle is *not* their entire army. Brough has three times that. No wonder they've been able to hold them."

It was all very startling information, something that changed their outlook on the situation considerably. Juston considered everything he'd been told and what had been speculated. He rubbed his hands together against the chill of the morning, contemplating his next step.

"So," he said after a moment, "we cannot expect reinforcements from Brough and I will assume the same from Appleby Castle because it, too, is along the same road, only further north of Brough. I will assume they tangled with Carlisle as well. Chris, what about Pendragon Castle? It is not too terribly far from here but it is very small. They normally do not carry more than a few hundred men at any given time. I wonder if they would send men to staff Bowes when I take the bulk of my army away to meet Durham."

Christopher shook his head. "Pendragon belongs to the Lords of Coverdale," he said. "Although they are loyal to Richard, Pendragon guards the road between Brough to the north and the Wensleydale pass to the south. In fact, that road comes out of the pass just south of Richmond, so I would not think the commander of Pendragon would be willing or able to supply us with men. Richmond is still a threat. Truly, Juston, we have enough men – even if we leave two hundred men here to guard the castle, that still means we will be fielding over one thousand against Durham."

Juston knew all of that but Christopher merely confirmed his own thoughts on the matter. So... Brough had prevented Carlisle from coming down on them. Pendragon wasn't an option because she was needed to hold that small pass for Richard. Juston could still send to Netherghyll for reinforcements but they were at least four days away, if not more. He didn't think they had that much time. Something told him Durham was coming, and coming soon.

Juston looked around at the men at his command; the de Lohr brothers, inarguably two of the finest knights to ever walk the earth, and Marcus Burton, a genius in his own right. Then there were Maxton and Kress and Achilles, his Unholy Trinity, men who would fight and die for him without question. He joked about their darkness, the edginess that each one of them seemed to have, but that edginess was a fuel for their talents.

Finally, there were Gart and Erik and Gillem. Odd how his knights seemed to travel in threes. Gart wasn't even a knight yet but he was treated like one and he could fight like one. There was no one more talented than young Forbes. Erik came very close, however, and he was a full-fledged knight, a man of honor and intelligence.

Then there was Gillem who, of course, had his own issues with Juston. Juston had to admit that he'd considered putting Gillem out front in a battle, many times, with the hope that he would catch a blade he could not defend himself from, but the truth was that Gillem was excellent in battle and to lose him would be a loss felt, indeed, simply for his skill and strength. It was an odd dynamic between them but as long as Juston could maintain control over the man, he was satisfied.

These were the men in his stable, the finest stable of knights that had surely served any lord. Juston was proud of them all, proud that such talented and loyal men were sworn to him. Now they were facing something that was possibly more dangerous than anything they'd faced in a very long time. He knew what he had to do.

And so did his men.

"Erik," he turned to de Russe. "When you came here, it was under Richard and Eleanor's instruction, but I am sure they did not realize what a serious situation you were entering. Therefore, you will take Tristan and go south to Netherghyll. Keep the boy there. Right now, the fortress is commanded by one of my senior soldiers. I will send you with a missive to him that will put you in charge of the fortress until I return. Keep the boy safe there and remain until you hear further word from me. Do you understand?"

Erik frowned. "But, Juston...."

"That is my command."

A command that clearly frustrated the knight. He looked around at the other men, who were looking back at him expectantly. *Expecting* him to obey. De Royans didn't give orders that were meant to be refuted. But Erik didn't want to go.

"Do you truly think it wise to be down one knight when you anticipate going into battle, my lord?" he asked, giving it one last try. "Tristan will be locked up in the keep, safe from harm. You *need* me."

Juston smiled faintly. "Of course I need you," he said. "But that boy is more important than I am. You must remove him immediately."

Erik was stubborn. He shook his head, clearly displeased. "Please, my lord. You must...."

Juston put up a hand to cut him off. He eyed the messenger, still standing there, so exhausted that he was trembling.

"Go inside and eat something," he told the messenger. "Find a corner to sleep in and rest. Your services have been greatly appreciated."

The messenger nodded swiftly. "Thank you, my lord."

As the soldier staggered off towards the keep, Juston maintained silence among his men for a few moments longer to ensure no one could hear their conversation. From this point on, the subject matter would be very private, indeed.

"Gillem," Juston looked to the red-haired knight. "Go with the messenger and see if there is anything more he knows that he has forgotten to tell us. He seems very exhausted; it is possible that something has slipped his mind. Report back to me after you are convinced he has told you everything."

Gillem couldn't help but notice he was the only knight being sent away. It was an insult as far as he was concerned but he begrudgingly followed the messenger as the man headed for the keep. Once he was far enough away, Juston spoke again.

"There is something you should all know about the lad Erik

brought with him," he said quietly, looking around the host of curious faces. "Some of you may already know this, but for those of you who do not, the young boy that accompanied Erik is none other than the son of Henry and Princess Alys of France. I am sure you are all well aware that Alys has been Henry's mistress for some time and there has always been the rumor that she bore Henry a child, but it seems those rumors are confirmed. Richard and Eleanor are now in possession of the child and they sent him north with Erik, to me, for safe keeping. But now it would seem it is not safe to remain here so that is why I am asking Erik to take the boy south to Netherghyll. You will, of course, never repeat what you have been told but I am telling you this so you understand that young boy's life is to be protected above all else."

Everyone was registering various level of surprise at the news but no one commented other than to cast their expressions at each other, silently confirming their shock at such information. *Henry's bastard son!* It was astonishing to all concerned, a rumor that, for once, had been born in truth. Eventually, Maxton spoke.

"I agree with you, Juston," he said. "That lad's worth is immeasurable. Do they intend to ransom him to Henry?"

Juston shrugged. "This I cannot tell you," he said. "With Eleanor involved, I would say ransoming the boy is not out of the question but, more than likely, she and Richard will threaten him somehow in order to force Henry to do their bidding. They are not beyond such things."

That was the truth. Eleanor, in some ways, was far more ruthless than her son and threatening a child, if it would gain her what she wanted in the end, was a definite possibility.

"Then the lad should not be in a castle that is facing a potential siege," Maxton said. "If something happened and he was injured, or worse, the ax of Eleanor would fall on your neck. She would have your head for it and Richard could not protect you."

Juston glanced at Erik. "Are you hearing this?" he asked. "I will take the fall if anything happens to the boy, not you. Therefore, you will take him out of here before midday. Gather your things, ready your mounts, and head for Netherghyll."

Erik knew he had no choice. He glanced at the knights around him before finally looking to Juston.

"Very well," he said with great reluctance. "I will go. But I will not take the road to Netherghyll that passes close to Richmond; I will travel another way. It will take me longer to reach Netherghyll."

"So long as you reach it."

Upset, Erik left the group, trudging back towards the keep as the wind picked up around them and the sky began to darken. A storm was approaching. Juston glanced up at the heavens, sensing the change in the weather, before returning his attention to his men.

"You had your orders last night," he said. "Nothing has changed. Durham is still coming and we must still meet him. Continue along with your tasks but I should like to have the army prepared to move out by dawn. Chris, you will select the men to remain here. You told me that thirteen hundred and forty-three men survived the initial battle. Of that group, leave two hundred of them here, including twenty-five archers. They may be needed if there is a siege. Everyone else goes with us, so ensure the men are prepared."

"Who are you leaving in command of the castle, Juston?" Marcus, standing next to Christopher, asked.

Juston's gaze lingered on him. "Are you volunteering?"

"I am *not*."

Juston knew it was going to be difficult to convince one of them to remain behind in command. These were fighting men and if there was a fight, they wanted to be in it. He didn't like that whoever he chose would cause him grief about it, much as Erik had just done. They were anxious now, smelling the scent of battle. In fact, knowing that the man he chose to remain behind would resist his wishes irritated him greatly.

"Then if you are not volunteering, I shall make the decision," he said, his manner bordering on snappish. "I wish I could take all of you into battle with me, but the truth is that there needs to be someone here in command. Since Gillem is not here, let it be him. Someone tell him and if he says one word to the contrary, I will lash him to the walls of the vault and leave him there to rot. He will remain in command of the castle because, God help us, if Durham is able to move past us, I will need a seasoned knight here to hold the castle. Now, the rest of you, on with your tasks."

With that, he turned on his heel and headed for the keep. The wind whistled through the bailey, blowing his tunic around as he went. In the gatehouse, the knights were pretending to move away but the truth was that they were not. They were still lingering on the most eventful news that had been delivered to them. Only when de Royans was out of earshot did they dare speak on it.

"Henry and Alys' son?" David finally blurted to his brother. "I cannot believe it!"

Christopher was clearly astonished as well. "Juston did not mention anything to me," he said, "and he usually tells me things of that nature. I wonder why he did not tell me."

"Because no one was supposed to know," Gart said. He was listening to the astounded voices and, in Christopher's case, perhaps offended voices. "Erik told me and Gillem after he'd had a little too much to drink. He swore us to secrecy. The lad doesn't know his parentage, Chris. I suppose Juston felt the fewer people that knew, the better. But now you know."

It was a heady realization. "Do you have any idea the price that lad could command?" Marcus muttered, leaning against the cold stone of the gatehouse. "To sell the lad off to Richard's supporters? To Henry's supporters, even? That lad is more valuable than anything in England, I'd wager to say. Mayhap it is a good thing he does not know his parentage. Such bloodlines are a curse."

That was the truth. The knights mulled over the true identity of the lad in the vault for a few moments longer before shifting their focus. There were tasks at hand to complete, things that would not wait, and they soon began to break off from the group, heading off to accomplish the tasks that had been assigned to them. There was a battle to fight, one that required their complete attention, and a small lad bearing royal bloodlines from England and France could be pondered at a later time. In fact, no one envied that child his position in life. As Marcus had said, it was a curse.

Christopher and Gart were the last to leave the gatehouse, but Gart had planned it that way. Before Christopher could walk away completely, Gart put his hand on the man's arm.

"Chris," he said quietly. "Wait a moment. I have need to speak with you."

Christopher paused, his attention on Juston's squire. "Of course," he said. Then, he grinned. "If you think to ask me if I am upset with you for the fact that you knew about the boy and I did not, the answer is nay. But I am concerned that de Russe ran off at the mouth as he did with drink in him. If he is harboring such a secret, then he should watch his drink intake."

Gart nodded. "I know," he said. "He and I have had those discussions before, even before the event of the boy. In any case, that is not what I wished to speak with you about. It is Juston I am concerned with."

"Why?"

Gart cleared his throat softly before proceeding. "When the messenger came this morning, I went looking for Juston," he said. "I assumed he was in the master's chambers and I was correct. But he was not alone."

Christopher didn't see anything shocking in that. "A woman?"

"Aye."

"That is not terribly unusual."

"It was Lady Emera."

That brought Christopher some pause. "I see," he said. "He has shown a great deal of interest in her since our arrival. In fact, the night we captured Bowes and she was brought to him, he tried to force her to service him. She refused. Now I see she is no longer refusing him."

Gart could see the humor in Christopher's eyes. He wasn't feeling it. "There is something more to this," he said. "I have served Juston for many years. I know his moods. I have seen him with women; we all have. But this... this is different. I cannot tell you how different, but there is something more there than is usual."

That brought about Christopher's interest. "What do you mean?"

"I mean I think he feels something for her."

Christopher's humor faded. "You must be mistaken," he said quietly. "Juston de Royans does not have feelings for anyone other than himself. I have known him longer than you have and I was there when Lizette was murdered. Juston went through hell for years afterwards so I cannot imagine he would permit himself to feel something for another woman, least of all an enemy."

Gart shrugged. "I can only tell you what my instincts are telling me, Chris. If I am correct, then he bears watching. He will become too emotional about it."

Christopher sighed faintly. "He was useless for an entire year after Lizette's death."

"And now we are facing a major battle with Durham. An enemy that de la Roarke was allied with."

Christopher could see where this was leading. "And she is the sister of de la Roarke's wife," he said. "Is it possible she is trying to weaken him somehow? That she is working on Henry's behalf?"

Gart shook his head. "I do not think so, but I do not know the woman. All I am saying is that this bears watching."

Christopher couldn't disagree. "Thank you for telling me," he said. "I will take close notice of what goes on from this point forward."

"As will I."

The knight and the squire separated at that point, each heading off to complete his duties. But one thing was for certain now – they would be watching the lovely Lady Emera far more closely.

The enemy within that could ultimately ruin them all.

CHAPTER EIGHTEEN

S HE COULDN'T KEEP the smile off her face.

Even though Emera had been alone in the great master's bed when she'd awakened, she hadn't truly been alone. Juston had left her food and a fire, so it wasn't as if he hadn't been thinking about her. She was positive he'd only left her out of necessity. Perhaps that was a foolish thought, but at the moment, she wasn't thinking particularly clearly. Everything in her head had to do with Juston and their encounter the night before.

Clad in a clean shift and a surcoat the color of mustard, she had taken more time than usual to dress that morning. It was cold and dark outside as she sat by the fire and warmed some water, running a rag and soap over her hands and face. She couldn't bear to wash her body, however, and wash away the scent of Juston that was still on her. She could smell him all over her and it was enough to make her giddy heart flutter away.

She knew she should have been ashamed for what had transpired the night before, but she honestly couldn't bring herself to feel shame over something that had been so life-altering. Aye, her life was changed, for the better she hoped. She had met a man who felt for her the way she felt for him, a wild and unrestrained attraction that was seldom seen. She'd known married women, plenty of them – her sister, her mother, and other female relatives – but she'd never seen any of them happy with their partners.

As much as Jessamyn pretended to be content with Brey, Emera knew that was a lie. Jessamyn only accepted her life as it was and made the best of it. Perhaps Emera had never thought to marry because she was equating marriage with unhappiness. But all of that changed last night; to actually feel something for a man – to yearn for him, to tremble at his touch – was something Emera never thought she would know. She counted herself extremely fortunate. To be married to such a man was a dream few women knew.

But the big question hung in the air, unspoken because she was afraid to ask it – dare it be love? Was she in love with Juston, and he with her? After last night, something about the man was cemented deep inside her soul, something she knew she could never shake. Even if she left here tomorrow, Juston de Royans would be embedded in her heart as surely as if a spiny-tipped arrow had been shot right into it, never to be removed. But it was of no matter to her, for she never intended to remove him.

Ever.

After her toilette, she wrapped herself in a heavy woolen robe, lined with sheep's skin, and headed down for the vault. She was tired of being cold all the time and the heavy robe, although bulky, would be good insulation. It was actually Jessamyn's robe and she hoped her sister wouldn't take it from her when she saw it. Jessamyn could be possessive that way.

Jessamyn....

Her sister would wonder why she hadn't come to bed in the vault last night. She would have to tell Jessamyn something so she supposed there was nothing she could do except tell the woman the truth. She had denied any feelings towards de Royans to this point but she could no longer do so. In fact, she wanted to shout to the world that her heart belonged to Juston but she had to admit that she was dreading Jessamyn's reaction.

As it turned out, she had been right in that fear.

Jessamyn nearly exploded when Emera, very quietly, told her what had happened the night before. But Jessamyn was wild with outrage over the advantages de Royans had taken over her sister and, finally, Emera had to put her hand over the woman's mouth and drag her back into their little alcove where their possessions were stored. There, she explained what had happened and she further explained that she wasn't sorry in the least, that she belonged body and soul to Juston de Royans. She was mad for the man. She adored him.

She was in love with him.

Aye, she was, but it had taken Jessamyn's rage for her to admit it. Stunned, that bit of news seemed to shut Jessamyn up. Then, she broke down into tears and Emera found herself comforting the woman and assuring her all would be well. But their animated conversation had attracted attention and Emera looked up to see Tristan standing in the doorway to their alcove. His big brown eyes were wide with concern.

"Good morn to you, Tristan," Emera said steadily. "Do you require something?"

The child shook his head, timidly venturing towards the sisters. "Nay," he said. "I heard crying. Why is Lady Jessamyn crying?"

Emera cast her sister an imploring expression to be quiet before answering the boy. "She is fine," she assured him. "Nothing is the matter. Sometimes ladies weep for no reason at all. 'Tis silly, but it is true. You are kind to ask, but please go about your duties. Jessamyn will be fine."

Tristan was puzzled. Lady Emera's words didn't match Lady Jessamyn's actions. He'd spent several days with these ladies, helping with the wounded, and he'd grown rather attached to them both. They were kind and they listened to him. They let him help and gave him duties. Therefore, he was concerned that something was amiss with Lady Jessamyn. He scratched his dirty red hair, sticking up like straw.

"Do you want me to go to the kitchen and get the food for the men?" he asked. "They are hungry. It is time to break their fast."

Emera nodded, giving her sister a final glance before rising to her feet. "I will go with you," she said, making her way to the boy. "Mayhap we will take a few of the wounded men to help us. Many of them are able to walk around, thanks to your good care."

Tristan puffed up like a peacock. But then he looked concerned. "I heard Sir Erik say they are prisoners," he said, looking around nervously. "Are they permitted to leave the keep?"

Emera looked at the men strewn about the vault, too. Forty-seven of them in all with most of them well on their way to healing. But as she looked at them, she began to realize that they were looking back at her with a myriad of expressions on their faces; suspicion, glee, even some that could be considered rather lascivious. She knew a few of them by name – Arthos, Kenelm, and Edgard, for example –who had been free with their gossip. Now, she was coming to realize that the soldiers must have heard her conversation with Jessamyn, especially when her sister was angrily shouting de Royans' name. Since these men had already been spreading rumors about her and de Royans, it would seem they had a little something more to whisper about.

"Nay," she said after a moment, uncomfortable with all of the staring going on. "They are not. I must ask de Royans first before allowing the men from the vault. We can find a servant up in the hall to help us."

Tristan thought that sounded like a good idea and he skipped on ahead of Emera, heading for the spiral stairs. He was just about to run up the steps when a knight was coming down and he had to jump back as Erik emerged from the darkness. His gaze fell on Tristan immediately.

"Where are your possessions?" he asked the boy.

Tristan pointed back into the vault. "In there," he said. "Why?"

Erik turned the boy around by the shoulder. "Go and retrieve them," he said. "And dress warmly. We are leaving."

Tristan's face fell. "Why are we leaving?"

"I said go!"

Erik boomed at him and Tristan scampered away like a frightened rabbit. Emera watched him dash off before turning to Erik.

"He has been an excellent helper while he has been here," she said, sensing the knight was agitated. "He is a thoughtful and obedient boy."

Erik's gaze moved to her, that beautiful woman that had bewitched de Royans. At least, that was what everyone was saying. He could see what had de Royans attracted; she was quite lovely, even in the shadows like this. There was something alluring and mysterious about her.

"Thank you for watching over him during our stay," he said politely. "I am pleased that he was of some help to you."

"He is a fine lad," Emera said. An awkward silence settled and she spoke again, simply to fill the uncomfortable pause. "Are you taking him home now?"

Erik shook his head. "I am taking him to Netherghyll Castle."

He fell silent again and Emera didn't feel as if she could probe the man any further. He didn't seem to want to talk or elaborate on his plans with Tristan. It all seemed quite mysterious to her.

"Then I wish you safe travels," she said. "I pray the weather holds for you."

"Thank you, my lady."

More uncomfortable silence, but she endured it until Tristan returned with his meager belongings because she wanted to bid the lad a farewell. They had spent so much time together over the past few days that they had formed something of a bond, so she gave the child a hug and wished him well.

Tristan was a little teary-eyed and she could tell that he was upset about leaving, but she assured him that Sir Erik would take great care of him and that another adventure awaited him. The last she saw of Tristan was him following Erik up the spiral stairs, rubbing the tears from his eyes.

Her thoughts lingered on the sad little boy as she continued along her way, heading up to the great hall so that she could see to the wounded's meal. The hall was relatively dark and empty at this early morning hour and she paused to find a servant to stoke the fire before continuing on her way. Taking the stairs down to the inner bailey from the keep, she was met by Juston as he was coming in.

They saw one another and, for a moment, neither one said a word. Neither one even moved. It was a magical moment of appreciation and, quite possibly, of joy. Emera's heart was so light at the sight of him that she swore that she was walking on clouds. Nothing in the world could keep the smile from her face.

"Good morn to you, my lord," she said.

The same giddy smile on her face also played on Juston's lips. "And to you, my lady," he said. "Are you well this morning?"

Her grin broadened, if such a thing was possible. "Very well," she said. "And you?"

"Perfect."

She laughed softly. "You do not need to convince me of that," she said, "for I am under the same opinion."

He dipped his head gallantly, as if to thank her. "I am flattered," he said. "Where are you going? Mayhap you will allow me to escort you."

"I am going to the kitchens. And I would be honored if you would accompany me."

She began to walk and he fell in beside her. Around them in the early morning, the whole of Bowes was very busy with departure preparations. In fact, Emera couldn't help but notice that men seemed to be moving in almost a frenzy-like fashion. It was most curious.

"Everyone seems so busy," she commented.

Juston was walking next to her but he wasn't touching her, not even to politely take her elbow. He wasn't sure that he could stop at merely her elbow. One touch and he would want to pull her into his arms and he couldn't do that out here for everyone to see. When she commented on the state of the bailey, he looked around also.

"Men are preparing to depart," he said. "Do you remember what I told you yesterday about anticipating an attack from de Puiset?"

She nodded. "You wanted me to go to Netherghyll so that I would be safe."

"That is true. But I also mentioned that I was removing my army from Bowes to set up a defensive line against de Puiset."

"I remember."

"That is what we are preparing for."

Emera came to a halt and faced him. "*Now?*" she asked, concerned. "Are you going right now? Is that why Sir Erik is leaving and taking Tristan with him?"

"What did he tell you?"

"That he was taking Tristan to Netherghyll Castle but he did not tell me more than that."

Juston could see the fret in her eyes. She was worried. He did reach out, then, to take her elbow. He forced her to continue walking, but not unkindly.

"It is as I told you last night," he said quietly. "It is my belief that de Puiset is coming very soon. I must be able to set up a line of defense to meet him. If he gains too much ground, he will be on our doorstep before we realize it. We are, therefore, leaving at first light tomorrow. My men have the day to prepare and then we must leave. I am leaving Gillem here in charge of the castle, however, and you are to obey him. I know that obedience does not come easily to you but, for my sake, please listen to him. It might mean the difference between life and death."

Emera didn't even know what to say. Everything was happening so quickly and she was struggling to process it all. "As you wish," she said quietly. "I will do all I can to be of assistance to Sir Gillem."

He squeezed her elbow gently. "I would appreciate that. I do not want to have to worry over you."

"You will not."

They rounded the side of the keep in silence with the kitchens looming before them. Juston could sense Emera's melancholy and it took him back to the days when Lizette would beg him not to go to battle. It brought him an odd sense of comfort knowing that a woman was worrying about his safety. He remembered what those days were like, knowing there was someone waiting for him when the horror and gore of battle was over. But he also remembered what happened the last time he'd left a woman to go into battle.

He had survived, she had not.

With that thought, something made him reconsider his departure with Emera. He had only planned to leave her with a few words but now he wasn't so sure. He'd left Lizette that day without telling her that he loved her and it had haunted him. He assumed she knew he loved her even though he couldn't honestly remember ever telling her, but now with Emera, he didn't want to leave her without saying something... well, something meaningful. He had known her barely a week but in that week, she had managed to mark him. Last night only confirmed it. There was so much on his mind that it was difficult to know where to start. Perhaps if he just started talking, it would come to him.

"Emera," he said quietly, coming to a halt. "I am not one to make great speeches when I depart for battle, but I would like to say that... that it has been an honor to know you."

That wasn't what he'd wanted to say but he'd lost his courage the moment he'd looked into her eyes. Now he felt like an idiot. Predictably, Emera's brow furrowed.

"That sounds final, as if you do not intend to come back," she said.

He shook his head. "I will, indeed, come back," he said. "But when I am successful in chasing off Durham, it is quite possible I will head to Brough to help them do away with Carlisle. I may not return for quite some time."

Now she was greatly concerned. "Carlisle?" she repeated. "What do you mean?"

He knew she hadn't heard what the messenger at the gatehouse had told him. He didn't want to frighten her but he supposed it was her right to know considering Bowes was in the middle of all of these skirmishes. It was only fair she be aware of the situation in case Carlisle somehow managed to trickle through and come to Bowes.

"As you are aware, messengers were sent from Cotherstone Castle

when I began the siege of Bowes," he said. "We speculated as to where
the messengers could have gone and it seems that one made it to
Carlisle Castle. I received word this morning that Carlisle, on their way
to assist Bowes, was repelled by Brough Castle. Brough has held them in
check to prevent them from coming to us, so it is my duty to assist
Brough once Durham has been repelled."

Emera stared at him, her blue eyes big and full of anxiety. "Then
you will not return to Bowes until you have helped your allies at
Brough?"

"That is correct."

"How long do you suppose that might take?"

He shook his head. "There is no way to know."

It was clear that Emera was upset by the information. She averted
her gaze, fumbling with her hands. "You have been doing this for a very
long time, have you not? Fighting battles, I mean."

He watched her lowered head. "Aye. For nearly twenty-five years."

Her head came up, astonished. "You are not that old!"

He smiled weakly. "When I was fourteen years of age, I was taken
by my master, Sir Luc de Vini, to France in support of King Henry and
his claim on French lands," he said. "I had fostered at Warwick Castle
until that time and I considered it my home. De Vini was an excellent
master and he taught me a great deal, but he mostly taught me how to
survive. Consequently, I am more comfortable than most in battle.
Have confidence that I shall, indeed, return, Emera. You needn't
worry."

Emera fell quiet, pondering his statement. It wasn't a prideful boast
more than it was simply a statement of truth. There was no way she
could disbelieve such confidence and experience. But still, she was
worried.

"And then what?" she asked. "Will you continue your lordship over
Bowes?"

"Aye."

"And will I remain at Bowes?"

"Aye."

"In what capacity?"

He cocked an eyebrow. "As chatelaine," he said. "Have you forgotten?"

Chatelaine. She didn't mind that so much but considering what had happened last night, she wasn't going to let him get away with anything less than what she expected of him. He'd danced around the subject before. But no more.

"I have not," she said. "But only last night, you told me your intentions are honorable. An honorable man does not tell a woman that only to bed her and nothing more. An honorable man will hold true to his word."

A smile flickered on is lips. "I gave you no word other than telling you that my intentions were honorable." When her face turned red and she coiled up for a fight, his grin broke through and he put a big hand on her face to soothe her. "I told you that you must be patient with me. Of course you will be more than my chatelaine, in time."

Her building outrage was soothed simply by his touch. But she still wanted to hear it from his lips. "Tell me, Juston. Tell me that I shall be your wife."

"In time."

Her eyebrows lifted. "Can you not even say it?"

"Why should I? You just did."

She growled in frustration, turning away from him. "You are the most maddening man I have ever met," she seethed. "Can you not say what is in your heart?"

Grinning, he watched her stomp away. "You are."

She came to a halt, agitated. "I am *what?*"

"In my heart."

With that, he turned away from her and headed back towards the keep, leaving Emera standing there, watching him with her breath caught in her throat. That was the effect his words had on her; that fluttering heart was beating like mad and her breath caught in her throat.

Her giddy smile returned as she resumed her trek to the kitchens. He may have been frustrating and arrogant, but he was learning how to melt her heart.

That Evening

IT WAS THE first time in weeks that pork hadn't been served for every meal because all of the pigs that had been slaughtered for Juston's projectiles had finally been consumed. The cook had proceeded to slaughter four fat, old sheep, which yielded a great deal of meat. The cook had two massive cauldrons in the kitchen yard boiling cuts of mutton in well-salted water and still more cauldrons of iron boiling turnips, cabbage, and carrots. The smell of baking bread also filled the air and the bread ovens built against the inner wall were working furiously to churn out enough bread for the mass of men who were hungry for it.

Emera could smell the bread from the second floor chamber where she and Jessamyn had retreated, dragging their satchels up from the vault and putting their possessions back into Emera's chamber. Even though Jessamyn had occupied the master's chamber before with Brey, they were both well aware that Juston now occupied that chamber. They made no attempt to settle in it. However, Jessamyn had raided the big wardrobe in the chamber for the remainder of her clothing and possessions, but she left Brey's clothing in there as if someone else might want it. She surely didn't. As far as she was concerned, that was a closed chapter in her life and she mourned it as no more than that.

Therefore, the ladies settled down in Emera's chamber, emerging from the vault now that Juston and his army were heading off to intercept Durham. There was no reason why they shouldn't sleep in a comfortable bed and Emera was certain that Juston would approve. The man no longer had a reason to keep them in the vault and, to be truthful, they were both relieved and grateful not to have to sleep there any longer now that the wounded were becoming mobile. Somehow, it wasn't seemly for them to sleep there with some of the men now able to move about.

Moving into the private chamber also allowed them to bathe and dress in private, which they did happily for the first time in weeks. While they had the servants drag up the big copper tub, Juston's knights had prepared an entire army. While the ladies bathed and washed their hair, a luxury and a rarity in the winter time, Juston's knights had gone about their duties of securing Bowes. It wasn't right that the women should worry about the castle, anyway, and there wasn't anything they could have done. But as they found a few moments of leisure time and Juston's men prepared to depart, down in the vault where the wounded were housed, there were hints of rebellion in the air.

A rebellion that had started nearly the day Bowes was captured for Richard. The wounded, so mistreated by Maxton's orders, had harbored that resentment deep. Men died because of his command and even when they were moved into the vault, only a mildly better location, men still died. Lady Emera and Lady Jessamyn had worked feverishly to keep them warm, but still, men succumbed. That resentment grew among the wounded who suffered non-mortal injuries and as they healed, a rebellion began to take root. Though they gossiped about Lady Emera and the enemy commander, the truth was that their gossip was a cover for something far more sinister.

A plan to take back the castle was coming from within.

Cowling, the man who had served with Juston years ago, had heard the rumblings. They mostly came from a few men who had been with de la Roarke before he ever took charge of Bowes. Arthos, Edgard, and Kenelm were older soldiers that were doing the most muttering and planning, listening to the women for any hint of information that might be important to them and also asking the servants about the army of

Juston de Royans. Most of the house servants wouldn't speak to them but one did, a younger man who hadn't yet learned to keep his mouth shut.

It was through this servant that the wounded of Bowes learned that de Royans was taking his army out to meet the Bishop of Durham in the field. The servant thought that perhaps tomorrow was the day but he wasn't certain. Most of the army had been prepared, he said, with only a hundred or so that would be left behind to guard the castle.

As the evening settled, cold and dark, Cowling sat against the wall of the vault, in the shadows, listening to the three soldiers use that information to plot to retake Bowes.

"If de Royans' men are left behind, then we canna take the entire castle," Arthos was whispering to his comrades. "But we can take the keep and hold it."

"The keep!" his friends hissed in excited agreement. "We can hold the keep until Durham can retake the castle!"

They were seemingly in agreement, whispering among themselves as they plotted. Cowling listened as they laid out the plan to rise up and seize the keep, which was more than possible – it was probable. With all of de Royans' men spread thin on the battlements, it wouldn't be a difficult thing to do to seize the keep. But the men were speaking with haste, not having thought the plan through completely. Cowling was finally forced to speak up.

"And what shall you eat once you bottle up the keep?" he asked the trio, who looked at him in various stages of surprise and suspicion. "That's right; I heard you. I have been hearing you for days now. You speak like fools, like men who have never had to thoroughly plan out anything because you always follow and never lead. How are you going to eat?"

The three of them looked at each other, confused. "We can store food down here," Edgard pointed out. "Look at all of the turnips down here. We can eat them!"

Cowling nodded with impatience. "How will you cook them?" he asked. "What about water? The well is outside of the keep. If we have no water in here, we will die."

That shot arrows into their plans but it wasn't enough to destroy it. "There are cisterns on the roof of the keep," Arthos said. "That will supply us with water."

"It is winter. They are mostly frozen over."

"We can heat the water!"

"With what?" Cowling wanted to know. "You must have fuel to do that."

"We will get it!" Kenelm insisted. "We will store it down here along with food and then we will strike."

Cowling thought they sounded rather idiotic, visions of glory and no concept of the reality of such a thing. "What about weapons?" he asked. "If you take the keep, de Royans is going to want it back. He is going to fight for it. How will you fend him off?"

Emera and Jessamyn chose that moment to enter the vault, bringing the evening meal for the wounded as they were followed by a few servants bearing hot food. They were very nicely dressed, cleaned and combed, in stark contrast to their appearance the last several days.

In fact, they looked quite beautiful. Emera checked on a few of the weaker men while Jessamyn began handing out the food. Cowling couldn't help but notice how the three rebels were looking at the women. In fact, when Arthos saw that Cowling was looking at him, he grinned in a wicked fashion.

"We will not need weapons," he said. "I doubt de Royans will harm us if we have the lady with us."

Cowling frowned. "What do you mean?"

Kenelm snorted while Arthos spoke. "Everyone knows she's his whore," he said quietly because she was coming near. "I would wager that he'll not do a thing to harm her if she is our hostage."

Cowling shook his head. "'Tis a low man who would hold a woman hostage," he said. "I agree we can hold the keep for Henry, but we'll do it as men. Not as animals."

Because Cowling was a senior man, and stronger and smarter than the rest of them, the trio of insurgents didn't argue with him on that point. They wanted, and needed, his help, so they were willing to keep quiet about the women for the time being. But Arthos had little doubt that Lady Emera was the best possible weapon they had against Juston de Royans.

When the time came, he intended to use her no matter what Cowling said.

CHAPTER NINETEEN

"GOD'S BONES," MAXTON muttered, mouth full. "Something other than pork to eat. I swear, any more pork and I was destined to grow a snout."

He and the other knights, including Juston, were seated at one of the big feasting tables, situated near the hearth so the warmth could heat their cold flesh as they stuffed their faces with boiled mutton. The weather had frozen over again and there was sleet falling, melting before it hit the ground and creating great puddles of icy mud. The wind, which had been blustery most of the day, had settled down and now everything was mostly still. But the freezing weather was concerning Juston.

Much of Juston's tactics depended on fire. As with the siege of Bowes, Juston used animal fat to light up his projectiles or, in the case of field battle, he had any number of other tactics he used to do damage. On the field of battle, he would often have his men stand shoulder to shoulder, protected by shields, and move archers forward that way. He could launch flaming arrows into the heart of any infantry, but when the weather turned freezing like this, it made it difficult to use his favored weapon – fire.

Therefore, he sat at the end of the table with a cup of hot wine in hand, worrying about the coming fight as he watched his men as they shoved meat into their mouths. Around him, the hall was jammed with soldiers who had come in from the icy weather to eat and warm their bones. A few of his men had even brought instruments into the hall and they sat in a corner, playing lively tunes as men ate, gambled, and even danced around them.

In all, the hall portrayed a scene of jubilation and relaxation when the truth was that these were men living life to the fullest because tomorrow, they were heading into battle. This was essentially their last chance for a moment of peace before the storm hit. Juston and the knights knew that better than most as they sat quietly, eating and drinking with a roof over their heads and a fire in the hearth. The days of uncertainty in a battle encampment were soon to come.

"I did not see Erik leave with the boy," Marcus said, seated on Juston's right next to Christopher and David. "Did he take the boy and go?"

Juston took a drink of wine. "Aye," he replied. "He left this morning while you were off with the quartermasters. He is heading straight to Netherghyll and that is where he shall remain."

"I did not have the opportunity to speak with the boy very much," Christopher said, "although when we were traveling to Gainford yesterday, he spoke quite a bit with Lady Emera. It seemed as if he had a good deal to say to her."

Juston wasn't particularly interested. "Why shouldn't he?" he said. "She is intelligent and easy to converse with."

Christopher shoved a piece of crusty bread into his mouth, chewing. "The boy speaks like Erik does when he has had too much to drink," he said. "He runs off at the mouth. I was riding near the wagon and meant to tell you this, but I had forgotten. He told the lady that a man named Dorian Lusignan murdered your wife. De Russe had better watch what he tells that lad because he has no control on what he repeats to others."

The mention of that subject, that name, had Juston's attention but before he could speak, Gart spoke up from across the table. "Erik is aware what happens to him when he drinks too much," he said to

Christopher, defending his friend. "I am sure he will be careful from now on."

Christopher opened his mouth to reply but Juston interrupted him. "The boy told her about Lusignan?" he asked. "Great Bleeding Christ, I wish I'd known. I would have had the lad sit in the other wagon. That is information he should not be repeating."

Christopher nodded. "I realize that," he said. "I monitored the conversation and that was the only inflammatory thing he said, I assure you. The rest of the time, he was just babbling."

Juston still wasn't happy. "I already told her about what happened with Lusignan and my family. She did not need to hear it again."

It was apparent to all who were listening that Juston was very concerned about the lady, perhaps *too* concerned. Normally one to speak unemotionally about most subjects, his conversation when speaking on the lady was quite impassioned. It was a definite indication that, perhaps, there was something more than just polite regard. Although Gart and Christopher passed knowing glances, considering the conversation they'd had earlier in the day, the person who was listening most closely to Juston's tone was Gillem.

Seated down the table from Gart, and well into his food and wine, he couldn't help but hear Juston as he spoke about the lady and it only served to upset him even more than usual. He had heard the rumors that morning about Juston and the lady, rumors started by servants in the keep as they had seen Juston carry Lady Emera up to his chamber the night before. It didn't take a great intellect to figure out what had happened after that, which only served to fuel Gillem's bitterness towards Juston and the lady.

It was disheartening, really. He'd thought he'd discouraged Lady Emera sufficiently, but evidently what he had said to her was of little matter. In spite of his warning, she was falling into Juston's web most willingly, knowing full well what had happened with Sybilla and their child. That meant that the lady had no respect for Sybilla if she was willingly falling under de Royans' spell.

And that realization was a catalyst for Gillem in that he knew simple discouragement wouldn't chase the lady away. She would not leave willingly. She had the interest of a wealthy and powerful man and had no interest in discouraging him. If she was infatuated with Juston, or even in love with the man, then she would forgive him anything.

All of this meant that Gillem had to step up his means of removing the woman from de Royans' temptation. Since he had been ordered to remain at Bowes while Juston took the army out into the field and the lady was to remain behind at Bowes, also... well, anything could happen while the army was away. All Gillem had to do was call it an accident and no one would be the wiser.

If the lady would not remove herself, then Gillem would do it for her.

While Gillem simmered in his deadly thoughts, the lady in question made an appearance. With her sister by her side, Emera moved in with pitchers of warmed wine and a platter of small cakes that smelled strongly of cloves and cinnamon. They headed straight for the end of the table where Juston sat, distracting the men from their wine and conversation.

"Good eve, my lords," Emera said as she set the cakes down in front of the knights. "The cook has made these for you. She says they will bring you luck in your endeavors tomorrow."

The knights all leaned forward to inspect what she had brought them; they were little oat cakes flavored with honey and cloves and cinnamon. They even had walnuts in them and the knights immediately plowed into the sweets. Emera had to laugh as David nearly shoved her over in his haste, bumping her straight into Juston, who was sitting back in his chair. He was the only one not grabbing for the cakes. His attention was on Emera.

"My lady," he said, his voice deep and soft. "How kind of you to join us."

Emera smiled at the man, not even thinking that anyone looking at her face would see how smitten she was. Even if she had known, she might not have cared.

"The wounded are tended and fed," she told him. "My sister and I thought to attend the knights in the hall. After all, you depart tomorrow. We might not have another opportunity for quite some time."

She was speaking as if she was part of their group, not a captive. It was an interesting dynamic, and an unusual one, considering that she was, indeed, a prisoner of Juston's conquest. But Juston didn't see it that way; he hadn't for a while. When he smiled sweetly at her, David happened to catch it. He elbowed Marcus, who saw the gesture as well. On down the line – Maxton, Kress, Achilles, Gart, Gillem, and even Christopher could see the expressions passing between Emera and Juston.

If anyone had been oblivious to the rumors floating around about the pair, the light in the eyes of Emera and Juston as they looked at one another was a bit of a shock. Even those who had been aware of the rumors were still caught off-guard, for the expression on Juston's face was no ordinary expression.

The Lord of Winter, the man with the heart of ice, was in love with his captive.

Since no one had the nerve to comment, as it was safer not to, the oat cakes disappeared off the trencher with blinding speed as the knights simply stuffed them into their mouths, anything to keep busy and pretend they weren't looking at Emera and Juston. It was difficult not to stare, however, purely out of morbid curiosity. No one really thought Juston was capable of such things, especially those who had known him the longest. It was truly a sight to see.

As the knights pretended not to notice the besotted pair, Jessamyn went around the table refilling cups and having a polite word for the men who had taken the castle from her husband. In truth, she harbored no ill-will and hadn't for days. After the initial shock of Brey's death, and the capture of the castle, Jessamyn had been resigned to her future. Emera seemed to be optimistic about it and some of that was rubbing off on Jessamyn, although she still wasn't completely comfortable with the relationship between de Royans and her sister. But she, too, saw the looks between them and she had to admit that de Royans didn't look like a man who was taking advantage of her sister.

Perhaps there really was something to it, after all.

Juston wasn't entirely oblivious to the fact that his men were looking at him. They weren't as clever in hiding their surprise as they thought they were. But for the first time since Lizette's death, Juston's heart was light and he didn't much care what his men thought. It felt good, in fact, to be attracted to a woman. It was a warm, happy feeling he never thought he'd experience again.

"Have you eaten?" Juston finally asked Emera after staring at her for a few long, pleasurable moments. "If not, please join us. I realize you may feel uncomfortable joining men who seized your home, but today we are no longer enemies. Are we?"

Emera shook her head. "You never were," she said. "When the first knight entered the great hall to announce the castle was now the property of the Count of Poitiers, Anjou, and Maine, I assured him that we would not resist. The first time I met you, I assured you of the same thing. Therefore, we were never enemies, my lord. I will ever be grateful to you for saving me from a hellish existence."

She was correct; she never had resisted their conquest. Emera had always been cooperative. Well, for the most part. Juston didn't blame her for not being cooperative on the day they met when he demanded she service him. In fact, Juston was rather glad she resisted. He never would have seen her strength otherwise.

He would have never realized just how sweet the eventual conquest actually was.

With a smile, he indicated for Emera to sit on the bench beside him and she did. While the knights lost themselves in conversation, knowing that Juston wouldn't hear anything they said, anyway, with lady in his presence, Juston was predictably focused on Emera as if no one else in the room existed.

"There is music in the hall tonight," he said to her. "Do you dance?"

Emera shook her head. "Sweet Mary, no!" she gasped, giggling. "It would be an abomination!"

He grinned. "I do not believe it. Not even a little bit?"

"Not even a little bit."

He swirled the wine in his cup. "Do you sing?"

"I sing worse than I dance."

"Then what do you do that is pretty and graceful, as befitting your beauty?"

He was flattering her again and she pretended to be thoughtful. "I can draw a little," she said. "My mother would permit Jessamyn and me to paint when we were young. My mother also had a fine garden, which I tended after her death but I had to leave it when I came to Bowes. I have often wondered what happened to my garden. I was sad to leave it."

Juston drained the remainder of his cup and sat forward, closer to her, and lowered his voice. "Netherghyll has a garden," he said. "The castle has been built up over the years and the design of it is somewhat strange, but there is a garden in the middle of it that has had no one to tend it since my mother passed away. You are more than welcome to make it your own."

Emera's face lit up. "I can?" she said. "I do not know what to say. That is incredibly generous, Juston. You do not think your mother would mind?"

He shook his head, daring to reach under the table and put his hand on her knee. "Not at all," he said. "She loved her flowers. She even had grapevines in the garden and pear trees. When my brother and I were younger, we would steal fruit from the trees. My mother would laugh but our nurse would chase us with a switch. I miss those days."

Emera smiled. "I had forgotten you had a brother," she said. "Quinton is his name, correct?"

"Aye."

"Is he like you?"

Juston shook his head. "Not much," he said. "Quinton is shorter and uglier. But he is a very good knight."

"Why does he not serve you, then?"

Juston snorted. "Because Richard could not bear to part with both of us. He had to keep one of us by his side, and that was Quinton."

"Fortunate for me."

"Why do you say that?"

"Because I would not have met you otherwise."

Under the table, Juston rubbed her knee affectionately. It had been so long since he'd sat in sweet conversation with a woman that he was nearly giddy from the joy of it all. He couldn't even think of leaving her tomorrow and perhaps not seeing her for a very long time. It was the first time in his long and distinguished career that he found himself wishing he didn't have to leave for battle. He wanted to stay here, with Emera, and have more conversations like this one. Already, he was looking forward to the night, eager to take her to his bed once again. His heart, that hard and cold thing, had been completely thawed by the lady and, in fact, it was far more than thawed. It was liquid now, hot and flowing, eager for more experiences with Emera. To her he owed the joy that he thought he'd lost. He couldn't explain it any other way.

Before he could continue the conversation with her, however, Juston caught sight of people entering the smoky, noisy hall. Even though he was far from the door, he was facing it and he was the first one to see two of his soldiers enter, men that were coated with ice and nearly frozen half to death. The expression on his face caught Christopher's attention and, very quickly, the other knights as well. Everyone was looking over at the entry with Maxton shooting to his feet. He stood up on the bench, waving the men over.

"Those men were part of a patrol I sent out earlier," he said as he jumped off the bench. "They have returned far too quickly for my taste."

Suddenly, the relaxed atmosphere of the table plummeted and the knights rose to their feet as the soldiers approached. With pinched-red faces and mail coated with ice, the first of the pair headed straight for

Juston.

"M-my lord," he said through chattering teeth. "We bear news of Durham's approach."

Juston didn't like the sound of that at all. Something told him that the news was very, very bad. "Where is he?" he demanded.

The soldier was quivering so badly that David and Marcus began helping the man remove his gloves. Gart did the same for the second man because it was clear that both men were too frozen to articulate very well.

"We have been monitoring the road to Gainford," the soldier said. "Earlier today, we saw some commotion within the castle and then people began fleeing the town. I caught one man and he told me that Durham's army was entering the town from the east."

Juston's heart began to pump, just a bit faster. "How far behind you are they?"

The soldier paused as David pulled the man's helm off, which was frozen to his head. In fact, ice from the helm and the man's hair had become one, and they had to break off the ice in order to get his helm off.

"They are not behind me," the soldier finally said as someone shoved a cup of hot wine into his hand. "That is what I came to tell you; de Balliol would not let de Puiset's army come through Gainford and use the bridge. He turned them away and they had to go north. The next bridge to cross is north of Cotherstone and it should delay his army by at least a day if not more."

Juston looked at his men, who were gazing back at him in various stages of concern. This was a most unexpected twist but it was actually a blessing; had Durham's army not been turned away by de Balliol, then they would have descended upon Bowes already. Even Juston was surprised at the speed in which de Puiset's army had assembled. Therefore, he viewed the situation as something good – Durham's delay would be his victory. His mind began working quickly.

"Let us assume de Puiset is resting his army for the night," he said to his men. "He'll take the bridge in the morning and it will take him at least the day, if not longer, to make the trek south to Bowes."

"That means we must depart tonight if we are to intercept him." Christopher said what they were all thinking. "If he does *not* rest his army tonight, then we will have to stop him by morning."

"Only an insane man would march his army at night, through a storm."

"That is what we are about to do, isn't it?"

Christopher had a point. Departing at night in a storm wasn't exactly what Juston had hoped for, but they had no alternative. The familiar scent of battle began to fill his nostrils again and there was no hesitation in his decision.

They had to move.

"Assemble the army," he told his men. "Every man in here, get them outside and into formation. We leave before the hour is up."

The knights broke away, filtering around the room of men and shouting commands. Suddenly, the music stopped and the hum of conversation ceased as Christopher and Maxton shouted concise commands to the roomful of men, most of whom had had too much to drink. But that was of no consequence; plans had been altered and they had to adapt. Hearts pumping with the rush of battle, men struggled to sober up and grab what possessions they'd brought with them into the hall.

Soon enough, they were rushing from the keep in groups as the knights herded them out. As Emera and Jessamyn remained by the feasting table, wide-eyed at all that was going on, Juston found Gillem and pulled the man aside.

"You have been told that you have command of the castle, have you not?" he asked.

Gillem nodded. "Chris told me," he said. "Have you specific orders, my lord?"

Juston nodded. "The western outer wall is still weak," he said. "You cannot depend on it to hold in the event that Durham's army is able to get past us and lay siege. Therefore, seal up the outer wall, the gate-house, and the outer bailey as best you can but be prepared to fall back to the inner ward and the keep in the event of an attack. You will not open that gatehouse for anyone but me or any of my knights. Is that clear?"

"It is, my lord."

Juston cast a glance over at Emera and Jessamyn, still standing by the table. "The Bowes wounded are down in the vault and you will keep them there, but Lady Jessamyn and Lady Emera have free run of the castle. Keep them to the keep and inner ward, but they have all due freedom. They should be able to help you with wounded or other tasks."

"Aye, my lord."

"And you will protect them with your life."

"I will, my lord."

"Go about your duties."

Gillem departed, heading out of the keep, as Juston turned for the ladies. When Jessamyn saw him approach, she scattered, leaving Emera standing alone at a cluttered, dirty table that was once filled with men. She watched Juston anxiously as he drew near.

"Is the bishop nearly upon us, then?" she asked fearfully.

He shook his head, putting a comforting hand on her arm. "Nay," he said quietly. "But he is coming. I knew he would be coming soon but this is sooner than I had expected. It simply means I must move my men sooner, 'tis all. He will be coming south on the road from Cotherstone and we shall be ready for him."

He sounded confident, which made Emera feel some confidence as well. Still, she had seen what a battle could do. She'd seen three weeks of Juston's siege on Bowes and it wasn't pretty. But there was nothing she could do other than summon her bravery and bid him a farewell because, one way or the other, he was going to battle.

"Is there anything I can do for you before you go?" she asked. "Do you need any supplies or anything else I can help you with?"

He smiled faintly at her. "Nay," he murmured. "But I thank you for asking. It is kind of you."

Emera wasn't sure what more to say. He was touching her arm, still, so she reached out to rest a gentle hand on his chest.

"Then Godspeed, Juston," she whispered. "I shall pray for you."

"It is appreciated."

"And we shall hold Bowes. I am not beyond taking up a sword."

He laughed softly. "Somehow, I believe that implicitly. You do well with an ash shovel, too."

He was referring back to the battle they'd had through the hearth, slapping at each other with ash shovels. She grinned. "If pushed, I can most definitely use the ash shovel."

He just stared at her a moment, grin fading. Then, he reached out both hands to cup her face, gazing deeply into her brilliant eyes.

"I am not very good at finding the right words in a moment like this," he said quietly. "I have said all I needed to say."

"I know."

He started to open his mouth again, hesitated, and then bent down to kiss her sweetly on the lips. It was a tender kiss, warm and soft and lingering. It was nearly enough to cause Emera to swoon.

"I will tell you that I will count the moments until I see you again," he murmured. "I never thought I would feel this way again, Emera. To know that I have your heart… it means everything to me."

Emera leaned into him, her forehead against his chin. "You have *all* of me, Juston. Not simply my heart."

"I know."

It was an arrogant statement in a tender moment. She looked up at him, then. "Have you nothing more to say to me than that?"

His eyes took on that impish twinkle. "Why should I?"

"Because I have asked you to."

The arrogant knight swallowed his pride a bit. He was forever pressing her to tell him her feelings, always backing off when asked to fully tell her of his. He kissed her on the forehead and let her go.

"You have all of me as well."

With that, he headed for the entry of the keep, leaving Emera standing by the table, her heart swelling with adoration and joy, everything she could possibly feel. He turned to her, once more, before leaving the great hall and she blew a kiss towards him. He flashed her a smile and was gone.

Slowly sinking onto the bench that he had previously occupied, Emera prayed hard for what was to come.

CHAPTER TWENTY

"COWLING! WAKE *UP*!"

Cowling had been in a deep slumber when he heard someone calling his name. His mind misty, he had to shake off the cobwebs as he rolled onto his back, trying to see in the darkness of the vault. In the black, he could make out the outline of Arthos.

"What is it?" Cowling demanded, irritable. "What do you want?"

Arthos huddled down next to Cowling's head so he wouldn't have to shout. "The army is moving out," he hissed. "In the dead of night, they are pulling out to meet de Puiset. The Bishop of Durham must be coming to save us!"

Cowling sat up, pushing Arthos away because the man was too close to him. He didn't like breathing in that foul breath. But the impact of Arthos' words settled in to his sleepy mind.

"De Royans' army is leaving?" he repeated just to make sure he heard correctly. "Who told you this?"

Arthos pointed up, to the floor above. "We could hear them," he said. "They were feasting and then something happened because they fled the hall. I went up to see what had happened, peeking into the hall so they could not see me, and there were very few men left in the hall. They all went outside. Now, the army is assembling! They have already opened the gatehouse and the infantry is leaving!"

It was startling news. Cowling rubbed the sleep from his eyes and stood up, unsteadily. Around him in the darkness of the vault, he could see that the other men were awake and whispering, some of them standing, all of them excited with the prospect of retaking the keep. Finally, they would take back what rightfully belonged to them in a perfect moment of weakness for de Royans. Cowling scratched his head.

"But who told you de Puiset was coming?" he asked. "Has this been confirmed?"

Arthos nodded his head. "The servants in the hall said they heard men speaking of Durham coming to Bowes," he said. "Why else would de Royans remove his army?"

He had a point. But Cowling still didn't seem excited about it, merely confused. "Did you bring in more supplies since we spoke?" he asked Arthos. "We cannot hold the keep if we have no supplies."

Arthos had the glow of victory in his eyes. "We will not only take the keep, but the inner bailey as well," he said excitedly. "The servants have said they are all with us. The well and the kitchens are within the inner bailey. We can lock ourselves up and wait for help to arrive."

Cowling shook his head. "Do you not think de Royans' men can mount the inner wall if you try to hold it?" he asked in frustration. "You are not thinking clearly. The keep is the only thing we will be able to hold because, surely, a hundred de Royans men will overwhelm less than fifty wounded men. You must only think on holding the keep and nothing more because we have no weapons for anything larger."

Arthos wasn't thrilled with Cowling's dissention but the man had a point. They had no weapons to hold the inner ward should de Royans' men try to regain it. That meant the keep, as Cowling had said, was their best option. He was disappointed at that realization, unable to hide it.

"Then the servants can bring food and other things into the keep," Arthos said, disgruntled. "As I said, they are willing to help and they can move without suspicion. They have already brought us what weapons they could steal – we have several bows, arrows, and swords they managed to steal from the pile of weaponry taken from our dead men that de Royans is keeping near the stables."

He was scrambling to prove to Cowling that he knew what he was doing and that the planned rebellion left nothing to chance. But Cowling still wasn't certain. So many things depended upon preparation and timing, of which they'd had little. Hastily planned ventures like this never succeeded but he knew he couldn't discourage the men. They were set on it.

"Then if you are truly going to take the keep, do it quickly," Cowling said. "Tell the servants to bring any and all food into the keep, and pots to warm water and cook food, and peat. We will need lots of peat or we will freeze to death."

Arthos nodded. "Are you with us, then?"

"I have never been against you."

That was good enough for Arthos. He scurried off to discuss the situation with the rest of the wounded as Cowling wondered if this would be successful. Was Durham really coming to aid Bowes? Or was that pure speculation on Arthos' part? One thing was for sure – if the wounded of Bowes regained the keep, it would spell trouble for Juston de Royans to have a battle on two fronts. As much as Cowling admired and respected Juston, he had been serving Henry too long to change his loyalties for a man who had once also served Henry. Cowling didn't know how Juston had come to serve Richard, but it didn't matter. Henry was king and Bowes belonged to Henry.

Nothing personal to Juston.

After that, the wounded of Bowes worked through the night obtaining what they needed in order to survive their rebellion. When morning finally came, that dull gray sky that signified yet another day had risen, the wounded of Bowes rose up out of their vault and filtered into the hall.

The time had come.

With hemp ropes, shovels, fire pokers, and anything else they could use for weapons, they managed to kill three de Royans' soldiers who had been in the great hall, tossing their bodies out into the inner ward and leaving a fourth soldier to tell the others what had happened. They then lit the wooden staircase of the forebuilding on fire and shored up the entry door, effectively sealing off the keep from any type of counterattack. Small windows, walls that were impossible to scale, and an iron entry door that could not be burned or rammed made the keep of Bowes quite impenetrable.

For Gillem and the two hundred men left behind by Juston, the seizure of the keep came as a great surprise. They had been up all night, watching the army depart and fade off into the darkness before securing the gatehouse and reinforcing the outer defenses of Bowes as best they could. Their concern was the outer ward because of the weakened western wall, never the inner ward or the keep, so a panicked soldier describing the Bowes wounded that had killed his comrades had been a nasty shock. Now, the keep of Bowes was in the hands of men who had not been considered a threat. It had been a terrible oversight on Juston's part.

Worse still, kitchen servants and other Bowes servants, who had been thus far serving de Royans and his men without question, now turned into an army of the wretched who tried to fight off Gillem and his soldiers with fire pokers and pitchforks. Shocked by the insurrection but quickly realizing that this rebellion had been well-planned, Gillem didn't hesitate to kill those opposing him. He did away with the fat cook and two kitchen servants personally while his soldiers took care of the rest.

Seventeen servants in all, including grooms from the stables and the castle's carpenter, were killed in the rebellion and their bodies left scattered so those in the keep could see what had happened. Now, Gillem was furious with what had happened and he was going to make those who had organized it pay. Leaving the bodies of the murdered rebels in full view of the keep was a message to those inside... *this, too, shall be you!*

As the night progressed and headed towards a stormy gray dawn,

Gillem was quite certain Juston's whore was the leader of the rebellion. He had no doubt in his mind, certain that she and her sister were inside the keep, more than likely laughing at the chaos they had caused.

Gillem wasn't too unhappy about that realization, in truth, because he could then kill the woman and be justified. *She was a traitor*, he would tell Juston, and he was certain that Juston would thank him for his cunning and intelligence. Gillem felt a good deal of satisfaction at the thought of breaching the keep, finding that black-haired vixen, and slitting her soft white throat. It became his one and only thought.

He was going to kill her and Juston would brand him a hero.

The murder of an innocent woman was the last thing on Gillem's mind when an arrow, fired from one of the lancet windows that dotted the hall, found its mark in his neck. In the end, it was Gillem whose white throat had been pierced by a sharp edge and it was his rich, red blood running out onto the frozen ground of the inner ward.

The death count at Bowes grew by one.

EMERA DIDN'T THINK she'd be able to sleep that night, but she had.

Lying next to her sister in her small but comfortable bed, she lay awake long into the night, gazing into the fire as it flickered in the hearth, thinking about Juston as he rode out with his men on this dark and frozen night. Because of the limited view from the keep, with small windows and, in the case of her chamber, windows that were facing the wrong direction, she couldn't watch the army as they left the castle. All she could do was pray for Juston's safety as he headed out to prevent the Bishop of Durham from coming to Bowes.

The day leading up to the army's departure had, truthfully, been exhausting and it was Jessamyn who eventually pulled her into bed at a late hour. Snuggled down beneath the warm coverlet, her back to her sister's back, the two of them kept each other warm as the icy winter chill filtered in through the chamber window. All was quiet and peaceful in the chamber even if the world outside was in chaos.

"Emmy...," Jessamyn said quietly. "Do not become angry with what I am to say, but it is clear that de Royans is smitten with you. I suppose I did not realize just how much until I saw the expression on his face tonight."

Staring into the flames, Emera smiled. "Why would I become angry with you for saying that?"

"Because the man is a soldier. This is not the first castle he has conquered nor will it be his last. Do you not fear he will simply grow tired of you and then find a new lady to be smitten with at the next castle he seizes?"

It was a depressing thought, one Emera had never entertained. Was it possible he'd grow weary of her at some point? Was it possible that the giddy desire they felt for one another would someday be extinguished by another woman's flame?

Damn her sister for being logical about the situation!

"He told me that he has not had feelings for another woman since his wife was killed," Emera said, some uncertainty in her voice. "I do not believe he will become tired of me. He said that I have his heart."

"Does he even have one to give?"

"That is cruel, Jess."

Jessamyn sighed. "I am sorry," she said. "I am only thinking of you. I do not want you to be hurt."

Emera softened. "I know," she said softly. "Aye, he has a heart to give. He had a wife several years ago that he had given it to, but his wife and children were murdered by a knight bearing the name of Lusignan."

Jessamyn rolled over, looking at her sister even though Emera was still facing away from her. "Lusignan?" she repeated, shocked. "That is terrible! What happened?"

Emera sighed. "I do not know," she said. "He only said they were murdered. And then when we traveled to Gainford, Tristan told me that Sir Erik had told him that a man named Dorian Lusignan had murdered Juston's family."

Jessamyn gasped. "Dorian Lusignan!" she cried softly. "Emmy, we have an uncle by that name!"

"I know."

"You did not tell de Royans, did you?"

Emera shook her head. "Nay," she said sadly. "I will never tell him and neither will you. It does not matter, does it? His family is still dead. Telling him we have an uncle by that name will not bring them back."

Jessamyn was looking at her sister's back, still, sensing there was more to it. "You do not want him to know, do you?" she asked softly. "You are afraid of what will happen if he finds out about Uncle Dorian. That, mayhap, he will end up hating you because of your ties to the man."

It was the truth. Jessamyn knew her all too well and Emera closed her eyes tightly to the selfish suggestion.

"Aye," she muttered. "I am afraid of what he will do if he knows the truth. I could not bear it if he hated me, Jess. Now that I have found… now that he and I… oh, Jess! Of course I could not bear it if he were to end up hating me!"

She began to sniffle and Jessamyn put a hand on her back, soothingly. "Emmy, do you love him? Do you truly love him?"

Emera wiped at her eyes. "I… I think so. He is generous and humorous and intelligent. He is brave to a fault. I have not known him for very long, but what I do know of him, I love. I could not bear to lose that. I have never known such happiness before, not ever."

Jessamyn patted her on the back before rolling over so her back was once again wedged in against her sister's. "I never thought you would ever feel anything for a man," she said quietly. "I have watched you grow up, Em. You were always so serious, so bold. You told me you wanted to follow in mother's footsteps as a healer. You even spoke of going to the charity hospital in Sherburn. But I never thought I would see the day when a man turned your head and softened your heart."

Emera could hear awe in her sister's tone. "Nor did I," she said.

"Please, Jess... never mention Uncle Dorian. If Juston ever asks you, plead ignorance. I do not want him to know what we suspect."

"I will never tell, I swear it. If it means so much to you, it will never pass my lips."

"Thank you."

After that, the conversation died as the fire continued to snap in the hearth. The night deepened and somewhere in that icy, stormy night, Emera fell asleep, warm and comfortable. It was a rarity. But as a cold dawn loomed and the fire in the hearth burned low, someone pounded on their chamber door.

It was loud, angry pounding. Jessamyn, still half-asleep, staggered out of bed and made her way over to the door. Throwing the bolt, the panel was shoved open from the other side, so hard that Jessamyn was thrown into the wall. As she screamed, Emera sat bolt upright as a collection of men flooded into the chamber. She recognized every one of them – the wounded men of Bowes.

Somehow, they were no longer in the vault and were now crowded into her chamber. Startled, she was genuinely fearful for them because they were not allowed out of the vault. They were prisoners, all of them, and if Juston's men discovered what they'd done, it could go very badly for them.

"What is the meaning of this?" she demanded. "You are not permitted to come out of the vault!"

The man at the head of the group was a man she had been acquainted with throughout her residency at Bowes – Arthos was his name. He was a simple soldier, an older man, who never seemed to have much to say. She had thought him rather quiet. But he was standing inside her chamber now, surrounded by other men with healing wounds, and all of them carrying some kind of club or pike in their hand. It seemed that the quiet soldier now had plenty to say.

"'Tis a new day, ladies," Arthos said. "We have reclaimed Bowes for Henry."

That was not the answer Emera expected to hear. She looked at the men who had barged into her chamber, and the weapons in their hands, and her initial confusion turned into something dark and deep. She was starting to get a very bad feeling about all of this. Tossing back the coverlet, she climbed out of bed, making sure she was closer to the fire poker in her chamber than they were. Something told her that she might very well need to defend herself.

It was just a feeling she had.

"What is happening?" she asked steadily. "What have you done?"

Arthos kept his gaze on her. "The keep is ours," he said. "De Royans took his army away and we reclaimed what belongs to us."

Emera looked at the man as if he was mad. "But de Royans left men behind to secure the castle," she said. "He even left a knight behind. Where are they?"

Before Arthos could answer, Cowling pushed his way to the front. He wasn't armed and he seemed to be much less worked up than the rest of them, gripping their weapons and shuffling about. Cowling was showing no signs of aggression.

"The knight is dead," he told her calmly. "We killed him a short while ago."

Emera's eyes widened. "You killed Sir Gillem?"

Arthos nodded. "Cowling shot an arrow from window in the great hall and took him down," he said, somewhat proudly. "With the knight gone, the army has no commander. The other men that de Royans left behind are still here, but they cannot get into the keep. We have burned the exterior staircase and we will hold the keep until de Puiset arrives."

Now, Emera was starting to get a clear picture of what had happened. Her jaw dropped. "What's this?" she gasped. "Are you *mad*? De Royans will discover what you've done and kill you all when he returns!"

That wasn't what Arthos wanted to hear from her. He was suddenly moving in her direction and, panicked, Emera grabbed the fire poker and swung it at the man, clipping his hand. He yelped angrily as she backed up against the wall, wielding the poker defensively.

"Get out of here, all of you," she hissed. "How dare you barge into my chamber like a pack of wild dogs? Get out of here this instant!"

Arthos was still rubbing his hand where she'd hit him. "You have no right to call us names when it 'tis you who have bedded with the enemy," he snarled. "Everyone knows you have betrayed us, that you have allied yourself with Juston de Royans like a common whore. Don't think we don't know that you side with the enemy!"

"Hold," Cowling commanded quietly, holding up his hands and putting himself between Emera and the mob. He could see that this was going to get out of hand, very quickly, and hastened to ease the situation. "Lady Emera tended your wounds; she tended the wounds of all of you. If she is a traitor, then she is a traitor who was kind to you. Who wiped your dirty arse, Arthos? It was her when you could not do it yourself. Do not be so quick to judge her. Think of the good she has done for you."

What he said was true and the men began to shift around, nervously, looking at each other with uncertainty. Kenelm, who was standing behind Arthos, elbowed the man to get his attention.

"We need her to chase de Royans away," he said. "You cannot forget that."

Arthos knew that. He was frustrated, now with a throbbing hand where the woman had hit him. He scowled at her. "This keep belongs to us," he said to her. "We will hold it until de Puiset arrives and then we will turn the castle over to him. If you are not a traitor, then you will do what I tell you to do."

Emera knew she wasn't going to obey the man, no matter what. "And if I refuse?"

Arthos didn't say anything for a moment. He turned around and looked through the mob behind him, seeing Jessamyn over against the wall where she had stumbled when the door hit her. He marched over to her and grabbed her by the arm, yanking her against him as she screamed.

"If you refuse, I will throw your sister from the top of the keep and let de Royans' soldiers pick up the pieces," he declared. "What do you have to say now?"

He yanked on Jessamyn again and she yelped as he hurt her. Gazing at Arthos, Emera didn't doubt that the man meant what he said. He was part of this mob now and the mob evidently had rather radical ideas. Throwing a woman over the battlements would mean little to them but it meant a great deal to her. She looked at Cowling, who was still standing between her and the restless rabble.

"Are you with them?" she asked, disbelief and pain in her tone. "Are you truly part of this madness?"

Cowling's expression suggested he wasn't so certain. "Aye," he said. "Bowes belongs to Henry, my lady. It is our duty, as soldiers sworn to Henry, to do all we can to regain control of the fortress."

It was probably the best explanation she'd heard about what was going on and she quickly weighed her options. If she resisted, they would kill Jessamyn and probably her as well. She didn't want to die, not when life had shown her what true happiness could be. Sweet Mary, it was all so unfair! Her first true taste of love and happiness, and now this? She couldn't decide if she was furious or devastated, but one thing was for certain – she had to survive and the only way to do that was to go along with the mob. Or, at least let them *think* she was. It was a gamble, but one she had to take.

She tossed aside the fire poker.

"Very well," she said. "Release Jessamyn. I will not resist."

No one moved. Cowling turned to look at the group, still hanging on to Jessamyn. "Did you hear her?" he said. "Release Lady Jessamyn. The ladies will not be any trouble."

Arthos' gaze lingered on Cowling. Instead of releasing Jessamyn, he passed her over to another soldier.

"I'm not entirely sure you are with us," he said to Cowling. "You seem to want to defend the women and especially Lady Emera. You know she's thick as thieves with de Royans, don't you?"

Cowling didn't need this group turning on him as well. Therefore, he tried to sound as neutral as possible. "Out of necessity," he said. "She is the one who had us moved into the vault when de Royans' knights moved us into the bailey. She has gone to fight for us against him and if that makes her as thick as thieves with him, then she did it to save your miserable life. Show the woman some respect!"

He was booming by the time he finished, which shook up the mob. Most of the men weren't truly wicked. They were weary and still recovering from wounds, but they were passionate about their loyalties. Bowes was meant for Henry and it was their duty to hold it for Henry. They'd listened to Arthos' rhetoric for days now and he had them worked up, but Cowling's shout had them seeing more clearly. The man holding Jessamyn let her go, pushing her back in the direction of her sister. Emera put her arms around her terrified sister.

"Now," Emera said steadily, "we will do what we can. We will still tend those of you who have not quite recovered from your injuries. We will prepare whatever food there is. We cannot fight but we will continue to tend you as we have."

Arthos didn't seem too convinced but with Cowling standing there, a man he very much wanted on his side, he eased back a bit. But not completely; he pointed a finger at Emera.

"You had better," he said. "If you do not keep your word, then I'll throw both you and your sister off the roof. I do not tolerate traitors."

With that, he turned around, shoving at the men who had filtered in behind him, herding them all out of the chamber and back into the big master's chamber beyond. Emera and Jessamyn could hear things tipping over and crashing as the men rifled through the chamber before leaving. Those clothes of Brey's that Jessamyn had left in the wardrobe found a home with some of the wounded Bowes soldiers.

Cowling was the last one out of the chamber but he didn't say anything to the women. He simply followed the mob out, silently, leaving a mood of confusion and fear in his wake. The mob didn't shut the door to the stairwell when the left, instead, leaving it open wide and the ladies could hear the grumbling and shouting as the men descended into the great hall below, settling in for a long wait.

Waiting for de Puiset to come and free them.

When both chambers on the second floor were empty and quiet, Jessamyn turned to her sister in a panic.

"We are at their mercy!" she gasped, tears overflowing. "What shall we do?"

Emera wasn't entirely sure. She was fairly certain the wounded didn't trust her or her sister in spite of the fact that they had nursed a few of those men back from very serious injuries, Arthos included. She struggled against the terror that was claiming Jessamyn, for it would have been very easy to give in to it.

"We do nothing," she whispered, shaking her sister and forcing the woman to look at her. "Jess? Listen to me. We do only what we said we were going to do. We continue to help the wounded men and we do not do anything other than that. We must not give them a reason to mistrust or harm us. Do you understand?"

Jessamyn nodded, trying very hard to calm herself. "I do," she said, gasping. "I do, I swear it. I will not do anything foolish."

Emera patted her sister on the cheek as she released the woman from her embrace. "I know you will not," she said. "Trust me when I tell you that Juston will come back to rescue us. As soon as he hears that Brey's men have retaken the keep, he will come back. We simply need to stay alive until he does."

Jessamyn was calmer now and she sat heavily on the bed, contemplating their situation. "Do you really believe that?"

"I do."

Jessamyn looked at her sister. "It seems strange that the man who killed Brey should come back to save us."

Emera's lips twitched in an ironic smile. "I told you before, Jess," she said softly. "He freed us from Brey's tyranny. I will never look at him as anything other than that – our savior."

Jessamyn nodded, feeling shaky and weak as she lay back down on the bed. "Em?"

"Aye?"

"When you marry him, may I come live with you? I do not think I want to stay here."

It was an unexpected light moment and Emera grinned. "Of course you will come and live with us," she said. "Keep the faith that we shall live through this and that we shall go to Netherghyll Castle. Juston says there is even a garden there."

"That is a lovely thought."

Emera thought so, too. As Jessamyn closed her eyes, simply to regain her strength after their harrowing experience, Emera went about putting cold water from the bucket into the iron pot over the hearth, stoking the flames to heat the water. All the while, however, she could only think of one thing – *survival*. In the beginning of Juston's reign, she had done what she needed to do in order to survive. Now, she would do the same.

She had no doubt that Juston would return for her and she wanted to live to see that day.

God help them both.

CHAPTER TWENTY-ONE

One mile south of Cotherstone
To the west of the village of Lartington

A RMAGEDDON HAD ARRIVED.
     Again.

Juston had taken the high ground against the advancing forces of Hugh de Puiset, who fielded an army about the same size as Juston's. Laying siege to a castle and fighting a battle in open warfare required very different tactics, but Juston was a master of both. Taking up position on a rise with a small valley and a frozen creek running at the base of it, he had been informed by his scouts that de Puiset was moving in from the north. Juston set up his defensive lines so when morning came and light fell over the landscape, de Puiset could clearly see that there was an army between him and his destination of Bowes.

It would be a shocking moment for Durham, which is exactly what Juston intended.

By morning, the sleet had stopped but the heavy, gray clouds hung in the sky, threatening to let loose at any moment. Juston, however, was ready. Shortly after their arrival to their prime position, his men had gone into a nearby forest and had cut down eight large trees, stripping them of their branches. Hemp ropes were anchored onto the ends of trees and they were carried over to the main defensive line where they were lined up, one next to the other, so they formed, literally, a line of trees.

It was all part of Juston's field tactics. The tree trunks were slathered in sheep fat that he'd had his men collect from the sheep that had been slaughtered at Bowes. Behind the line of fat-coated trees came Juston's army, shoulder to shoulder with their shields raised and fitted together, seamlessly, for better protection for the men. Behind the shield men were the archers, protected by the shields. They, too, had the tips of their arrows dipped in fat and ready to ignite at Juston's command.

It was a fine line of precise men in Juston's army as he sat astride his war horse behind the lines with Christopher, watching David and Marcus, Maxton and Kress and Achilles position the men. Gart was up in the front with the men who had the fatted trees, waiting for the command to ignite them. That command wasn't long in coming; even though the trunks had been damp from the winter weather, the fat burned hot and heavy, sending black smoke into the air, and burning to the wood underneath that wasn't damp. With eight massive logs burning heavily, Juston watched the approach of de Puiset's army.

"He will want to *parler* first," Christopher said confidently. "Look at the way he's holding his army; they are simply hanging back. He is making no attempts to put them into formation. We have caught him off-guard."

Juston was watching the army to the north as well. "As we intended to," he said. "Now he sees that he must go through me to get to Bowes."

"De Puiset is not an aggressive tactician if, in fact, he is even riding with his army," Christopher said. "It is my guess that his generals are in charge while he remains at Auckland."

Juston nodded. "That would not surprise me in the least," he said. "We have been staring at each other for about an hour. I will give him a few minutes more before I send a messenger out to him. Find your brother and bring him to me. I will send him."

Christopher nodded, reining his war horse to the west where he could see David in the distance. Reaching his brother, a few words were exchanged before David headed in Juston's direction, wrestling with his excitable, young stallion. Christopher wasn't far behind him.

"My lord?" David said as he reined his horse next to Juston. "You wanted to speak with me?"

Juston nodded. "When Durham sends a messenger, you will meet the man in the middle. Our terms are as follows: de Puiset is to return to Auckland and remain there. He is not to come near Bowes and he is to keep any and all allies away from Bowes. Bowes is now held for Richard. If he does not agree to these terms, we will destroy him and his army this day, and when we are finished, we shall march on Auckland Castle and raze it. Make sure he understands."

David nodded shortly. "I will, my lord."

"I am sending you because you will not try to negotiate. If I send your brother, he will listen to their pleas and if I send any of the others, they will grow impatient and slay de Puiset's messenger. You will go in, deliver the message, and be done with it."

"Aye, my lord."

As David moved aside, awaiting the order to move forward to meet de Puiset's messenger, Christopher reined his horse alongside Juston.

"I will *not* listen to their pleas," he said, miffed. "I am not so weak."

Juston cast him a long look. "Nay, you are not weak, but you have more of a heart than most," he said. "What were we discussing at the conclusion of the siege of Bowes? How I lack mercy? I told you that too much of it can be deadly."

"I do not have too much mercy."

"You are the Great Communicator, Chris. You could negotiate God off his mighty throne. But today, I am in no mood for negotiations. De Puiset will fight or he will leave. There is no alternative."

Christopher had been insulted and complimented in close succession. Not having anything to say to Juston's statement, he fell silent and continued to watch the distant army. Oddly enough, the clouds that had hung so low and heavy in the sky abruptly parted, leaving spots of blue sky beyond. Sunbeams descended to the wet, frozen earth, like glowing fingers, illuminating the landscape.

The minutes passed as the clouds continued to part, leaving more and more blue sky, but on the earth below, there was suspicion and anxiety between the two opposing armies. Juston was nearing the command to send David out to deliver terms when he began to see movement in de Puiset's army.

As Juston and his men watched, the army of the Bishop of Durham began setting up offensive lines. The infantry was placed in three long lines that stretched about two hundred men each. One line was behind the other, meant to fill in should the line in front of them fail. Behind the infantry, the archers were brought in because Juston could see the standards that would deliver commands to the archers when lowered. Behind the archers, the cavalry took up position.

"So they will not send a messenger to *parler*," Juston muttered to Christopher. "It is their intention to simply go to war. I will, therefore, comply. Be ready to relay commands, Chris."

Christopher and David spurred their horses, charging off across the lines, preparing to ride out with the infantry. Some commanders, like de Puiset, preferred to send the cavalry in after the initial clash, but Juston didn't – a man on foot was no match for a man on a horse and he liked to strike hard and heavy in the initial stages of a battle.

When he saw Durham's lines began to move forward, he waited until they had covered nearly half the field. He needed them in a prime position in order to effectively cripple them as he intended to. Once they hit the bottom of the small valley and began to make their way up towards him, he gave the command his men had been waiting for.

It was time for the battle to begin in earnest.

The fire logs, in a long line at the very front of his army, were rolled forward by the men in charge of them. Rolling, flaming logs began to gather speed as they rolled down hill, turning into massive flaming projectiles, and de Puiset's army predictably began to run from them. Six hundred infantry turned and began to run as fast as they could, trying to escape the flaming logs, and that was when Juston let loose with his archers.

Flaming arrows now filled the sky, hitting the fleeing men and anyone else who happened to be in range. Between the flaming logs and the flaming arrows raining out of the sky, de Puiset's infantry dissolved into chaos. That was when Juston gave the command for his infantry to move.

Trapped and burning, de Puiset's army was already beaten when Juston's infantry descended. The knights plunged into the thick of it, cutting men down, killing those who tried to run, and when de Puiset ordered his cavalry to finally engage, it was nearly too late – Juston's cavalry, and his knights, had already thundered down the hill and were now engaging de Puiset's army right on their lines. Beneath the blue sky with puffy clouds, a slaughter of the Bishop of Durham's army was taking place with astonishing skill.

Juston sat at the top of the hill, watching everything and scrutinizing every section of fighting men, looking for an issue or a weakness. He still had about one hundred cavalry he'd held back, men he could send in quickly should the need arise, but all of his knights were engaged in a fierce battle. He could see the de Lohr brothers battling some of de Puiset's knights, and he saw clearly when Achilles, who had evidently been knocked off his horse, charged through the mass of fighting men, snapping necks and driving his sword into anyone who was unfortunate enough not to get out of his way fast enough.

It was a gruesome sight, but a satisfying one. Confident the battle was being won by his men, Juston nonetheless remained vigilant. He couldn't become too pleased with the progression yet, but he was hopeful. If he could only end this today, he could head to Brough and help them chase off Carlisle. His men would be weary, of course, but they were strong and they were professional. He had little doubt that they could help Brough's army triumph over Carlisle once and for all.

"My lord!"

Someone was calling his name and Juston turned to see some of his cavalry soldiers pointing off to the south. He reined his horse around because he couldn't see what the men were pointing at, but he soon saw the approach of a single rider from the south, heading up the road towards them at breakneck speed. He pointed to the rider.

"Intercept him," he commanded. "Go!"

Two cavalrymen spurred their horses onto the road, galloping towards the rider that was approaching them. Juston returned his attention to the battle, not particularly giving the incoming rider a great deal of thought, until several minutes later when the rider arrived. Juston heard his men muttering behind him and he turned to see that the rider was one of his own soldiers. It took him a moment to realize it was one of the men left behind to guard Bowes.

Apprehension filled him. There was no reason why a soldier from Bowes should be here... unless Bowes was somehow in danger.

"Why are you here?" he demanded. "What has happened at Bowes?"

The soldier, cold and dirty, was out of breath. "My lord," he said. "I have been sent to tell you that the wounded of Bowes, the men who had been kept in the vault, have risen up to take the keep. They have killed Sir Gillem and a few other men, and they now hold the keep for Henry."

Juston's mouth popped open in astonishment; he couldn't help it. "The *wounded* have taken the keep?"

The rider nodded, his expression between sick and ironic. "They were not so wounded, after all, my lord," he said. "They have sealed the keep up and we cannot get into it. They burned the stairs. With Sir Gillem dead, we have no commander except for senior solders. They continue to hold everything but the keep, but we need help."

Juston closed his mouth. *Sir Gillem is dead and we need help.* Realizing there had been an uprising from men he'd not considered a threat, he was consumed by rage he had never before experienced. Rising up from his toes, it filled his entire body like raging, liquid fire. He was so angry that he actually began to sweat.

This is what he'd meant when he told Christopher that mercy could be deadly – this situation was a perfect example. Wounded he had taken pity on by moving them into the vault had showed their gratitude by killing his knight and seizing his property.

He'd never been so furious in his entire life.

"How long ago did this happen?" he asked through clenched teeth.

"It started before dawn, my lord," the rider answered.

"Did you see any other army approaching? While we are off fighting de Puiset, no one else is coming for Bowes?"

"Nay, my lord. We saw no one else approaching but the patrol that was sent out at dawn has yet to return."

Juston sighed heavily; it was entirely possible de Puiset's army was just a ruse to lure him away from Bowes. He'd considered that, of course, but he felt the risk of leaving Bowes had been less than the need to remain. He was fairly confident that the uprising of the wounded was isolated. At least, he would proceed on that premise. Then, the most pressing question of all came forth.

"And the other occupants of the keep? The ladies?"

"They are trapped in the keep, my lord."

That was enough for Juston. He sent two cavalrymen out to find his knights. One by one, the knights began to trickle up the hill to his command. Christopher and Marcus were the first ones to reach him, with Marcus sporting a nasty gash on his right forearm. Their faces were alight with curiosity, flushed with the rush of battle.

"We should have the battle concluded by the end of the day," Christopher said, assuming that was why Juston had summoned them. "Their infantry was hit hard by our archers. Now it is a matter of bringing the cavalry to their knees."

Juston was still so furious that his lips were white. "I have just received word that the wounded of Bowes have risen up to capture the keep," he said. "They killed Gillem in the process."

Expressions of shock appeared on Christopher and Marcus' faces. "Gillem is dead?" Christopher repeated, astonished. "God's Bones… what happened?"

Juston struggled to keep his fury under control. "All I know is that they have taken the keep and that the women are trapped inside," he said. "I will, therefore, be returning to reclaim it. I will take Maxton, Kress, Achilles, and two hundred men with me. If it is just the keep, then that should be more than enough men. I will leave the rest of you to clean up this battle and send de Puiset back to Auckland in shame."

Christopher and Marcus nodded in agreement as they were joined by David, Gart, and Maxton. Christopher, however, was still focused on Juston and what he'd just been told.

"Juston," he said quietly as Marcus explained to the other what had happened. "Is it possible that Lady Emera and her sister are part of this revolt? They may not be trapped inside the keep as much as they are there willingly."

Juston didn't want to admit that; God help him, he couldn't admit that. To admit that Emera might be part of the rebellion would be to admit he'd been duped by her. He'd been made a fool of. Nay, he couldn't admit that at all. Until he saw evidence with his own eyes, he would go on the assumption that she was an unwilling victim in all of this.

Any other thought would destroy him.

"Although I cannot speak for the sister, I will say that Lady Emera is not part of this," he said quietly. "If she is trapped in the keep, then it is as a prisoner. The woman hated de la Roarke and she has no ties to Henry. There is no reason for her to participate in a revolt."

Christopher could see the anguish in Juston's eyes even though the man was trying desperately to hide it. Christopher knew why; proud, arrogant Juston de Royans couldn't admit that a woman may have fooled him. More than that, he would never admit to a woman breaking his heart.

Therefore, Christopher didn't press him. He simply let the subject go, sitting back and listening when Juston explained the situation to all of the knights, who had now joined him. There was outrage among the knights but, as Christopher could tell, there was also suspicion.

They were all suspicious of Lady Emera, who was conveniently trapped in the keep with a hoard of rebels, men she had been loyally tending since the siege of Bowes. Nay, it was just too much of a coincidence for Juston's knights, now worried that somehow the lady was luring Juston back to Bowes and to his death. If Juston couldn't see that, then the knights would have to make sure to protect the man.

They would be on their guard even if Juston wasn't.

As Christopher watched Juston, Maxton, Kress, Achilles, most of the reserved cavalry, and about one hundred soldiers head south, he couldn't seem to shake the sense of foreboding he was feeling. It all seemed like the perfect trap to capture Juston, who would make a fine prize for Henry's operation. Perhaps this had been planned all along because the timing of it just seemed far too coincidental.

A lady who had seduced Richard the Lionheart's most powerful knight, perhaps paid well by Henry's loyalists… de Puiset, Richmond, even Carlisle. Dear God… perhaps that's why Carlisle had been coming… to take away what would inarguably be Henry's most valuable prisoner, Juston de Royans.

All Christopher could do was sincerely pray that he was wrong. But one thing was for certain – he intended to wrap this battle up quickly and head back to Bowes as fast as he could.

If Henry's loyalists wanted Juston, it would be over his dead body.

CHAPTER TWENTY-TWO

Bowes Castle

T HE DAY WAS clear, which meant Arthos could see them coming.

To the north, he could see a small army approaching, following the road through the small hills that dotted the area, and his first thought was one of glee – *de Puiset was coming!*

Up on the roof of the keep, he had an unobstructed view of the countryside in all directions and now that the sun was shining, he could see for miles. When he saw the approach of the army from the north, he began jumping up and down, yelling in excitement, and the de Royans men who were surrounding the keep below were greatly concerned. The men on the battlements of the outer wall could see the approaching army, too, and it was a race between the factions to see who could identify the army first.

Was it de Puiset?

Was it de Royans?

Arthos was convinced it was de Puiset as he looked down at the de Royans soldiers in the inner bailey, drawing a finger across his throat in a slicing motion and then laughing gleefully. He was thrilled that they were soon to be aided in their quest to retake Bowes as Cowling, alerted by the yelling, emerged onto the roof.

Up until that point, he had been in the hall where Lady Emera and Lady Jessamyn were warming boiled pieces of mutton for the nooning meal. Cowling had tried to take charge of the rebellion but men like Arthos and Kenelm and Edgard would listen to him half of the time, ignore him the other half. They had no concept of conserving supplies and had been happily gulping the precious wine stores all morning, making them quite drunk. It didn't seem to occur to them that the wine might be needed over the course of days or even weeks.

In fact, they'd been running amok the entire day, like animals who had been released from their cages and had no idea what to do with their freedom. It was enough to cause Cowling to rethink joining them because it was clear they had no plan in mind. They thought they were holding the keep for Henry when, in fact, they'd only retaken the keep for themselves. With that understanding, Cowling could see that all of this was doomed to failure. He didn't want to be part of it.

So, he'd taken up space in the hall below while Lady Emera and Lady Jessamyn worked around him, silently preparing the coming meal, not saying a word to him as he sat and brooded. It was coming to occur to him that he should more than likely assist the women in escaping because once those men became too terribly drunk, they might set their sights on the only women in the keep. Cowling wasn't sure he could convince the men not to rape the women, especially Lady Emera because of her alleged ties to de Royans, so as he watched the women work, a plan began to form.

He had to get them out of the keep.

But then the shouts came, shouts from the roof two stories above. They were so loud that he could hear them quite plainly, so he left the hall and made his way up to the roof of the keep. Opening the trap door that was lodged in the floor of the roof, he emerged into the cold, brilliant sunshine as men ran about.

The roof itself was built of wood, pitched slightly to allow for drainage, with the angle of the pitch preventing the weight of snow or water to form upon it and lead to a collapse. Therefore, only the perimeter of the roof allowed men to walk on it and Cowling made his way around the sides to the northeast corner of the keep where Arthos and several other men were gathered, looking off into the distance. Immediately, Cowling could see the approach of the army.

"Look!" Arthos cried out gleefully. "It is de Puiset! I told you he would come, Cowling! Now, what have you to say? Henry will once again hold Bowes. By sunset, we shall be drinking a toast to the king!"

Cowling didn't reply. He shielded his eyes from the sunlight, watching as the tiny black dots on the horizon became bigger dots with arms and legs. Men on horseback could be seen, riding furiously, but until he saw the standards, he couldn't get excited about it. In fact, he didn't want to get excited about it because if it was de Puiset's army, that meant they were in for another battle when the de Royans men, who still held the majority of the castle, fought back. Either way, they were in for a battle.

"It is possible that it is de Puiset," he said reluctantly, still watching the group approach in the distance. "It is equally possible that it is not."

Arthos went from happily laughing to frowning in an instant. "Is that all you have to say?" he demanded. "Have you no joy for the fact that de Puiset has come to save us?"

Cowling's gaze never left the incoming army. "If it is him, I shall be properly joyful," he said. "But it also means there will be a battle here tonight because de Royans soldiers still hold much of the castle. Keep that in mind before you become too giddy with excitement."

Arthos pursed his lips irritably at the man. "You are too much doom and gloom, Cowling," he said. "You depress me."

Cowling didn't respond. He kept his focus on the incoming army as the others around him drank and cheered their beliefs that help had arrived. But the closer the group of riders came, the more Cowling was certain that they were not de Puiset.

Seeing the blue de Royans tunics confirmed it.

But he didn't say anything. He knew that if Arthos and the others knew de Royans was returning, things could go very badly in general. Most certainly, Cowling was afraid for the women now. He was increasingly convinced that drunk rebels and a grudge against Lady

Emera would spell disaster. Therefore, he left the roof and disappeared back down the hatch.

Time was pressing as Cowling quickly took the spiral stairs down to the great hall. He was moving with such haste that he nearly tripped, entering the great hall just as Emera was taking a very large pot off of the fire. He rushed up as she set it on the ground, using her apron to guard her hands against the searing iron.

"Ladies," he addressed hurriedly. "There is no time to explain, but you must come with me now. Please."

Jessamyn, on her knees before the fire, sat back on her heels and looked at him curiously. "Why?" she asked. "What is the matter?"

Emera was wiping her hands off on her apron, peering at the man who seemed to be almost panicked. Her brow furrowed.

"Cowling?" she asked. "What has happened?"

Cowling sighed with some frustration. He had told them there was no time to explain, yet that was exactly what they were asking him to do. He realized he had to tell them, as rapidly and as concisely as he could, what was transpiring. It was either that or drag them out of the hall, screaming, and if that happened it would most assuredly attract attention. He tried to be brief because, for the women, this was life or death.

"The de Royans army is returning, or at least some of it is," he said quickly. "Someone must have gotten a message to de Royans about the rebellion. I have a feeling when they realize it is de Royans who has come, those drunken fools might try to make examples out of you both. If you want to live, then you will come with me."

Emera and Jessamyn didn't need to be told twice. Hurriedly, they dropped what they were doing and scampered after Cowling as he led them up to the second floor, very aware of the cries and laughter still coming from the roof. Slipping into the master's chamber, he bolted the door to the stairwell. At least that would give them a little time before the rebels realized where they were and broke the door down. Quickly, he hustled the ladies into the second smaller adjoining chamber and bolted that door as well.

"What are you going to do?" Emera asked anxiously. "Why did you take us in here?"

Cowling immediately went to the window, sticking his head out and seeing how far the drop was to the bailey below. It was far too big a drop to make unassisted and he began to look around the room for something to help him lower the ladies from the chamber. His gaze fell on the bed and he rushed to it, yanking off the coverlet to reveal a variety of linens beneath.

"Quickly," he hissed. "We must tie the linens together and make a rope so that you may escape from the window."

"A rope?" Jessamyn gasped. "But we will fall to our deaths!"

"Would you rather face the mob?"

They wouldn't. Fed by a frightening sense of urgency, Emera and Jessamyn swung into action, yanking the linens off of the bed and tying the ends together. End after end, they tied, and Cowling tested the ties, having to re-tie some of them. But the linen rope wasn't nearly long enough and he unbolted the chamber door so they could strip the master's bed as well.

As Cowling secured the ties, Emera and Jessamyn pulled the linens from the master's bed and dragged them into the smaller chamber for Cowling to secure to the rope. It was the three of them, working madly to make a rope of linens as the whooping and yelling on the roof suddenly went silent.

It was not a good silence.

That's when Cowling knew they were in trouble.

"DE ROYANS!" ARTHOS screamed. "It's de Royans!"

The men on the roof could hardly believe their eyes, but there before them, illuminated by the unexpectedly sunny day, was a contingent of heavily armed men led by none other than de Royans himself.

The High Sheriff of Yorkshire was hard to miss because he wasn't wearing a helm, so his dark blonde curls waved wildly in the wind as he galloped up the road towards Bowes. Leading his pack of armed men, he stood out as a mountain of a man, riding like the wind, in control of both himself and his mission.

It was an imposing sight, indeed.

"It *cannot* be!" Kenelm gasped. "How could he have come instead? Where is de Puiset?"

No one had an answer. All of the revelry and wine drinking came to an immediate halt as the wounded of Bowes watched in horror as de Royans led his army right up to the gatehouse. They could hear the creaking from the portcullis as it was raised, old ropes straining to lift the weight, and it was then that the reality of the situation began to sink in.

De Royans, in the flesh, would soon be upon them.

"Nay!" Arthos breathed in disbelief. "I cannot believe it!"

His cohorts, Kenelm and Edgard, were equally shocked. The wine that had made them so happy was now making them wildly paranoid and fearful.

"What should we do?" Kenelm begged. "De Royans will gain access to the keep and then he will kill us! What should we do?"

Arthos was struggling to think clearly. There was too much wine in his head, making his thoughts spin, but he grasped at the most obvious idea. De Royans had arrived to reclaim his keep, and his whore, but the whore had to be used to ensure the safety of the rebels. That was the obvious solution until he could think of a way out of this for them all. He shoved past his fearful comrades.

"Where are the women?" he bellowed. "Bring them to me!"

The men began to scatter, all of them trying to make it through the hatch that led to the spiral stairs and all of them bogging it up, fighting, each man trying to push past the other. Finally, one man managed to make it down, followed by another man and still another. Soon, all of the drunkards who had been on the roof made it down the stairs one at a time and without killing each other in their inebriated state.

They were on a hunt.

The first place the group went to was the hall because that's the last place the women were seen. When the hall proved empty, they split up, half going to the vault and the other half heading to the second floor where the sleeping chambers were. When they realized the master's chamber door was bolted from the inside, they began to yell at the group below, telling them to bring axes or pikes, poles, anything that could be used to break the door down.

They continued to pound on the oaken panel, demanding that whoever had locked it should open it, but their demands were met with silence. That infuriated the mob further as Arthos beat on the door until his hands hurt, screaming at whoever was inside.

He *knew* it was the women.

The interior doors of the keep were heavy wood held together with iron strips, but the bolt that locked the door and held it to the stone wall was too small for the size of the door. It was a design flaw that King Henry's architects had overlooked when they'd upgraded the keep several years ago. With a door that size and weight, a bigger bolt was needed, and as the drunken wounded pounded on the door from the landing, splintering the wood, it was only a matter of time until the small bolt gave way.

Inside the smaller chamber, Cowling and Emera and Jessamyn could hear the pounding and they knew it was only a matter of time before those pounding on the door managed to break it down. Cowling was working furiously to secure the last piece of linen, his big fingers deftly tying off the knots. Even with the considerable length of the rope, it would still dangle several feet off the ground, but that couldn't be helped. They were out of time.

Finishing with the knot, Cowling grabbed the nearest woman, which happened to be Emera.

"Come, quickly," he said, looping the linen around her waist. "I must lower you from the window. There will be a bit of a gap at the end, but it shouldn't be too much. You can fall to safety."

Emera balked, pulling the linen off her midsection. "Nay," she said. "You must lower Jessamyn first. Get my sister out of here!"

Cowling frowned. "Lady Emera, you are the one they want," he said. "I must remove you immediately. There is no time to argue about this!"

The pounding on the door grew louder and they could hear objects hitting the floor. Chips of wood were flying off the door as the wood splintered.

"Please," Emera begged, fearing that the men might break through at any second. "I am of some value to them, at least, but my sister is not. I am afraid they will throw her off the roof in their rage, so you must help her to escape first."

Cowling was beside himself. "My lady, I cannot...!"

"You *must*!"

"But you do not know what they will do to you!"

"If they think they can use me against Juston, then I will be safe, at least for a time. But my sister will not be!"

Cowling was torn, miserable. "My lady, please...."

Emera would not hear him. "*Do it!*"

She began wrapping the end of the linen rope around Jessamyn's waist as the woman stood there and gasped in panic. When Cowling tried to remove it to put it on Emera again, Emera simply moved out of arm's length, thrusting her sister at the man, and Cowling had little choice. He had to get one of them out and Emera was making it most difficult. With great reluctance, he began to tie the linen around Jessamyn's waist. Emera was giving him no say in the situation at all.

Meanwhile, Emera was coming to realize that she needed to buy her sister some time because the drunken mob were nearly through the door. The second door, which covered the portal to her chamber, wasn't as big or as strong as the one currently being pummeled. More than that, with the pass-through hearth, all those fools had to do was come in through the weak fire to capture them. Being that they were desperate and angry, she couldn't imagine that the small fire in the hearth would prevent them from coming through it.

Clearly, they had very little defense once the master chamber door broke down and with that thought, Emera grabbed the heavy fire poker and went to her chamber door, throwing it open. Seeing the state of the other door, nearly broken through, she turned to Cowling.

"Lower my sister to freedom," she half-hissed, half-begged. "I will hold them off as much as I can."

Aghast, he tried to plead with her. "My lady – you must not!"

"Do not argue with me! Do as I say!"

With that, she was gone, dashing through the master's chamber and wielding the poker like a club, pounding on those who were trying to get their fingers inside the door to lift the bolt. As she whacked and smacked, listening to Arthos and his men cry out in pain and rage, Cowling watched her in awe for a moment before slamming the smaller chamber door and bolting it.

"God's Bones," he grunted as he finished securing the knot around Jessamyn's waist. "I would never have believed it had I not seen it with my own eyes. Your sister's bravery is that of ten men."

Jessamyn was terrified for her sister. "She is doing it to save me," she wept. "Please… do not allow anything to happen to her."

Cowling rushed Jessamyn to the window and lifted her up onto the sill. "I will do my best, my lady, I swear it," he said. "So brave a woman, I dare not disappoint. Now, out with you, lass. Do not let your sister's sacrifice be in vain!"

He pushed Jessamyn out, listening to her weeping with fright, as he lowered her foot by foot, slowly so that she would not drop. The keep was fifty feet in height, quite considerable, so it would not do to have Jessamyn fall as he tried to lower her out. As Emera tried to hold off those who were breaking down the master chamber door, Cowling lowered Jessamyn as far as he could. There was no more rope left. Looking out of the window, he could see that she was still several feet from the bottom.

"Untie yourself!" he called down to her.

Jessamyn was holding on to the rope with a death grip. "I'll fall!"

"If you do not untie yourself, you will die! Please, my lady!"

Weeping, Jessamyn struggled with the knot, finally managing to undo it and falling to the ground several feet below. She landed, unharmed, but her struggles had attracted attention and several de Royans soldiers, having heard the commotion, came around to help. Cowling was vastly relieved when he saw the men helping Jessamyn out of the mud. Now, he knew she was safe.

With one lady down, he reeled in the linen rope and turned his attention to Lady Emera. He could still hear the struggle at the master chamber door and he opened the smaller chamber door at nearly the same time as someone managed to lift the bolt on the master chamber's door.

Men poured in and Emera was swallowed up by them. Cowling lost sight of her although he could hear her resisting whatever they were trying to do to her. The next thing he realized, Arthos was storming at him with a fire poker in-hand, the same poker that Emera had been using. He shook it in Cowling's face.

"Where is the other woman?" he demanded.

Cowling shook his head. "She is not here," he said simply. "What are you doing with Lady Emera?"

Enraged, Arthos ignored the question, pushing past Cowling and going into the smaller chamber. Clearly, Lady Jessamyn was not there. He looked under the bed and even in the trunk, but there was no sign of the lady. It was as if she had vanished. He came out of the chamber, red in the face.

"What did you do with her?" he snarled.

Cowling remained calm. "I did not do anything with her," he said. "How do you know she was even here? Mayhap she is in the vault."

"She is *not* in the vault," Arthos barked. "Do you think me blind? She is not in the vault and she is not in the hall, yet you were in here with the whore. *Where is Lady de la Roarke?*"

Cowling merely shrugged. If the mob didn't know, or at least suspect, then he wasn't going to tell them. They were a stupid bunch, anyway, but he was very concerned that the stupid bunch had Emera, trapped by several men who were using hemp rope to tie her up. She was kicking and fighting for all she was worth.

"If you do not know where Lady de la Roarke is, surely I do not, either," he finally said. "Tell me why you are tying Lady Emera up. What has she done?"

Arthos had finally reached his limit. Infuriated, and still quite drunk, he took the fire poker in his hand and rammed it straight into Cowling's belly. The tip of it was sharp and pierced his flesh quite easily. He plowed the poker all the way through Cowling, even as the man fell to the ground, mortally wounded. Arthos' rage was so great that he didn't care that he'd just killed a man he had greatly respected. All he saw was a man who was against him.

Cowling's last recollection was hearing Emera's screams as she was taken from the chamber.

CHAPTER TWENTY-THREE

THE GATEHOUSE OF Bowes opened wide for Juston, admitting him into the vast outer ward as the soldiers he left behind swarmed around him. The men he'd brought with him filtered in and he dismounted his steed, grabbing the first soldier he came across.

"Who is in charge now?" he demanded.

The soldier, a younger man, pointed to an older warrior who was coming from the gatehouse. Juston recognized the older man as a soldier who had been with his army a very long time. Tomas was his name. Pushing through the men and horses, he made his way to Tomas.

"I received word that the keep has been taken by rebels," he said. "Gillem has been killed?"

"He was, my lord."

"There was nothing you could do for him?"

"Nay, my lord. He took an arrow to the neck."

"Where is he?"

"Over near the stables. We put him over there and covered him up with straw."

Juston sighed, shaking his head with some regret. Although he was sorry for the loss of a good sword, he found that he wasn't particularly sorry that he'd lost Gillem. At least he wouldn't have to worry about the man's conniving any longer and that was a burden relieved.

"Very well," he said after a moment. "What is the situation now?"

The old soldier glanced at the top of the keep, seen over the top of the inner wall. "The wounded from the vault have arisen and claimed the keep in the name of Henry, my lord," he said. "Since Sir Gillem was killed by an arrow from the keep, we know they have some manner of weapons, which keeps us in the outer bailey. They are trying to kill everyone that comes within range but a few minutes ago, one of the women escaped through a window."

Juston's heart caught in his throat. "*Which* woman?"

"Lady Jessamyn."

Now he was swept with disappointment to hear it wasn't Emera. "Where is she?"

The old soldier motioned for him to follow. "Come with me, my lord."

Juston did, with Maxton and Kress and Achilles behind him. Together, the group followed the old soldier through the muddy outer ward and back to the cold, dark gatehouse.

They were taken to a small room, a guard room where a fire blazed brightly in the hearth. The room was only big enough for six or eight men at a time, and Juston crowded in with his knights behind him only to see Jessamyn sitting on a three-legged stool next to the fire, trembling as she tried to warm herself. When she looked up and saw Juston, she burst into tears.

"They have her," she wept. "They have my sister!"

Juston struggled not to feel sick. He crouched down next to her, trying to keep his manner calm and soothing. "Lady Jessamyn, what happened?" he asked. "We received word that the wounded rose up and took the keep."

Jessamyn wiped at her nose. "They did," she said. "I do not know what happened, to be truthful. Emmy and I were sleeping when the wounded soldiers burst into our chamber and announced they had taken the keep. They called Emmy your whore and they seemed to be very angry with her, but she swore she was not a traitor. We had to help them or they would have killed us."

"Then… then she did not have anything to do with this uprising?"

Jessamyn shook her head. "Never," she insisted. "Emera is not the kind of woman to rebel. Surely you know that about her by now."

He did, but to hear it from Jessamyn's lips was the confirmation he needed. He hung his head for a moment because there was a massive load off of his heart and mind to realize that Emera hadn't anything to do with this rebellion, that she had simply been caught up in something she couldn't fight off. He felt foolish that he'd let his suspicions get the better of him.

Truthfully, he'd known of her innocence all along or at least he'd hoped he'd known. He hadn't wanted to doubt her, to have faith in the relationship they were building. At Jessamyn's words, something inside of him felt vindicated.

"I know," he said after a moment. "But I needed to hear it from you. Who is leading this rebellion, then?"

Jessamyn was deeply troubled. "Men who have served my husband for a very long time," she said. "Wounded men that my sister and I nursed back to health. We had no idea they were planning something like this, I swear it. Never once did we hear utterings to that regard. We were completely surprised when they burst into our chamber and told us they now held the keep for Henry."

Juston was listening intently. "Where was Emera when you escaped?" he asked. "Why did she not come with you?"

Jessamyn teared up again. "A sympathetic soldier helped me to escape by making a rope of linens and lowering me from the chamber window," she said. "He tried to send Emera first but she refused, insisting that I go instead. The wounded were at the chamber door, pounding it, breaking it down, and she went to fight them off so that Cowling could lower me from the window."

Juston was shocked by what he heard. "Cowling?" he repeated. He knew the name of the man who had once served him, a man he respected. "He was the one who helped you?"

"Aye."

"He was not involved in the rebellion?"

"I do not know for certain. He did not seem to be as much as the others were."

"And Emera... the last you saw of her, she was fighting the rebels?"

Jessamyn nodded. "She is brave that way. She is braver than I could ever hope to be."

Those few words were an understatement as far as Juston was concerned. He felt a great deal better knowing that Cowling was on the inside, possibly helping Emera, but hearing that she had fought against those who had taken the keep... the mere thought was overwhelming him. He could just see her using whatever weapon she could to strike back at those threatening her and Jessamyn, and he'd never been so proud or so angry all at the same time. Angry with Emera for risking her life, but proud just the same. She was selfless to a fault, this time for her sister.

He could only pray it didn't cost her everything.

Wearily, he stood up. He wasn't particularly physically exhausted, but mentally he was nearly at his limit. The last time a woman he loved was in danger, he hadn't been able to help her. That terrible reality kept rolling over and over in his mind, pounding it home. But this time, he made it back before anything could happen to the woman who held his heart. At least, he prayed that was the case because he intended to save her or die trying.

There was no question in his mind.

He turned to Maxton and the other knights, wedged in behind him.

"You heard her," he said. "Rebels hold the keep. We must find out if they have a price for their safety and release."

Maxton nodded, motioning Kress and Achilles out of the cramped room. Juston followed. When the four knights were outside, they joined into a quiet huddle, away from the other men. With just the four of them, they could lay out their plans.

"Achilles, if Lady Jessamyn was lowered from a chamber window, mayhap there is a way to get back into the keep," Juston said. "I would like to think that while I keep the leaders of this mob occupied, you and Kress could find a way in."

Achilles nodded. "We can try, but that is a very tall keep," he said. "We could build a ladder to reach the hall entry but that would take time."

Juston shook his head. "If they have the door bolted, which I am sure they do, then it must be opened from the inside before you can gain admittance," he said. "I am talking about any of the windows. If we could only get Cowling to lower that linen rope again, we could use it to climb up."

"I think that we should get a look at the keep first and see the state of it for ourselves," Maxton put in. "If we cannot get in through the hall entry, then we shall have to get in another way."

"There *is* another way."

Kress had spoken those words and they all looked at him expectantly. "The latrines in the hall," he continued. "The ones on the top floor. They have large shoots and wooden seats. If we come up through them, we can easily break the seats away."

Maxton and Achilles gave him such a look that Juston had to fight off a grin. "You know it will be us going up those shite holes, correct?" Maxton said, his expression wrought with disgust. "We will be climbing through other men's piss!"

Achilles pointed a finger at Kress. "You will go first," he said. "You can clear the way and then I shall follow. This is *your* foolish idea."

Juston put up a hand to silence their annoyance, although he did find it rather humorous. "Enough," he said quietly. "If going up through the privy chute is the best way to gain access, then so be it. But if you can find another way, I suggest you try. Meanwhile – Maxton, you will seek a *parler* with whoever holds this keep. I wish to speak with them."

Maxton cast a long glance at the inner bailey. "Aye," he said in resignation. "Give me a shield so they do not try to shoot me with an arrow like they did Gillem. Juston, I cannot say that I ever liked Gillem, for we all know how the man tried to manipulate you using his sister, but I am sorry to hear of his death. In spite of what we all thought of him, he was a good knight."

Juston nodded in a fashion that suggested he was thinking the very same thing. "Indeed," was all he said. "Get on with it, Max. Time is wasting."

They waited while Maxton went back to his horse to retrieve his shield. When he had it up in front of him, well-fortified, he proceeded through the inner wall and came face to face with the enormous keep. Cold, foreboding, and stretching to the sky, he could quickly see what the rebels had done to the forebuilding, burning the wooden stairs that had been protected by stone. The ground around the keep was still littered with dead and he recognized a few of the servants. Holding the shield up, he shouted to those in the keep.

"I come on behalf of the High Sheriff of Yorkshire, Juston de Royans," he boomed. "I wish to speak with whoever is in command."

No one replied right away but he could hear movement. He just wasn't sure where it was coming from. He could hear voices, muffled, and shuffling around. It took him a moment to realize that there were men on the roof and he stepped back, raising his shield to ensure nothing came hurling down at him from that angle. He called up again.

"Who is in command?" he bellowed. "De Royans wishes to speak with him."

A head leaned over the side of the keep, but only partially. There were other heads up there, too, but Maxton couldn't really see them or make out features. The man nearly directly above him shouted down to him.

"What does de Royans want?" he said.

"To whom am I speaking?"

A pause. "My name is Arthos. I have nothing to say to de Royans. If he does not abandon Bowes completely, there will be serious consequences."

From where Juston was standing, he could hear what the man said and he didn't like that in the least. That threat had him moving towards the inner bailey already but Kress stopped him, forcing him to wait until his shield was retrieved. Once he had it in-hand, he held the shield high and took off at a run into the inner bailey.

Maxton didn't hear Juston until the man was upon him and it startled him so badly that he nearly drew a dagger on the man. Heart pumping as he saw who it was, he also knew why Juston had come.

There will be serious consequences....

"I am de Royans," Juston called up to the keep. "I will not make an aggressive move against you, but I want to be able to reach a peaceful settlement. What is it that you want?"

The rebel in command leaned further over the side of the roofline, exposing most of his head. He was an older man with long, dirty hair. "I told you," he yelled down to them. "You must abandon Bowes. That is what I want."

"I cannot go against Richard's order. He wants me to hold the castle. Surely you can understand that I have my orders."

More chatter and scuffling on the roof. Juston and Maxton looked at each other with some curiosity and apprehension. There was evidently some discussion going on up there. Abruptly, the rebel commander leapt up onto the wide edge of the roofline, exposing his entire body. But he reached down and, with help from a few of his comrades, pulled up another figure next to him. Juston was trying to see what they were doing without exposing his head too much, but he caught a glimpse of long, black hair blowing in the breeze.

His heart sank.

"Great Bleeding Christ...," he hissed.

Maxton, too, caught sight of Emera on the battlements next to the rebel leader. She was gagged and bound around the torso, with a great deal of rope wrapped around her body. In fact, she couldn't move at all but she was propped quite dangerously on the edge of the roofline as the rebel leader held on to her arm. Beside him, Juston flinched and

Maxton threw out an arm to prevent the man from leaving the safety of his shield.

"Nay, Juston," he said, blocking the man from moving. "They are trying to draw you out. They probably have archers trained on you this very moment, so do not move. It would be suicide."

Juston's gaze was riveted to Emera, trussed and gagged, and his heart was breaking. He couldn't even imagine what the rebels had already put her through and, in truth, he couldn't think about it. As it was, he was barely holding his composure. As he struggled not to rush out and get himself killed, the rebel leader shouted down from the roof.

"We have your whore, de Royans," he yelled. "Take your men out of Bowes or I will throw her down into the bailey and all you'll have left of her is pieces. Do you understand me?"

Juston closed his eyes against the threat, as if to block it out. *God, why?* Why did this have to happen again? He'd found happiness. Aye, he'd found love again but now something was threatening to take her away from him, just as Lizette had been taken away from him. Here he was in a pivotal moment, a precipice from which there was no escape – he'd been unable to save Lizette. He'd never had the chance. But with Emera, he had the opportunity to save her. And he would, any way he could.

Now, the rage was starting to build. These rebels had signed their own death warrants when they decided to use Emera has a hostage. Juston de Royans was a man of action. He rarely negotiated because he never had to. He was decisive in everything, correct in his decisions, and this would be no different. Now was the time to put that perfection to the test.

He had to save Emera.

"Max," he muttered. "I will keep them occupied but you must find a way into the keep. Can you do this?"

Maxton felt Juston's burden. He could see the panicked look in the man's eye but he was doing an admirable job of trying to hide it. The knights had been worried that Lady Emera might somehow tear Juston down and perhaps this was the way she was going to do it. It was unintentional on her part, but still, Juston was willing to do anything to save her. That much was clear. If Maxton didn't find a way into the keep, then Juston would make a run at it and more than likely get himself killed in the process.

Now, Juston's burden became Maxton's.

"I can try," he whispered. "But do not do anything until I send you a signal of some kind. You must give me time to find a way in."

Juston didn't look too confident in that request. "I am not sure how much time I can give you," he said quietly. "But I will try. Max... I know it is a lot to ask of you, I truly do, but I must tell you that Emera means everything to me. Call it infatuation, or foolishness, or whatever you will. I do not care. I am telling you the truth when I say that I love the woman. I cannot let her die."

Maxton was hit by the sincerity in Juston's eyes, nearly as astonishing as the confession itself. Guilt swept him. Had he thought wrongly about Lady Emera, then? Had they *all* thought wrongly about her? She was the enemy, that was true, but Juston de Royans wasn't in the habit of making bad decisions. Perhaps they should have trusted his judgment when it came to the lady, for if she had been able to thaw out Juston's frozen heart, then perhaps she was worthy of their faith. Perhaps, just this once, Juston needed a guardian angel to ensure that he didn't lose another woman that he loved. One thing was for certain, however – Maxton couldn't stand to see the agony in Juston's eyes.

He had to help.

"You will not," he assured him with renewed courage. "I will find a way in, but you keep the rebels distracted. Do what you must."

"I will."

At that point, they separated. Maxton could hear Juston calling up to the rebels again, gaining their attention, as Maxton fled the inner bailey. He was nearly to the entry in the inner wall when he happened to see something over on the corner of the keep, something white and lengthy. The wind was blowing a bit and whatever it was had apparently blown the other way, or so he thought. When the wind gusted again, he caught sight of it clearly –

A rope made out of bed linens, hanging from an upper window.

Perhaps that guardian angel was a reality, after all.

COWLING KNEW HE was dying.

The fire poker that Arthos had rammed into his body had done horrific damage, but it hadn't killed him immediately. After the initial injury, Cowling had fallen to the floor and passed out, but he emerged from that hazy blackness to find himself still alive and staring at the ceiling. He tried to move but the pain was tremendous and, from the odd buzzing sensation in his legs, he suspected his time on this earth was very limited. But he didn't want to die here, in a nest of rebels, because his name would be forever associated with the fools who tried to retake the keep. That, he couldn't stomach.

He had to get out.

But leaving the keep was impossible since the stairs to the entry had been burned. Over to his left, he could see the bed linen rope, coiled up where he had left it. If it was good enough to lower Lady Jessamyn to the ground, then perhaps he could use it to escape from the window, too. His strength was waning and he knew it was more than likely an impossible task, but he had to try.

Slowly, he dragged himself across the floor, towards the linen rope, smearing blood across the wood floor as he went. It was pure agony to move but he was determined to escape. Grasping the rope, he tied it to the leg of the bed, hoping the bed was heavy enough to support his weight as he climbed down to freedom. All he could think of at the moment was getting clear of the keep and not necessarily of his safety in doing so. He was a dead man, anyway. All he wanted to do was get out of there.

But his fingers wouldn't work properly. Deprived of blood, it took him several tries to tie a knot that could possibly hold. Then came the matter of standing up; he was still on the ground and he used every last remaining bit of strength he had to sit up, using the bed as leverage.

Breathing heavily, and in excruciating agony, he paused for a moment, digging deep to summon more strength to stand and go to the chamber window. He found himself looking around the chamber, wondering where Lady Emera had been taken and praying that whatever they did to her, she was dead before they did it. The men he saw this day were not the men he'd known for the past several years, men he'd fought with and lived alongside. They were desperate animals. He was ashamed to have been a part of their madness.

Gripping the bed, he rolled to his knees, saving his last remaining strength to crawl to the window because he couldn't seem to stand. He had the end of the rope in his hand and he gripped the windowsill, pulling himself up as he tossed the end of the rope through the window. He fed the rope through until there was no more rope to feed, and with the hope that he could climb down the rope without falling the entire way, he hoisted himself into the windowsill.

But it was too much for his dying body to take. Cowling was in the windowsill, preparing to take the rope in hand, when his vision dimmed. He tried to hold on to the windowsill but he couldn't, his body giving out as he fell back into the chamber, crashing to the floor in a heap of blood and bones and flesh.

For a brief moment, he felt the disappointment of not being able to climb out of the window, but that disappointment soon faded. A warm light enveloped him and the last thought that crossed Cowling's mind as his body gave out was that death wasn't such a horrible thing, after all.

It was the warm, white light that finally helped him escape for good.

MAXTON WASN'T SURE if the rebels on the roof of the keep had seen him move, but no one seemed to be shouting or pointing, or drawing attention to him. He considered that a small victory of sorts.

After seeing the linen rope blowing in the breeze, Maxton had casually made his way back into the inner bailey but he'd stayed to the south side of the keep, away from the northeast side where Juston was yelling to the rebels. Maxton could hear talk of a great battle lord in the north, Ajax de Velt, and monetary compensation to the rebels, and he knew that Juston was simply trying to keep them busy. It was a negotiation tactic, of finding a common ground with an enemy to ease a volatile situation, and Juston was very good at it.

Keep them talking!

Pressed against the keep on the south side, he was out of the line of sight of the rebels on the roof. He could still see the linen rope blowing in the breeze but he realized that the end of the rope was several feet off the ground, perhaps even beyond his reach. He began to inch towards it when he caught movement out of the corner of his eye; Kress and Achilles were at the entrance to the inner bailey and they could clearly see him as he pressed himself up against the keep. Maxton held up a hand to prevent the two of them from coming to him but, loyal friends that they were, they ignored him, darting across the inner bailey and into the shadow of the keep. Maxton was furious.

"Why did you come?" he hissed. "God help us if those rebels on the roof saw us."

Achilles was pressed against the cold stone. "We could not see them from where we were standing," he said. "Juston is up by the northwest corner of the keep, speaking to the men on the roof. I think I saw Lady Emera up there with them."

"You did," Maxton said. "They have her as a hostage and are threatening to kill her if Juston does not leave Bowes and take his army. He is trying to distract them while I find a way into the keep, so we have little time. We must save the woman. But the angels must be smiling upon us because someone has lowered a rope for us to use."

Kress and Achilles strained to see what Maxton was talking about.

The wind was picking up now and dark clouds were starting to blow in, undoubtedly a foreshadow of the bad weather to come. But the wind had one advantage; it blew the linen rope around so they could see it swaying gently in the breeze.

But if they could see it, chances were the rebels on the roof might be able to see it if they shifted position. Quickly, they began to move.

With speed and stealth, the trio rounded the side of the keep and came face to face with the rope, hanging from a third floor window. It dangled about seven or eight feet off the ground and Maxton had Achilles boost him up so that he could get a grip on it. With his great upper body strength, he climbed the rope up to the window it was hanging out of, peering inside to make sure this wasn't some manner of trap. He didn't see anyone, nor did he hear anyone, so he hoisted himself through the window and leapt out into the chamber beyond.

The first thing he saw was a dead man lying on the floor of the chamber with a fire poker through his midsection. Obviously, there had been an altercation in the chamber and his senses were attuned to his surroundings. Since he knew the wounded of Bowes held the keep, at last count there were under fifty of them, which meant somewhere in this keep – or spread throughout it – were almost fifty men. As good a knight as he was, and he was one of the best, even he wasn't sure he could take on fifty men. Therefore, he waited for Kress and Achilles to follow.

Behind him, the bed suddenly shifted, startling the hell out of him, but he realized that it was because of extreme tension on the linen rope. Guessing his comrades were both on the rope at this point, he threw his weight into holding the bed steady as Kress first appeared in the window and then Achilles. They both entered the chamber, seeing the dead man on the floor, and looked at the surroundings as if they were on the hunt.

Or being hunted.

"What happened?" Kress hissed, pointing to the body on the floor. "Did he attack you?"

Maxton shook his head. "He was dead when I arrived," he said. "These two chambers are empty but if my calculations on Bowes' remaining wounded are correct, there are close to fifty men in this keep as part of the rebellion. We must proceed carefully."

Kress and Achilles nodded, their bodies coiled with caution and anticipation. "Do we have a plan?"

Maxton nodded as he made his way to the chamber door. "Make it to the roof and save the lady," he said dryly. Then, he glanced at his companions. "I am going to assume that not all of the rebels are on the roof, which means we must prevent any of them on the floors below us from reaching it. Achilles, that will be your task. Kress, you come with me. Between the two of us, we should be able to fight off whoever is on the roof and reach the lady. She will be my target, Kress. The rebels are yours."

Kress cocked an eyebrow. "Fifty men in this keep, you say?"

"Aye."

"This should be simple."

He meant it with great irony, something that was keenly felt by all of them. Three knights, fifty men... no problem, indeed.

"What weapons do we have?" Achilles asked.

Maxton shook his head. "None that I know of," he said. "Unless you want to take the fire poker from that corpse."

Achilles didn't hesitate. He yanked the bloody fire poker from the body and wielded it like a sword. "Let us proceed," he said.

Maxton made Achilles go first since he had the only weapon between the three of them. Emerging into the master's chamber, they noticed the shattered door immediately and there were several large, sharp pieces of wood lying on the floor, heavy wood that was perfect for a weapon. Maxton selected a big, sharp piece and Kress picked up another. Now, all three of them at least had something to use should it be needed.

And they had no doubt it would be needed.

The spiral stairs were dark and quiet. The men paused, listening for voices or sounds, anything to give them any indication where the rebels were. They thought they heard something down in the great hall but they couldn't be sure. Regardless, their target was on the roof and Maxton and Kress moved for the roof hatch while Achilles covered their back.

The roof hatch was ajar. The closer Maxton and Kress came to it, the more they could hear shouting. It was ajar enough that they could see what was happening and what they saw wasn't encouraging; a rebel had jumped on to the crenellation of the roofline and Lady Emera, bound hand and foot, had been hauled up beside him. He was holding on to her and another man stood behind her, supporting her also, while no more than fifteen rebels wandered around on the roof. In fact, a pair of them were heading towards the hatch and Maxton quickly motioned Kress and Achilles down the stairs and into the master's chambers, where they pressed themselves against the wall on either side of the broken door.

They could hear the rebels coming down the stairs from the roof, talking between themselves, and they lay in wait until the pair came to the landing in front of the master chamber door. Then, they ambushed them, pulling them into the chamber and killing them, stealing their weapons. Both of the rebels had been armed with short swords, which were infantry weapons used for close quarters fighting. Now, Maxton and Kress were properly armed.

"Hold this stairwell at all costs," Maxton instructed Achilles. "But if you hear too much commotion on the roof, come up and help us."

Achilles nodded. The three of them went back out to the stairwell again as Maxton and Kress, once again, moved to the roof hatch. It was fully closed now so they had to take the chance to raise it slightly so they could see. Still, the scene on the roof showed the lady on the battlements with a rebel beside her. The rest of the rebels were gathered up around them, looking over the side of the keep. Maxton turned to Kress.

"The moment they realize we are after the lady, her life is forfeit," he whispered. "I am going to run for her and no other. You make a break for the north side of the roof as a distraction. Kill anything that moves. Chances are, they'll be so surprised to see us that the lady will not go over the side immediately. It's those few precious seconds I need to reach her."

Kress got a good grip on his sword. "Understood."

"I will go first."

Kress simply nodded. Now, the moment was upon them and each man knew what he had to do. A lady's life hung in the balance and, in a sense, so did Juston's. He couldn't lose a woman he loved a second time. Taking a deep breath, Maxton lifted the hatch.

Because the rebels weren't expecting any manner of ambush or attack, no one gave notice when the hatch opened. Men had been coming through it all day, so it was a normal occurrence. Maxton was able to lift the hatch completely and he and Kress were able to make their way out onto the roof without any issue.

In fact, they made their way up to the rebels without anyone noticing until someone happened to turn and catch a glimpse of Kress. Kress ran the man through immediately before he could sound the alarm but the noise from his body hitting the roof alerted the others.

From that moment forward, the battle was on.

CHAPTER TWENTY-FOUR

SHE'D GIVEN THE wounded a fight but, in the end, it hadn't been enough. There had been too many of them and they had been able to overwhelm her. But Emera didn't give up; she'd fought and twisted, bitten and screamed, as they'd tied her up tightly with hemp rope.

Some fool kept kissing her head and petting her like a dog, telling her to quiet down and be calm. That had only made her angrier and the next time he tried to pet her, she bit him. That's when someone had shoved a piece of cloth into her mouth to gag her. Terrified and furious, Emera had been effectively corralled.

Now, her future was cloudy. She had no idea what the wounded intended to do with her and there was a great part of her that was insulted by their behavior. After she'd risked her health to remain with them and tend their wounds, their manner of gratitude involved ropes and mistrust. Still, there was a greater part of her that understood their motives. They knew, as everyone at Bowes knew, that she and Juston were attracted to each other. Since Juston was the enemy, that made her an enemy as well.

The only comfort she had was in the fact that Jessamyn had escape, so at least her sister wasn't at risk of being thrown off the roof. But that comfort faded when she realized that was exactly where they were taking her – to the roof of the keep. Four of them carried her up the spiral stairs, through the roof hatch, and into the bright, cold day beyond. The sun was bright, the wind blowing dark clouds around, and it was a rather glorious day but for the fact she was in such danger.

Just because they could no longer throw Jessamyn off the roof didn't mean they weren't considering that same fate for her.

There was a good deal of yelling and activity going on, but the voices weren't simply coming from the roof. They were coming from the bailey below. As they were carrying her over to the edge of the roof, one of her captors squeezed her breast and she howled in spite of the gag, trying to twist and kick. She could hear lascivious laughter all around her when, suddenly, they tilted her up and propped her on her feet, right on the edge of the roof along the crenellations.

Emera yelped when she realized that she was right on the precipice of the roof, with a fifty foot drop in front of her. She was absolutely terrified. She could feel hands on her, gripping her to prevent her from falling, but that could change in an instant, she knew. Closing her eyes tightly, she began to pray furiously.

And then she heard it.

Juston's voice! Her eyes flew open and she dared to look down, seeing Juston standing below with a second knight. Their shields were raised, no doubt to protect themselves against rebel projectiles, and she tried to scream and call out to him but it was impossible with the gag in her mouth. Therefore, all she could do was stand there and listen to the exchange, praying she wouldn't be thrown to her death right in front of Juston.

Please, God! Please do not let this be my last moment on earth!

"We have your whore, de Royans," a rebel yelled down to Juston. Emera thought she recognized the voice but she could not be sure. "Take your men out of Bowes or I will throw her down into the bailey and all you'll have left of her is pieces. Do you understand me?"

There was quite a delay before Juston replied. The second knight with him moved away, fading out of Emera's line of sight. Evidently, the delay was excessive because the rebel spoke again.

"Well?" he yelled. "What have you to say?"

There was a bit more of a delay until Juston spoke again. "That would not be wise on your part," he said. As those on the roof watched, Juston began to move towards the north side of the keep, pointing to the dead bodies that littered the ground. "Do you see these fools? Such will be you and your men if you harm one hair on Lady Emera's head. The fact that she is alive and whole is the only reason I am not storming the keep and slitting your throat. Are you listening? Keeping her alive is the only thing keeping *you* alive."

Tears popped to Emera's eyes as she watched Juston down below. The sound of his voice was comforting and soothing even if his words were not. When she turned her head slightly to see what the rebel leader's reaction was, she could see that it was Arthos. That foolish, chatty man who had been the source of much of the gossip about her and Juston. Disgust and disappointment filled her heart.

"You are a fool to threaten us when we have captive that which you hold dear," Arthos shouted down. "The only way she will live is if you take your men and leave."

Juston shook his head. "I will not leave without her," he said. "So let us determine the best way for you to get what you want and me to get what I want."

"There is no other way."

"Aye, there is. I can give you more money than you have ever seen in your lifetime but you must give me the woman. Then, I will leave."

Arthos frowned but his rebel companions began hissing excitedly at him. He waved them off. "What money?"

Juston shifted the shield he was holding, holding it at more of an angle so he could more clearly see those he was speaking with. "My money," he said simply. "If you want to keep Bowes running sufficiently after I am gone, then you will need money to do that. In that instance, money will be more valuable to you than a hostage."

Arthos actually appeared to be considering it; a man like de Royans was enormously rich. But he quickly shook his head. "If I keep the lady, it is a guarantee you will not come back. *She* is more valuable."

Juston snorted. "Mayhap I will not come back, but Richard has any number of supporters who will march on Bowes and they will not care that you hold one small woman hostage. The House of de Lara might march on you or even the House of de Velt. How would it be if the Dark Lord broke from the north and came down here to lay siege to Bowes? You know what he does to his enemy, don't you? He will put you all up on poles, rammed through your body, and leave you for the ravens to pick at your flesh. Is that what you want?"

The rebels began to look at each other with uncertainty. No, that wasn't what they wanted. They certainly didn't want the army of Ajax de Velt to end up on their doorstep. Perhaps accepting money for the lady wasn't such a bad exchange, after all.

"Then let us say I am willing to take your money," Arthos said. "How much is your whore worth?"

"You will stop calling her that or I will not negotiate."

Arthos frowned. "Then you must not want her back very badly!"

"I want her returned more than you can ever know. But if I leave this place without her, I can promise you that I will send word to de Velt for the man to send his army down here. I will take great pleasure at his men shoving a spiked pole into your body and leaving you to die a slow and painful death."

Two threats in as many minutes of Ajax de Velt's army coming to Bowes. Arthos couldn't be completely sure the man wasn't bluffing. "De Velt would not bother with Bowes," he said with more courage than he felt. "Tell me how much money you will give me for your wh -... I mean, for the lady."

Emera had remained largely silent until this point, listening closely to everything that was being said. But the moment Juston offered to pay the rebels for her release, she started to feel a great deal of resistance. She didn't want Juston to drain his coffers for her because it would devastate him militarily. Armies were expensive. As a great general, his army defined him and princes depended upon him. She simply couldn't let him give it all up for her.

So she began to shake her head, crying out even though her voice was muffled by the gag. The rebels began to note her agitation and Arthos shook her to force her to stop moving, but she didn't heed. She continued to shake her head and try to yell to Juston, which aggravated Arthos. Reaching out, he slapped her across the cheek, not particularly hard but enough to sting. Her head snapped sideways and her black hair ended up over her eyes. Down below, Juston lost some of his carefully held composure.

"Strike her again and I will scale this keep with my bare hands, find you, and pulverize your head into dust," he snarled. "I will make sure you feel every blow and every pain as your skull slowly cracks into a hundred pieces and your brain becomes mush. Is this in any way unclear?"

Arthos knew he meant it. Already, he was coming to suspect that turning the lady over to de Royans would not sate his bloodlust against those who had taken the woman hostage. He looked at Emera, with her hair across her face and a wet gag in her mouth, and he muttered to her.

"You will tell de Royans to leave me his money and then go in peace," he said, squeezing her arm painfully. "He must take his army and leave, and I will release you tomorrow. Tell him that he must go now."

Emera shook her head and looked away. Arthos nearly slapped her again but thought better of it. If de Royans was at all capable of scaling the keep with his bare hands, which Arthos wasn't so sure the man couldn't, then he didn't want to take that chance. Frustrated that these negotiations weren't going exactly as he'd hoped, Arthos turned to Juston.

"Leave your money and take your army away from here," he shouted, annoyance evident in his voice. "Do it today and tomorrow I will release the lady to you unharmed."

Down below, Juston shook his head. "I am not leaving without her."

"I told you I would release her!"

"You will release her now if you want me to leave."

Arthos' temper flared. He shook Emera hard enough to cause her to lose her balance and she screamed as she started to pitch forward, over the side of the roof. Hands held her legs steady, however, and those men standing behind her were the only things keeping her from falling to her death.

"Do you think this is a game, de Royans?" Arthos nearly screamed. "I hold what you want! If you do not obey me, then I shall throw her from the keep and she will die in front of you! If that is what you wish, then continue arguing with me. I grow weary of your refusal to obey!"

Emera was starting to believe he might actually do it. Her heart was pounding in her ears, the terror of a frightening death filling her mind. These past two years, working alongside these men, tending their wounds, only to find out that her diligence and kindness towards them meant nothing. They were willing to sacrifice her for their foolish cause. And Juston... pitiful Juston. He'd been unable to prevent his wife's death and now he was facing the possibility of watching another woman he adored die. She could only imagine the fear in his heart. Truth was, she felt far more concern for him than for herself. Thoughts of Juston dealing with yet another death flooded her thoughts as a very odd thing happened.

Emera was aware of scuffling and shouting behind her. It sounded like a fight. Men began screaming. Suddenly, she was pitching sideways, she thought, but she closed her eyes tightly, afraid she was about to plummet to her death, so she really wasn't sure what was happening or which direction she was falling. All she knew was that she was going down and someone suddenly grabbed her from behind, around her legs, and she was being hauled away.

More fighting. More sounds of scuffling. She opened her eyes to see blood on the roof of the keep as someone carried her away. She caught glimpses of weapons and then she saw one of Juston's knights, Sir Kress, as he sliced his way through several rebels with a sword. She didn't see Arthos but she saw his companions, Kenelm and Edgard, dead at Kress' feet. But that was about all she saw because whoever was carrying her lowered her down into the stairwell and then carried her down to the master's chambers.

There was more fighting in the stairwell. She could hear the fighting both above and below as the man who had rescued her now plopped her onto the master's bed. He loomed over her as he removed the gag and began untying her hands.

"Sir Maxton!" Emera gasped. "Sweet Mary... how did you get in here?"

Maxton ripped off the rope around her hands and went to work on the ties around her ankles. "Someone lowered a linen rope for us," he said quickly, unraveling the rope around her legs. "Was it you?"

Emera sat up, helping him remove the last of the rope. "Nay," she said. "It must have been Cowling. That was how he helped my sister to escape!"

"And that is how we are going to escape now," he said, taking her hand and pulling her off the bed. "Come along, now. Hurry!"

They raced to the linen rope, still hanging from the window. Maxton climbed into the windowsill and held out a hand to her. "Come," he commanded softly. "We are going to climb down together. I will help you."

Emera was looking at Cowling's body, sickened at the sight. She knew the man must have somehow sacrificed himself for Jessamyn and she was greatly saddened. But Maxton was beckoning her and she could not delay, mostly because he was terrified the rebels were going to rush into the chamber at any moment and recapture her. She would have jumped out of the window to avoid such a thing, so she climbed up onto the windowsill, following Maxton's instructions as he helped her to climb from the window.

Holding tightly to the rope, Maxton was half-supporting her as they inched down the rope together, bit by bit, until they reached the bottom. He let go, falling the last several feet to the ground, and ended up on his feet. He held out his arms for Emera and she released the rope, falling right into him.

Setting her feet on the ground, Maxton took Emera's hand and pulled her along the south side of the keep, keeping her tight to the stone so those in the keep wouldn't have a clear shot at her. The moment he came to the southeast corner, he peered around the side of the keep only to see Juston still standing where he'd left him.

Juston was standing over a dead body and Maxton immediately recognized it to be the rebel he'd been negotiating with. Kress must have somehow thrown the man from the roof, only to land at Juston's feet, a fitting end to the man that had threatened to do the same thing to an innocent woman. In fact, Maxton knew that Juston would be mad with worry over Emera's fate so he emitted a sharp whistle between his teeth, catching Juston's attention.

Emera, still in Maxton's grip, peered around the big knight in time to see Juston running in their direction. The man was moving like the wind. When he came around the corner and saw her, the shield fell to the ground and he drew her up into his arms, her feet dangling off the ground, squeezing her so tightly that she couldn't breathe.

Happy sobs filled the air as Emera wept, her arms around Juston's neck and her face buried against his. It was a joyful reunion of the most glorious magnitude, relief and delight and utter delirium filling the air. As Maxton left the couple and made a break for the inner ward entrance, Juston backed her against the keep, shielding her with his big body, protecting her as he hadn't been able to do until now.

It was happiness he'd never felt in his life.

"Are you well?" he asked, his voice hoarse with emotion. "Did they hurt you?"

Emera shook her head. "Nay," she assured him. "I am not injured. Is Jessamyn well? Did she make it?"

He released her, taking her face between his two big hands. "Jessamyn is well," he said, gazing into her face. Words failed him for a moment and he choked up as he looked at her. "I... I was not entirely certain I would ever know a moment like this again."

Emera could see his eyes welling. She threw her arms around his neck again, kissing his cheek. "I am unharmed," she said. "All is well, Juston. Did you truly believe a few foolish rebels could keep us apart?"

He cleared his throat, struggling against the lump in it. "I had hoped not."

She looked at him, her hands on his face, soothing the man who evidently needed more comfort than she did. She could see how shaken he was. "Nay, they could not," she whispered. "Nothing can ever keep us apart again, for I shall be by your side for always. Do you believe me?"

He nodded as she flicked an errant tear from his right eye. "I believe you."

She smiled. "Good," she said, "for I love you dearly."

He swallowed hard. "I know."

Her smile fled. "Is that all you have to say to me?"

He took her cold hands within his big warms ones, bring them to his lips. "What more would you have me say?"

"That you love me, too."

"Why should I? Is not my presence here proof enough of that?"

With a growl of frustration, she tried to yank her hands from his grip, but Juston held her tightly. He began to laugh; the more she tried to pull away, the more he laughed. Behind them, de Royans soldiers, led by Maxton, began pouring in through the inner ward entrance, some heading to the front of the keep while still others ran past Juston and Emera on their way to the linen rope that still hung from the window. On the roof overhead, Kress and Achilles were already declaring victory. The recapture of the Bowes keep was in full swing as Emera finally stopped trying to pull away from Juston only to plant her soft lips on his, a kiss that was as pure and passionate and promising as when the world was first new.

The kiss of a love realized.

For the arrogant battle lord with the damaged heart and the lonely maiden with a stubborn streak, it was also a kiss that foretold of great promises for the future. There was a bright new life ahead for them both. When Emera finally pulled away from him, simply to catch her breath, her expression told him everything that words couldn't. Juston gazed into those bright blue eyes, feeling more gratitude and adoration than he'd ever felt in his life.

"Emera?" he asked softly.

"Aye, Juston?"

"I love you."

"I know."

"Is that all you have to say to me?"

She nodded, laughing, as he scooped her into his enormous arms and carried her off into the setting sun.

The Lord of Winter was frozen no more.

EPILOGUE

September, Year of our Lord 1188 A.D.
Netherghyll Castle

DE ROYANS KNIGHTS were congregating in the great hall of Netherghyll Castle, a vast and elaborate hall that had been built by Northmen forbearers, so the hall tended to mimic a longhouse more than a Norman hall. Exposed beams on the ceiling were elaborately carved with Northman gods and other scenes until Juston's grandmother had decided they were sacrilegious in nature and demanded her husband chisel them out.

Creighton de Royans, a wise and just man, wouldn't damage the carvings but he did end up wrapping some of the beams with hemp fabric to cover up some of the more offensive scenes. The result was a very unique, and mostly beautiful, great hall that the de Royans family had occupied since the Norman conquest.

And it was very much a busy place at the moment. Juston sat exhausted but elated at the end of the large feasting table, wolfing down a meal of boiled beef and carrots, and downing copious amounts of alcohol. There was great celebration at Netherghyll on this day and the knights who hadn't already been at Netherghyll had journeyed there for a most momentous gathering.

The birth of an heir.

None was more thrilled with the event than Juston, but there was also something of a rub. His beautiful, stubborn wife had her heart set on a name for their son that didn't quite fit into Juston's plans. Every de Royans male was given a name ending in "ton", as that had been a family tradition for over two hundred years. Lady de Royans wanted to name their son Sebastian and Juston wanted to name him Brenton in following with family tradition. Now they were at an impasse and while Lady de Royans slept after the rather difficult birth, Juston was trying to figure out how to convince her that family tradition had to be followed.

"*Has* the problem been solved, then?" Christopher asked over his second cup of wine.

"It has not," Juston said frankly, swallowing the food in his mouth. He wiped his lips with the back of his hand. "My wife feels that the name Sebastian better suits the lad, but I have told her that there is no choice. Every de Royans male must have a traditional name."

The knights gathered around the table were all grinning to varied degrees. "You are the husband, Juston," Christopher said. "Simply be firm about it. She must bow to your wishes."

Juston scoffed. "You have not yet married," he pointed out. "When you have a wife, then you will see that being firm with her is not so easy."

"My wife will obey me implicitly."

"You have no idea what you are talking about."

Soft laughter came from the knights at Christopher's expense. Even though Christopher shook his head in disagreement, he refrained from verbally sparring with the new father. As Christopher went back to his wine, Juston continued eating and glanced over at the lad sitting next to him.

"Do you hear me?" he said. "Be very careful who you marry. Make sure she will not fight you on every decision."

Tristan grinned at Juston, a man he had lived with for the past several months. "I shall marry a lady who listens to me," he declared.

Juston wriggled his eyebrows at him. "Then I wish you well, lad."

"Can I go and see the baby now?"

Juston shook his head. "He is sleeping," he said. "You can see him soon."

Tristan was thrilled with the new addition. When Erik brought him to Netherghyll back in December, it was evidently to stay because Tristan remained even though Erik eventually left, returning to Richard in March while leaving Tristan in safe hands with Juston and his new wife, Emera. Emera was already attached to the lad, having worked so closely with him at Bowes, so it was the most natural of things for Tristan to remain with her and, eventually, Juston grew fond of the boy as well. He found Tristan obedient and eager to learn, but the closer he drew to the lad, the more he worried about the day when Richard and Eleanor would want the child returned to them to use against Henry.

In fact, he was very much dreading that day. It hadn't come yet but he knew, eventually, it would. When the day came, he was fairly certain he would not turn the boy over for their nefarious plans. That mercy Christopher had long accused him of not having had reared its ugly head in the form of pity and fondness for a lonely child who was now more like one of the family. What was it he had told Christopher? That mercy can be deadly? He wondered if those words were going to come back to haunt him.

He hoped not.

But it wasn't something he thought of regularly. He had much more than just Tristan to occupy his mind. In addition to Henry and Alys' son living under his roof, there was another lad who had his father's curly, dark blonde hair and enormous green eyes. Even now, the child sat on Tristan's other side, sharing treats with him. Looking over Tristan's head, Juston could see his now four-year-old son with Sybilla happily munching oat cakes, one in each hand. He grinned at Juston, his face full of crumbs, and Juston could feel his heart melt.

But it wasn't always like that. Thornton de Royans, or Thorn as he was called, had come to live with his father sometime back in the spring when two haggard d'Evereux servants had come to both deliver the child and the terrible news that his mother had died of a fever in

January. The little boy had evidently been sick as well and wasn't particularly healed at the time he'd been brought to Netherghyll. Juston remembered looking at the pale child, shocked by his appearance and terrified of how Emera was going to react to him.

But he should not have worried. While Juston had been reluctant to accept the child right away, there had never been a question in Emera's mind. Juston had watched, amazed, as the woman accepted his illegitimate son as if he was her very own. Emera had nursed Thornton back to health and Juston had inevitably drawn close to the little lad who looked and behaved exactly like him. He was a sweet terror, bright and loving. It was true that Thornton's very existence brought about terrible memories for Juston, memories of manipulation and betrayal, but with Emera's generous heart leading the way, he had been able to be generous, too.

It wasn't Thornton's fault that the circumstances of his birth had been less than pleasant.

Therefore, Juston was busy these days with a new wife, a new family, and a happiness that was greater than anything he'd ever known. For the moment, Yorkshire was peaceful. Bowes Castle was his, garrisoned for Richard, and de Puiset remained in north Durham, far away from the activity in the southern part of the shire and far away from Bowes. Carlisle had been tamed, Richmond had never been a factor, and both Richard and Henry supporters seemed to be holding station for the time being. The battle outside of Cotherstone had been the last battle Juston had been involved in, and he was content with that. He'd learned over the past few months that there was much more to life than battles and advancing Richard's cause.

For now, he was happy to remain at Netherghyll.

But that wasn't the case for his knights. Even though they were sworn to him, they were loyal to Richard overall, and changes were coming. Stirrings were coming from Henry and Richard again, changes that threatened to separate Juston from his knights.

Changes Juston wasn't looking forward to.

"Let us put aside talk of women and children for the moment," he finally said. "Although I thank you for coming to celebrate the birth of my son, that is not the only reason you have all come. I received a missive from Richard recently outlining some changes that are blowing upon the wind. It seems that I am to remain in England to secure his legacy here while he will take some of you with him to France and points beyond. Chris, you and your brother and Marcus are headed for France, are you not?"

Christopher nodded, although it was clear that he didn't seem thrilled about it. "Aye," he replied. "We will be joining up with Arthur Barringdon's army in Worcester and moving on to France with him. I have been told that Henry wants to bequeath the Aquitaine to Richard's brother, John, but Richard will not relinquish what he feels is his birthright. I have a feeling we will see a good deal of action to that end."

Juston knew of the tensions building over the Aquitaine. "I am sorry to see you go," he said quietly, "but I understand why you must. I have not seen Arthur in years; you will give him my best wishes when you see him."

"I will," Christopher said, feeling a melancholy mood settle as he thought this might be the last time he would see all of these men together in one place. Specifically, he looked to Maxton, seated across the table. His eyes glimmered with mirth. "We have enjoyed a great many adventures together, all of us. I think it is most important to remember that, although we may not have always agreed, we were, nonetheless, always willing to lay down our lives for each other. That is what I will remember the most. The camaraderie in this band of knights is greater than any I have known. I shall miss most of you. Not all of you, but most of you."

That brought a grin from Maxton although he tried to conceal it. He poured a measure of wine into his cup from the pitcher on the table. "A sentiment I wholly agree with," he said, looking not only to Christopher but to Juston as well. "Kress and Achilles and I are off to the Levant. Since the fall of Jerusalem to barbarian armies, Richard feels that our skills could be best used there. I am under the impression that he will be following us shortly."

Juston nodded. "As am I," he said. "If Richard goes to the Levant, it will be a great crusade, indeed. I am not entirely sure I will go, however, because with Richard away from England and his territories in France, someone must remain behind to make sure they remain his properties. I will, therefore, remain here, at Netherghyll, holding the north."

It was a rather sad idea to think on Richard's greatest knight, a man who was one of the greatest warriors of his time, sitting out the great action that was happening in France and would soon be happening in the Holy Land. But given how Juston put the situation, it made sense. Someone had to hold England on Richard's behalf.

That someone would be the great Lord of Winter.

"Your sword will be missed, Juston," Maxton said. "I cannot recall a campaign in recent memory that you were not at the head of. Do you truly think Richard will keep you in England?"

Juston shrugged. "Even if he does not, I will ask to remain," he said. He noticed the surprised faces around the table and he grinned. "I am much older than the rest of you. I was fighting back before some of you were born. Nay, I have earned my reputation. I have proven my worth. Now, I wish to remain home and enjoy my family. I wish to see my sons grow up and become great knights. I never thought I would see the day when my desire for peace would outweigh my desire for battle, but it is true. My time has come and gone. Now, it is your time to make names for yourselves. Christopher, you have a great destiny to fulfill, as do David and Marcus. I cannot teach you anymore than I already have. My job is done. Max, Kress, and Achilles – you are my Unholy Trinity. There is such darkness in you three, but there is also such greatness. I cannot explain it any better than that. You must find it out for yourselves."

His words settled around the men, a bittersweet moment to realize their group of knights would now separate and move on to other things. It was their time to find their own greatness, as Juston had said.

He had already found his.

"What about me?" Tristan asked, breaking the downhearted silence. "What will I do?"

Juston grinned at the boy. "You and Thorn will become the greatest knights of all," he said. "I will teach you myself and you can both serve Richard in his legions."

"That ought to give Henry fits," Christopher muttered.

The others covered up smiles as Juston simply lifted his eyebrows in agreement. "Mayhap he will never know," he said. "If I have anything to say about this, he will not. Tristan will grow up a great knight and I will see to it."

It sounded rather final and also rather defiant. The knights knew that Juston had grown fond of the lad and their impressions were that the boy was now under his control, not Richard and Eleanor's. But no one questioned him; Juston de Royans was a warrior big enough and powerful enough, to defy even the royal family. It would make for interesting dynamics if it ever came down to a battle of wills.

As the men considered that possibility, Christopher turned his attention to Gart, sitting silent at the end of the table. He was the only one who had remained largely silent through this gathering, a big and silently brooding man who had been knighted around the first of the year by Juston. Now a fully-fledged knight, he'd been given great responsibilities. But he hadn't spoken of any of them or of his future plans.

"How does it feel being a garrison commander in a castle surround-ed by Henry's supporters, Gart?" Christopher asked. "We have all spoken of our futures, but we've not yet heard from you. Are you planning on staying at Bowes in definitely?"

Gart looked up from his cup. "I will remain there as long as Juston requires it," he said. "I rather like commanding my own castle."

Maxton leaned over the table. "What of Erik?"

"He is in France with Richard, the last I heard."

"And if Richard calls for men to go on the great quest to the Levant, will you go? Or will you remain with de Royans, guarding Richard's holdings?"

Gart's gaze moved to Juston. "That depends on him," he said. "As he has said, we must find our greatness for ourselves. I might find mine on the sands of the Levant."

Juston could see the longing in Gart's eyes. He wanted the adventure and the glory of it. "You are young and talented," he said. "If you wish to go on Crusade, I will not stop you."

"Then join us," Maxton said. "Come with us to the Levant when you tire of Bowes."

"That might not be for a year or two yet."

"I have a feeling we will still be in the Levant. Join us when you can."

Gart gave the man a weak smile, returning to his wine. It was true that he was very young and Bowes was his first command but, like the others, he found that the adventures in France and the Levant were calling to him. He wasn't content to remain behind.

Juston knew that. He could see it in all of their faces. But he was precluded from commenting when Jessamyn suddenly appeared from a side door of the hall. She was smiling as she entered, a host of faces turning to her and, in Juston's case, it was anxiously. It had been Jessamyn and a midwife who had delivered his son so he knew she came bearing news of those nearest to him. He set his wine aside and stood up from the table.

"How is my wife?" he asked, struggling not to sound too eager. "Is she well? How is my son?"

He couldn't quite pull off being calm in his questioning and Jessamyn laughed. It was a very happy day in her life in a series of months that had been the happiest she'd ever known. Living at Netherghyll had been a blessing as far as she was concerned. She'd never realized just how miserable she had been at Bowes, married to Brey, until she'd come to the de Royans fortress. Now, life had never been better.

"Your wife is fine," she said patiently. "Your son has been fed and now he is sleeping peacefully. In fact, I have come on behalf of your wife. She has a proposal and I have been authorized to negotiate for her."

Juston's eyes narrowed. "What about?" he asked. "The name? My son's name *shall* be Brenton."

Jessamyn shook her head. "Lady de Royans does not like the name," she said. "But she is willing to not name the child Sebastian if you will agree to another name of her choosing."

"What is it?"

"Ashton de Royans."

The name gave Juston pause. He turned to look at his knights, seeing that half of them were agreeing with the name. He sighed heavily, stroking his chin in thought as he turned back to Jessamyn.

"She will agree to Ashton?"

"She will. It was suggested by the midwife and she likes it very much."

Juston continued to be thoughtful. "Tell her I will agree if I can name the next son without any interference from her."

"I am sure she will agree to it."

"Good. Then I will agree to Ashton."

Finally, the downy-haired infant had a name and Jessamyn returned to her sister with a big grin on her face and two little boys in tow because Tristan and Thornton wanted to see the baby. As the knights in the hall continued to celebrate the birth of little Ashton de Royans, Emera was pleased that her husband had agreed to her chosen name. If it meant giving up her naming rights with her next son, she supposed it was a small price to pay. But she was fairly certain that Juston wouldn't completely cut her out of the decision making the next time.

It was just a hunch she had.

As it turned out, a healthy little girl was born to Juston and Emera a year and a half later, a tiny lass with black hair and a scream louder than anything Juston had ever heard. It positively set his hair on end. But she was beautiful and he was in love, and he didn't even mind that his wife named the child without even consulting him. In fact, he didn't care at all.

Lady Wynter de Royans had quite a ring to it.

ೋ THE END ಎ

ABOUT KATHRYN LE VEQUE

Medieval Just Got Real.

KATHRYN LE VEQUE is a USA TODAY Bestselling author, an Amazon All-Star author, and a #1 bestselling, award-winning, multi-published author in Medieval Historical Romance and Historical Fiction. She has been featured in the NEW YORK TIMES and on USA TODAY's HEA blog. In March 2015, Kathryn was the featured cover story for the March issue of InD'Tale Magazine, the premier Indie author magazine. She was also a quadruple nominee (a record!) for the prestigious RONE awards for 2015.

Kathryn's Medieval Romance novels have been called 'detailed', 'highly romantic', and 'character-rich'. She crafts great adventures of love, battles, passion, and romance in the High Middle Ages. More than that, she writes for both women AND men – an unusual crossover for a romance author – and Kathryn has many male readers who enjoy her stories because of the male perspective, the action, and the adventure.

On October 29, 2015, Amazon launched Kathryn's Kindle Worlds Fan Fiction site WORLD OF DE WOLFE PACK. Please visit Kindle Worlds for Kathryn Le Veque's World of de Wolfe Pack and find many action-packed adventures written by some of the top authors in their genre using Kathryn's characters from the de Wolfe Pack series. As Kindle World's FIRST Historical Romance fan fiction world, Kathryn Le Veque's World of de Wolfe Pack will contain all of the great story-telling you have come to expect.

Kathryn loves to hear from her readers. Please find Kathryn on Facebook at Kathryn Le Veque, Author, or join her on Twitter @kathrynleveque, and don't forget to visit her website at www.kathrynleveque.com.

39848426R10208

Made in the USA
Middletown, DE
27 January 2017